W9-BUL-736

DEAD RINGER

Books by Annelise Ryan
(who also writes as Allyson K. Abbott):

A Mattie Winston Mystery:

Working Stiff
Scared Stiff
Frozen Stiff
Lucky Stiff
Board Stiff
Stiff Penalty
Stiff Competition
Dead in the Water
Dead Calm
Dead of Winter
Dead Ringer

Helping Hands Mysteries (a new series
featuring Hildy Schneider!)

Needled to Death
Night Shift (coming in August 2020)

Books by Allyson K. Abbott
(who also writes as Annelise Ryan):

A Mack's Bar Mystery:

Murder on the Rocks
Murder with a Twist
In the Drink
Shots in the Dark
A Toast to Murder
Last Call

DEAD RINGER

Annelise
Ryan

KENSINGTON BOOKS
www.kensingtonbooks.com

This book is a work of fiction. Names, characters, and incidents either are products of the author's imagination or are used fictitiously. Any resemblance to actual persons living or dead, or events, is entirely coincidental.

KENSINGTON BOOKS are published by

Kensington Publishing Corp.
119 West 40th Street
New York, NY 10018

All Kensington titles, imprints and distributed lines are available at special quantity discounts for bulk purchases for sales promotion, premiums, fund-raising, educational or institutional use. Special book excerpts or customized printings can also be created to fit specific needs. For details, write or phone the office of the Kensington Special Sales Manager: Kensington Publishing Corp., 119 West 40th Street, New York, NY, 10018. Attn. Special Sales Department. Phone: 1-800-221-2647.

Library of Congress Card Catalogue Number: 2019951385

Kensington and the K logo Reg. U.S. Pat. & TM Off.

ISBN-13: 978-1-4967-2255-3
ISBN-10: 1-4967-2255-8
First Kensington Hardcover Edition: March 2020

ISBN-13: 978-1-4967-2256-0 (e-book)
ISBN-10: 1-4967-2256-6 (e-book)

10 9 8 7 6 5 4 3 2 1

Printed in the United States of America

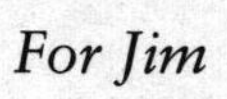

For Jim

DEAD RINGER

CHAPTER 1

The dead woman in front of me is a stranger. I've never seen her before and I don't know her name or where she's from, but I can tell she hasn't had an easy life. Yet by the time I'm done with my job for the day, I will know her with a level of intimacy few can understand.

My name is Mattie Winston, and helping my boss, Izzy, a forensic pathologist, figure out how people die is what we do. It requires knowing someone both inside and out in every sense of the word. In the current case, this began with a call in the wee hours of the morning that got my husband, Steve Hurley, a homicide detective, and me out of bed. This was because a county sheriff cruising along a country road not far outside of Sorenson, the Wisconsin town where I live and work, came across what he thought was a dead deer alongside the road. This is not an infrequent site in Wisconsin, where the deer population might well outnumber the people.

This body, however, wasn't a deer. It was human, a woman, lying on her side with her arms flung out as if in a plea for help. But nothing could help her anymore. It became apparent as we examined the body that she had been dead for some time. She was pale and cold—colder than the unusually warm April temperatures we've had the past few days could explain—and her back was dark from blood that had settled there when her heart stopped. This discoloration, along with the lack of blood in the ground around the body, told us that she had been dumped there on the side of the road after being killed elsewhere. She had been killed lying on her back and left that way for some time before being tossed away here, like a piece of trash.

I loaded her body into a bag with the help of a local funeral home and followed their hearse to our office in Sorenson, arriving there just as the sun was starting to light up the sky. Now Izzy and I are in the process of trying to figure out what happened to her.

She has been x-rayed from head to toe while still in her body bag. When she first arrived in our office, I opened the bag enough to get to her eyes, so I could remove vitreous samples—the liquid within the eyeball. This can often tell a story about how and when a person died. Now she is on our autopsy table and we have removed her clothing: a pair of worn and torn blue jeans, cotton underpants with stretched-out elastic, a thin blue T-shirt stained with blood, and a faded brown puffy coat, torn in two spots where it is bleeding stuffing. We have also removed a pair of plain cotton socks and dirty athletic shoes that have seen better days. All her clothing is filthy and worn. Not surprisingly, she is not wearing any jewelry.

The woman's skin is a pale gray color along the front of her body, though I can see the edges of the darker coloring that marks her back and buttocks. Her body is a bag of bones, the skin loose and sagging in places, indicating a large weight loss. The ends of her blond hair are ragged, as if she cut it herself. Her nails are cracked and jagged; yet there are chipped remnants of a mauve-colored polish on them. Seeing how ravaged her body is now, I find it hard to imagine she ever cared for it enough to polish her nails, but she did. This lingering vestige of pride and vanity she clung to in the weeks before she died saddens me. I wonder what her life was like before it all started to fall apart.

One of the most obvious indications that she has led a less than stellar life is the fact that she only has three teeth in her mouth—one of them broken, all of them brown, her gums inflamed and spotted with pockets of infection. It's a classic example of meth mouth, and the methamphetamine abuse has also left red, scabby sores on her face. There are pockets of festering infection tracking down both of her arms and along one foot, evidence of an IV drug habit. It's an all-too-common story of drug use and abuse: heroin, sometimes laced with other narcotics to mellow out, and methamphetamine to amp back up again. Both are highly addictive and horribly destructive.

How she died appears obvious, though it's not what one might expect at first glance. It wasn't the drugs, an infection, or malnutrition that killed her. There are five stab wounds in her torso, each one deep with bruising around the wounds to indicate that the hilt of the knife came into brutal contact with the skin. Two of the wounds are located just above her breasts, the left one—likely the cause of death—over the heart. There are two more wounds in her abdomen at the same height as her navel, about six inches apart. The final wound is centered in the lower abdomen, just above the symphysis pubis.

All the wounds appear deep enough to have reached and injured underlying organs, but none of them, other than the one by the heart, were likely to be fatal, at least not immediately. Based on the bloodstains and a cursory examination of the surrounding tissue, all the wounds appear to have been inflicted while she was still alive, and her blood was still pumping. She was stabbed through her clothing and there are two denim fibers from her jeans embedded in the right-sided chest wound, suggesting that the single wound in the pelvic area was inflicted first.

Notably lacking are any of the defense wounds typically seen in a stabbing like this: slashes and cuts on the forearms, hands, and fingers as the victim tries desperately to ward off the knife blows.

"Someone really didn't like this woman," I say to Izzy, who is across the autopsy table from me. He is standing on a stool, which enables him to reach everything he needs to, because he is barely over five feet tall.

I, on the other hand, need no such accommodation as I have a full foot of height over him. I hit five-foot-twelve (it sounds shorter that way) at the age of twelve, earning monikers like Giraffe, Beanstalk, Amazon, and my personal favorite, Timber, which some of my schoolmates would holler at me whenever they passed me in the hall. This is because I have very large feet that made me clumsy back in the day. Okay, they still tend to make me clumsy at times, but you try walking around on snowshoes all day and see how well you do.

The size thing also led to the nickname Sasquatch, a version of which my husband has adopted for his own, calling me Squatch as a form of endearment. I should probably be offended. However, the way the name typically rolls off his tongue with a ton of love, and a hint of lust behind it, makes it easy to tolerate.

Izzy and I are the yin and yang of coworkers: He's short and I'm tall; he's swarthy and I'm fair-skinned; he's dark-haired and I'm a pale blonde. Despite the physical differences, we are a lot alike in the way we think and function, right down to our shared predilection for men. It has made us the best of friends and great colleagues.

"How old do you think she is?" I ask.

"Hard to say," Izzy says, straightening up from his close

exam of the wounds. He arches his back and lets out a little sigh.

"Are you okay?"

"I'm fine," he says dismissively. "Just a bit of a backache. One of the many joys of getting older." He studies the woman's face for a moment. "I'd guess our victim is late twenties or early thirties," he says after a bit. "Can't be very precise with the level of damage to her body. Hopefully, your husband can come up with an ID for her soon."

No doubt Hurley was currently working hard on that very thing, even though the body was dumped in a location outside of his typical jurisdiction. There is a lot of overlap on this sort of thing, and since the body dump site was close to town, and my office does all the criminal autopsies for the county, Hurley took over the investigative part. The county cop looked more than happy to give it up, since they've been short-staffed of late and an investigation into a Jane Doe such as this one was likely to be long, tedious, and frustrating.

Izzy once again bends over the body to examine the knife wounds more closely. He is looking at the one over the heart when I see his brow furrow. "Can you open this wound a little for me?" he says, handing me a small speculum.

I carefully insert the end of the speculum into the wound and push the handles together ever so slightly, separating the edges. "What the heck is that?" I say, peering into the wound at what appears to be some type of yellow debris.

Izzy picks up a small, narrow forceps and reaches into the wound. When he pulls the instrument out, there are two small yellow bits of something grasped in its end. Izzy holds the forceps aloft and we examine the debris in the light. I think at first that it looks like tissue, but something about it isn't right. Izzy sets the debris on a towel-covered Mayo stand beside him; he uses the forceps to unravel and flatten the small chunks and then straighten the edges. The result is two vaguely fan-shaped bits of delicate-looking material.

"I think they're flower petals of some type," he says, staring at the bits. He then picks them up and drops them into a glass container before once again going into the wound. This time he comes out with three pieces, and he drops them into the container as they are. Setting the forceps aside, he peers at the debris through the glass.

With the mention of flower petals, something in my brain shifts, like an elbow nudge in the ribs. My first impulse is to ignore it, but then it nudges again and a memory, hazy but distinct in parts, surfaces. I sort through the pieces of it, and as I'm doing so, I become aware of Izzy staring at me.

"What is it?" he asks. "You're onto something, aren't you?"

"Maybe," I say. "Could those be petals from a carnation, by any chance?"

Izzy eyeballs the debris again and his eyebrows rise. "They certainly could be." He shifts his gaze to me and narrows his eyes in curiosity. "Why?"

I look down at the woman's torso, at the arrangement of the wounds, and the memory gels a bit more in my mind. "These wounds, they form a sort of triangle, or chevron shape."

Izzy glances at the wounds, then back at me. "They do," he says cautiously.

"I recognize this MO."

Izzy frowns. "I don't. Was it a case you did with Otto?" he asks, referring to Otto Morton, a forensic pathologist from Madison who job-shares with Izzy.

I shake my head. "No, it wasn't one of our cases. It was one I heard about. It was at that forensic conference in Milwaukee I went to last fall. I was in the bar one night, chatting with a guy from Eau Claire, and he was telling me about a case he worked on with that serial killer from up there. I can't remember the killer's name, but it was in the papers last year. You remember, don't you? I believe he killed four women."

"Ulrich?"

"That's it!" I say, trying to snap my fingers, an impossibility with gloves on.

Izzy frowns and shakes his head. "I think the stabbing pattern was similar to our victim, but I don't remember anything about any flower petals."

"That's because that fact never came out. The guy I talked to said he was part of a new program in Eau Claire where they're trying to set up a forensic pathologist for the area by training someone with local interest. It's through the U of Dub."

"I heard about that," Izzy says. "Most of the outlying areas don't have forensic pathologists, so they send all of the bodies that need autopsies to Madison or Milwaukee. Those places are getting overwhelmed, and because of the success we've had here, they decided instead to implement a rural training program a few years ago. They send forensic pathologists to these outlying areas to provide training to interested physicians, sort of a residency program. Sounds like your guy might be in one of those programs."

"That sounds about right," I say with a frown, "though, truth be told, my memory of my chat with this fellow is hazy at best, as I might have had a little more to drink than I should have." I shrug and give Izzy a guilty smile. "I was feeling carefree and a smidge wild, given that I had two days and one night with no mothering or other responsibilities."

Izzy gives me a mildly chastising look.

"Anyway," I go on, "something I remember this guy telling me was that the flower petals were never brought to light because the prosecution couldn't connect them to their suspect. They couldn't figure out where he might have obtained them, and the murders took place during a time of the year when the flowers wouldn't be available in the wild.

Given that they couldn't tie them in, and afraid the defense might try to use this lack of a connection to create reasonable doubt, they buried the evidence. I think he said it was made available to the defense team, but he didn't know if they'd found it or understood the significance of it. Apparently, the prosecution felt like the case was strong enough without the flower petal evidence, and it would seem they were right, given that Ulrich was convicted."

"And the flower petals in this Ulrich case were stuffed inside a wound?" Izzy asks.

"They were," I say with a nod. "I remember him saying that the stab wounds were in a triangular pattern that was wide at the chest and narrowed down to one wound in the pelvis, and the petals were in the one over the heart." I gesture toward the body in front of us. "There was something about these wounds that was nagging at my brain, but I didn't make the connection until you found the flower petals."

Izzy holds up the container with the petals in it and studies them again in the light. "Did your fellow happen to mention what type of flower petals they were?"

"He did. He said they were yellow carnation petals."

Izzy sets the container to one side. "Do we have a copycat killer?"

"Only if the information about the flower petals got out somehow." I stare at the face of our victim as something occurs to me. "We also have to consider the possibility that Ulrich didn't do the other murders, don't we?" I give Izzy a worried, partly panicked look, a sinking feeling in my stomach. "Oh, hell, did the wrong guy get convicted again?"

CHAPTER 2

Our legal system is good, but it's far from perfect, and the harsh reality of that is all up in my face right now. That's because I started my day yesterday by apologizing to a man who was wrongly convicted, someone I helped put behind bars because, for a long time, I was thoroughly convinced he was guilty.

I can admit it when I make a mistake, but I don't like having to. It's not a pride thing; it's that some mistakes are bigger than others. During my career as a nurse, working first in the ER and then in a surgical suite, a mistake had the potential to cost someone their life and cost me my job, my license, and my livelihood. That's a lot of things at stake and the responsibility of it has made me a careful, thoughtful person.

At least now the possibility of making a mistake that could directly kill someone is no longer a risk for me, since my clients are already dead. But while the stakes aren't quite as high, it's not risk-free. A mistake could mean a killer goes free, or a cause of death goes undetermined. Letting a killer avoid justice might cost someone their life in the long run if that killer decides to practice his or her trade again.

While I know that in the course of carrying out my current

job, I no longer run the risk of killing anyone if I make a mistake, I've discovered that I can destroy a life. An erroneous assumption I made robbed a man of his freedom. My guilt is mitigated a bit by the knowledge that the error wasn't mine alone, and that the stage was set through the conspiratorial efforts of some very bad people. But *mitigated* isn't *assuaged,* and the knowledge of my role in the whole mess still stings.

The victim, a man named Tomas Wyzinski, was convicted largely on the testimony given by Bob Richmond, one of our local police detectives, and me. Neither of us lied about the facts, which were straightforward and admittedly damning, considering that we found the head of a murder victim in Wyzinski's refrigerator. My assumption that Tomas was guilty colored the observations and conclusions I made on the day of that first encounter, as well as my observations, assumptions, and testimony later.

But he wasn't guilty.

Eventually the wrong was righted, and just yesterday morning, I sat across from Mr. Wyzinski at a table in our office library—which also serves as office space for me and the person with whom I job-share—atoning for my mistake. I was relieved and glad that Wyzinski was no longer in prison and delighted that he had been rejoined with his brother, Lech, who is mentally challenged. The two of them were accompanied by two U.S. Marshals, who were ready to take them to a secret location, where they would embark on a new life in the Witness Protection Program.

"I'm so very sorry, Tomas," I told him with all the sincerity I could muster. I was tempted to try to explain my erroneous assumptions, to paint a picture of the damning scene I encountered that day when I first met him, but I refrained at the last second for several reasons. He'd heard it already the day I testified in court, it made no difference in the end, and I recognized the impulse for what it was: an attempt to explain away my blame. I didn't want to explain it away; I needed to own it.

"I jumped to conclusions and closed my mind to the possibilities," I told him. "And you paid the price for my ignorance. I'm sorrier than you will ever know and will regret it for the rest of my life."

Lech, whom I'd visited several times while his brother was in prison, smiled at me. Tomas did not. "You helped us," Lech said with a big, beaming smile. "And that's a good thing."

I smiled back at him, but it was hard to feel happy about any of this.

"Your part in this was very minor," Tomas said finally. "In some ways, you were as much a victim of the puppet masters as I was. I don't hold any grudges, and I don't blame you for what happened. What's more, I appreciate what you did for both me and my brother. Particularly what you did for Lech. You made sure he was safe."

"It was the least I could do," I said with a wan smile. "I knew he was your weak link and suspected it was threats of harm to him that were keeping you in line."

"And you were right," Tomas said. He closed his eyes for a moment and took on a pained expression. "I was so afraid of what they would do to . . ." His eyes opened, and he looked at his brother with sweet affection. "Of what they would do," he concluded, presumably not wanting to spook his brother.

"The marshals were really nice," Lech said with an emphatic nod. "They gave me a new house to stay in. They got me really good food, too. I got to eat ice-cream cake!"

Tomas smiled at his brother, and it transformed his face. These two obviously bore a deep mutual affection for one another, and I knew that the role I played in nearly destroying that relationship would haunt me for the rest of my life. I hoped it would also serve as a reminder to me in the future, a precautionary note for any time I found myself tempted to jump to conclusions or close my mind to possible scenarios.

"Thank you for your understanding, Tomas," I said, getting up from my chair. "I'm not sure I deserve it, but I'm truly happy to have it." I glanced at my watch and sighed. "I need to get to work and you guys need to get going. You won't be able to contact me, and I'll likely never see you again, but know that I'll be thinking about the two of you often, hoping that you're enjoying your new lives."

"Thank you," Tomas said, giving me one last smile.

"Thank you, Mattie," Lech echoed. He rose out of his chair, came around the table, and wrapped his arms around me, hugging me for all he was worth.

I hugged him back, my eyes closed to contain burgeoning tears. When Lech released me, I swiped at my eyes and saw that Tomas was also on his feet. He walked to and then past me without another look my way. No hug, no good-bye, no comment of any sort, but then I hadn't expected one. Lech followed him out of the room, one marshal leading the way, the other falling into step behind the two men.

I'd stayed in the room to give myself a moment or two to get my emotions under control and to give the marshals and their charges time to leave. Then I went into the locker room, changed into scrubs, and headed for the morgue fridge to retrieve the body I'd put there during the night.

I'm normally somewhat immune to cold temperatures, in part because you adapt to it if you live in Wisconsin for any length of time, and in part because I come with plenty of my own insulation. But yesterday morning, when I walked into the morgue fridge on the heels of my meeting with the Wyzinskis, I was wracked by a violent shiver that made me hug myself. I made quick work of getting the body out of the fridge, the air in there feeling colder than the look my ex–mother-in-law,

Stella, had given me when I'd ran into her—quite literally—at the grocery store the night before.

My marriage to Stella's son, David Winston, a local surgeon, ended because he cheated on me. Despite that, I've somehow become the enemy in Stella's eyes. She is here in town now because David has remarried and his new wife, Patty, just had a baby. It's Stella's first grandchild, as David is her only child and he and I never had any children.

I have them now, however: a seventeen-year-old stepdaughter named Emily—a surprise arrival in Hurley's life a few years ago, given that he never knew he had a child before then—and Hurley's and my two-and-a-half-year-old son, Matthew.

I'd had Matthew with me when I ran into Stella at the grocery store, and Matthew, in what seems to be his modus operandi of late, was having a meltdown in the cereal aisle, screaming and thrashing about in the cart because I wouldn't buy a box of Frosted Flakes. He was sobbing that he wanted "Tony Tiger" with all the angst of a kid who's just been beaten and threatened with death. I was refusing to buy them because I'd done so once before, and Matthew hated the stuff. But there was no way to explain that to the other shoppers, who were watching us with hooded, judgmental eyes, and expressions that clearly communicated their displeasure.

Desperate to get Matthew to stop, I had bent down close to his ear, telling him in a stern but low voice that if he didn't knock it off, I was going to run Tony Tiger out of town and he'd never see him again, not even here at the grocery store. It wasn't my proudest parental moment, but I find that logic and kindness tend to disappear from the equation when dealing with a temperamental toddler amid societal condescension and judgment.

As I was muttering my Tony-cidal threat to my sobbing son,

I steered the cart around an end cap and into the next aisle, eager to leave the row of cereals behind. I wasn't watching where I was going and ran the cart into someone else's. An expletive escaped my lips before I could stop it, uttered right near my son's ear. At least this, combined with the shock of the collision, got Matthew to stop crying. It took me a second to place the woman behind the cart I'd hit, as I'd only seen Stella twice before: once when David took me to Chicago to meet her and announce our engagement, and again at our wedding.

Stella is a large and imperious woman who *literally* looks down her nose at people. A wealthy widow—her husband died of cancer when David was in medical school—she is a class-conscious snob. I never felt accepted or good enough when I was around her, a feeling reinforced by the fact that during seven years of marriage, she never came to visit us or invited us down to Chicago to visit her.

"I'm sorry," I'd uttered automatically postcollision, focused on disentangling my cart from the other one.

The only response I got was a dismissive "Hmph."

It was then that I looked up at my victim. "Stella! What are you doing here?" I asked, feeling momentarily disoriented. Then I remembered. "Oh, wait, you came up to meet your new granddaughter, didn't you? Congratulations."

Again there was no response, just a glacial stare delivered from a head that was tilted back ever so slightly to give that look-down-my-nose-at-you posture. After a moment, she gave a derisive glance toward my son, who was gaping at her with a startled yet fascinated expression.

I whipped my cart around, aiming for the next aisle over. With one last glance over my shoulder, I said, "Tell David and Patty hi for me." Then I hightailed it out of there and hid in the baked-goods aisle for half an hour before venturing on.

* * *

As I tally up my encounter with Stella, yesterday's meeting with the Wyzinskis, and the current realization that the body we are working on is providing evidence of yet another possible wrong conviction, my emotions feel tighter than the SPANX I wore to my sister's Christmas party.

"Let's try to get ahead of this case," Izzy says, nodding toward the woman's body between us and refocusing my thoughts. "Call Arnie and have him come down here to collect some of this trace. And then call your husband and get him up to speed on this right away."

I nod and step back from the table, stripping off my gloves. I wash my hands, flexing my fingers a few times to test my dexterity. For some reason, my fingers have been swollen for the past couple of weeks, making my rings so tight that I had to take them off. I suspect it's due to the ten pounds I put on over the holidays and have yet to take off. It's now April and those extra pounds are taunting me, reminding me that shorts and bathing-suit season is right around the corner.

First I use the phone on the desk by the far wall to call Arnie down from his second-floor lab, and then to call Hurley. I get Hurley's voice mail and leave a message telling him we need him to come to the autopsy suite ASAP. By the time I'm done, Arnie has arrived.

"What's up?" he says, eyeing the body on the table through his thick-lensed glasses.

After cutting off his ponytail as payment for a lost bet, Arnie is trying to grow his thinning hair long again, and it's not a good look for him. The long, thin strands hanging down around his head are prone to static and it makes him look like the love child of Mr. Magoo and a sea anemone.

"You haven't cut yet?" Arnie says, coming close to my own thoughts, though mine are regarding his hair, not our body.

"Getting ready to," Izzy says. "But we found something in

one of the stab wounds that I want you to take a closer look at right away." He holds up the jar that contains the flower petals, and Arnie walks over and takes it from him.

"Flower petals, I believe," Arnie says, turning the jar around in his hand. "Yellow ones, maybe from . . . a carnation? That could be potentially significant since the yellow carnation symbolizes rejection, or disappointment."

"You know that off the top of your head?" I say, surprised. I hadn't given him a clue as to why Izzy wanted him to come down here.

Arnie smiles at me. "I know a lot of things," he says cryptically. "This particular tidbit I know because it's part of an RPG I play a lot that has mystical and mythological overtones based on real folklore."

"RPG?" Izzy says.

"Role-playing game," Arnie and I say at the same time. Then Arnie says, "You found them inside a stab wound?"

Izzy nods. "Mattie says she remembers hearing about a case at the conference she attended last year that also had these flower petals embedded in the stab wounds."

"And the same stabbing pattern we see here," I add, making Arnie look again at the body.

"Does that ring any bells with you?" Izzy asks Arnie. "Have you and your evidence tech cronies chatted about anything that sounds like this?"

Arnie's brow furrows in thought. "Not the flowers, but I remember a case out west that involved a unique stabbing pattern. I think they determined it was a pentagram. Ended up being a twisted devil worshipper. This is morc of a triangular shape, though. Didn't that recent serial killer in Eau Claire stab in a similar pattern?"

"He did," Izzy says with a grim smile.

I gather he's pleased that Arnie made the connection without any prompting or clues from us, but also worried about the questions it raises regarding Ulrich's guilt or innocence.

"I don't recall any mention of flower petals in that case, though," Arnie says, looking bemused. He rubs his chin and stares at the petals in the jar. "Wait . . . does this mean—"

Before Arnie can finish his question, the door to the autopsy suite opens and my husband walks in. As always, the mere sight of him gets my heart to racing, that long-legged stride, those sky-blue eyes, that thick black hair. I sigh and smile, hoping my reaction to the sight of him never wanes. Then I wonder if he has a similar reaction when he sees me.

"What's going on?" he asks, walking over to where Arnie and I are standing. He glances at the body on the table and frowns. "You haven't opened her yet?"

Izzy counters, "You haven't identified her yet?"

The two men stare at one another and then collectively sigh with such coordinated timing you would have thought they'd practiced it.

"We have some interesting findings," I say to Hurley, hoping to disperse the tension in the room. I then explain it all to him, beginning with the pattern of the stab wounds, finding the flower petals, the discussion I had with the fellow at the forensic conference last year, and the fact that the flower petals were never mentioned during Ulrich's trial.

Hurley listens with little reaction and without interruption. When I'm done, he says, "Are you saying you think our case might be tied to the guy who killed those women in Eau Claire?"

"It appears that way on the surface," I say.

Hurley looks over at Izzy, who nods his agreement.

"And if I remember right," Arnie says, "all the victims of the guy in Eau Claire were of a physical type, the same as our girl here. Blond, tall, late twenties, early thirties." He pauses and eyes the woman's body with this last bit. There is a hint of doubt in his voice and on his face. I get why. It's hard to estimate her age based on how she looks.

"Hmm," Hurley says. "A copycat perhaps?"

"You'd think so," Arnie says, "given that the guy convicted of the Eau Claire murders is in prison serving a life sentence without the possibility of parole."

"Except for the flowers," I say. "I remember this guy at the conference telling me that the prosecution never raised the presence of the flower petals during the trial, and apparently, the defense attorney either missed it or didn't think it was relevant."

Hurley rakes a hand through his hair and I realize he's overdue for a cut when he ends up with a Mohawk. He looks over at Arnie. "Your thoughts on this?"

"You mean other than the fact that another innocent man may be in prison?" Arnie says.

"Another . . ." Hurley starts to speak, but then stops himself and looks at me. "Right."

There is an awkward silence until Arnie clears his throat and says, "There is some symbolism associated with yellow carnations." He then tells Hurley what he told Izzy and me earlier.

"Sounds like it's personal for the guy," Hurley speculates, once again turning his attention to the dead girl. "Is Arnie right?" he says, looking at me. "Did this guy you talked to say that the other victims shared a physical resemblance?"

"I can't recall," I say. "I don't remember a lot of what we discussed, but we didn't get into any in-depth details about the case other than the flower thing. It was one of those late-night bar chats, just shoptalk. Nothing official. You know how that goes. We were discussing interesting oddball cases we'd encountered."

Arnie and Izzy both nod, but Hurley arches his eyebrows at me. "You had late-night drinks with a guy in a bar?"

Izzy clears his throat and suddenly becomes very focused on our victim's body. Arnie pulls at his chin and pretends to look away, but he can't quite pull it off. A second later, he's watching to see how this one is going to play out.

"I did," I say, offering no additional explanation.

Hurley and I stare at each other for a few seconds.

"Why didn't you mention it before?" he asks.

I shrug. "Didn't think it was important. Until now, of course. Now the conversation is very important, wouldn't you agree?"

Hurley pins me with those blue eyes. They are intense, but I also see a hint of a twinkle there and know he's teasing me, at least partially.

"Sounds like you two should find this guy Mattie talked to," Arnie suggests. There is a hint of voyeuristic interest in his voice, as if he thinks this talk might somehow explode into something more emotionally fraught that he'd like to have a ringside seat for. And maybe a tub of popcorn.

The tension in the room is crackling so much that I swear I can feel it sparking on my skin. Then Hurley's phone rings, and just like that, the tension dissipates.

"Detective Hurley," he says.

All of us watch his face eagerly, trying to discern the nature of the call and if it relates to our case. When Hurley says into his phone, "Hold on a second and I'll ask," I feel certain it does.

My suspicion is confirmed when he says to Izzy, "Does she have some kind of wine mark, a birthmark on her head, near her left temple?" Hurley looks a little confused by the question, but I know immediately what he's asking about. Izzy does, too.

"A port-wine stain," we both say at the same time.

Izzy starts rooting through the girl's dirty hair, pulling the strands taut so he can see her scalp. After a moment, he looks at Hurley and says, "She does."

"That's confirmed," he says into his phone.

Izzy and I exchange excited looks. I feel certain we are about to identify our victim, a huge step in trying to figure out who killed her.

"That would be great," Hurley says, and then he disconnects his call.

"Was that—"

Hurley puts up a hand to stop me, staring at his phone screen. "Hold on," he says. After a few seconds that feel like an eternity, there is a ding from his phone and he swipes at the screen. He looks for a moment, then carries the phone over to the victim, holding it up next to her face.

"What do you think, Izzy?" he says, scowling. "This picture is a few years old and before she got serious about the drugs."

Arnie and I walk over and peer around Hurley's arm at the picture. I see what he means. On his phone is a photo of a young woman with blond hair who looks to be in her early twenties. She is pretty, with a wide, bright smile, unblemished skin, a full set of straight white teeth, and about thirty more pounds on her than the woman on our table.

Izzy sighs. "Hard to say. The basic physical characteristics, such as hair and eye color, fit, but that's about all I can confirm. Well, that and the port-wine stain, but those types of birthmarks are more common than you might think. And the location of this one is also quite common. It's not enough for a definitive ID, but perhaps a tentative one. I'll need to get DNA if we can."

Hurley nods. "There may be DNA available, according to the cop who sent the info. The mother of this missing girl has all the teeth she lost as a child, as well as her hairbrush and some other items that might be helpful."

"Who is she?" I ask.

"Her name is Lacy O'Connor. She's from Viroqua and she's twenty-seven. She's been missing for two years, and for a year and a half before that, she was hanging with a guy named Dutch Simmons, who was heavy into drugs. Lacy started using and things escalated. Her mother tried interventions a couple of times—apparently, the father is dead—but

Lacy kept running away and hooking up with Simmons again. Then Lacy went missing. The cops in Viroqua think she and Simmons hooked up with a group of traveling druggies that move from town to town, performing purse snatches and home break-ins so they can get money for more drugs."

Arnie's eyes grow big. "Since she was found here, does that mean they're in this area now?"

"Could be," Hurley says. "I'll check with Junior Feller to see if he's had an uptick in robberies recently. And we should check out Troll Nook."

Troll Nook is a 1950s-era motel/camp comprised of a collection of individual cabins that were popular with families when it was first built. The cabins used to border a small lake, but it was a man-made lake that dried up in the '70s when the water was diverted upstream for farm irrigation. In the decades since, the place has fallen into disrepair and it now attracts a different type of crowd, thanks to the "kitchen facilities": a microwave, a sink, and a hot plate, which many of the current residents use to cook things other than food.

"I doubt a group of drug-addicted people would have any motive, not to mention the wherewithal, to create a copycat murder of one of their own," I say. "That means we still have the issue of this girl's murder matching the MO of the guy the Eau Claire cops put away."

Hurley nods, sighing wearily. "I might need to have a chat with our Mr. Ulrich," he says. "And it looks like I'm going to be taking a trip to Eau Claire."

"I'd like to go with you," Izzy says.

It's a surprise proclamation to me, and judging from the looks on their faces, I see also to Hurley and Arnie.

"Eau Claire is one of the counties that still has a coroner system in place, at least for now, though they're piloting a training program there for forensic pathologists. I'd like to see how it's going, and maybe review the autopsies on the victims in the Ulrich case," Izzy says.

Hurley looks over at me. "Are you up for a road trip?"

"Absolutely, assuming we do it tomorrow. Christopher's on for the next few days." My job-sharing coworker, Christopher Malone, and I split the weekdays between us, overlapping on Wednesdays and alternating coverage on the weekends, since our job also entails answering death calls at all hours of the day and night.

"Does tomorrow work for you, Izzy?" Hurley asks.

Izzy nods. "As luck would have it, tomorrow is Otto Morton's first day back after his accident."

Otto Morton is a forensic pathologist who was readying for retirement, until Izzy had a heart attack several months ago, and someone else had to step in. Otto found he liked our office and the work here, and he decided to stay on when Izzy made the decision to come back to work on a part-time basis only. This decision was triggered in part by the fact that Izzy and his partner, Dom, had adopted a baby girl named Juliana. During a bad winter storm several weeks back, Otto was involved in a car accident and broke his arm, putting him on the injured reserve list for a while.

"Oh, goody," I say. "It sounds like we're up for a road trip."

Hurley says, "I'll get it set up, and I'll also look into this boyfriend of Lacy's, see what I can find." He cocks his head to one side and looks at Lacy with a sad, tired expression. "Do you have a time of death for me, Izzy?"

"Not exact, but I can narrow it down some. She's already gone through full rigor and it's nearly receded completely at this point. I can't be sure how much temperature played a role, because we know she wasn't killed where she was found, but we don't know how long she was by the road, or where she was before that. But based on rigor alone, I'd say she was killed sometime between the hours of ten p.m. and six a.m. the night before last."

Hurley goes off to make the arrangements while Arnie

gathers up the flower petals and other trace evidence we collected earlier from Lacy's clothing and hair. Arnie heads back to his lab, and I re-glove and start to help Izzy with the autopsy.

We spend a long time combing over Lacy's body surface, looking for more trace evidence and documenting every bruise, needle mark, sore, and cut she has. And there are a lot of them. Several of the bruises on her arms, neck, and face appear to be new, suggesting that they might have been left by the killer. We photograph each one and then swab them on the off chance that there might be some foreign DNA left behind.

Lacy also has several clusters of raised red wheals on her arms, legs, and torso. "These look like bedbug bites," Izzy says. "They tend to leave a distinctive pattern of three bites in a cluster, with two close together and the third a little ways off." He points out two such clusters on the girl's arms. "Sometimes they form a line like these." He points to another cluster and I shrug my shoulders to eliminate the crawling sensation I suddenly feel.

"That's one more reason to check out Troll Nook," I say. "I talked to one of my friends who runs with EMS the other day and she was telling me about all the overdoses they've picked up out there. She mentioned that they have a very bad bedbug infestation. They've had to practically rip apart the insides of their ambulances a couple of times to get the bugs out."

Beneath Lacy's broken, ragged fingernails, we find bits of what look like dirt, decayed leaves, and moss consistent with the area where her body was dumped. We'd found more of the same material in her clothing and hair during our initial exam, and even though we know it's unlikely to be of any great evidentiary value, we photograph, document, and collect it all. The only unexpected thing we find is a small piece of gold thread snagged between the two broken bottom teeth she has.

When we finally open Lacy to examine her insides, we've been working on her for over two hours. The actual autopsy reveals little in the way of surprises. Lacy's lungs show evidence of her smoking habit—both cigarettes and drugs—her liver is cirrhotic, and her heart is enlarged and shows evidence of a simmering endocarditis. Without intervention, that would have likely killed her within the year, had someone not stabbed her to death first.

Notification to her mother would have to wait until we can get the DNA results, but it's a good bet she already has a strong suspicion, given that the local cops in Viroqua have asked her for samples for DNA comparison, as well as a description of any identifying and distinctive birthmarks, tattoos, or scars. Based on what Hurley told us about her, it sounds like Lacy's mother tried her best to turn Lacy around, to no avail. How heartbreaking this must be for her. I feel for her, but as a parent, I also fear being in her shoes someday. What makes a kid go astray?

I've seen some situations where the parents can easily be blamed, but I've also seen others where the parents and the home situation seemed ideal, yet the kid went off the rails anyway. It raises the whole question of nature versus nurture, and based on what I've seen, heard, and read, there are no easy answers to that question. There are no training classes for being a parent and raising kids, so most of us function on what we've seen and experienced ourselves. We learn as we go, do the best we can, and sometimes make mistakes. I've personally known some family situations, my own included, where I think it's pure luck that the kids turned out okay, given the way they were parented, which makes me lean more toward the nature side of the equation.

By the time we're done with Lacy's autopsy, Hurley has called to let us know that he has spoken to Mason Ulrich's current lawyer, who has arranged for us to meet with Ulrich at the Columbia Correctional Institution, where he's serving his life sentence. Our appointment is for nine o'clock the following morning, so we will need to leave around eight.

Hurley has also arranged for us to meet with and talk to the detective in Eau Claire who oversaw the Ulrich investigation, and then visit with the doctor who performed the autopsies. I'm surprised the autopsies were done locally, given the nature and seriousness of the case. Izzy, however, tells me that the training program there requires a board-certified forensic pathologist to supervise any procedures. That means the autopsies were overseen or perhaps were conducted by someone who might have performed them if the bodies had been sent to Milwaukee or Madison.

Christopher comes in at noon and we settle in at the conference table in the library so I can fill him in on the case. I end it with the caveat that I plan to stick with the investigation for now and will be going with Hurley tomorrow to talk to both Ulrich and the Eau Claire detective.

"Sounds like quite the can of worms," Christopher says.

"Speaking of cans of worms," a male voice says from the door to the library.

We turn and see Junior Feller, another of Sorenson's detectives, standing there. Junior was a patrol officer for many years, but was promoted to detective two years ago. His focus is on vice crimes, but the vices typically indulged in by Sorenson residents are neither serious enough nor frequent enough to keep Junior busy all the time. That being the case, he often helps Hurley and the other homicide detective, Bob Richmond, with their cases and investigations.

"Hurley wants me to help him out today with this Jane Doe case," Junior says. "Though I understand she's no longer a Jane Doe."

"We don't have DNA yet," I say, "but we're pretty certain about her ID."

Junior nods. "Hurley's tied up with getting some police reports from Eau Claire, or something like that. He said he wanted me to check out Troll Nook to see if our victim might have stayed there."

"I think it's quite possible," I tell him. And then I explain about the bedbugs. Junior shivers and subconsciously brushes at his arms while I'm describing the bites, and I suppress an urge to do the same.

"So, which one of you is going with me?" Junior asks, looking back and forth between Christopher and me.

"That would be me," I say, my enthusiasm waning some. "Give me a second to grab my scene kit and then we can go."

CHAPTER 3

Junior offers to drive and I follow him out front to a four-door dark blue sedan that looks like it was pulled from the prop department for a movie about unmarked police cars.

"If we don't find what we want at Troll Nook, I have some other leads on this Dutch Simmons guy this girl was hanging out with," Junior says. "I think he might be an associate of some drug dealers in the area that we've been trying to bust."

During our drive, Junior fills me in on some facts about Troll Nook. "It's currently owned by a man who lives in Milwaukee, but there is an on-site manager named Clyde Rivers, who lives in one of the cabins and is supposed to handle the rent collections, repairs, maintenance, and other issues. The rents are cheap and available on a daily, weekly, or monthly basis. As a result, for the past six years or so, the cabins have served as temporary housing to a variety of desperate people and societal lowlifes. Drug use is rampant and we get called out to the place nearly every week for overdoses."

The place is even smarmier-looking than I had imagined. Judging from the condition of the grounds, which is mostly dirt spattered with a few scrubs of grass bravely clinging to life, I figure maintenance isn't high on Clyde's list. Based on complaints Junior tells me about from some of the residents, repairs aren't a priority, either. But if the stories of the residents can be believed, Clyde is apparently quite persistent when it comes to collecting the rent money.

"He's kind of a scary dude," Junior says.

There are only two cars parked out front when we pull into the lot, but this doesn't mean the place isn't busy. A lot of the people who stay here don't own a vehicle. Clyde's cabin is at the center of the front row of cabins. It has a hand-painted wooden sign hanging cockeyed over the front door and it says MANGER. Apparently, spelling isn't high on Clyde's list, either, though based on what I've heard about the condition of some of the cabins, it's quite possible that the inside of Clyde's resembles a straw-filled barn.

I follow Junior to Clyde's front door and stand back a few feet while Junior knocks. We hear rustling inside, and then a loud bang followed by a muffled curse. Then the door opens and Clyde is revealed in all his glory.

I've never seen or met Clyde, though I've heard stories about him. In the past, I've heard him described as "scary-looking" and "intimidating," but without much in the way of specific description. Now I see why. Clyde is huge, standing six-eight at least, with legs the size of tree trunks extending out from a pair of cutoff sweatpants. His hands look like two canned hams, and his broad chest is covered with a tattered, holey T-shirt. WTF? is written on it in six-inch-high letters. His feet are bare, filthy, hairy, and huge—at least a size seventeen, I'd wager. Here is someone who makes my feet look small, and that's no easy task. There's a reason Hurley's nickname for me is Squatch.

Despite all this oversized flesh, Clyde has a surprisingly small head; so much so, it looks like it belongs to someone else and he just borrowed it to have a head for the day. Or maybe he just returned from a vacation to an island inhabited by head-shrinking natives. His facial features are small, too: a tiny nose, little rosebud lips, and small, close-set eyes. His expression is flat, utterly devoid of emotion. The ears make up for it all, to some degree; he apparently borrowed those from Dumbo. But the overall look of the man is oddly unsettling. He just looks . . . wrong.

"Mr. Rivers," Junior says, his head tilted back to look up at the guy. "I'm Detective Feller with the Sorenson Police Department and I'd like to talk to you. May we come in?"

I'm hoping Clyde says no, because there is no way I want to go inside this cabin. I try to see past the bulk of Clyde's body to the interior to prep myself, just in case, but I can't see anything. It's dark as night in there.

"Not much room in here," Clyde says, delivering his second surprise.

I expected a deep, rumbling voice to emanate from that body, something that sounded like a volcano erupting. Instead, his voice is breathy, soft, and slow, each word carefully enunciated and barely above a whisper. It's somehow creepier than the booming voice I expected.

"What you want to know?" Clyde asks. He takes a step forward and pulls the cabin door closed behind him.

Junior is prepared. He has a picture of Lacy with him and shows it to Clyde. "Has this girl ever stayed here?"

Clyde stares at the picture, taking hold of it in his canned-ham hand. The five-by-seven-inch picture looks wallet-sized inside his massive grip. "Yup, she's been here," he says, handing the picture back. "Rented cabin eighteen last week. But I haven't seen her for a couple of days. She owes me some rent money, so I'm guessing she ran out of cash." He hands the picture back to Junior.

"She ran out of life," I say, and it's all I can do not to take a step back when Clyde raises his head and fixes his beady eyes on me. "Someone killed her."

For a split second, Clyde's face softens, morphing into something resembling sadness. But then it corrects itself and becomes expressionless again. "That means the boss is going to hit me up again," he says.

"Hit you up?" Junior echoes.

"Yeah, if I don't get the rent money up front, the boss man takes it out of my pay. And I let Lacy slide for a couple of days. She's been good for it before, so I figured she would be again. Lesson learned."

Based on what Junior told me about Clyde, he's not known for his magnanimity or patience, so I'm betting the reason he let Lacy "slide" is because she paid him with something other than cash. The thought makes my stomach turn.

"Did she stay here by herself, or was someone with her?" I ask.

Clyde looks at Junior, then back at me. "Why you want to know?"

"Like the lady said," Junior answers, "someone killed her."

"And it's possible it was a serial killer, one who kills both men *and* women," I add. This is essentially a lie, but I want to hit Clyde where it might hurt. "The reason you didn't get Lacy's rent money is because she died. Your other tenants are at risk, too."

Clyde scowls at this. "Yeah, she has a guy fella who runs with her. They been together nearly a year, I think. Goes by the name of Dutch."

"Do you know his last name?" Junior asks.

I wonder why. It's not like there's a whole bunch of people by the name of Dutch running around.

Clyde shakes his head.

"What does he look like?" Junior asks.

Clyde shrugs and blinks slowly, like a slow-motion picture. "Dark hair, wears it long, has a beak nose. He's not very tall."

I can't imagine anyone looks very tall in Clyde's world and wonder what this means to him. I'm about to ask him to clarify when he does a karate chop motion on his chest just below the nipple line. "Comes to about here on me."

Junior pulls a picture out of his pocket and shows it to Clyde. "Is this him?"

"Yup."

"Is Dutch staying here?" Junior asks with a hopeful tone, returning the picture to his pocket.

"He was, but when Lacy didn't return, neither did he."

Junior's shoulders sag with disappointment. "Has anybody else stayed in that cabin since Lacy left?" he asks.

"No, business is a little slow right now. And I figured Lacy might come back. She left some stuff in there."

"We need to take a look at her cabin," I say.

Clyde scowls again. "What for?"

"There might be something in there that could help us catch this serial killer guy," Junior says, playing along with my ruse. "The sooner we can catch him, the better your rent collections will be. You can't collect rent from dead people."

Clyde looks intrigued, now that we're speaking his language. "You looking for evidence, like that *CSI* stuff?" he says, scratching at his armpit.

"Something like that, yes," Junior says.

"Yeah, okay." Clyde turns and reenters his cabin, shutting the door behind him. We wait, assuming he's gone to get a key, but then I start to wonder. There's a little too much chlorine in Clyde's gene pool for my comfort. Just as I'm about to tell Junior to knock again, the door opens. I'm expecting Clyde to go with us to cabin eighteen, but to our surprise he holds out one incredibly long arm and I see a key hanging from his ham fist. "Bring it back when you're done," he says, dropping the key into Junior's hand, which looks infantile next to Clyde's. Then the door shuts again.

I'm glad Clyde gave that key to Junior, given that he was holding it with the same hand that had been scratching at his armpit moments before. Lord knows what else he was scratching when he was inside that cabin.

Junior seems unfazed, or perhaps just unaware. He turns and looks at me with an anticipatory smile. "Shall we?"

CHAPTER 4

Cabin eighteen is in the back row behind the ten cabins out front. After getting my scene-processing kit from Junior's car, we follow a dirt path between Clyde's cabin and the one next to it. Then we head down the row behind. Many of the cabins' numbers are missing, but number twenty has survived, so it's easy enough to identify ours by counting backward. Before unlocking the door, we both don gloves. Since we still don't know where Lacy was killed, we need to treat this room as a crime scene.

The exteriors of the cabins have held up over the years reasonably well, but the same can't be said for the insides. The interior of this cabin is dark and smells of mildew. Junior reaches for the switch inside the door and flips on an overhead light. Two of the four bulbs in the light are dead, but this is probably a blessing in disguise. I'm certain this room looks much better in dim light. The floor is carpeted, but it is threadbare and worn down to reveal the wooden planks in several places. The bed, a double, is covered with an old-fashioned bedspread that at one time had a rim of fringe around its edges. All that remains now of the fringe are mangled, tangled clumps of thread that hang from the edge of the spread like tiny turds. The blanket's color is a mix of gray and yellow, and it's hard to guess what the original color was, though I'm thinking it was either white or beige.

A cheap pressed-wood credenza, with six drawers in it, is on the wall opposite the bed. The handle on one of the drawers is missing, and there is a screwdriver thrust into one of the holes where the handle used to be, providing a makeshift way to open the drawer. A plastic shopping bag is on top of the credenza, whose faux-wood laminate is peeling and broken. A razor, two toothbrushes, and a used bar of soap, with one short, dark, curly hair dried onto its surface, are inside it. The sight of the hair makes me gag.

There is no TV—this place is a bare-bones level of existence—but there is a small refrigerator in the far corner, with a one-burner electric hot plate on top of it. A round table, with the same laminate top as the credenza, and two mismatched wooden folding chairs are near it.

The entrance to the bathroom is in the far corner and the room is tiny. There is a sink, a toilet, and a stall shower, with a hinged glass door on it, all of them jammed so close together that one could practically shit, shower, and shave all at the same time. At first, I think the glass in the shower door is opaque, but then I realize it's covered with soap and lime buildup from a lack of cleaning and the effects of the hard water we have in this area. The tile floor has years of grime ground into the cracks where the grout used to be.

A wave of nausea comes over me as I look at the filthy floor and I clamp a hand over my mouth. I back out of the room and walk over to the bed, feeling the nausea subside. Once I feel like my stomach is under control, I reach down and pull back the covers on the bed. The sheets are gray and thin, and when I look along the sides of the bed, where the fitted sheet is rolling back from the mattress seams, I see the telltale reddish-brown residue of bedbugs.

My stomach lurches again and I look away, letting my head roll back. I see a spot on the ceiling above me that has a similar reddish-brown color and I quickly step back, thinking it's one of the bugs. But then I look closer and see that the shape isn't quite right, and it isn't moving.

"Junior? Come over here and look at this. Does it look like blood?"

I point up at the spot and he stares at it. It's too high for either of us to get a close look at it, and after looking around the room, Junior says, "We need something to stand on. And I think we should spray this room with luminol, see what shines."

"Okay, but let's get some pictures of everything as it is now before we do that."

For the next twenty minutes, I work my way around the room, snapping pictures of everything from the hair on the soap bar in the bag to the mildew in the corner of the shower. I find a hypodermic needle, uncapped, lying behind the toilet and very carefully retrieve it and place it in a glass evidence jar. Junior helps me collect and label the bag and its contents, and then we swab all the likely spots for DNA. Given the poor quality—or apparent lack—of maid service in the place, I'm guessing those swabs will be a veritable primordial soup of DNA remnants.

Just for grins, I make Junior lift the mattress on the bed. He nearly drops it when a half-dozen little brown bugs go scurrying for cover. "What the hell are those?" he says, backing his feet up. "Cockroaches?"

"No, bedbugs. Hold on, I want to capture one or two of them. Since they like to dine on human flesh, maybe they'll be good sources for DNA."

The bugs are fast and skittery and it takes me four tries before I manage to scoop a bug into an evidence jar. I decide one will do and quickly screw on the lid. Junior lets the mattress drop and then shudders, brushing at himself.

I continue photographing, bagging, tagging, and swabbing everything I think is appropriate, while Junior hunts down Clyde and rounds up a small stepladder. The ladder is rather rickety-looking, so I let Junior do the climbing and swabbing of the spot on the ceiling as I hold the ladder steady. When that's done, I take out my luminol and start by spraying the ceiling above the bed, extending several feet beyond the perimeter of the bed itself. I then spray the wall around the headboard and then the headboard itself. The surface of the bed is next, and then I spray the rug around the bed. I do all of this as fast as I can, and then I give Junior the nod. He flips off the overhead light and I turn on my special flashlight, aiming at the ceiling first.

"Wow, look at that," I say. "I think we have our crime scene."

Along the ceiling, there is a line of tiny luminescent spots that runs above the bed from one side to the other, extending a tiny bit behind us. Junior is taking pictures and I shine the light on the wall and headboard next. Here, there is surprisingly little to see, a few random, minuscule specks of luminescence on the wall and only three on the headboard—spots so small, we didn't see them with the naked eye.

As soon as Junior is done shooting pictures of that area, I move the light to the rug, where we again find some random drops and one curved line that looks like it might have been made by the edge of a shoe. Junior again snaps away, and when he's done, I turn the light to the surface of the bed, where I expect to see a giant pool of glowing evidence.

There is nothing there. I give Junior a puzzled look. "Let's pull back the covers and spray some more, and if that doesn't show anything, we'll flip the mattress," I say.

Junior helps me do just that, but despite our efforts, we still come up empty on the bed.

"He must have used some kind of plastic barrier," Junior says. "We have castoff on the ceiling and walls, some drips on the carpet and floor, and part of a footprint, so clearly something happened here. But the void on the bed means he covered it with something. He came prepared."

I frown at this.

"What?" Junior says, seeing my expression. "You don't agree?"

"No, I do. I agree with everything you just said. But that shoots a hole in a theory I had. If we assume Lacy wasn't a copycat, and the same man who killed the women in Eau Claire killed her, I figured her death was one of opportunity. I imagined the guy was trying not to kill anymore, knowing it might raise questions, but Lacy kind of fell into his lap. He couldn't help himself because she fit his victim profile. But if he had plastic to cover the bed, and the flower petals to stuff in the wound, then that means her death was planned. It was premeditated and carried out in an area some distance from all the others." I pause and swallow hard. "He's starting up again."

"If that's true, there will be more victims," Junior says. "But where?" The two of us stand there lost in thought for a moment. Then Junior hands me the camera and takes out his cell phone. "I need to call Hurley."

Junior jabs at his phone screen, but his gloved fingers won't do the trick, so he removes them. Then he jabs at the screen some more and curses under his breath. "No signal in here," he says. "I'm going to step outside."

He walks over, opens the cabin door, and stops dead in his tracks. "What the . . ."

A short man with long, dark, greasy hair and a beak nose is standing on the threshold. He looks startled as he stares up at Junior, then at me standing behind him.

"Are you Dutch?" Junior says.

Dutch, or the man we assume is Dutch, answers by spinning on his heel and taking off at a run.

CHAPTER 5

"Damn it!" Junior mutters, and then he takes off after the guy.

Good thing Junior's willing to run—because I'm not. I hate running. I'm not built for it, and if anyone ever sees me running, they should run, too, because it means something really awful is chasing me.

I step outside just in time to see Junior disappear around the end of cabin ten. I turn right and hurry down toward the middle path we followed to the back row of cabins. When I emerge out front in the parking area, I find our fleeing man prone on the ground with his face in one of those desperate clumps of grass, Junior's knee in the small of his back.

"I'm going to let you up," Junior says, mildly breathless. "I just want to talk to you, but if you try to run again, I'm going to arrest you and throw you in jail."

I think Junior is bluffing; as far as I can tell, this fellow hasn't broken any laws that we know about, at least not yet. The cops are allowed to lie and most of them, Junior included, do it convincingly. Besides, I'm thinking that for anyone who has been forced to stay in one of these cabins, a jail cell with three squares a day and no bedbugs might seem more like a gift than a threat. But our man seems adequately kowtowed, and when Junior takes his knee off his back, Dutch rolls over and sits up.

"What the heck, man," Dutch mutters, frowning at Junior and rubbing one of his elbows.

"I'm going to ask you again, is your name Dutch?"

"Yeah," he utters with a scowl. "Why?"

"You've been hanging with Lacy O'Connor," Junior says.

"I was," Dutch says, his scowl deepening. Then his expression brightens. "Oh! Do you guys have her? Is she in jail? I wondered why she didn't come back."

Junior looks at me and I shrug. The guy sounds convincing to me, but these druggies are amazing actors at times.

"Yeah, Lacy is with us, in a manner of speaking," Junior says. "When did you last see her?"

"Night before last," Dutch says.

"Where?" Junior asks.

"Right here, in her cabin."

"Why did you come back here to the cabin today?"

"I left my shaving stuff behind," Dutch says, rubbing at the scruff on his face.

I recall the plastic bag with the razor and hairy soap, which was on the credenza. So far, his story seems reasonable.

"Does Lacy need bail money?" Dutch asks. "'Cause I know a guy who might front her some green if she . . ." His voice drifts off and he looks around frantically for a second. "She might be able to work a deal with the guy," he says finally.

I have a terrible feeling I know exactly what type of deal he's talking about.

Junior bites his lip for a second and then decides to spill the beans. "Dutch, Lacy is dead."

"Dead?" Dutch echoes with disbelief. "Did she OD? Aw, damn. Didn't anyone have any Narcan? Hell, that stuff is

everywhere now. Why didn't someone have Narcan?" Dutch looks angry and like he's about to cry.

"No, she didn't overdose," Junior says. "Someone killed her. Stabbed her to death and left her by the side of the road like some trash." If he's hoping to elicit some righteous indignation from Dutch, he's disappointed.

"I didn't kill her," Dutch says emphatically. Then he finally musters up some tears—either that or he's starting to go through withdrawal. "I love that girl," he says sadly.

"Yeah, you love her so much that you got her hooked on drugs and took her away from her family," I say.

He shoots me an irritated look. "I admit I led her over to the dark side," he says, "but I'm trying to get us both clean now. I even went to the ER here and told them I needed help. That's where I was when Lacy disappeared."

Junior looks at me with an unspoken request. I nod and step away, taking out my cell phone and dialing the number of the ER at the hospital in Sorenson. I worked there for six years, so I still know many of the docs and some of the staff there. I get lucky and my call is answered by one of my old friends, Phyllis, aka Syph, a nurse who has been working in the ER since she was born.

"Hey, Syph, it's Mattie."

"Mets," Phyllis says, using the nickname I had in the ER years ago, "what sort of trouble are you getting into today?"

"I'm at the scene of a murder and one of the cops is talking to a suspect, a guy named Dutch Simmons. He has an alibi, claims he was in the ER as a patient on the night in question, and I'm wondering if you can verify that for me."

"Sure, what night?"

"Night before last. That would be the evening of April fifth, morning of April sixth."

I hear Syph tapping away at a keyboard and after a moment she says, "Yep, he was here, all right. Ambulance brought him in as an overdose just before eight at night on the fifth and we shot him up with some Narcan. That got him going through withdrawal. He spent several hours here in the ER and then was admitted upstairs. He was discharged at nine this morning."

That covered the entire estimated time of death for Lacy. I felt a twinge of disappointment, but also a trill of excitement. Ruling Dutch out made the case more complicated, but it also left the door open for a case of mistaken conviction for Ulrich. "Thanks, Syph. I owe you one."

"Drop by anytime. You know you miss this place."

Oddly enough, she's right. I do miss the ER at times. The unpredictability, the fast pace, the unexpectedness, the variety . . . was all stuff I enjoyed most of the time. By contrast, the OR had been something of a snore, given that most of the cases were preplanned and followed a predictable course and pattern. Plus, there was little interaction between staff and patients, since most of the patients were anesthetized into oblivion and covered up with sterile drapes that reduced them to a patch of iodine-bronzed skin.

I disconnect the call and go back to Junior and Dutch. "He's covered," I say. "He was in the hospital from eight o'clock in the evening on the fifth until nine a.m. on the sixth."

Junior sighs. "When was the last time you saw Lacy?" he asks Dutch, who is busy brushing dust off his already-filthy pants.

Dutch stops brushing, looks at Junior, squints his eyes, and then groans as if the effort hurts. He rubs his forehead with his two middle fingers, making a circle where a cyclopean eye would be if he had one. "We scored some stuff from a guy in a bar."

"What bar?" Junior pushes.

"Somewhere," Dutch says, wavering a little. Though this sounds like an evasive answer, it's not. Three of the bars in

Sorenson have the names Somewhere, Anywhere, and Nowhere, which can make a discussion about a night out sound like an Abbott and Costello routine.

"You mean the Somewhere Bar, right?" Junior asks to clarify. Dutch nods. "How did you pay for the drugs?" Junior asks.

Dutch looks at him with what I imagine is supposed to be a wry smile. He wags a finger and his eyes become fixated on it for several seconds, making him nearly fall over. "I can't tell you that 'cause you'll arrest me."

"You have amnesty for the moment," Junior says, impatient. "Anything you tell me right now comes with a get-out-of-jail-free card."

Dutch apparently finds this hilarious; he leans forward and bellows out a laugh. The motion gives him just enough momentum that he staggers away, loses his balance, and ends up sitting on the ground. He tries to get up and falls down again. Then he gives up, crosses his legs, and leans forward, elbows on his knees.

"There's this group of people," Dutch begins. "They travel around and scope out neighborhoods in smaller towns where people are used to leaving their doors unlocked during the day. We hooked up with them and hit up a neighborhood of nice older homes, with a mix of family types. Lacy and I cruised the neighborhood on foot after dark had settled, knowing we might draw unwanted attention if we did it during the day. We saw an elderly couple step out of their house with their dog and head up the street, and we waited until they were out of sight and then walked up to their front door like we owned it. Sure enough, the front door was unlocked, and we just waltzed inside. We found the woman's purse sitting on a table in the foyer, and we found the man's wallet sitting on his dresser. We took all the cash they had and then hightailed it out of there. Total time, less than five minutes.

Total haul, over five hundred bucks—and no one paid us the least bit of attention." He pauses and smiles smugly, clearly proud of the crime they pulled off.

"We got lucky with that one," Dutch continues. "Those two had a lot of cash on hand. That tends to be the way with some older folks, though. They don't trust the banks and don't like using credit cards."

Dutch's story makes me angry. He and those like him are taking advantage of neighborhoods in towns like Sorenson that suffer from something of an identity crisis. Many of their inhabitants still think of them as insular communities populated with friendly, kind people who have old-fashioned, small-town values. This is still true to a large extent, but it's changing rapidly. Despite the steady uptick in crimes like the one Dutch and Lacy committed, plenty of people still leave their houses and cars with the doors unlocked.

"So you took the cash you stole and used it to buy drugs?" Junior says.

Dutch nods. "We scored at the Somewhere Bar and then went down by the river and got high. After that, we headed back here, but our car broke down out on the highway. Lacy got out and started walking back to our cabin. I must have passed out in the car, 'cause next thing I know, an ambulance is there loading me up and taking me to the hospital."

If Dutch's story can be believed, Lacy might have been picked up by her killer as she was walking along the road. Had he then driven her back to her cabin here at Troll Nook and killed her? The lack of any defensive wounds suggests that Lacy was incapacitated in some way when the stab wounds were inflicted. That makes me wonder.

"Dutch, did you have drugs left over when you and Lacy got in the car to drive back here?"

"A little bit," he admits. "I guess Lacy took it with her, 'cause when I went looking for our car, someone at the hospital told me the cops had it towed. No one said anything about finding anything illegal in it, so I'm guessing Lacy took what was left of what we bought."

Junior walks over to Dutch and holds out his hand. "Get up," he says.

Dutch takes the proffered hand and staggers to his feet.

"Turn around and put your hands behind your back," Junior says, taking a pair of handcuffs from his pocket.

Dutch gapes at him. "You said I had amity," he protests.

"The word is 'amnesty,'" Junior says irritably, "and I lied." He proceeds to recite the Miranda warning to Dutch and then walks him to the car, tossing him into the backseat. "Do we need anything more from the cabin?" he asks me.

I shake my head. "I think we're okay for now. I just need to get my scene kit and tape the place off."

"I'll let Clyde know he's got one less rental to worry about for now."

Fifteen minutes later, we are on the road, headed back to Sorenson, listening to Dutch cuss us out from the backseat.

CHAPTER 6

I check in with Hurley when I'm ready to call it a day and tell him I'll pick up Matthew and meet him at home. We briefly discuss dinner, but before we can come to any kind of agreement, Hurley has a call on his office line and our conversation is cut short.

By the time I drive to Izzy and Dom's house to pick up Matthew, it's after six and Izzy is already home. Izzy's life partner, Dom, is my primary source for childcare. When Matthew was born, I lived in a cottage behind Izzy's house. It had been built for Izzy's mother, Sylvie, who had broken a hip and needed closer supervision. Sylvie rallied, and after a year, she moved out. I'm sure she would have preferred to continue living close to the son she dotes on, but Sylvie struggles with the fact that Izzy is gay. To this day, she continues to bemoan the fact that he hasn't found himself a nice girl and settled down.

In the beginning, Sylvie ignored Dom for the most part, but now that he and Izzy have Juliana, Sylvie has come around some. She still lives in her world of denial and acts as if Dom is simply a male nanny hired to care for Izzy's child, but she knows that if she wants to spend time with Juliana—and she does—Dom is part of the package.

Dom has certainly done his part to win her over. The man was born to be a caregiver, and he loves to be a homebody. His cooking skills are divine (I have the thighs to prove it!), his sense for interior design is exquisite (as I learned when trying to decide on the décor for the new house Hurley and I had built last year), and he is an easygoing and natural parent. His ability to woo Sylvie—though "tolerate" is probably a better word—has done wonders for their relationship. Good thing, as Sylvie's health has again taken a turn and she is now back in the cottage, this time for good.

I lived in that cottage for the better part of two years, hiding there after I left David. Having discovered his dalliance by accident, and in an undeniably shocking way, catching him in flagrante delicto with a woman who was a coworker of mine at the time, it took me some time to figure out what I was going to do. Since he and I also worked together, I fled my job at the local hospital at the same time I fled my marriage. The drama behind the dissolution of our marriage is still fodder for gossip at the place, and I'm glad I never went back.

Izzy's assistant at the time had just quit, so he offered me the job. Since I knew how to slice and dice and had a better than average understanding of human anatomy, it was a good fit. My basic nosiness also made the investigative part of the job a natural for me, and after several seminars and educational programs, I have advanced my career and can now call myself a medicolegal death investigator. The title is a mouthful that basically means I spend a lot of time with dead people and I get to stick my nose into other people's business. I also get to work with my hubby, an additional perk.

When Matthew was born, using Dom for childcare came easily and naturally, since I lived mere feet away at the time.

Now that Hurley and I have built a home just outside of town, the commute is longer, but Dom is still my primary childcare person. Hurley's daughter, Emily, who lives with us now that her mother is dead, and my sister, Desi, another person who was born to be a parent, fill in as needed. Emily has been particularly useful for those middle-of-the-night calls that both Hurley and I get, because we can leave Matthew asleep in bed and not have to drag him out. That's going to change in the not-so-distant future, however, since Emily will be going away to college in another year.

One of the delights of having Dom as a caregiver is that he's always cooking or baking up something sinfully delicious. I've envied Izzy on more than one occasion. Being able to come home to one of Dom's delicious meals is a little slice of heaven. Not that Hurley can't cook. He can and does, but his offerings tend to be a bit more pedestrian than the stuff Dom makes. Not that I have room to criticize, since my own cooking skills are limited to what can be boiled, poured from a can, or ordered from a restaurant. For tonight, Dom is fixing a meal of beef tenderloin, baby red potatoes, asparagus, and homemade sourdough bread. The smell of his kitchen is the best aromatherapy I can imagine. Apparently, my son agrees, because he doesn't want to leave and come home with me.

"Izzy said you guys are going to Eau Claire tomorrow, so I'm assuming you'll be dropping Matthew off in the morning?" Dom says to me as I help my son put on his jacket.

"Yes," I say. "We'll be by around eight to pick up Izzy and drop off Matthew."

"You can leave Matthew here for the night, if you want."

"Maffew stay!" Matthew says, trying to wriggle out of the jacket sleeve I just got his arm into.

The offer is tempting, but I decline. As it is, it seems like I have so little time to spend with Matthew, and it's the same for Hurley. Our family unit is a bit ragtag at times, with all four of us going in different directions, particularly now that Emily has her driver's license and her own car. We see less and less of her as she opts to spend more time with her friends and with her boyfriend, Johnny Chester, whom Hurley refers to as Chester the Molester. It's an unfair moniker to hang on the kid, who has proven to be smart, trustworthy, and well-behaved. But he comes from a family that has cell blocks named after them at most of the state's prisons, and Hurley is convinced Johnny will one day follow suit and join the family business: Felonious Crimes, Inc.

Emily is home when Matthew and I get there, and Hurley arrives twenty minutes later. Faced with the rare opportunity to have all four of us together for dinner, I offer to cook, but both Hurley and Emily quickly nix the idea. Though I'm not known for my cooking skills, I've been trying to improve and learn. For the past six months, I've been experimenting with new recipes and techniques, with admittedly mixed results. Even our dog, Hoover, has turned his nose up at some of the leftovers from meals I've fixed, and he's been known to eat anything.

Given the vociferous objections to the idea of me cooking, I call one of our favorite restaurants in town, Pesto Change-o, and order a variety of our favorite Italian dishes. There are audible sighs of relief from both Emily and Hurley. After I go out and get the food and return home, bearing my packages, Matthew claps his hands with joy and says, "Pasketti!"

My son loves spaghetti. Unfortunately, he likes doing more than simply eating it. Something about that long, stringy pasta brings out the artist in him. He decorates himself and everything around him with it. Hoover has become quite adept at slurping noodles that are hanging off the edge of the table or Matthew's arm.

I decide tonight to try giving Matthew spaghetti without tomato sauce, hoping to minimize the mess, but he has a major meltdown over it. After squalling about his "bad pasketti," and resisting my encouragement to just try it, he takes the entire plate of spaghetti and turns it upside down on top of his head. The plate slides off and lands on the floor, some of the pasta falling with it, the rest of it draping itself over Matthew's head, shoulders, and lap. Since I had buttered the pasta, Matthew's hair and clothing are now greasy.

I tell him in my stern mommy voice to knock it off, but not satisfied with his degree of protest thus far, Matthew climbs down from his chair and pushes it over on its side. Hoover is at his side in a flash, trying to grab the pasta hanging from him. Hurley yells at Matthew, and then Matthew utters a word he might have heard me say a time or two, even though I try not to say such things aloud. It's not standard two-and-a-half-year-old vocabulary and it's the kind of word that makes other mothers gasp in horror, as if they don't say the same things at times.

In the brief, silent aftermath that follows this utterance, Hurley and I both stare at one another. Showing an uncanny ability to size up the situation and take advantage of it, Matthew runs from the room and goes upstairs, leaving a trail of "pasketti" behind him. Hoover is busy vacuuming it up, living up to his name. Emily, also no slouch when it comes to home combat survival, quietly slides off her seat and heads upstairs as well.

"Where did Matthew learn a word like that?" Hurley asks.

"Oh, come on, Hurley," I say, rolling my eyes. "You know very well that we've both said things in front of him that we shouldn't. How does that saying go? 'Little pitchers have big ears'?"

Hurley looks like he wants to argue the point, but then he takes on a faraway look, which tells me he's summoning up some memories. Apparently, they are memories involving his role in this, because his expression softens and he smiles at me.

"We need to be more careful in the future and make it

clear to Matthew that such words are inappropriate," he says.

"I agree." I reach over and give his hand a squeeze, hoping the doubt doesn't show on my face. Fact is, we've been trying to focus on this for a while now. So far, our efforts have produced mixed results. Cussing comes easily to Hurley and me.

Hoping to change the subject, I ask Hurley, "Did Junior fill you in on our talk with Dutch?"

"He did. Interesting, but not much help in figuring out what happened to Lacy between their time in the car and when she was killed in that motel cabin. Though Dutch is apparently singing to help lighten his sentence, and that will help solve several home robberies that have happened around town lately."

"You know, Lacy had no defensive wounds of any sort, yet her stab wounds were inflicted pre- or perimortem. We can't be sure of the exact order of the stab wounds, but there were fibers from the pants she was wearing inside the chest wounds, indicating that the pelvic wound was administered before the chest ones. It's as if she just lay there and let the killer do what he wanted."

"It sounds like she was pretty high when she and Dutch parted company that night," Hurley says.

"And she left with the rest of the goods they had bought. If she shot up some more, or someone shot her up, it might explain the lack of defensive wounds. It will be interesting to see what her tox screen shows."

With work talk out of the way, I clear the table and do the dishes while Hurley heads upstairs to "prep for tomorrow."

Despite his "pasketti" meltdown, or perhaps because of it, Matthew goes to bed more easily than usual. Pleased that we've avoided the drama that sometimes accompanies his bedtime, I head for our own bedroom, where I find my husband sitting up in bed wading through some files. The headboard for our king-sized bed is a large bookcase that contains shelves, cubbyholes, and overhead lights. Hurley and I both take our work to bed at times, probably more often than we should. We have a fourth bedroom on the upper floor that currently serves as a home office. Late nights in our bedroom, however, is the one place in the house where we can have privacy and discuss the cases we're working on, the details of which are often too gory and graphic for the tender ears of our son.

Emily would likely love to eavesdrop on our work conversations because she is intrigued by what we do. She's been talking about pursuing an education in forensic science, with a secondary focus on art. The girl has an amazing talent for drawing, particularly faces. A few years ago, when she was sitting in the library in my office waiting on her father, she focused on a skeleton hanging there and used the skull to draw a woman's face, not knowing that a portrait of the woman whose skeleton it was hung in another part of the office. The bones belonged to the wife of a previous pathologist who, at his wife's request, had donated the skeleton. Emily's drawing was notable not only for its resemblance to the once-living person, but also because she had no idea whom the skeleton belonged to or even if it was male or female. Somehow she had intuited the details and then rendered them with amazing precision and accuracy. The kid has an amazing talent; it's an innate ability that I think will segue nicely into a forensic pathology career.

As I approach our bed, I see two glowing orbs beneath it. It's one of our two cats, Tux and Rubbish, both of whom were rescues I took in while living in the cottage behind Izzy and Dom's house. The cats seem to take great delight in hanging out under our bed, but only if Hurley is in it. Hurley doesn't like cats. He's afraid of them, truth be told, but he's asked me not to say this to people. I think he's afraid it will have a deleterious effect on his macho image. The cats, conniving creatures that they are, seem to sense Hurley's fear and take delight in lurking beneath the bed, making just enough noise for Hurley to know they are there.

I've tried to quash Hurley's fears by pointing out how the cats lovingly attempt to make sure we are fed and cared for by bringing in any number of fresh kills to feed us—mice, moles, voles, baby rabbits, the odd bird or two, and, recently, a small turtle. They always leave them on Hurley's side of the bed, often on his pillow. But he continues to interpret their attentive kindness as a subtle form of intimidation. He's convinced the cats want him to move out—though there are times when he's said he thinks they want him dead—so they can have me all to themselves.

It's a true testament to his love for me that Hurley tolerates what he refers to as "those vile creatures," and lets them share his space. The fact that I also brought our dog, Hoover, to the mix has helped. Hurley and Hoover bonded early on. Hurley has Hoover keep guard on the floor next to our bed at night when the cats are stalking from beneath it. This gives Hurley a false sense of security, because Hoover is even more afraid of the cats than Hurley is.

I climb onto our bed from the bottom, crawling on my hands and knees toward my husband, who looks incredibly sexy wearing the new cheaters he's had to buy because his close-up vision is starting to go. I think the glasses make him look professorial, wise, and a tad bit nerdy. Oddly, this look turns me on.

"Hey, handsome," I say, reaching up and taking the folder from his hands.

He smiles down at me with one eyebrow arched. "I should study up on this case before we go to Eau Claire," he says with an obvious lack of conviction.

"We can do that tomorrow, in the car, on the way," I say,

pushing up his T-shirt and planting a kiss on his belly. "Right now, I think you need to study some anatomy."

With that, he tosses the pile of folders onto the floor, and then reaches down and pulls me up toward him, kissing me on the lips. And then he proceeds to earn an A+ in his anatomy class.

CHAPTER 7

I awaken the next morning at a little past six to find Hurley rolling out of bed and heading for the bathroom. My own bladder is feeling impatient, so I toss back the covers, get up, and head down the hall to the other bathroom. Matthew and Emily are both still asleep, and I figure Hurley and I might have an hour of peace-and-quiet time to enjoy our morning coffee before the chaos kicks in.

Once I'm done in the bathroom—which includes another failed attempt to get my rings on and a tense exchange with my scale, where I learn that I've not only *not* lost any weight, I've gained another five pounds—I head downstairs to the kitchen. There I turn on the coffee maker, which I'd set up the night before. We have a fancy De'Longhi espresso machine, which makes lattes and cappuccinos, but the effort involved is more than I feel I can deal with first thing in the morning. I sometimes make exceptions on the weekend mornings if I'm off duty, but the fancy machine gets most of its use in the afternoons or after dinner. Good old-fashioned drip coffee is our morning staple on most days.

Hurley comes downstairs a moment later, his unshaven face and tousled hair making him look scruffy and sexy at the same time. I'm in the process of taking two mugs down from the cabinet over the coffee machine when he comes up behind me and snakes an arm around my waist, pulling me into him.

"Good morning, beautiful," he says into my hair.

I arch my neck and turn my face around to kiss him, but before I can, my stomach lurches threateningly. I quickly face front again and lean forward, bracing myself with my hands on the edge of the counter.

"What's the matter, Squatch?"

I rub a palm over my stomach and swallow hard. "I'm okay," I say tentatively. "I got hit with a wave of nausea there for a moment. I hope I'm not coming down with something."

Hurley's hands settle on my shoulders, where they begin a slow, soothing massage. I close my eyes and relish the delicious feeling as he kneads my muscles. After several seconds of this, his hands suddenly stop moving and his fingers tighten ever so slightly.

"What is it?" I ask, opening my eyes and turning to face him. I'm quite tuned into my husband's body language, and I know that some idea, some significant thought, has just struck him. I assume it has something to do with our current case, but Hurley proves me wrong.

"Could that nausea be an indication of something else?" he asks in a hopeful tone.

I catch his meaning immediately and my eyebrows rise in astonishment. I flash on the swollen fingers, the weight gain, the intermittent nausea I've had recently. *Oh, dear.*

"It could be," I say, looking at him again, a tentative smile forming on my lips.

Hurley's mouth forms into a smile of its own. "Are you late?"

I think back and try to calculate, but it's no use. "I might be," I say finally. "I don't keep track of my periods very well. Do you remember when I had it last?"

Hurley makes a face like I just asked him to eat from the cat's litter box. "Lord, no. That's your job."

Technically, but we are in this together. I feel oddly irritated by his response, and the uncharitable thought pops into my head, but I manage to subdue it before I voice it.

"Do you have a test?"

"I do. I bought four of them two months ago when they were on sale." Hurley looks at me with a questioning expression, clearly implying that I should do the test right away. "I just peed," I say. "I need to drink a cup of coffee so I can go again."

"But isn't coffee a no-no?"

I sigh, the mere thought of giving up coffee makes me want to scream or kill someone. "It's fine in moderation," I say, which is true, though it still feels like a lame excuse. And then, before Hurley can come up with any more protests, I proceed to pour coffee into both mugs, though guilt prompts me to fill my own cup only halfway.

I hand Hurley's mug to him and we settle in at the table in our breakfast nook. It's one of my favorite spots in our newly built house, an outset area with windows on three sides. It offers a view of the woods that border us on one side, and of an area that runs down the side of the house that I plan to turn into a flower garden. For now, the view is of a great expanse of mud waiting for the spring planting of grass that will eventually create a lawn. Since the house was completed in early December, there hasn't been time yet to do any landscaping, though now that it is early April, the planting is about to begin in earnest.

We have to be careful with spring plantings here. Snowstorms in April are not unheard of; in fact, it's darn near a certainty that we'll have at least one. Beyond the muddy moat that currently surrounds our house is a bluff that overlooks the countryside out front, and rolling fields that once yielded corn, soybeans, and tobacco out back. We bought five acres from a farmer who was no longer working the land and whose family was selling it off one parcel at a time to finance the old man's nursing home–based retirement. Some of the surrounding acres have been sold to hobby farmers and are still being used for plantings. I'll know it's safe to start planting preparations when the first sure sign of spring comes around: the smell of cow manure. It's the local farmers' favorite fertilizer.

Despite the lack of any natural beauty to take in at the moment, the nook is still a cozy, warm place, thanks to its southeastern exposure. I want to sit and bathe in the morning sunlight for as long as I can, leaving the rest of the world behind. Hurley, however, is staring at me with puppy-dog eyes—eager, excited, and impatient. Desperate to escape from that optimistic and expectant—pun intended—scrutiny, I ask him if he learned anything useful last night in the time he had to study what he had on the Eau Claire serial killer.

"I was reading some police reports when you so delightfully interrupted me," he says with a salacious wink. He eyes me over his mug of coffee and his gaze sobers. "Was this guy you talked to in the bar at the conference married?"

I nearly spit my coffee out, surprised as I am by the question. "What difference does that make?" I ask a bit irritably.

Hurley shrugs and props his elbows on the table, holding his mug up in front of his face with both hands as if to hide from me. But I can still see his eyes and they tell me we aren't done with this discussion. "I don't suppose it matters," he says after a moment. "Did he flirt with you?"

His tone is even, not angry or upset, but the question clearly is a provocative one. I shrug and hold my coffee cup the same way he is, obscuring part of my face. Two can play at this game. "Are you jealous, Hurley?"

Another shrug. "I don't like the idea of you sipping drinks till all hours of the night in an out-of-town bar with some good-looking guy," he says. Now his tone is wounded, worried, but still not angry.

"Who said he was *good-looking?*" I ask. I suppress a smile. Hurley's image of me as some seductress or femme fatale amuses me because it couldn't be further from the truth. I didn't date a whole lot before I met my ex, David Winston, and the dates I did have were mostly disasters. I had one serious relationship before David that happened while I was in nursing school, but aside from that, the highlight of my dating experiences was a fellow who boasted that I was the best date he'd ever had. Sadly, he was one of my ER patients, someone I had to put in four-point leather restraints and shoot up with Haldol.

My courtship and subsequent marriage to David occupied most of my adult life, and he was clearly the one in charge during the whole thing. Typical of his surgeon's type A personality, he is and always has been a take-charge kind of guy who has no qualms about steering his life in the direction he wants it to go. The one time he couldn't do that was when I left him after discovering he'd been cheating on me with my coworker.

I sometimes wonder if we might have tried to work things out, had I discovered his indiscretions via the pervasive and surprisingly accurate grapevine at the hospital, as opposed to the way it happened. I walked into a dimly lit operating room one evening, thinking my husband was working late saving lives. I was bringing him a goody basket, since he'd missed dinner, but I found him with the nurse in question. She was on her knees in front of him, eagerly exploring *his* goody basket. The shock and pain of that moment seared my brain and heart, slamming shut the door on my relationship with David.

For two months, I hid out in Izzy's cottage and experimented with things like how long I could go without bathing before I truly began to smell, how many pints of ice cream I could eat in one day before I had to worry about weight gain, and how long I could sit on a pity pot before I became laughing stock for a big helping of pathetic soup. Finally I emerged from my self-made prison and began my current job.

"So this guy was ugly," Hurley says hopefully.

He hadn't been—quite the opposite if memory serves. Though when it comes to that night, my memory is serving minuscule portions, like they do in those extremely fancy, expensive restaurants where they put one scallop on a plate and then decorate around it and call it an entree. As far as I'm concerned, that barely qualifies as an appetizer.

I dodge. "I'm starting to think you don't trust me, Hurley." It's not an answer, but I'm hoping my deflection will keep Hurley from noticing this. It's wishful thinking on my part. My husband is an experienced interrogator.

"You didn't answer the question," he grumbles. "And it isn't you I don't trust, it's men in general. I know how we think."

I give him what I hope is a reassuring and understanding smile.

"You're not wearing your rings again," he says.

"They're too tight," I say, flexing my fingers. "I've put on a few pounds. I think I'm going to have to get them resized."

Hurley scowls, and I figure this conversation has about as much promise of turning out well as did the offering of the dead chipmunk Rubbish left on Hurley's pillow a few days ago, though it has been entertaining listening to Matthew natter on about the dead "pimpchuck" ever since. I decide to switch gears.

"I think I can pee now," I say, getting up. "Be back in five."

The diversion works. Hurley's developing scowl immediately morphs into an expression of hopeful anticipation. I make my way upstairs to the bathroom off our bedroom and retrieve one of the pregnancy tests I have stashed in a cabinet. After a brief review of the instructions, I position myself and proceed to pee on both the stick and my fingers. I set the test stick on top of a wad of toilet paper and leave it on the edge of the sink while I wash my hands. I glance at the clock on the wall and calculate my waiting time.

The idea of having another kid is one I've come to, somewhat reluctantly. Hurley has been eager to have a second child—though technically for him it's his third—ever since Matthew was born. I, on the other hand, have been on the fence. I didn't enjoy my pregnancy all that much, and I still recall the mental and physical exhaustion I felt during those early months of Matthew's life. Granted, things would be different this time. When I had Matthew, I was still living in the cottage behind Izzy's house and was essentially functioning as a single parent. It wasn't because Hurley didn't want to help; he did. But I was in a strange place then, mentally and emotionally, still struggling to deal with my failed marriage to David and unconvinced that Hurley's proposals were based on anything more than a sense of obligation.

Don't get me wrong. Hurley is a great hands-on dad and I absolutely adore my son. I would do anything for him. But Matthew really tests my patience at times, and I get tired at the mere thought of doing it all over again. There's also the fact that Emily will be moving out of the house in another year or so, taking with her one of our most convenient babysitting resources. It's already hard enough trying to balance Matthew's needs with those of my job and marriage. Adding another kid to the mix isn't likely to make things easier.

Hurley's persistence wore me down, however, and in a desperate attempt to come up with a decent birthday gift for him, I agreed that we would try for another child. I've become resigned to the idea at this point, though I also realize that my body may not be as willing as my mind. I'm pushing forty and keenly aware that the risks to any child I might bear and to me increase with every month that goes by. I'd be lying if I said there isn't some part of me that is hoping this pregnancy test will be negative.

I glance at the clock, see that my time is up, and brace myself before looking at the test stick. The answer is crystal clear, and after taking a moment to absorb it all, I get up and head back downstairs.

I'm on my way out of our bedroom when Matthew comes tearing down the hall and smashes into my legs, wrapping his arms around them. "Morning, Mammy," he says, using his unique combination of Mattie and mommy.

"Good morning, Matthew." I reach down and scoop him up, balancing him on my hip. He is the spitting image of his father, with his black hair and blue eyes. He has his father's nose and mouth, too, though he did manage to inherit my dimples . . . the ones on my face, that is.

"Maffew hungry," he says. This is his latest affectation, talking about himself in the third person.

"Well, then, we best go feed that monster in your belly before he starts to growl." I tickle his tummy, making him laugh and squirm to be let down. I set him on the floor and watch as he dashes off toward the stairs. "Be careful!" I holler. It's a wasted warning. The kid always tears down those stairs like they aren't there. My son is a constant ball of energy and inquisitiveness, a cross between two of his favorite cartoon characters: the Tasmanian Devil and Curious George.

As I reach the top of the stairs, I hear the delighted squeals of Matthew greeting his father good morning, and it makes me smile. Then I remember the test stick.

Hurley is busy fixing Matthew a bowl of cereal when I enter the kitchen. Our kid has some odd tastes when it comes to food. He doesn't like milk on his cereal, and for a time, we had to give it to him dry, lest he dump the entire bowl on his head in protest. Then one morning he decided to pour his apple juice into his bowl of Cheerios—his favorite cereal—and eat that. Now that's how he wants his cereal every morning, and it's what Hurley has prepared for him.

Hurley looks at me expectantly, a half-smile on his face. "Well?" he prompts when I don't say anything right away.

"I might have to start limiting my coffee intake," I say glumly, giving him a wan smile.

He gives me a bemused look. "Meaning . . . you're pregnant?"

"I am."

"Woo-hoo!" Hurley whoops, pumping one fist in the air. He walks over and gives me a big hug, nearly lifting me off the floor.

Matthew mimics Hurley's holler with one of his own. "Woo-woo!" he says, throwing both of his arms up in the air and then laughing hysterically. Unfortunately, he is holding a spoonful of apple-juiced Cheerios when he does this, and the oat circles go flying in all directions. Hoover knocks over a chair as he makes a mad dash for the scattering cereal bits, and our cat, Rubbish, comes flying out of the laundry room and starts running after rolling oat bits, too. This makes Matthew laugh even more, and before I know it, he's dug his spoon into the bowl and gathered up more cereal, which he then tosses across the floor.

"Matthew, stop that," Hurley says in a calm voice.

Matthew does, looking properly chastised. It amazes me how Hurley can do this, as I often have to repeat my commands several times, getting sterner with each one, before Matthew will listen to me. And then it's even odds as to whether he'll listen to me at all.

Though my feelings on the pregnancy matter are still mixed, it's hard not to get caught up in Hurley's excitement. Clearly, he is thrilled. Matthew appears to be, too, though he has no idea what all the excitement is even about. I wonder what he'll be like as a big brother.

Hurley gets solicitous suddenly. He releases me from his bear hug and steers me toward the breakfast table, where he rights the chair that Hoover knocked over, and directs me to take a seat. "What would you like for breakfast, my dear?" he asks.

My first inclination is to tell him not to bother. I'm not a big fan of being fussed over. But I hold back and think about it for a moment, realizing that it would be unfair to deny Hurley this bit of excitement and celebration. "How about some scrambled eggs and toast?"

"Coming right up." Hurley heads for the refrigerator and gathers what he needs. Then he heads for the stove and starts cooking.

I sit and watch as Hoover finds and scarfs up the last of the apple-juiced Cheerios, and then I look at my son, sitting across the table from me. The morning sunlight dances in his hair, his delight over the celebration still evident on his face, even though I don't think he has a clue what all the hubbub is about. My heart swells with love for him, and for a moment, I worry that I won't be able to love another child the way I love Matthew. It's hard for me to imagine doing so, but I shrug the feeling off and tell myself that surely nature has a way of dealing with these things.

Then again, nature is also responsible for things like tornadoes, volcanoes, and certain breeds of animals that eat their young.

Twenty minutes later, breakfast is finished, and we are all headed upstairs to get dressed. Hurley, still riding his high, offers to take care of dressing Matthew while I hop in the shower. I typically get first dibs on the shower that Hurley and I share because my routine takes longer than his. I have more surface area to shave, more hair to shampoo and condition, and then there's the whole styling thing, which Hurley doesn't have to do. He simply runs a comb through his hair and calls it good, letting it air-dry. I have a lot of hair, particularly for a blonde, but the individual strands are very thin and prone to frizz. If I were to do what Hurley does, my head would look like a dandelion puffball gone to seed.

We are ready to head out a little after seven-thirty and Hurley is still on cloud nine. He is whistling, smiling, and has such a lilt to his step that I half expect him to start skipping. Matthew's mood, on the other hand, has moved to the other end of the spectrum. He has a mercurial temperament and it's now making itself known as he fusses, pouts, and kicks his legs in irritation as Hurley fastens him into his car seat, whining that he doesn't like his shoes.

We are taking Hurley's pickup truck, since my car, a midnight-blue hearse with relatively low mileage and a reinforced body that rivals the president's limo, will remain at home. There's no point in taking two cars, since it's technically my day off, and my only plans for the day are to go with Izzy and Hurley to the prison and Eau Claire.

The driving arrangements hadn't been easy to agree to yesterday. Izzy loves to drive, and he has a beautiful and lovingly restored Impala. Unfortunately, the Impala has a bench front seat, so by the time Izzy has the seat positioned so that his short legs can reach the pedals, neither Hurley, who is six-four, nor I can comfortably fit in the front seat without risking a dislocated hip or a knee colliding with a chin. That meant both of us would have to ride in the backseat. Initially Izzy seemed okay with this idea, but when I started making goo-goo eyes at Hurley, rubbing his arm sensuously, and commenting about what we could do in the backseat of the car, Izzy finally saw the wisdom in letting Hurley drive.

The drive to Izzy's house is a little less than ten minutes under good conditions, but even this length of time is too long this morning because Matthew is all about trying my patience. His build takes after both Hurley's and mine, with his long legs—long enough that he can easily reach the back of my seat with his feet from his spot in the backseat of Hurley's king cab. The minute he is strapped in, he starts wheedling that he doesn't like his shoes, and when he sees that he isn't getting the attention he thinks he should, he starts kicking the back of my seat.

I try my hardest to ignore him, but his kick is powerful, and his whining grates on my nerves, which seem ultraexposed this morning. Two minutes into the ride, I snap. "Matthew, stop it!"

"I can't," he whines petulantly. "I hate my shoes."

I turn around and glance behind me to see what he's wearing. He has on a perfectly good pair of children's athletic shoes, ones he has worn dozens of times before without complaint. "What's wrong with your shoes?" I ask in that tone of frustrated patience known to parents everywhere.

"They have green on them," Matthew says. "I don't like green."

"You do, too, like green," I tell him. "One of your favorite shirts, the one with the dinosaur on it, is green."

This color fixation is one Matthew has demonstrated before. I have no idea what triggers it, which makes it even more maddening because there is no rhyme or reason to it. A color he adores and insists on wearing one day becomes a supervillain the next. The irritation spectrum changes from day to day.

"Your shoes only have a little bit of green on them," I say, hoping to rationalize the situation. This is a clear sign of mental illness on my part, because everyone knows toddlers aren't rational. However, the kicks to my back stop momentarily, and that gives me hope that I'm getting through somehow.

A minute of silence ensues, and I relax in my seat with a smile, confident the battle has been won, or we've at least reached a cease-fire. Silly me. I am about to say something to Hurley when a shoe flies from the backseat into the front. It lands at my feet and I lean forward to pick it up. "Matthew!" I chastise in my best warning voice, uttered through gritted teeth. I turn around to scold him and that's when the second shoe hits me in the side of the face. The pain it triggers, combined with the simple audacity of the act, makes something inside me snap.

"Matthew Izthak Hurley!" I yell. "Stop being such a little brat! Do you know how lucky you are to even have shoes? There are kids in foreign countries who don't have shoes. Maybe I should take your shoes away from you, let you walk around barefoot on gravel for a while and see what *that* feels like. I'm betting you won't mind the green when your feet are all bloody and sore." I shake the shoe I have in my hand at him through the entire rant, functioning on raw, reactive anger, only vaguely aware of what I'm saying and doing.

Hurley, who has remained seemingly oblivious up until now, sitting in the driver's seat wearing that dumb-assed grin that's been stamped on his face ever since he found out I was pregnant, turns his head and looks at me warily. "That's a bit over the top, isn't it?" he says.

I straighten in my seat, lean my head back, and squeeze my eyes closed. I drop the shoe I'm holding and clench both hands into fists so tight that I leave moon-shaped fingernail marks on my palms. My reaction *was* over the top, and I know it, but I'm too angry and upset to admit it and can't seem to let go of my ire.

"Matthew, tell your mother you're sorry," Hurley says, his stern voice filling the car.

"Maffew sorry, Mammy." He says this hurriedly with a hitch in his voice.

I open my eyes and turn to look at him. He stares back at me with tears brimming, doubt and a hint of fear on his face. For one second, I think, *Good, you should fear me*. Then his expression sucks all my anger away.

"I'm sorry, too, Matthew," I say. "Sorry I lost my temper."

"It's okay," he says in a comforting, nurturing tone that breaks my heart and brings tears to my eyes. I feel instantly ashamed, convinced I'm the world's worst mother.

Fortunately, Hurley has pulled into Izzy's driveway, and

once he's parked on the wide paved area behind the house, he wisely gets out and makes quick work of extracting Matthew from the truck.

As I get out of the truck, I give the cottage a wistful look. The time I spent there was confusing, marking as it did a painful and unsettling period in my life. But it was also a time of growth for me, and was rewarding in many ways. It was my first experience living truly on my own and I discovered that I'm not an easy person to live with. It was the place where I was forced to reevaluate my life, my priorities, and my goals. I discovered my priorities in life weren't what I once thought they were. It was where I learned that I could be shallow and selfish, that I had an addiction to ice cream and gambling, and that I'd been foolish in trusting my financial future to my husband. It was where I lived when I met Hurley, and it was where I gave birth to Matthew, literally, in the bathtub.

I miss it, I realize. Or maybe it's the relative simplicity of my life back then that I miss. Not that my life was all that simple. During that time, I lost my job, my husband, my future, and, in many ways, my identity. Yet, despite all that, the only thing I really needed to worry about, the only person I had to take care of for most of that period, was me.

Now the cottage is once again a home for Sylvie. I don't think she'll be leaving this time, at least not under her own power. Sylvie has always been a small woman, but now she's a tiny wisp of a thing that looks like she could be blown over by a sneeze. She's still able to get around on her own, using her walker, a device she also wields surprisingly well as a weapon at times, but she's much slower than before. More frightening than her physical decline is the mental one. Her mind makes frequent trips back in time to when she was a child or young adult, and often stays there. And lately she's been witnessed doing things like trying to make a phone call with her hand mixer, loading dishes into the oven instead of the dishwasher, and getting herself out of bed and all dressed up for church at two in the morning on a Tuesday.

Despite her difficulties, Sylvie has remained stubbornly independent. Any attempts to or even hints at placing her in a nursing home, or having her live with Izzy and Dom, have failed. I think Sylvie would love to live with her son if Dom wasn't there, though Dom has made remarkable strides in wearing down Sylvie's bias against him. He checks on Sylvie multiple times during the day, bringing her treats and inviting her over to what she calls the "big house" whenever he can.

Juliana has had a lot to do with the softening of Sylvie's heart, and even though Sylvie knows on some level that Juliana is adopted and not Izzy's biological child, when she's in the throes of her dementia she makes constant reference to all the physical characteristics Juliana shares with Izzy, referring to him as Juliana's father and Dom as the "man nanny."

Hurley waits for me to catch up to him at the garage door to Izzy's house and I punch in the code. We make our way through the garage and enter the house without knocking. I've known the door code since back when I first moved into the cottage, and now that Dom regularly takes care of Matthew for us during the day, we've adopted something of an open-door policy on those days when we're expected.

We enter the kitchen and I'm not surprised to see Sylvie seated at the breakfast table with Juliana. Sylvie is still in her pajamas: a top and bottom made of white flannel and adorned with tiny blue flowers. Sylvie will wear these heavy nightclothes all summer long, even on those rare July and August days when the temperature gets into the nineties. The woman has no fat on her body to serve as insulation; simply opening a refrigerator door near her will send her into a spasm of shaking chills. This is the exact opposite of Izzy and me. Both of us possess enough insulation to survive on the frozen tundra sans coats for a good long while. If someone harvested our fat, they'd have enough to deep-fry a whole herd of moose.

"Good morning," Dom says cheerily. He is standing in front of the stove cooking French toast from thickly cut slabs of the sourdough bread he baked yesterday. A rasher of cooked bacon is sitting at the back of the stove on a plate lined with paper towels. Dom is who I want to be, if I ever grow up: a great cook, a nurturing spouse, and a loving, capable, patient parent. Dom would never threaten his kid with bloody feet.

"Want to join us for breakfast before you head out?" Dom offers. "Izzy should be down in a few minutes."

The smells of bacon, butter, and cinnamon mix together in a tantalizing aroma that makes me imagine a cartoon miasma wafting toward me that hooks me by my nose and floats me to one of the chairs at the table.

Being a bit less imaginative, Hurley says, "Thanks, but we already ate."

I'm tempted to ask him what that has to do with anything, but I refrain. I try a different tack instead. "If Izzy still needs to eat, it won't hurt to sit down and have a nibble, will it?"

"Izzy ate already," Dom says, and I curse to myself.

As if on cue, Izzy walks into the kitchen. "Good morning, all," he says cheerily. He kisses Juliana on top of her head—a smart move, given that her face is covered with syrup—and then walks over and gives Dom a peck on the cheek.

"Hi, Unca Itsy," Matthew says. Matthew hasn't mastered his *z*-sounds yet, and his version of Izzy is apropos, given Izzy's short stature. I've heard other people use it in the past, either intentionally as a joke or because they thought that was Izzy's real name, and it never went over well. Izzy has always been quick to correct anyone who uses it—anyone except my son, it seems. He likes Matthew calling him Itsy. Go figure.

Izzy walks over and gives Matthew a kiss on top of his head and my son beams. "Unca Dom is making friend toast," Matthew says.

"I know. I had some earlier. It's very good." He looks at us then and says, "Do you guys want to eat before we head out?"

I'm about to jump at this second invitation, but Hurley again beats me to it.

"We ate already, and I want to get going, if that's okay."

I give Hurley a disappointed look. Clearly, he has forgotten what I do for a living and the fact that I know all kinds of clever ways to kill someone and get away with it.

"That's fine," Izzy says, and then the two of them turn to leave as if I'm not even there. I pout for a millisecond and consider playing the pregnancy card to get some French toast, but it's too soon to let that cat out of the bag. Resigned, I kiss Matthew good-bye as my stomach growls in protest, tell Dom we'll see him later, and then dutifully follow the two men out the door, but not before snatching one slice of bacon along the way.

CHAPTER 8

There is a moment of debate about who is going to sit where, but Izzy quickly relinquishes the front seat to me. The backseat of Hurley's truck has a surprising amount of leg room, not that Izzy needs much, but with Matthew's seat secured on the passenger side, the backseat rider has to sit behind Hurley, and his long legs require having the front seat pushed back as far as it will go. I could fit behind him, but not comfortably, and Izzy fits just fine.

Our first stop is the Columbia Correctional Institution, the prison Mason Ulrich, the convicted Eau Claire serial killer, now calls home. The drive takes a little over half an hour, and Hurley fills the time by sharing some of the facts of the case and summarizing the conversation he had yesterday with Barney Ledbetter, Mason Ulrich's current lawyer.

"Ledbetter was hesitant to talk to me at first, much less allow us to talk to his client," Hurley says. "But when I told him we had some new evidence regarding the case, he was at least willing to listen. Once he found out there's another victim that appears to fit the same MO as all the others, he got very interested."

"Did you say anything to him about the flower petals?" Izzy asks.

Hurley shakes his head. "I didn't. We danced around the issue the entire time. Ledbetter kept asking me for specifics on the evidence we had and why we felt it was connected to his client's case. I told him about the wound pattern, the physical resemblance to the other women, and the fact that our victim was a transient, like three of the four women Ulrich is accused of killing."

"What was different about the fourth victim?" I ask.

"She was someone Ulrich knew and dated," Hurley says. "And not a transient. The working theory was that this woman dumped Ulrich and his anger over that fact made him kill the first three women, who all looked like the woman he had dated. Then they think his anger grew to the point where killing the substitutes no longer did it for him, so he went after the real thing."

"What kind of evidence did they have on him?" I ask.

Hurley gestures toward a large brown envelope on the front seat between us. "There are some summaries in there."

I pick up the envelope and open it, sliding out the pages inside. The first thing I find is a police report and I scan it, summarizing it aloud. This is mostly for my own and Izzy's benefit, since I assume Hurley has already read much of the stuff in the envelope. But I did interrupt him last night, so maybe he wasn't able to read it all.

"It looks like they found some evidence near the body of the first victim, Mary Ellen Clark, age thirty-two. Mary Ellen was a transient, homeless, and a drug addict, who was originally from Detroit, but hadn't been seen or heard from by family and friends for nearly a decade. The body was found along the banks of the Chippewa River, within sight of I-94, on March 9, 2017. The evidence they found was a fishing license belonging to our Mr. Ulrich, but Ulrich said he'd been fishing along that part of the river three days earlier and that he lost his license, presumably when he took a pack of smokes out of his pocket, the same pocket that had the license in it. It was confirmed that Ulrich was fishing in that area, or at least that his phone was in that area three days before the body was found. The cops know this because Ulrich offered up his cell phone and showed pictures of the fish he caught that day. Those pictures clearly show the location."

"Did they look at his cell phone data—" Izzy asks.

"For the day of the murder?" I finish. Hurley looks over at me and smiles. "They did. Ulrich had his GPS turned on and it showed he, or at least his phone, was at home all day."

"Convenient," Izzy says.

"Apparently, that's what the cops thought, too," I say. "They theorized that he purposely left his phone at home during the time of the murder, so it would provide an alibi for him. He received several phone calls during the time of the murder that weren't answered and went to voice mail. The cops think that's proof Ulrich didn't have his phone with him."

"What did Ulrich say about the calls?" Hurley asks.

"He said he was working on a car in his garage for several hours that day, some older-model Mustang that he was trying to restore."

This piques Izzy's attention. He has a love of old cars, particularly the muscle cars of the sixties, and he spent the better part of two years restoring his Impala.

"He said he never bothers bringing his phone out to the garage because he's usually too busy, too greasy, or some combination of those things to answer it," I reply.

"Makes sense," Izzy says, shrugging. "What were Ulrich's connections to the other victims?"

"Let's see," I say, shuffling through some papers. "The second victim was a woman named Jane Doe 03252017." I pause and look at Hurley. "That's a big number," I say.

"It's the date she was found, most likely," Izzy says, and Hurley nods. I look at the report and see that this is correct.

"Okay, that makes sense, I guess," I say. "Jane Doe turned up a little more than two weeks after Mary Ellen, and her body was found in a wooded area across the street from a cemetery in Eau Claire. She'd been there for a few days, and since the weather was warm, there was some decomp. That explains why it took a while to ID her—that and the fact that she wasn't originally from the area, although they did turn up a connection between her and Ulrich. It was a week before they figured out who she was, and that was through a tattoo and a unique scar on her leg that was deep, wide, and twisted. The ID was later verified with DNA and she was identified as Linda Marie Elwood, twenty-nine and from the Green Bay area originally, though she'd been gone from there for at least two years before she died. Her parents said she got involved with a group of drug users, and despite attempts at interventions, they were unable to turn her around."

"A sad but all-too-common story these days," Hurley says with a frown. "Makes you afraid to have kids sometimes, you know?"

I shoot him a look, wondering if his thoughts on the matter are because of my newly discovered pregnancy. He looks over at me and smiles, reaching out to give my shoulder a squeeze. "It will be okay. I'm speaking in generalities."

Izzy watches this little interchange with interest and after a few seconds says, "Are you two pregnant?"

I look at him in surprise, though I shouldn't be shocked that he figured it out. Izzy is one of the smartest people I know, and he knows me better than anyone else in my life, except for maybe my sister, though Hurley is catching up. I also told Izzy I agreed to try for another child.

Hurley sputters, "How . . . the . . . Why . . . What . . ."

Izzy chuckles. "I take it the answer is *yes*?"

"It is," I say. "We just found out this morning and it's

early, very early. So we don't want to say anything to anyone yet."

"Understood," Izzy says. I feel reassured because Izzy can be trusted to keep a secret.

Hurley, on the other hand, is a bit more circumspect on the matter. "That means not telling anyone," he says. "Not even Dom."

"I got it," Izzy says, sounding mildly insulted. "And congratulations."

"Let him tell Dom," I say. "He can be trusted, and, besides, if I know Dom, he'll figure it out in no time on his own. He figured it out last time."

Hurley capitulates with surprising ease. "Okay," he says, shrugging. There is a hint of a smile on his face and I begin to suspect he doesn't care who finds out. He's happy to share the news.

"Okay," Izzy says. "Back to bodies and such. How was Ulrich connected to this Elwood woman?"

"He went to college with her," I say.

"She went to college?" Izzy says, his voice rife with skepticism.

"For a year, then she dropped out. She attended the UW campus in Eau Claire and she and Ulrich were in some classes together. It doesn't sound like there's any proof they ever interacted, and the classes were freshman pre-reqs, so there were probably lots of students in them. Plus, the classes were ten years ago."

"Did Ulrich graduate?" Hurley asks.

I flip through the pages in the folder and scan several other reports before I find an answer. "He did," I say. "A bachelor's degree in history and a minor in English lit, with a teaching certificate. He was teaching history at the local high school at the time of his arrest."

"Let's go back to the victims before we get too involved

with Ulrich," Izzy says. "It will help me keep things straight in my head."

"Okay," I say, shuffling papers again. "Let's see . . . the third victim was Darla Ann Marks. She was found by a fisherman on April 18, 2017, along the banks of the Chippewa River, on the north side of Eau Claire near the Chippewa Valley Regional Airport. The location of her body suggested that the perp had dumped it there after he killed her, and the site of her actual murder remains unknown." I pick up another sheet of paper and add, "That's the case with all of the victims, it seems. All of the bodies had been dumped where they were found, and the actual sites of the murders were never determined."

"Odd," Hurley comments, and Izzy and I both nod in agreement.

"Anyway, it was surmised that the killer gained access to the dump site by boat, since the body was found in a boggy area with narrow fingers of land that extend into the river and aren't easily accessible from land. Darla was twenty-five years old and tested positive for cocaine and opioids, with evidence of IV drug use. She was from a small town in Minnesota and had no immediate family. She was a foster-system kid."

"The fourth and final victim was Caroline Marie Helgeson, age twenty-nine, found on April 28th, 2017, in a wooded area alongside a road just outside of town. Unlike the other victims, she wasn't a drug user or a transient, though she was shot up with a large dose of heroin. In fact, she and Ulrich dated for a while, so he knew her. He swears things ended amicably, that they liked one another, but didn't have any real spark between them and decided to remain friends. But one of Caroline's friends said that Caroline told her Ulrich wanted to keep dating her, and when she refused, he didn't take it very well. Caroline told this friend that Ulrich stalked her for several weeks after the breakup."

"When was the breakup?" Hurley asks.

"Just before Christmas, in 2016."

"So the guy had a thing for Caroline, and in his frustration, he starts killing other women who look like her?" Hurley says. I can hear the skepticism in his voice.

"Just to verify," Izzy says, "all of the victims had the same knife pattern and they all had the flower petals in one of the wounds?"

"Correct," I say, after I pull out another sheet. "Each of the women had a series of five knife wounds that formed a *V* with the point being over the symphysis pubis and the top of the *V* located in or above the breasts. The petals were always found in the wound over the heart, which was the fatal wound in each case. There were five petals stuffed into the wounds of each woman. It doesn't say anything about the order of the stabbing, and there's no mention of any defensive wounds on any of them, but these aren't autopsy reports, so I don't know if it's just not mentioned or they weren't there."

"I definitely want to examine the autopsy results on all of these women," Izzy says.

I shift through the papers and find one with four pictures on it, each one labeled with the name of one of the victims. "Wow, the victims certainly did resemble one another," I say, struck by the similarities. I hold up the paper so both Izzy and Hurley can see the pictures.

"The guy has a type," Hurley says.

"I'll say," Izzy comments. "Those women look enough alike that they could be sisters. They're all light blondes with pale complexions, blue eyes, small noses, high cheekbones, and a broad facial structure."

"And they're all quite pretty," Hurley observes.

I can't help but smile at their descriptions. Izzy's is about the anatomy, whereas Hurley's is all about aesthetics. "You guys do realize that you're describing a good portion of the female population in this area," I say. "With all the Scandinavian blood in and around Wisconsin, there must be thousands of women who look like these four. Heck, I look like them. These girls are all tall, like me. Not as tall, and not as heavy, but still . . ."

"Your comments are meant to suggest that the killer might have simply picked victims who fit the odds, that he wasn't choosing them based on physical parameters?" Izzy says.

"It's possible, isn't it?" I say.

"I suppose it is," Hurley says, "but I'd find that easier to believe if it was only two victims. Maybe even three. But four?"

"And now it might be five," I point out.

Hurley shoots me a worried look and a shiver races down my spine as I realize that the real killer may still be out there. What's more, I fit the description of the type of victim he's looking for.

CHAPTER 9

The Columbia Correctional Institution is in Portage, Wisconsin. The red-and-brown brick main building with its state and national flags flying from poles situated in a well-manicured lawn across from the front door looks like any other government building in Wisconsin—my office building and the police station in Sorenson included. That is, as long as you look past, or block out, the razor wire–topped fence surrounding the sides of the building and the guard tower looming up behind it.

Hurley advises us to leave our cell phones in the truck, as well as our keys, wallets—or purse in my case—except for a picture ID. "They'll take them away from you if you try to bring them in," he says. "Plus, you'll set off the metal detectors."

The mention of metal detectors causes me a moment of panic as I recall my visit to Tomas Wyzinski in a different prison not that long ago. I'd left all the aforementioned items behind in my car, but I kept setting off the metal detector anyway. As it turned out, it was my underwear that was the problem. The underwires in my bra were not only enough to set off the alarms, they were considered usable as a weapon. I was forced to remove the bra to make it past the front desk.

"Um, I need to remove some clothing," I say to no one in particular, and then both Hurley and Izzy stare in awe at me as I remove my coat and then sneak my bra straps down over my arms one at a time, snaking them out from beneath my sleeves. Once that is done, I reach one arm behind me to undo the clasp and then reach under my blouse and pull the garment out.

"Impressive," Izzy says. "I've heard about women doing that, but I've never seen it done."

Hurley is staring at my chest, where my newly exposed nipples are reacting to the cold. "You can't go in there like that," he says with a frown. "Why did you take it off?"

"There are wires in it, metal stays that run under the cups. I discovered that they set off the metal detectors when I visited Tomas," I explain, shrugging back into my jacket. "I'll keep my jacket on and it will be fine."

Hurley looks skeptical.

As we approach the main entrance, I try not to feel intimidated by the place, but its history and the razor wire enclosure make that hard. I did some research yesterday and learned that it's where Jeffrey Dahmer was imprisoned and subsequently killed. With ten 50-cell maximum-security units, and a 150-bed minimum-security unit, all of it sitting on 110 acres of land, the place resembles a college campus, albeit one occupied by over 800 lawbreaking men. Some of the inmates are as horrifyingly scary as Dahmer, while others might be incarcerated here for lesser crimes.

As expected, the check-in requires us to go through a metal detector, and even though I've taken the necessary precautions, I wince as I step through, half expecting the thing to go off. Hurley frowns the entire time because I was required to remove my coat before stepping through, since the zipper would have triggered the alarm, and my headlights are on high beam. One of the interesting and occasionally annoying things about pregnancy is that, in the early months, the breasts become exquisitely sensitive and reactive. As soon as the pockets have been searched by a guard, I quickly shrug my coat back on and zip it up tight.

The three of us make it through without incident, and after showing our ID and signing in, we are escorted to a room furnished with a heavy wooden conference table and six chairs, three on either side. There is a second entrance to the room on the far wall, presumably the one the prisoner will use.

We have barely entered the room when someone else comes in behind us, bursting in like a hard gust of wind, the door flung open so wide it bangs against the wall. I jump at this flurry of noise and activity, letting everyone know how jangled my nerves are. Prison might not be a deterrent for some folks, but I know I'll always think twice before committing any offense that could land me in a place like this.

When I turn around, I see the culprit behind these shenanigans: a man with a briefcase, making me guess that this is Ulrich's attorney. He scurries past us and makes his way to the far side of the table. I see that his shirtfront sports a large brown stain that looks like coffee. He slams his briefcase down on top of the table and I see that it is old and battered, a faux-leather brown thing that is peeling along the edge and corners.

"Good day, folks," he says, several decibels louder than necessary. "I'm Barney Ledbetter, Mr. Ulrich's counsel as of last week. His prior attorney of record is no longer involved, thank goodness, since he clearly didn't provide my client with a decent defense."

He sits and then proceeds to snap open his briefcase. When he lifts the lid, it nearly comes off as one of the hinges falls partway off. But it clings tenaciously to its base, cockeyed and not lining up quite right.

As I take one of the seats, I see that Barney doesn't quite line up right, either. This is due in part to the fact that his shirt is buttoned wrong and tucked into his pants, so his button line makes a diagonal run across his torso toward the right. The left lapel of his suit jacket is curled under, making it appear shorter than the right one. On his head, Barney is sporting what appears to be a very cheap toupee, which has slid to one side and rotated slightly. The overall effect of all this misalignment is quite disconcerting—it's like looking at a Picasso painting—and I can't help but wonder if Barney looks this way intentionally for that very reason.

He reminds me a lot of Lucien, my brother-in-law, whose crass language, ballsy tactics, and slovenly appearance are an act designed to disarm and mislead his court opponents. In Lucien's case, it's all very effective. He is quite successful and rarely loses a case. I hope for Mason Ulrich's sake that Barney will be the same.

Barney removes a stack of papers from his tattered briefcase and slaps it down on the table. Then he scoots his chair up to the table in an awkward dragging manner, which makes a screeching noise like fingernails on a blackboard.

When he's done, he looks at Hurley, then at me, with a big, cheesy smile on his face. "Aren't you two adorable?" he says, wrinkling his nose into a cutesy face like one might use on a baby. "How nice it must be for the two of you to be able to work together, given that you're married. Though time apart is important in a relationship. Do you ever feel like you have too much together time?"

Barney has put us on notice that he's done his homework. Hurley, without hesitation but with a hint of irritation in his voice, says, "No, not at all. And we don't work together all the time. Just on some cases."

Barney chuffs a laugh and waves away Hurley's answer. "What do I know?" he says with exaggerated self-deprecation. "I've been married and divorced four times, so I think it's safe to say that relationships aren't my strong suit. Now, then . . ." He looks at Izzy, narrowing his eyes. "Sorry, I'm not sure who you are?"

"Dr. Izthak Rybarceski. I'm the medical examiner in Sorenson." Izzy doesn't offer his hand. In fact, his arms are folded over his chest.

Barney flashes a smile and then looks down at the papers in front of him, flipping through them. The three of us take the seats on our side of the table and wait.

"You said that you want to talk to Mr. Ulrich about the women he's accused of killing, is that right?" Barney says after a minute or two.

"It is," Hurley says.

"And will you be recording this little Q-and-A session?"

"We will not."

"Can you give me an idea of the nature of the questions you're intending to ask?"

"We're mainly interested in hearing his explanation for the evidence that was used against him. And we also want to ask him about the flower petals."

Barney raises his eyebrows at that. "You know about the flower petals." It isn't a question. "How?"

"We have our ways," Hurley says cryptically.

If he's hoping to annoy Barney with this nonanswer, he's disappointed. The man simply shrugs and says, "They tried to bury that evidence beneath a pile of other crap during the trial. My predecessor should have used the petals as part of the defense, because the inability to connect my client to those flowers creates reasonable doubt. I'm sure the judge reviewing our appeal will agree."

"Why didn't your predecessor bring up the flower petals?" I ask. "Did he miss them?"

Barney rolls his eyes. "He knew about them, but didn't want to use them. Some jibberty-jab about how it could lead to a lot of psychiatric voodoo that the prosecution could use. He figured by the time all the cuckoo-crazy crap was presented, the jury wouldn't care that no one could figure out how my client came by the flower petals." He sighs and shakes his head woefully. It makes his toupee slide a little more, but he reaches up and tugs it back into place. Sort of.

"What is your interest in the flower petals?" he asks. "Have you guys managed to connect them to my client, when no one else could?" There is a hint of worry in Barney's voice when he asks this. Clearly, he's hoping those petals are going to be his client's ticket to a new trial or an overturning of his conviction.

"We have not," I say.

Barney sags ever so slightly, visibly relieved. "Then why are you interested in the flowers?"

Even though Barney is looking at Hurley and me when he asks this, it's Izzy who answers.

"I have a murder victim in my morgue who has the same pattern of stab wounds as all of Ulrich's supposed victims, and I found flower petals in the same wound they were in on all the other women."

Barney's eyes narrow as he turns his laser focus on Izzy. "When was your victim killed?"

"Two days ago."

"What kind of flower?"

"Carnation, according to my lab tech."

"Color?"

"Yellow."

"How many petals?"

"Five."

Barney's eyes roam between us and there is a new shine to them as he leans back in his chair. "Well, now, this *is* interesting," he says. He licks his lips and I can feel his excitement growing. He looks at Hurley. "Do you think it's a copycat of some sort?"

"Unlikely," Hurley says, "given that the flower petal information wasn't widely known or released to the public."

Barney eyes all of us again, a look of suspicion on his face. "This is for real?" he says finally, like he thinks we're punking him.

"For real," Hurley says. "If it puts your mind at ease, let me state up front that we are exploring the possibility of your client's innocence."

Barney shifts nervously in his seat. His fingers are fiddling with the stack of papers, several of which I now see look to be blank. His little stack is a prop, I realize, and the knowledge makes me smile.

"Okay, then," Barney says finally. "I do need to set some ground rules because I'm filing appeals. This conversation is off the record and cannot be recorded. You are not to ask my client if he killed any of the women in question. You cannot ask him if he's guilty. I don't want you asking him any questions that might be self-incriminating. Understood?"

Hurley and I both nod as Izzy just sits there and stares at Barney, who doesn't seem interested in Izzy's opinion.

Hurley says, "You can stop us anytime you like and tell your client not to answer any questions you don't like."

"Right," Barney says, narrowing his eyes thoughtfully. Then he slaps his palms on the table. "Let's get to it then." He gets up, walks over to the door we came in, and knocks on it. A guard looks through the window and Barney nods at him. Then he returns to his seat.

The four of us sit in awkward silence, trying not to stare at one another for the next several minutes. Hurley and I both squirm in our seats, and Izzy sits straight and still, staring at the wall. Barney seems right at home with the tension in the room. He sits in his chair, hands clasped behind his neck, a smile on his face. He lets his gaze wander around the room, focusing on the table, the walls, the door, the floor, the ceiling, and, on a few occasions, each of us.

Finally the door behind him opens and a guard ushers in our prisoner.

CHAPTER 10

Mason Ulrich is a hollow shell of a man dressed in a baggy orange jumpsuit. His dark hair is shaved close to his head, revealing several scars, some of which appear to be fresh. His face looks haggard; his cheeks sunken and hollow; his color pale, but for the dark stubble gracing most of his lower jaw and the bruise encircling his right eye and the bridge of his nose. His eyes are brown, yet somehow pale, as if some of the color has drained out of them along with his hope. As he walks, or rather shuffles, into the room, I see that his shoulders are rounded and slouched. His cuffed hands and spindly fingers hang limp near his crotch, a chain connecting them to the shackles around his feet.

He drops into his chair, and the guard who brought him in takes a position behind him.

Barney shifts around and eyes the guard. "This is a confidential session between attorney and client. You can wait on the other side of the door."

The guard doesn't look at Barney or in any way acknowledge that he heard him. In a low voice, but one carrying a degree of menace in it, Barney says, "Now."

Five seconds tick by and then the guard pivots, takes two

big steps, and exits through the door he came in. Not once does he look at any of us. My respect for Barney is growing.

"Now then, Mason," Barney says, turning back to the table, "these people want to ask you some questions. I will tell you if they ask you anything I don't think you should answer, okay?"

No response. Barney shrugs and gives Hurley a go-ahead nod.

"Mr. Ulrich," Hurley says, using the more formal title as a show of respect. He does this a lot, I've noticed. At one time I thought it might create a wall of distance between him and the people he talks to, but his demeanor and tone of voice work to ease that formality, creating an atmosphere of cordiality.

Ulrich stares at the tabletop, his eyes lifeless and dull. If he heard Hurley, he gives no indication.

Hurley continues anyway. "My name is Steve Hurley. I'm a detective with the Sorenson, Wisconsin, Police Department. This is Mattie Winston, a medicolegal investigator for the medical examiner's office in Sorenson, and her boss, Dr. Izthak Rybarceski, the medical examiner for our county. We're here today because we'd like to talk to you about the women you've been convicted of killing."

Ulrich doesn't blink. He doesn't move. I'm forced to stare at his chest to make sure he's still alive and breathing.

"To start with," Hurley goes on, "I'd like to ask you about the flower petals that were found in the women's wounds. It's my understanding that you've denied any knowledge of them, but I'd like to know if you ever mentioned them to anyone else. Maybe a family member? Or another visitor of some sort?"

We all stare at Ulrich, waiting, but he doesn't answer.

"Mr. Ulrich, we have another dead woman who has the same pattern of stab wounds and the same flower petals stuck inside the wound."

No response, but I decide to elaborate on Hurley's comment. "She was killed just days ago, so we know you didn't do it."

Ulrich blinks. I count it as progress. And then, he slowly raises his head, shifting his gaze to me.

"Help us help you," I say. "Talk to us. Please."

Ulrich's eyes do a slow slide toward Hurley, then to Izzy, and finally back to me. I hold his haunted gaze, even though every nerve in my body is screaming at me to look away. And then he speaks. "Don't give me false hope." His voice is heartbreakingly flat and dead.

"We can't give you any hope at all yet," I say. "We don't have enough facts. What we have are some new questions. Obviously, you didn't kill this latest victim, and yet the MO for her death is identical to the ones for the other women. Most of the details could have been picked up by reading up on or attending your trial, but the flower petals are a special situation. We're trying to figure out who knew about them, since their presence wasn't discussed at the trial or released to the public. What did your attorney tell or ask you about them?"

"Don't answer that," Barney says.

I give him a frustrated frown and he just shrugs.

"Let's try a different tack," Hurley says. "Can you explain to me how your fishing license ended up next to one of the bodies?"

Ulrich emits a weary sigh. "I've gone over this a million times already."

"Humor me," Hurley says.

Ulrich looks at Barney, who nods his okay. "Like I told the cops, I was in that area fishing in a gravel pit pond three days earlier. I had my license in my back jeans pocket, but I also had a pack of cigarettes in there. When I took the smokes out, the license must have fallen out and I didn't notice it. I realized it was missing that night when I got home."

"Did you try to get a replacement for it?" Hurley asks.

Ulrich shakes his head. "I was going to have to get a new one by April first anyway."

"Okay," Hurley says. "Talk to me about Caroline Helgeson. How many times did the two of you go out together when you were dating?"

Ulrich gives him a painful smile. "The only reason I can answer this question is because the cops who interrogated me told me how many times it was. I wasn't keeping track. According to them, it was nine times."

"How did you meet her?"

"It was at a friend's house. She was throwing herself a birthday party, and Caroline was there. We got to chatting over the hors d'oeuvres and I asked her out for the following evening. We did dinner and a movie."

"What did you do on your other dates?"

Ulrich leans back in his seat, looking weary. "We went out for dinner sometimes. In fact, other than one evening when we ate at Caroline's place, we ate out every time."

"Different restaurants each time?" Hurley asks.

Ulrich shakes his head. "Caroline liked the burgers at a place called Cully's, so we ate there three times. We did fast food a couple of times, and one night we went to a play and ate at a steak house."

"Who paid for the meals?" I ask.

Hurley shoots me a curious look, but quickly turns back to Ulrich to see his reaction. Ulrich's eyebrows arch in mild surprise, making me think no one has asked him this question before.

"I paid for most of them," Ulrich says. "Though on the night when we went to the play, Caroline paid for everything. The whole evening was her idea and she said up front that it was her treat." Ulrich pauses and gives me a curious look. "Why do you want to know who paid for what?"

I shrug. “Sometimes people can get ideas about things owed to them.”

Ulrich looks dismissive, then angry. “You think I expected Caroline to put out because I was buying her dinners?” His tone makes it clear how ridiculous an idea he finds this.

“Did you?” Hurley says, jumping on my bandwagon. “You wouldn’t be the first guy who got upset because he spent a lot of money on a woman with the expectation that there would be something in return.”

“That’s not me,” Ulrich says.

“What about the night when you had dinner at Caroline’s house?” Hurley asks. “It sounds like that was the first time the two of you were in a private location as opposed to out in public. Did things get intimate?”

Ulrich’s brow furrows with irritation. “That’s personal,” he grumbles.

“The lady’s reputation isn’t really an issue anymore,” I say, trying to sound empathetic.

Ulrich considers this and the wrinkles in his forehead relax some. “We kissed for a while, did some making out . . . you know.” He shoots me an embarrassed look.

“According to the police reports, Caroline’s friends said you tried to get it on with her and couldn’t,” Hurley says. “Your equipment didn’t cooperate. That had to have been awkward.”

This tidbit is a surprise to me, because I hadn’t come across it in the reports I scanned through earlier. Apparently, it’s a surprise to Ulrich, too, as he gives Hurley an appalled look and shakes his head in disgust.

“If that’s what she told her friends, she wasn’t being totally honest,” he says. “My equipment functioned just fine until Caroline’s cat sneaked into the room, climbed onto the bed, and tried to use my junk as a cat toy.”

I bite back a laugh, not only because of the image this triggers, but because of the look on Hurley’s face. He didn’t see this one coming, and Ulrich couldn't have picked a better comeback to set Hurley off his game. I can still clearly recall a time when Rubbish, who was a kitten at the time, decided to climb the inside of Hurley's pant leg all the way up to the family jewels. The look of utter terror Hurley had on his face still makes me smile, because at the time, it was so incongruous with my overall opinion of him as a tough, fearless, take-no-prisoners kind of guy. The expression on his face now resembles the one he had then, though it's currently mixed with a hint of empathy for Ulrich.

Ulrich seems to sense a shifting in Hurley's sympathies, and he cocks his head to one side and produces the barest hint of a smile. Then he continues with his explanation. "Caroline and I liked each other. We enjoyed one another's company. At least I thought we did, though if what the cops told me about what she said to her friends is all true, I gather Caroline didn't feel the same. But despite my liking to spend time with her, there was no romantic spark between us. I think we both realized that on the night of the cat attack. We'd just watched a James Bond movie, so we jokingly referred to the fiasco as *Procto-Pussy.*" He emphasizes the title with wide eyes and a deep, booming voice. "Sorry, ma'am," he says to me, and then he huffs out a small laugh. "When Caroline called me to say she wanted to move on and see other people, I totally agreed with her. It was an amicable discussion and breakup. I had no reason to dislike her, much less kill her."

I believe the guy. I'm not perfect when it comes to reading people, but I'm quite good at it, if I do say so myself. This is in part to living a good portion of my life with one of the best bullshitters I know: my mother. Mom has been a hypochondriac all her life: a well-informed and educated one. The woman possesses more medical knowledge than many med students, and when she is in the throes of one of her hypochondriacal episodes, she knows exactly what signs and symptoms she is supposed to have. As a child, I watched her either thrill to death or scare the bejesus out of many a provider as she slowly but steadily convinced them that she had some rare and exotic disease.

Aside from my mother, I spent six years working in a hospital emergency room. And hospital ERs have evolved into central station for bullshitters of all types: drug seekers, drug users, people with mental health disorders, and even simple attention seekers. Granted, it doesn't take a whiz kid to figure out that the woman who arrives in the ER claiming to have ten-out-of-ten abdominal pain—while playing Candy Crush on her phone, eating a bag of chips, and drinking a soda—might have an ulterior motive. Some of the actors and liars are far more sophisticated than that, but over time it gets easier and easier to ferret out the charlatans. So, while practice may not have made me perfect, it has made me darned good at sniffing out a liar. And Ulrich doesn't strike me as one. There is nothing artificial or disingenuous about him.

Of course I do have the advantage of my knowledge regarding the latest murder case to help me in my assessment of Ulrich. Could it be a copycat murder? Yes, it's possible. But the deeper we dig into this case, the more convinced I am that Ulrich is just another victim in all of this.

Having gathered his wits again after the mention of the dreaded *Procto-Pussy* debacle, Hurley shifts the focus with Ulrich. "Caroline told her friends you didn't take the breakup well, and that you kept after her to go out with you again."

"That's not true," Ulrich says calmly. "I did tell her that I enjoyed her company and wouldn't mind doing things with her in the future, but I agreed that our relationship was more of a friendship than it was anything romantic. I think she was expecting me to be more upset over her suggestion that we break up, because she seemed surprised when I agreed with her. I got the impression that she felt offended at first, like my ready willingness to part ways with her was an affront to her looks or sexuality or appeal or whatever quality it is that woman want to have." He pauses and shrugs. "Maybe she told her friends a different version of the events to make herself feel better," he suggests.

This sounds feasible to me. I can remember falling for a clichéd "I need to find myself" breakup line that a guy I dated in college fed me once. I was blind to the clues he'd been giving me—wrenching his head around so hard and fast to ogle other women's derrieres that he should have been in a cervical collar, complaints about the way I chewed my food or fixed my hair, and mysterious meetings that kept coming up, causing him to cancel a date at the last minute. I honestly (and stupidly) believed the "find myself" line. I later realized it was nothing more than a chickenshit euphemism for "I can't stand one more minute with you, but I'm too much of a coward to say so." Oblivious to the true meaning behind his words, I thought there was still hope.

I caught the jerk making out hard with someone else a mere two days after I sent him off on his journey to find himself. I then realized two things: one, he apparently thought his self was either down the throat or up the shirtfront of the gorgeous girl he was with, and two, if he really wanted to find himself, he should have had a colonoscopy, because I felt certain that's where he'd find his head.

Embarrassed by my naivete and vulnerability, I told a different version of these events to anyone who asked about our breakup. To this day, my sister thinks that I broke things off with that guy because he was too immature and flighty, and I'm fine with her believing that for the rest of her life. Given this, it seems perfectly reasonable that Caroline Helgeson might have told her girlfriends a slightly different version of the events that led to the breakup between her and Ulrich.

Hurley, who has probably never been dumped in his life,

moves right along. After all, what reasonable, intelligent woman would ever dump a man who is gorgeous, loving, considerate, kind, smart, and romantic?

"Caroline also told her friends that you were stalking her. She said you followed her to work on several occasions. She saw you tailing her in your car."

Ulrich chuckles, shaking his head. "Yeah, the cops mentioned that to me, and, I confess, it puzzled me at first. I couldn't figure out why Caroline would have said something like that. I wasn't stalking her, and she didn't strike me as the kind of girl who would make something like that up. She wasn't a drama queen or anything like that." He gives us an ironic smile. "Then I figured it out. I was a substitute teacher when I met Caroline. That meant my job site sometimes changed from one day to the next. While I got work at the high school most of the time, I occasionally got gigs at the middle schools, too. Caroline's workplace was on the same street as the middle school, and I did an eight-week stint there to cover someone's maternity leave right after Caroline and I decided to call it quits. My guess is she saw me driving to work and recognized me. For whatever reason, she thought I was stalking her."

Ulrich makes a pained face and shakes his head again. "I don't know why she wouldn't have just called me or sent me a text about it if she really thought I was following her. I swear, we parted on friendly terms and she had no reason to be afraid of me, or to think I was angry with her. Or that I would do anything like that, for that matter. I don't get it." His body sags and his expression turns sad as he adds, "And I guess now I'll never know why."

Ulrich and Hurley stare at one another, each gauging the other, neither of them showing any emotion. It's Hurley who finally interrupts this visual détente by looking away and asking another question.

"What about Linda Marie Elwood? You knew her, too?"

"So said the cops," Ulrich tells him. "They said she was in some of my classes back when I was in college, but if that's the case, I have no recollection of her. The name isn't familiar to me, her face isn't familiar to me, and the classes we supposedly attended together were basic required classes that were held in large classrooms with lots of students. Not to mention that it was nearly a decade ago."

"Do you own a boat?" Hurley asks.

"I did. Just a little fourteen-foot jon boat that I kept on a trailer parked alongside my house. The police confiscated it as evidence."

Hurley looks at Barney. "I haven't had time to read through all the police reports yet. Did they find any evidence in the boat that tied him to any of these deaths?"

Barney raises his eyebrows. "They tried. They took a sample of some river grass that was stuck to the boat and said it could only have come from the area where one of the bodies was found. But that same grass was found in two other areas along the river, one of which is right by the boat launch my client uses."

"What about alibis for any of the times when these women were killed?" Hurley asks next, turning his attention back to Ulrich.

Ulrich sighs. "I'm a bachelor. I have no family in the area. I lived alone at the time. My dating life was nonexistent after Caroline and I broke up, so I was sleeping alone. The cops said all these women were killed during the night, though I understand they couldn't provide very specific timelines for some of them. But since I was in bed alone, sleeping, every night, it didn't matter."

"However," Barney jumps in, "there's no motive, either. I know the cops tried to say that my client had an issue with the Helgeson woman that enraged him, and that he killed these other women because they looked like her and served as substitutes for his supposed rage until he finally killed the real deal. But that's a load of bull hockey. This case is mostly circumstantial."

"And yet here I am," Ulrich says, proffering his cuffed hands and giving us a bitter smile.

His eyes take on that cold, dull, almost-dead look again, much like Tomas Wyzinski's eyes had been in that courtroom. At the time, I thought that look in Wyzinski's eyes was a sign of malice, proof of his evil nature, but I now know it was the look of utter despair. I hope I can do something to put some life back into Mason Ulrich's eyes.

Satisfied that he's gotten all he can out of Ulrich, Hurley brings our meeting to an end. Barney Ledbetter thanks us for our time and asks us to keep him posted. We leave the room with the two of them sitting side by side, heads bowed together, discussing who knows what.

CHAPTER 11

Once we are outside the prison and back in the truck, Hurley says, "On to Eau Claire. What do you guys think so far?"

Once again in the backseat, Izzy says, "I think there's a good chance they got the wrong man. But there is a window of doubt here. The defense knows about those flower petals, and who knows how many other people might have learned of them? It's not beyond the realm of possibility that some kook decided to carry out a copycat killing."

"Or perhaps the defense did," I say. I see Hurley shoot me a bemused look and can feel Izzy doing the same. "Well, think about it," I say. "What better argument could Ulrich have for an appeal, or maybe a new trial, or even outright exoneration, than another murder that is identical in every way, including an obscure detail only a few people knew about? A murder where Ulrich finally has an alibi, an unassailable one, in fact. Barney said he took the case on just a week ago and—*wham!*—there's another murder." I pause, but neither of the men says anything. "And let's face it," I go on. "Barney seems a bit sketchy, don't you think?"

"I think 'sketchy' is a kind word," Hurley offers. "But that aside, I'm inclined to agree with Izzy. I think there's a chance

Ulrich is innocent, and, if so, that means the killer is still on the loose. Until we know for sure, we keep digging, agreed?"

"*Agreed,*" Izzy and I say in unison.

"When we meet with the folks in Eau Claire, let's try to find out what things about the first cases differ from ours," Hurley says. "We know the geographic area is different, though I'm not sure of the significance of that, given that three of the four original victims were drug users and transients."

"Our victim was a drug user and transient, too," I say. "Which means that the biggest difference, so far, is victim number four, Caroline Helgeson, the woman Ulrich dated. She's the only one who doesn't fit the profile."

"Good point," Hurley says, looking thoughtful. "If we take Ulrich out of the equation, the Helgeson woman doesn't fit at all. She only makes sense if Ulrich *is* the killer and our victim is a copycat."

"Unless someone is trying to frame Ulrich," I toss out.

Silence follows. This line of paranoid thinking is a bit out there, and it only seems reasonable to me now because I know it happened to Tomas Wyzinski. My thoughts feel muddled, and my stomach growls.

"Should we grab an early lunch somewhere?" I suggest.

"Good idea," Izzy says.

Hurley says nothing, but at the next exit, he turns on his indicator and gets off the interstate. We pull into an area that includes a gas station and a Subway restaurant. I'm proud of Izzy when he orders the salad version of one of the sandwiches. I have no such restraint, and not only order a sandwich but a bag of chips and a cookie as well. We eat in silence, each of us lost in our own thoughts, though I'm sure we're all thinking about the case.

When we get back in the truck, the sun beating down through the windshield and my full tummy combine to make my eyelids feel heavy. Moments after we are back on the road, I drift off. It seems like only seconds later that Hurley is gently shaking my shoulder and saying, "Mattie, we're here."

I sit up and rub the sleep from my eyes. We are parked in front of a sprawling white concrete building that looks like a prison façade. Instead, it is a municipal building that serves as home to the Eau Claire Police Department, as well as several other governmental entities.

After checking in at a glassed-in reception area, a uniformed cop meets us and buzzes us through a door and down labyrinthine hallways into a conference room. Standing inside the room, leaning against a large conference table, is a heavyset fellow wearing a white shirt, a plain blue tie, and a pair of navy dress pants with a sheen that suggests they've seen better days. He looks to be in his mid-forties, with a broad chest and a bit of a paunch over a pair of long, skinny legs. His dark, thinning hair is combed straight back from his forehead, which, like the rest of his face, is heavily lined. That, combined with a subtle scent emanating from him, tells me he's a smoker.

"Hello there," he says, pushing away from the table and extending a hand to Hurley. "You must be Steve Hurley. I'm Rick Stetson, like the hat."

Now that we're closer, I can see that Detective Stetson has lazy, hooded eyes in an odd shade of pale brown that is almost yellow. They remind me of a snake's eyes. I suspect the man does very well when questioning anyone, because his gaze is disconcertingly uncomfortable.

After shaking Hurley's hands, Stetson turns his attention to us.

"Detective Stetson was in charge of the Ulrich investigation," Hurley explains before doing the introductions. "This is Dr. Izthak Rybarceski, our medical examiner in Sorenson, and this is Mattie . . . um . . . Winston, one of the medicolegal investigators in the ME's office."

Hurley's verbal stumble makes me wince inwardly. The

fact that I haven't changed my last name to his, or at least reverted to my maiden name of Fjell, is something of a sore subject with him. However, even he admits it's handy to have two different names in situations where we have to work together, but don't necessarily want other folks to know that we're married.

When we first met, Hurley called me Winston all the time. Nowadays I never hear that name from him. It's always either Mattie or Squatch.

I don't want to take on Hurley as my last name, at least not yet. The two of us work together so much, it's bound to raise eyebrows and questions if we introduce ourselves with the same last name. Barney Ledbetter's knowledge of our relationship, and his reaction to it, is exactly the type of situation we don't want.

Hurley and I take great pains to avoid any circumstances that might create a conflict of interest, though sometimes they can't be helped. If people don't know to look for one, then so much the better.

"Please have a seat anywhere you like," Stetson says after the greetings are done. "Help yourselves to some coffee or water, if you like."

There are plastic urns at the center of the table, along with a half-dozen plastic water cups and an equal number of plastic coffee cups. Both urns have masking tape labels on them, one with COFFEE written on it, while the other says WATER. Next to the coffee urn and cups is a dish with about a dozen small containers of artificial creamer, and a two-sided plastic caddy of sugar and sugar-substitute packets.

Stetson heads around to the opposite side of the table, so the three of us settle into seats on our side, me in between Izzy and Hurley. I reach for the water first, and after getting nods from both Hurley and Izzy, I pour each of us a glass. When I'm done with that, I grab the coffee urn and give the two men questioning looks again. This time they pass. I pour myself a small cup, dump two of the creamers into it, and give it a sip. That's enough to tell me that the men were wiser than I.

I set the cup down a ways away from me. I should have known better. There isn't a cop house anywhere that's known for its coffee. Besides, Hurley is giving me raised eyebrows and I remember that I'm pregnant.

Stetson laces his fingers together, smiling at us as he watches the beverage action. "I trust you received the reports I faxed to you yesterday?" he says to Hurley.

"I did," Hurley says with a nod. "Thank you. I haven't had time to go through all of them yet, but got through enough to give me a good idea of the facts of the case. Though I'd be interested in anything else you might have."

"Of course," Stetson says, blinking lazily. He gestures toward a couple of boxes at the other end of the table. "I've pulled together as much of the file on Ulrich as I could find. You're welcome to look through it all, though I'm not sure how you think it's going to help you with your case."

Hurley takes a drink of water, stalling. "As I said on the phone," he says finally, setting his glass down, "we have a homicide victim in Sorenson whose wounds and manner of death appear to fit Ulrich's MO."

"A copycat," Stetson says in a tone that makes it clear he's stating the obvious.

Hurley rakes a hand through his hair. "That was my first thought, but Dr. Rybarceski found some evidence that suggests otherwise."

The door behind us opens and we all turn to look. A tall man dressed in a black suit and white shirt enters the room. He has dark eyes, brown hair slicked straight back from his face, a smile that looks plastic and forced, and a definite air of authority.

"Ah, this is our county DA, Pete Hamilton," Stetson says.

As Stetson relays our names and occupations to the newcomer, Hamilton walks to the head of the table and pulls out the chair there, barely acknowledging our presence. "Yes, yes, welcome," he says in an impatient tone. He doesn't look at us as he says this. Instead, he reaches for the carafe of water and one of the cups, then pours himself a drink.

I study his tie during this interlude, a slash of bright red against the white shirt that looks like a big, bloody wound. There are ladybugs printed on it, and I gather the design is to suggest a bit of whimsy, which I'm betting the man doesn't possess.

He settles into his chair after he's done pouring his drink and then takes a sip of the water. His movements are slow and deliberate, and I realize he's performing for us, much like he might in front of a jury. He runs a hand down that tie, smoothing it.

"I understand you folks might have a copycat killer?" he says, smiling at Hurley.

It's Izzy who answers him. "I'm not sure it's a copycat," he says. "I think there's a possibility Ulrich could be innocent."

Hamilton scoffs at this, giving Izzy a skeptical look. "And you think this why, exactly?"

"Because of some evidence we found on the body of our victim," Izzy says.

"I see," Hamilton says in a placating tone. "And what would this evidence be?"

"Debris I found in one of the stab wounds, the one over the heart. Plus, the pattern of the stab wounds matches those of the victims you had in the Ulrich case."

We have Hamilton's attention now. "This debris you found, it was what, may I ask?"

"Parts of a flower," Izzy says. "Five yellow carnation petals."

Stetson leans back in his chair, his hands dropping into his lap. He turns and stares at Hamilton, his body stiff as if he's bracing himself for a blow.

"That does match findings we had on all of our victims," Hamilton says.

"And yet, it wasn't mentioned during the trial," Hurley says.

Hamilton's smile is gone now. "We decided not to use that evidence because we couldn't figure out where Ulrich got the petals from. Mentioning them might have complicated the case by creating possible doubt about his guilt. Of course the defense had access to the autopsy reports, and I assume they knew about the petals. They could have brought them up, but I think the psychiatric experts we had lined up ready to testify about the meaning behind those particular flowers convinced them otherwise." He leans back and looks up toward the ceiling. "Though I must admit, they may have been smarter than I give them credit for."

"How so?" I ask.

He lowers his head and looks at me with an expression that is a mixture of condescension and patient tolerance. I get the sense that he's someone used to being in charge and getting his way. "Come now, Ms. Winston. Surely, you can see how this dead woman of yours casts doubt on Ulrich's guilt, opening the door for all kinds of appeals and motions."

"What are you suggesting?" I ask.

He shrugs. "I'm not suggesting anything. Draw your own conclusions." He says this with an inflection that suggests an inevitable outcome is obvious.

I try again to pin him down. "Do you think Ulrich might be innocent?"

"God, no," Hamilton scoffs. "That man is as guilty as the day is long. But I'm sure the defense will jump on this right away. How convenient for them." He smiles at me, his brows arched ever so slightly, waiting for me to get the inference in case I missed his first one.

I know exactly what he's thinking and implying—I'd had

the same thought myself earlier in the truck. The idea that a defense attorney would have someone killed to try and prove his client's innocence is an outlandish theory, and it's also not the first one I would expect someone in Hamilton's position to jump to.

I give him a look of disbelief. "Are you suggesting that the defense team somehow arranged for a murder to match the others purely as a strategy for an appeal, or to submit a motion for retrial?"

"Murder is a strong word," Hamilton says, making a face like he just tasted something awful. "Perhaps they took advantage of some poor vagrant girl with a drug problem who overdosed. It would be easy to create the wounds and stuff some flower petals in one of them."

"That didn't happen," Izzy says emphatically. "The wounds were definitely made perimortem, and the one over her heart was the one that killed her."

"Do you have her drug screens back yet?" Hamilton asks, looking a bit smug.

"We have some of them," Izzy says.

"Do you have the opiates test back?" Hamilton asks, and Izzy nods. "And were they present in your victim?"

"Yes," Izzy admits.

"Enough to have killed her?"

"I don't know yet," Izzy says. "But I do know that she was alive when she was stabbed," he says determinedly.

"Okay, if you insist," Hamilton says dismissively. "It doesn't mean your death wasn't committed by a copycat killer." He is wearing that plastic smile again and the room falls silent. Glances are exchanged, and the tension in the room is so thick, one could cut it with a knife. This gives me an idea.

"We have imprints around the wounds that appear to have been made by the hilt. Did your victims have similar markings? And did you match them up to the murder weapon?"

Hamilton and Stetson exchange looks.

"We never found the actual knife," Stetson says. "We know Ulrich bought a fishing knife the year before that fits with the type of wounds three of the victims had, though Ulrich claimed he lost it. He could have tossed it into the Chippewa River in any number of places and we'd never find it. But we have records of the purchase and know what the knife looked like. We bought one just like it, and the docs said the specs and dimensions of that particular knife fit with the victims' wounds."

"Three of the victims?" I repeat, zeroing in on that. "Are you saying a different weapon was used on one of them?"

Hamilton nods. "The first one. She was stabbed in a similar manner as all the others—same locations for the wounds, same depth, same flower petals—but the overall size of the wounds was different. The knife used on her was bigger, and likely had a longer blade, because there were no hilt marks on her body."

"And you didn't find either weapon?" I ask.

Hamilton shakes his head. "My guess is the first knife is at the bottom of the Chippewa River somewhere. It was his first kill and he likely got nervous and wanted to get rid of the thing. Then when he killed again, he used a different knife, but hung on to it this time, feeling more confident after getting away with the first murder."

"So you have no murder weapon, no witnesses," Hurley says, looking deep in thought. "Any other evidence? Or, rather, any evidence at all?"

Hamilton bristles; Stetson's face colors.

"Of course," Hamilton says. "And if you know about the flower petal evidence, I'm betting you have some source of information and know full well what other evidence we had."

Score a point for Hamilton, though things aren't as straightforward as he might think.

Hurley smiles. "I do have some information," he admits. "I know you found Ulrich's fishing license by one of the victims, and that Ulrich had connections to two of the victims."

Hamilton scoffs. "More than a connection in the case of the last victim," he says. "He dated Caroline Helgeson until she dumped him, and then he stalked her for weeks afterward. It's no coincidence that the murders started shortly after that, or that the first three victims all bear a physical resemblance to Helgeson."

"All circumstantial," Hurley says. "Given the violence of these crimes and the fact that it appears that all of the bodies were dumped, you'd think the killer would have transferred something to the victims or the sites. And yet there's nothing?"

Hamilton frowns and says, "Ulrich's fingerprints were found in Caroline's house."

"He readily admitted to being there, didn't he?" Hurley counters. "They were dating for a while, so that's of little to no evidentiary value."

Hamilton smiles, but the muscles in his cheeks twitch with tension. "There was the fishing license found near the first victim," he says, his voice tight, as if he's gritting his teeth. "And there was also a fiber found on one of the victims—I forget which one, off the top of my head—that was matched to the carpet in Ulrich's car."

"That was on Darla Marks," Stetson offers. "They think it got on her body while Ulrich was transporting her to the spot where her body was dumped."

"You searched his vehicle?" I ask.

Hamilton sighs with exasperation. "We did."

"And?"

"And we didn't find anything other than a match to the carpet fiber."

"So there was no other trace evidence in the car that he supposedly used to transport a dead body?" I say in disbelief.

"No, there was not." Now Hamilton's teeth are clenched.

"Let me see if I have this right," I say. "You're telling us that this Ulrich guy somehow managed to murder four women over a period of a few months in places unknown and transport all of their bodies to dump sites. So far, the only evidence you've been able to find against him is a fishing license, which he could have lost anytime, and a fiber that matches the carpet in his car—a carpet, I'm guessing, that could also be found in hundreds of other cars in the area?"

Hamilton shrugs off the question. "So the guy is smart," he says irritably. "Hell, if you watch enough crime shows on TV these days, it's easy to figure out how to get away with murder and avoid detection." He looks at us and huffs a humorless laugh. "Look, I know how excited you can get thinking you've discovered something big. A serial killer wrongly convicted! Wow!" he says in a mocking tone. "I get it. It's heady stuff. But it's just not true in this case. Ulrich did it. Is your death similar? I'll take your word for it. You all seem like competent professionals. But these flower petals aren't the big deal you're trying to make them out to be. Did they get mentioned during the trial? No. Were the petals public knowledge? Again, no. But our team knew about them, the defense team knew about them, and who knows how many other people heard about them?"

He pauses, and when no one says anything, he goes on. "Not to mention that Ulrich himself could be behind this. He's in a prison with some hard-core criminals, including other murderers. It wouldn't be the first time someone in prison arranged a killing on the outside."

All cogent arguments, and our faces must reflect this. Hamilton's next words, said with a sympathetic look in our direction, are "Go home. You're barking up the wrong tree here."

Hurley gives him a smile I've only seen a few times. It's a cold, calculating smile that makes a shiver run down my back.

"Thanks," he says in a hard, brittle voice. "But I'd like to draw my own conclusions."

There is a heated stare-off between the two men, and Hamilton has a look in his eye that makes me glad I'm not a defendant facing him. Then, in the blink of an eye, his face morphs into Mr. Friendly again. "Suit yourself," he says flippantly, stroking his tie. "Far be it for me to tell anyone else how to waste their time."

With one last glacial glare at Hamilton, Hurley turns to Stetson. "I'm curious, did Ulrich ever explain what was behind the pattern of the stab wounds?"

Stetson frowns and shakes his head. "A lot of what we have is speculation, some of it expert. We did have a shrink talk with Ulrich, or, should I say, he talked *to* Ulrich. Ulrich wouldn't speak to him. The shrink didn't come up with much about Ulrich personally because of that. He did say, though, that the V pattern of the wounds, leading down to the area of the female reproductive organs in a shape resembling the uterus, suggested some level of sexual frustration. We thought Ulrich had some sexual issues with Ms. Helgeson, and that added to both his fixation and his frustration."

"What sorts of sexual issues?" I ask.

Stetson shrugs. "Can't say for sure, since Ulrich wouldn't talk, but Helgeson supposedly told one of her friends that Ulrich couldn't get it up." He clears his throat, looks at me, and says, "Sorry, miss."

I wave away his apology. "Don't censor yourself on my account," I tell him. "I spent a lot of years working as an ER nurse, so you'd be hard put to say anything I haven't heard before."

"And the flower petals," Hurley says, frowning in thought, "they weren't mentioned because you couldn't tie Ulrich to them in any way?"

Apparently tired of being ignored, Hamilton pipes up. "That's right. We thought the lack of connection could potentially create enough doubt in the minds of the jury that they wouldn't be able to come to an agreement, or even worse, they might acquit."

Hurley doesn't look at Hamilton; he keeps his focus on Stetson. "I assume you checked out all the local florist shops?" he says.

"We did," Stetson says after a quick glance at Hamilton. "We checked all of Ulrich's online activity, too, thinking he might have made a purchase that way. I had my men search out areas in town where anyone might be growing the flowers in a hothouse somewhere, and we also pored over his financials, looking for any purchases that might have included the flowers. Even though the flowers wouldn't have been in season at the time of the murders, we checked out local gardens, just to be sure. There was nothing. We have no idea where those flowers came from."

"Did Ulrich ever say anything about them?"

Stetson scoffs a laugh. "Talking wasn't one of Ulrich's strong suits. He steadfastly denied having anything to do with any of these killings, and his denials were about the only thing he'd ever say."

"But in the end," Hamilton rudely interjects, "we had enough other evidence to make the conviction stick. We didn't need the flower petals. Ulrich dated one of the victims, and she dumped him after a few weeks. He had connections with another victim, and we found his fishing license at one of the dump sites. We know that the year before, he bought a fishing knife that fits with the type of wounds the victims had. Plus, he had no alibi for any of the deaths."

"I'm still surprised that the defense didn't bring up the petals," Hurley says.

Once again, Stetson and Hamilton exchange a look; then they shrug in unison. "We made all the evidence available to the defense team," Hamilton says with a hint of smugness.

I'm sure they did, but I'm also willing to bet they found a

way to bury the flower petal evidence in hopes that the defense would never find it. I make a mental note to find out who was Ulrich's original attorney and to ask him. Barney Ledbetter's explanation made some sense: They had likely seen the flower petal evidence, but were worried that the prosecution had some powerful psychological testimony lined up. They suspected it would be descriptive enough to make the jurors forget or simply ignore the fact that the flowers couldn't be traced to Ulrich.

"Was there evidence of sexual assault in any of the girls?" Izzy asks.

Stetson shakes his head.

"That seems odd if the man's motivation was some kind of sexual frustration," Izzy says.

Hurley nods. "I agree. Did you guys talk to any of Ulrich's previous dates, assuming he had any? Or any of his family?"

"Of course we did," Stetson says irritably. He folds his arms over his chest, distancing himself. "The guy saw other women over the years, but they all seemed to fizzle out after a date or two. One of them was a teacher at the high school where Ulrich worked, and she said the guy was too intense for her. He seemed all about getting serious, getting married, starting a family, that sort of thing. And she wasn't ready for that yet."

Hamilton snorts a laugh. "Bit of a switch there, eh?" he says.

We all turn to stare at him. "How so?" Hurley asks.

Hamilton casts an incredulous look Hurley's way, clearly astonished that he can't see the obvious. "It's always the chicks who want to make things serious fast," he says. "You know, they're all about commitment, and the ring, and the wedding. It's the guys who are usually backing away."

Once again, Hamilton and Hurley stare at one another. Hurley's frowning; Hamilton smiles at him, eyebrows raised, waiting for him to get the joke. Over the next few seconds,

Hamilton's smile fades and he looks over at me suddenly, as if he forgot that there was a woman in the room.

"Stereotypes," he says with an awkward shrug. "You know what I mean."

"No, can't say that I do," I tell him.

This isn't true, but I don't feel like letting the guy off the hook, if for no other reason than simply because he used the word "chicks."

"Did any of the other, um, *chicks* that Ulrich dated have anything interesting to add?" I ask him.

Hurley's eyebrows raise, and I see the corners of his mouth curl up the tiniest bit. Izzy hides a laugh/cough behind his hand. Hamilton just stares at me, his facial muscles twitching.

"Sorry," he says finally. "I didn't mean to be . . . I shouldn't have . . . oh, hell." He lets his head fall back and he stares at the ceiling, emitting a world-weary sigh. "No, the other women didn't have anything of interest to offer. They all said the same thing—they dated the guy, there wasn't enough of a spark there, and they moved on."

Hamilton lowers his head, but doesn't look at me. Instead, he smooths his tie again and then reaches for the water carafe to refill his glass. I get a strong sense that he wishes there were something stronger in that carafe than just water.

"Did any of the other women initiate the breakups?" I ask him.

"No. They all said things just petered out. They went on a couple of dates with the guy, the magic wasn't there, and they just stopped seeing one another."

"What did his family say about him?" Hurley asks.

Stetson jumps in to answer this one, since Hamilton is currently gulping down water. "Ulrich is the youngest of three kids, and the only boy. His dad died when he was in high school, and his mom said Ulrich took it hard, but seemed to do okay. She, of course, doesn't think he did any of this."

"So no big red flags in the guy's history?" Hurley says.

"Nope."

Silence falls over the room, and it's quiet enough that I hear Hamilton swallow just before he breaks the silence.

"You guys are convinced Ulrich is innocent, aren't you?" His tone makes it clear how ludicrous he thinks this idea is. "You don't think you have a copycat. You think you have the same guy that killed our girls here, don't you? Except that doesn't make any sense. Why would he suddenly relocate? Why would he stop killing for a while and then start up again?"

"All good questions," Hurley says. "But the bigger question, the one that bothers me the most, is how would anyone else know about the flower petals? If it is a copycat, how could they have known about the flower petals . . . not just their presence, but the specific number of them and the wound they were found in?"

"The presence of those flower petals wasn't a state secret," Hamilton says. "And I think the idea of Ulrich arranging something from prison is quite feasible. It makes a lot more sense than some random copycat."

"Except," Hurley says, pulling at his chin, "if Ulrich was hoping to arrange another killing to make himself look innocent, why do it so far from the area where the first killings took place? I mean, yes, the story was all over the news at the time it happened, but that was, what, almost two years ago? In this day and age of instant news cycles, that's a long time. It was pure happenstance that we made the connection."

"Yet you did," Stetson says, a hint of suspicion underlying his words.

"Yes, you did," Hamilton says thoughtfully. "Just how did you make that connection? Clearly, your focus is on the flower petals, yet, as you so succinctly point out, that information wasn't publicly available. How did you find out about them?"

My heart does a little flip-flop because I don't want the answer to that question to get out, at least not yet. The person who told it to me might get in trouble, and I don't want to be the cause of anyone losing their job. I'm afraid either Hurley or Izzy will let the cat out of the bag, so I jump into the fray in hopes of diverting attention.

"I'm sorry, gentlemen, but I need to excuse myself." I shove my chair back and give the men an awkward smile. "I need to pee something fierce," I say with false embarrassment.

My efforts have the desired effect. Stetson blushes and stammers something unintelligible, pushing his own chair back and standing in a gentlemanly manner. Hamilton merely shakes his head, smiles, and takes another gulp from his glass.

"Can someone show me to the nearest bathroom, please?" I say. "And can we hurry?"

CHAPTER 12

Stetson hurries around the table as I open the door to the room. I step out into the hallway and run smack into someone.

"*Oomph,*" a feminine voice says as I back up and start to apologize. A tall, redheaded, angry-looking woman around my age, is standing in front of me.

"Susan?" Stetson says from behind me. "What are you doing here?"

Belatedly I realize that Susan isn't alone. Two towheaded, toddler-aged girls, identical twins, are with her.

As the two little girls sing a chorus of "Hi, Daddy" to Stetson, Susan glares at me, giving me a head-to-toe assessment. Judging from her expression, I see I come up seriously lacking. Then she shifts her stare to Stetson.

"You were supposed to pick up the girls at noon, remember?" she chastises.

Stetson shoots me an apologetic look, points, and says, "The bathroom is down this hall and to your right." Then he grabs Susan by the arm and starts to pull her along with him in the opposite direction.

Susan wrests her arm loose of his grip and the two of them indulge in a short stare-down before Susan steps past Stetson and goes the way he'd wanted her to, in the first place. The two little girls are toddling along in her trail. Stetson, with head bowed, falls into step behind them until they disappear around a corner.

I hear an intense hiss of voices coming from that direction, though I can't make out what they are saying. Despite an overwhelming urge to be nosy and eavesdrop—I'm a nosy person at heart—I head for the bathroom.

By the time I get back to the conference room, I see that Stetson hasn't returned, but Hurley and Hamilton are chatting with a newcomer, someone I recognize. With blond hair, blue eyes, a muscular but slim build, and a tan—a definite rarity for this time of year in Wisconsin—he looks like he's from central casting, called up to play the role of California surfer guy.

"Hello there, Mattie Winston," he says with a smile when I walk in. "Long time, no see."

I see Hurley shoot me a curious look. I smile back at the newcomer, whom I recognize as the guy from that night in the bar at the forensic conference. I wrack my brain for a name. "Good to see you again, too," I say, stalling. I scramble madly through the detritus of my memories from that night. "Is it Tim?" I say, taking a stab after unearthing a vague, alcohol-fuzzed memory.

"Close," he says with a sideways nod, his smile broadening. "It's Todd. Todd Oliver, from the conference last fall."

"Right. Sorry," I say with an apologetic smile.

I watch Hurley's gaze turn steely-eyed as his head pivots toward Todd. I know he has deduced that this is the man I had drinks with in the bar, the one who told me about the Ulrich case.

"You two know one another?" Hamilton says, looking from Todd to me, and back at Todd again.

"Sort of," I say.

"Do tell," Hurley says, a hint of challenge in his voice. His steely-eyed gaze is back on me.

Izzy is sitting at the table, observing; there's an amused and curious expression on his face.

"Well, we met at a forensic conference in Milwaukee last fall," I say. I'm saved from any further explanations when Stetson walks back into the room, the two little girls with him.

"Sorry about that," he says to no one in particular. "Susan had an engagement and I was supposed to take the girls. I forgot." He looks over at Todd. "Thanks for coming over. Let me take these two to Mrs. Gilbert so she can entertain them for a bit while we finish here. Pete can bring you up to speed." With that, he takes his daughters by their hands and leads them off down the hall.

"What brings you up our way?" Todd asks me.

"A case," I say. "One that might be related to one of yours, Mason Ulrich."

"Really?" Todd looks intrigued. "Is that why Stetson called me over here?" he asks Hamilton.

"It is. These folks are from Sorenson and they have a case down there that is similar to the Ulrich murders."

"He had another victim we didn't find?" Todd says, wide-eyed.

"Not exactly," Hamilton says. "They have a recent victim, killed a couple of days ago. It appears she was killed by someone with an MO identical to Ulrich's."

"A copycat," Todd deduces, still intrigued.

"I don't think so," Izzy says.

I suspect that he, too, has guessed that Todd was my source for the flower petal information, and he's sensed that

I'm not eager to reveal that. But the facts are going to come out sooner or later.

"We understand that the presence of some flower petals in the wounds of your victims was a fact that wasn't generally known. We found the same flower petals in one of the wounds on our victim," Izzy says.

Todd looks over at Hamilton and his face flushes red. He makes the connections with amazing speed and earns my respect a second later.

"I told Mattie here about our case during the conference," he says, coming clean. "It was just the two of us, though, two colleagues who work in the same field, sharing data." Todd looks over at me. "Did you tell anyone else about it?"

"I did not," I state emphatically, eager to reinforce the trust he placed in me when he first shared the information. "To be honest, I'd kind of forgotten about it until this case turned up on our autopsy table. Then it came back to me because it was such an unusual finding."

This is true. The part I don't say is that on the night in question, in the hotel bar, I had a little more to drink than I should have. I was feeling no pain that night, though I felt quite a bit the next morning when I woke up. It was the first hangover I'd had in years, and at the time, I swore it would also be the last. What Todd and I had discussed the night before wasn't uppermost in my mind the next day, and many of the details regarding our conversation were a blur. To be honest, they still are, but the flower petal detail stuck in my mind."

"Oh, hell," Todd says, raking a hand through that thick blond hair. "Are you suggesting that Ulrich might be innocent?" His blue eyes grow wide and I'm struck by how handsome a man he is.

I guess his age to be around mine, maybe a bit younger. Vague flashes of memory from that night come back to me.

Had I flirted with him? Harmless enough if I had—nothing happened. But still . . . I probably shouldn't have done it. Feeling a twinge of guilt, I glance at Hurley and see that he's watching me. Can he tell what I'm thinking?

"That's what we need to figure out," Izzy says, and for one horrifying moment, I fear he's either read my mind or, worse, I've spoken my thoughts aloud. I feel my face flush hot and then realize Izzy is answering Todd's question about Ulrich's possible innocence.

Stetson returns. "Did they bring you up to speed?" he asks Todd, who then nods.

Hamilton blows out an exasperated breath and hoists himself out of his chair, making for the door. "This is absurd. You people are imagining things, building a case where none exists. And I, for one, am done with it. You're wrong about Ulrich. He's right where he belongs."

With that, he storms out of the room, slamming the door closed behind him.

"Llewellyn isn't going to be happy about this, either," Todd says, giving Stetson a worried look.

"Who is Llewellyn?" Hurley asks, and I feel my rigid stance relax a hair, now that I'm no longer the sole subject of his burning scrutiny.

"Cory Llewellyn is the county coroner," Todd explains. "Both he and Hamilton are up for reelection this fall, so neither of them is going to be happy to hear that the biggest case they've ever worked might also have been their biggest mistake."

"Let's not get ahead of ourselves," Izzy says. "We don't want to jump to conclusions until we've had a chance to review the evidence. While the odds of this being a copycat case are small, they aren't zero. We have to follow the trail of those flower petals and see what we come up with."

"Good luck with that," Stetson says tiredly. "We looked into those flowers quite thoroughly and came up with nothing."

"Except you did it with a suspect in mind," Hurley says. "Eliminate Ulrich from the equation and it opens up all sorts of new avenues."

Stetson frowns. "Such as?" he challenges, clearly put out by Hurley's suggestion that he might not have done his job as meticulously as he could have.

Hurley gives him a placating smile. "I'm sure you did a thorough job of searching the local area for greenhouses and gardens, but with all the online florist services out there, isn't it possible that someone other than Ulrich might have ordered those carnations?"

Scowling, Stetson doesn't answer. He looks like a kid who's just been caught in a lie.

"I did some research into those flowers," Todd says, and I'm grateful to him for veering the conversation down a different path. "There are meanings associated with many different types of flowers and this one seemed significant, given that it wasn't something that grew wild during the time of year in question, and the fact that the same color and type of petal was used in all of the cases."

"What did you find out?" I ask, eager to encourage this line of thought, and curious to see if he'll come up with the same things Arnie did.

Todd tips his head back and stares at the ceiling. "I may forget some things without my notes in front of me, but let's see what I can recall." There are several seconds of silence and as I watch Todd, I feel someone else's eyes on me. I look and see Hurley watching me. I smile and wink at him, and then turn my attention back to Todd.

"Yellow flowers, in general, are associated with happiness and joy," Todd begins, "though that doesn't hold true with carnations. Carnations are considered flowers of love and their meaning changes with their color. A white one is said to represent purity, luck, and loveliness, whereas a red carnation symbolizes admiration, affection, and adoration. Pink ones convey tenderness, like a mother's love. The yellow carnation, however, symbolizes disappointment, disdain, and rejection. So the fact that the yellow carnation petals were found in the wounds over the hearts of each victim would tend to imply that the killer either felt that the victim, or whoever the victim represented, had disappointed him and failed to prove worthy of love, or that the victim had rejected him. Given Ulrich's history with Caroline Helgeson and the fact that the earlier victims all looked like her, it made sense."

"Except Ulrich's version of events regarding Caroline Helgeson is quite different from the police version," Hurley says. "He told the police his breakup with Caroline was both mutual and friendly."

"And saying that the earlier victims all looked like Caroline is making a potentially erroneous assumption," I say. "It could be that all of the women, Caroline included, look like someone else entirely. Just because Ulrich had a relationship with Caroline and she appeared to be his last victim doesn't mean she's at the heart of all this. In fact, given the victim we have in Sorenson, it now appears that Caroline wasn't the last victim."

"Do the physical characteristics of your victim match the others?" Todd asks.

"They do," Izzy says. "They also match the physical characteristics of about half the female population in Wisconsin. Tall, blond, blue-eyed women are a dime a dozen in this area."

"Damn," Todd mutters with a pained expression. He stares

at the floor and again runs a hand through his hair. "Did I help convict an innocent man?"

I feel for the guy, and I have a strong urge to try to pull him back from the edge of a despair I know all too well. Eager to distract him from his thoughts, I say, "This background information on the meaning behind yellow carnations, it's not the sort of thing the average Joe would know, is it?" I say. "I mean, how many guys would possess that kind of knowledge?"

"Ulrich would," Stetson says. "Ulrich did. In addition to working as a sub at the high school and middle school, he moonlighted teaching classes at the UW campus here in town. And one of the subjects he taught was a class on mysticism and symbolism. I got a copy of his syllabus, and the meanings, uses, and symbolisms of various plants throughout history were some of the topics he covered in the class."

"Well, it's not hard to see why Ulrich was convicted," Izzy says with a woeful shake of his head. "The evidence may be mostly circumstantial, but it's also incriminating."

"It wasn't all circumstantial," Stetson says. "There were fingerprints, and a fishing license, and the carpet fiber."

"Let's think this through," I say. "We know Ulrich didn't commit this last murder. That means we need to figure out how our latest case fits in with the others, or maybe how it doesn't."

"You're welcome to all of our files, even our samples, if it will help," Todd says. "To be honest, Noah probably knows more about this case than I do."

"Noah?" Hurley and I say at the same time.

"Noah Larson. He's the pathology resident here. He's training to become a board-certified forensic pathologist. He did the autopsies, along with the guys who have been coming from Madison and Milwaukee to supervise and teach him. Of course I'm happy to help in any way I can, too. I'm Dr. Larson's assistant. I'm hoping to be the main medicolegal death investigator for the medical examiner's office here, once Noah finishes his residency and gets board certified. For now, I help with all of the autopsies and do what I can with the investigations."

"Mattie and I would very much like to speak with Dr. Larson," Izzy says. "I'm intrigued by this training program your Dr. Larson has started. I've been approached about doing something similar at our facility in Sorenson, to train other doctors in forensic pathology. Where is his office located?"

"We're at General Hospital," Todd says.

"I don't think we'll accomplish much by going there," Stetson says, scowling. "I can have Dr. Larson call you. And I can have him send you copies of the autopsies, if you like."

"I'd rather look at them now myself," Izzy says, garnering a frown from Stetson. "And I'd like to see the facilities."

"As would I," I say.

Stetson looks oddly out of sorts and I see him exchange a look with Todd. Todd then says, "I can take you there."

I look at Hurley, eyebrows raised in question.

He hesitates, frowning, and then says, "I think I'll stay here and sort through this material." He gestures toward the boxes at the end of the table. "If Todd can drive you two to the hospital, I can meet you there when I'm done. Or if you prefer, you can take my truck and come back to pick me up when you're done," Hurley suggests.

"I'm more than happy to drive you guys there," Todd offers with a smile directed at me.

I don't smile back. Instead, I turn toward Hurley, whose frown has deepened. "What if we finish before you do?"

"Then I'll drive you back here," Todd chimes in cheerily.

Hurley and I stare at one another for a nanosecond longer than what's comfortable. "I appreciate that," he says, finally shifting his gaze to Todd. He looks back at me and adds, "Let me know when you get done and I'll do the same."

Then he turns away, effectively dismissing us. "Show me what you got," he says to Stetson.

Todd waves for us to follow him, and Izzy and I do so, going back the way we came in and exiting out the front of the building. Todd's car is a black Honda SUV, and a quick survey of the contents tells me he likely doesn't have any kids. He isn't wearing a wedding ring; so for now, I'm going to assume he's single. Then again, I'm not wearing my wedding ring, either.

Even though Todd and I are close to the same height, I let Izzy have the front seat and I settle in behind him, not wanting to stare at the back of Todd's head. It's cramped, but sitting next to Todd would have cramped more than my legs.

"I take it Detective Stetson isn't a fan of the hospital," Izzy says once we're under way.

Todd makes an equivocal face, clearly debating what to say. "Rumor has it, he had some bad experiences at General Hospital a few years ago, even though his wife, Susan—she's his ex-wife now—worked as a nurse there at the time. His mother developed cancer and underwent treatment at the hospital, but something went wrong during one of her hospitalizations and she died. Stetson was very close to her, since he's an only child and his father died when he was a boy—I think he was twelve or thirteen when it happened. He lived with his mom for a long time, right up until he married Susan, and I've heard there was no love lost between the two women. His mom got sick right after Stetson got married, so there was some speculation that Stetson felt guilty because of that, like he somehow caused her to get the cancer. Even though Susan was pregnant at the time, his mother's death apparently signified the death of his marriage as well."

Todd shrugs and smiles guiltily. "I'm speculating some, because I wasn't here when it all went down. I arrived right after Stetson's mother died, so I don't know all the details.

But I've heard the gossip. Hospitals seem to be hotbeds for that sort of thing."

"Tell me about it," I say.

"And then there's all the political intrigue," Todd says. "Dr. Larson and I are caught right in the middle of it, big-time."

"How so?" Izzy asks.

"You haven't met the other player in this game yet, our esteemed coroner, Mr. Cory Llewellyn," Todd says. "As you probably know, coroners in Wisconsin are elected officials, and Cory has been the coroner in this county for the past twelve years. It's a position of some authority in these parts, and Cory basks in the attention it provides him. That, and the fact that he owns the Town's End Bar, the biggest bar in the area."

"Your coroner is a bar owner?" I say, admittedly surprised. I know that the position often has no real knowledge requirements attached to it, but I thought it would at least lean toward someone with a periphery of experience.

Todd chuckles. "It's a popularity contest, and you have to admit that the owner of a bar in Wisconsin is bound to be a popular person. I think Cory might have some goods on a few people around town as well, and no doubt he drags out threats to reveal around election time."

"So this coroner is the person who responds to the death scenes?" I say. Todd nods. "What kind of training does he have?"

"To be honest, I have no idea," Todd says, "other than the fact that he's been doing it for a dozen years or more. I can tell you he's none too happy about this new medical examiner program Dr. Larson has started, though Dr. Larson is well known here and has a lot of support. He had a job as a regular pathologist at the hospital, but when he found out that we ship bodies to either Madison or Milwaukee for autopsy, he thought that was ridiculous." He looks over at Izzy and winks. "Just between us, I think he was also a little bored with his current job, and he's never liked Llewellyn. He wrote up a proposal to set up a satellite training campus at the hospital in conjunction with UW four years ago and volunteered to be the first student."

"Smart move," Izzy says.

"It was. Dr. Larson is quite canny," Todd says with tones of admiration. "He owns a cabin on the river, though 'cabin' is a relative term, since I hear the place is very nice and hardly rustic. And he offered the cabin as a residence to any of the forensic pathologists from Madison or Milwaukee who were willing to come up here for a time and provide the necessary oversight, education, and instruction for the residency program."

"That *is* smart," I say. "I'm guessing he has no shortage of volunteers."

"You've got that right," Todd says. "The program has been running for almost three years now and Dr. Larson is getting ready to take his board exams. Once he does that, he'll be like you." Todd looks at Izzy and smiles broadly.

"And no more shipping of bodies out of town," I say. "Are there other people interested in the residency program?"

Todd nods. "Yes, there are. One is a physician interested in changing her focus. One is a doc who's looking to do something different as he closes in on his retirement years. He wants to move up north, where the lifestyle is a little more laid back. Others are just looking for a change. I think there are six physicians who have expressed an interest if the program is approved to continue. And all but one of them plans to practice their new vocation in rural areas that are currently served by coroners like Cory Llewellyn."

"I hope it does get approved," Izzy says. "Wisconsin is behind the times in that regard."

"Not according to Cory Llewellyn," Todd says. "He's done everything he can to try and make sure Dr. Larson's program fails. Wait till he hears about this case you guys have and the idea that Ulrich might be innocent. Llewellyn isn't known for his sweet temperament, and this will likely set him off like a gas-soaked firecracker."

I'm about to ask Todd for examples of what Llewellyn has done, but he pulls into a parking lot and says, "Here we are."

CHAPTER 13

Todd pulls into a gated lot, using his hospital ID to gain access. We climb out and walk alongside him toward the entrance. I fall into what I think of as my Izzy pace—slower, shorter steps so that my long legs don't force Izzy, with his shorter ones, to trot to keep up. After the heart attack he had last year, I'm very tuned into Izzy and the physical demands our job sometimes puts on him. Fortunately, Todd is an ambler and Izzy keeps up with us both with ease.

I typically walk like I'm an hour late for the most important event in my life. I think this is due in part to my nursing days in the ER when the job required a constant near run to keep up with things. That speed became my default mode. Hurley is an ambler, like Todd. Sometimes, when we're walking together, I'll suddenly realize that I'm five feet or more ahead of him, forcing me to stop to give him time to catch up.

Speed long ago became my default mode for eating, too. When I was working as an ER nurse, I never knew when I would get to eat or how long I'd have to do it. I learned to inhale my food, and all too often did it in stages, standing up. I've even been known to eat while sitting on the toilet. It's a hard habit to unlearn. As a result, I typically finish eating way ahead of anyone else at the table, no matter where I am. It's just one of the many ways that my career in nursing altered my lifestyle.

The main lobby area of General Hospital is an airy, brightly lit atrium with modern furnishings and a colorful décor. As is the case with most hospitals during the day, there are people hustling and bustling about—employees, providers, patients, visitors, vendors. All of them have a barely subdued sense of urgency about them. The business of treating illness and injury often comes at a hastened pace; at times, the buildings seem to pulse as if they, too, are alive.

Not surprisingly, the autopsy suite is in the basement, a common location for morgues. It's out of the way, far apart from the hustle and bustle of saving lives that takes place on the main floors. Death is often hidden away, as if by not seeing it, we might somehow avoid it—when, in fact, it is the one thing all of us can count on with absolute certainty. We may not know how it will come, or when, or if we'll have knowledge of its pending arrival beforehand. But come it will for all of us at some point.

Despite this inevitability, death often has no place in a modern-day hospital. It is hidden, spoken of in whispers, and never dwelled upon. To the people who work in hospitals, death is seen as failure. In many cases, it is a failure, but not always. Sometimes death is the normal and peaceful end to a life well lived, or much-needed relief at the end of a long, exhausting battle to beat a disease. Over the last few decades, the hospice movement has helped alleviate some of the shame and embarrassment of death. Hospitals, though, still use special carts to move dead bodies—carts that hide their cargo beneath what appears to be an empty stretcher with a well-draped sheet covering the hidden compartment beneath.

The fact that most hospital morgues and, if they have them, autopsy rooms are in the basement adds to the spookiness sometimes associated with death. Hospital basements are creepy places to be without the presence of dead bodies. Dark, windowless hallways, overhead pipes, clanking machinery, and an almost-unearthly silence compared to the bustle of the upper floors make hospital basements an uncomfortable place to be at times. Add some dead bodies to this mix and you have a relatively high fear factor.

The basement where Dr. Larson works is no exception. Access requires a badge, as if going down to the spooky level is a privilege, and the hallways, while brightly lit, possess shadowy corners of darkness caused by the lack of outside light. Todd leads us down labyrinthine hallways, and despite my efforts not to feel spooked, I map out the turns in my head, just in case I need a quick escape. I'm wondering how deeply buried the morgue area is when Todd turns a corner and stops so suddenly that I nearly run over Izzy, who is in front of me, but behind Todd.

"Dr. Larson," Todd says. "Just the person I'm looking for."

The person we have almost literally run into is a man who looks to be in his forties, with deep-set eyes that are a warm, dark brown color and a boyish mop of hair cut in a style reminiscent of the early Beatles. He is wearing khakis and an untucked short-sleeved green shirt with a straight hem. He is shorter than I am, but not by much. He flashes us a tentative smile and raises his eyebrows at Todd in question.

"These are the folks from Sorenson they told us about this morning," Todd says. "And you need to hear what they have to say. They have a murder case in Sorenson that matches the MO of the Ulrich victims"—he pauses and leans in for dramatic effect, adding sotto voce—"and that includes the presence of yellow carnation petals in one of the wounds."

Dr. Noah Larson somehow manages to make his eyebrows go even higher. He shoots a questioning look at me and I nod. Then he looks at Izzy. "You're Dr. Rybarceski," he says in a soft-spoken, almost-reverent voice.

"I am," Izzy says, stepping forward and offering a hand. Dr. Larson shakes it and Izzy adds, "Please call me Izzy."

"And I'm Noah," he says. He shifts his gaze to me and releases Izzy's hand. "And you are?"

Before I can answer, Todd does it for me. "This is Mattie Winston. She's a medicolegal death investigator who works for Dr. Rybarceski."

Noah extends his hand to me and I give it a shake. "Nice to meet you," I say.

"I met Mattie at the forensic conference in Milwaukee," Todd says. "It was that one last fall. We got to talking in the bar late one night and swapping war stories, and I told her about the Ulrich case, particularly the flower petals. In strictest confidence, of course."

"Yes," I say quickly. "I didn't repeat the information to anyone, but when our victim turned up, I vaguely remembered Todd mentioning something similar. That's how we got onto this case and ended up here."

Noah Larson gives Todd a look I can't quite interpret. The closest I can come is to say that it resembled the look my mother used to give me whenever I acted out in public. It was a wait–until–I–get–you–home warning look. That look made me think that Dr. Larson wasn't too happy with the fact that Todd had shared the information.

Dr. Larson dismisses Todd and shifts his attention back to Izzy. "You may not know this, but you are my hero," he says with a smile. "Your situation in Sorenson is what prompted me to submit the proposal for the forensic pathology program here. The fact that you were able to set up as a forensic pathology–certified medical examiner in your town was an inspiration to me."

"Nothing heroic about it," Izzy says. But there is a hint of pride behind his smile, nonetheless. "It was more a happenstance of opportunity and acquaintance. I happened to be friends with the governor who was in place ten years ago, and when I told them I was willing to set up shop in Sorenson and provide forensic pathology services for our county, he jumped on it. There was a shortage of forensic pathologists in Madison at the time, and they were terribly overworked, so any opportunity to ease some of their burden was fine with him. We set it up on a trial basis for the first couple of years, but it's worked out well enough that we are a permanent part of the budget now. No governor since has suggested a change, probably because we do a good job, and because we sometimes cover neighboring counties that still operate under a coroner system, like you do. People are finally starting to realize how antiquated and outdated that system is. I think people thought a system of forensic pathology–trained medical examiners would be more expensive, but we've proven to be quite cost-effective. It costs a lot of money to ship all those bodies out of town."

"Ah, yes," Dr. Larson says, rolling his eyes. "The almighty budget. I thought board certification was what I needed to become official, but I've since learned that getting to be a line item in the budget is a much stronger position."

The two men share a chuckle over that comment, and then Dr. Larson says, "I assume you're here to look through our files on the Ulrich victims' autopsies?"

Izzy nods.

"You're welcome to look at anything you want, and we'll be happy to make you copies of documents you need as well," Dr. Larson says. "But before we get buried in paper, can I give you a quick tour?"

"I would love one," Izzy answers.

Dr. Larson turns and takes off with Izzy on his heels. I'm not sure if I'm invited along on this little mutual admiration society tour, but when I look at Todd, he gives a sideways nod of his head and says, "Come on."

Dr. Larson takes us to his autopsy room first, and it's a surprising exception to the dim, shadowy light of the rest of the basement area. The surfaces gleam with silver stainless and white enamel brightness lit by two rows of fluorescent fixtures in the ceiling. There are procedure lamps overhead, too, a high-wattage bulb inside a reflective shade attached to the end of a movable arm so one can aim the light in dozens of different directions. The room is small and has only one autopsy table, which looks to be identical to ours. Also, like our autopsy suite back home, there are two entrances, one meant for those who are still walking and the other for those who enter feet first on a stretcher. A microphone for use in dictating findings during the actual autopsy hangs down from the ceiling over the table.

"Looking good," Izzy says.

It's a kind and generous comment, given that our autopsy suite is at least twice the size of this one, and our town is only one-fourth the size of Eau Claire. Using his admitted connections to the governor at the time, Izzy had somehow managed to talk the guy into investing a lot of money to convert what was once an old municipal office building into a modern-day medical examiner's office. I'm not sure exactly what Izzy's connection to that particular governor was, but it certainly came with a lot of influence and perks.

From the autopsy suite, Dr. Larson takes us to his office, one he shares with Todd. It's a big room, and even though they share the space, I think the Eau Claire team has one-upped us on this one. My "office" is a desk located in our library, and my job-share cohort, Christopher, also has a desk in the library. It's not very private, but Izzy's office is the size of a closet, probably because that's what it was at one time. There aren't any other spaces for offices in our building. Whatever funding Izzy got for the conversion of the building he poured into the autopsy suite and Arnie's lab upstairs, not into office space.

"We have a mix of old and new here," Dr. Larson says, once we're in the office. "We don't have any X-ray machinery down here yet, though there are plans to build a room for it, so we have to take all our body films using the machinery and staff upstairs in the radiology department. It makes for some interesting sleight of hand." He pauses and, with a sly smile, says, "Or perhaps 'sleight of body' would be the better term. But we make it work. We do have modern recording equipment installed, however, and we videotape all of our autopsies. I can show you the reports or you're welcome to review the tapes, if you like."

"The tapes would be great," Izzy says. "I'm sure your reports are thorough, but there's nothing like visualizing the actual autopsy for comparison. Since I just did the post on our victim yesterday, it will be interesting to see how the victims and the results compare."

Dr. Larson invites Izzy to sit at his desk and then provides him with a pair of headphones. Then he shows him how to access the videos on the computer and leaves him there. He tells Todd he'll be available on his cell if needed and steps out of the office.

Izzy looks mesmerized and there is a gleam in his eye that tells me this sort of documentation will be the next tech advancement for our office. He's in seventh heaven.

I turn to Todd. "While Izzy's watching the videos, I'd like to review the scene photos, autopsy photos, and evidence inventories for each of the cases. Can you help me with that?"

"I can," he says with a smile. "All that stuff gets scanned and uploaded to a secure server." He steps behind his desk and pulls the chair out. "Have a seat."

"I don't want to impose. Don't you have work to do?"

"Nothing that can't wait," he says. "Besides, I think it will be helpful if we review this stuff together, so I can answer any questions you might have. Wouldn't you agree?"

Before I can answer, the door to the office opens and a short, squatty fellow, with the physique of a fireplug, walks into the room. He looks to be in his fifties, and has red hair, bushy red eyebrows, and a red handlebar mustache. His blue eyes are bloodshot, and his bulbous nose is streaked with tiny superficial blood vessels, a sign of someone who has a close personal relationship with booze. He's dressed in a standard Wisconsin uniform: blue jeans, a plaid flannel shirt, and boots.

"What the hell is going on, Todd?" he says in a gravelly voice that is much louder than it needs to be.

I hear Todd curse under his breath as the man's eyes zero in on me, since I'm positioned closest to the door.

"Are you the one who's trying to stir up trouble in the Ulrich case?" he says. His face looks like he just sucked on a lemon.

Todd clears his throat and says, "Cory Llewellyn, meet Mattie Winston, a medicolegal death investigator from Sorenson, Wisconsin."

Cory Llewellyn gives me a rapid head-to-toe once-over, and apparently finds me lacking if the look of disgust on his face is any indication.

"What's the deal?" he asks in a challenging tone. "You urban yahoos think us dumb-assed country folk can't do the job right? Is that it?"

I open my mouth to answer, but Todd speaks before I can. "Looks like we might have gotten this one wrong," he says in a calm, soothing tone. It's a wasted effort.

"Aw, bullcrap," Llewellyn scoffs, glaring at me. "I talked to Hamilton about it and it sounds like you got yourselves a copycat. If you think for one minute that Ulrich is innocent, then you are dumber than you look."

"Sir, you owe Mattie an apology," Izzy says from behind me in a sterner tone than I've ever heard him use.

Llewellyn gives him a startled look, and I realize he didn't see Izzy sitting there, his short body hidden behind the computer screen on Larson's desk. "Who the hell are you?" he snaps.

"I'm *Dr.* Izthak Rybarceski, a board-certified forensic pathologist."

He puts emphasis on the "doctor," and the fact that he has given Llewellyn his full formal name tells me he doesn't like the man. When he likes someone, Izzy always tells that person to call him by his nickname.

"Who the hell are you?" Izzy counters in an ironically polite tone.

Apparently, he hadn't taken off his headphones before Todd's introduction, though I can't be sure. Izzy might simply be trying to take the man down a peg.

"I'm Cory Llewellyn, the coroner for this county these past twelve years." He puffs his chest out and takes on a dismissive expression. "I know you medical types think your system of doing things is the best way, but we've done just fine in these parts without costing the taxpayers a lot of extra money."

Izzy smiles at him. It's a forced, somewhat predatory smile I don't see often on him. But I know what's going to come next and I also know I'm going to enjoy watching it.

"Mr. Llewellyn," Izzy says, getting out of his seat and standing as tall as he can.

It isn't much, but there is something about Izzy when he's in this mode that makes him seem much bigger than he is. I've seen him do it in court before.

"You're in charge of an antiquated, embarrassingly faulty system that, in fact, costs the taxpayers more money in the long run because of your need to ship bodies to Madison and Milwaukee. Your 'just fine' system compromises evidence, puts the public at risk, and wastes time and resources. The only benefit I can see to your 'just fine' system is that it helps you puff up your ego. What's more, there's a very good chance that your 'just fine' system has put an innocent man behind bars for life. And that means the real killer is still out there, putting the public in danger. If you doubt me on the cost issue, I'll be happy to provide you with a detailed cost-benefit analysis of my system against yours. I think you'll see that the cash flows and outcomes are a little more complex than they are in the bar business. Any other questions?"

Llewellyn opens and closes his mouth like a fish out of water. His face is beet red and I swear I can see steam coming out of his ears. He wants to say something—that's clear—but the words aren't coming out. He is shifting from one foot to the other, his hands opening and closing into fists. Something about him seems very familiar, and a second later, I realize why: Cory Llewellyn is the spitting image of the cartoon character Yosemite Sam.

After several seconds of Llewellyn's stuttering posturing, Izzy says, "Now, as I said before, I think you owe Mattie here an apology."

Llewellyn stutters some more and finally says, "I don't owe anybody an apology. You people don't know what you're talking about. You come waltzing in here like you're some big authority on this death stuff, but I'm here to tell you that I know what I'm doing, and I intend to keep doing it."

"Mr. Llewellyn," I say, putting on my best plastic smile, "I'm sure you are the 'hootenest, tootenest, shootenest bobtailed wildcat in the West,' when it comes to being a coroner." I hear Izzy snort back a laugh behind me and know he gets the reference. He and I have watched Bugs Bunny cartoons together dozens of times—they were my favorite as a child and they are now my son's favorite, too—and this is a quote from one of Yosemite Sam's classic rants. "But things are going to change. You can change with them, or you can get left behind. That's your choice. The days of an elected coroner running the show in this area is coming to an end. You don't have to like it, but you're going to have to face it."

Llewellyn stutters some more and turns even redder. I'd wager his blood pressure along about now is in the high-risk-of-stroke category. I glance at my watch to mark the time, so

I can report the onset of symptoms to the ER staff if it happens. But in the next second, I realize that if it's going to happen, it won't be in front of me. Llewellyn spins around and storms out of the office, firing one last "You haven't heard the last of me!" shot over his shoulder.

"Wow," Todd says, grinning. "You two are scary awesome."

I shrug and smile at him. Izzy simply sits back in the chair behind Larson's desk and puts his headphones back on.

"That Llewellyn guy is a real jerk," Todd goes on. "When I go out on death calls, no easy task, since he somehow manages to keep me from being notified half the time, he does his best to keep me out of the loop. He lets Dr. Larson examine the bodies, but not much else, and whenever I try to do any scene investigation, he keeps telling me I don't have the proper authority or training. Several of the cops are on his side, too. It's one of those good-ole-boy networks around here at times."

"That has to be frustrating," I say.

"It is," Todd agrees with an exasperated roll of his eyes. "I can argue the training aspect. I've gone through all the necessary training to become a medicolegal death investigator for the state and I worked in the ME's office in Milwaukee for several years before coming here. But the question of authority remains unclear for now. The governor approved the program Dr. Larson is in, and the intent is to do away with the coroner system in this area, but it hasn't been legislated yet, in part because Dr. Larson hasn't finished his residency. That means I'm stuck in a kind of legal limbo for now."

"How involved were you in the Ulrich case?"

"I was at every scene and assisted with each of the autopsies. Llewellyn was always at the scenes, too, so I took my own photos, did my own drawings, and kept rigorous notes about each setting, the surrounding area, the people present, and the processes that took place."

"Were you involved in any sampling at the scenes?"

Todd gives me an ironic smile. "Only one of them. The victim that was found in the woods across from the cemetery."

I nod. "Linda Elwood."

Todd looks impressed. "You've done your homework," he says. "Anyway, she'd been there a while before she was found, so there was decomp. Llewellyn was all about letting me do the dirty work in that case."

"And who had control of the evidence, once it left the scene?"

"The bodies come under the direction of Noah and the docs working with him, but everything else falls to Llewellyn or the cops," he says. "Our hospital lab set up an area designated for running some crime scene samples, so I have access to a few things. The rest get sent to Madison. We have copies of the reports here and, of course, I have my own case notes."

"That's what I'd like to see first," I say, and he looks flattered.

"Most of them are right there," he says, pointing to a file folder icon on the computer screen. "There are a lot of them, so you might want to get comfortable."

CHAPTER 14

Nearly three hours later, I'm exhausted from reading and sorting through the files, and I have printed off a small stack of pages.

Todd's help proves invaluable, as he not only provides time-lines and explanations for some of the files and documents, but he serves as something of a Guy Friday for me. He primes Izzy and me with food and drink: cookies, coffee, and water.

Izzy's face lights up at the sight of the cookies. I smile as he takes two of them and mumbles something about sticking to his diet, only to steal a third and fourth cookie from the plate ten minutes later. He doesn't get to cheat often, so I don't be-grudge him this one. Dom has done a phenomenal job of watching Izzy's diet since the heart attack, at times to Izzy's dismay. Mine, too, since I used to share meals with them often.

Izzy has finished watching the autopsy videos, and Todd and I are going through the last folder, which somewhat iron-ically contains information on the first of the murders, when Hurley calls me.

"Hi, Hurley, how are things going on your end?"

"Not well."

I hear traffic noises in the background. "Are you in your truck?"

"I am. I'm headed for you and the hospital. I hope the folks on your end have been more helpful than mine were. Some people aren't taking too well to the idea that they might have convicted and imprisoned an innocent man."

"Let me guess," I say, smiling at Todd. "You met Mr. Llewellyn."

"What a gasbag he is," Hurley mutters.

"I'd have to agree with you there, and apparently he's been something of an obstacle for Dr. Larson and his team, too. But as it turns out, Todd and Dr. Larson have been very helpful. Todd even fed and watered us."

"And the poison should take effect any moment now," Todd says in a mock-wicked voice, wagging his fingers in a menacing manner and winking. Izzy shoots him a stern look, but the corners of his mouth are crinkling. Morgue humor.

"Are you about done?" Hurley asks.

"We are. Your timing is perfect."

"Well, at least something is going right," Hurley says. "Can you meet me by the front entrance?"

"Sure. Give us a few minutes and we'll be there."

I disconnect the call and relay the information to Izzy and Todd.

"I need to use a bathroom," Izzy says. "Is there one close by?"

"Sure," Todd says, "go down this hall and turn right. Halfway down on your right is a bathroom."

"Got it," Izzy says, and off he goes.

I turn to Todd with a smile. "Listen, there's something I need to say to you before Izzy comes back."

His eyebrows arch suggestively. "Have you had a change of heart?" he says teasingly.

"A 'change of heart'?"

"You're regretting the fact that you turned me down when we were at the conference, aren't you?" There is a comical tone to his voice that makes it hard to tell if he's being serious or not.

"Turned you down?" I say, confused. "What are you talking about?"

"When I invited you back to my room that night in the bar?" he says.

I gape at him, clueless.

"At the forensic conference?" he adds, prompting my memory.

"I'm sorry, I don't remember that," I tell him. "Though I have to admit, my memory of that night is a bit hazy. I overindulged on the alcohol."

Todd chuckles. "Doesn't matter. I was only inviting you up for a cup of coffee anyway, nothing nefarious. Just thought I'd tease you a little, since you said you wanted to talk to me before Izzy came back."

I stare at him, horrified that I was even *more drunk* than I remember that night at the conference. "I just wanted to say I'm sorry for breaking your confidence from that night at the conference, after what you told me in the bar about the Ulrich case. I never mentioned or shared it with anyone else until now, and likely never would have shared it if it hadn't been for our murder victim turning up with the same exact MO." I give him an apologetic smile.

"It's okay," he says with a dismissive wave. "Dr. Larson's great to work with, and I don't think he'll be too upset. It's not like the information ended up all over the Internet or something like that. I sensed that you were someone I could trust, and since you didn't tell anyone else about it until your case turned up, it proves I was right."

"You're not mad at me, then?"

"Heck no, though I am upset to think we might have convicted an innocent man." His expression turns uncomfortably troubled.

"Believe me, I know how you feel. I testified against a man recently and my testimony helped convict him. Then I found out later that he was innocent. Though in my own defense, the evidence *was* rather damning. I mean, he had the dead woman's head in his refrigerator."

Todd laughs. "I think anyone would make assumptions based on that evidence." He lifts the stack of papers that I intended to take with me and puts them in an empty box. Izzy appears a moment later, and Todd picks up the box and leads us back to the elevator and up to the first floor.

When we reach the main lobby, I see Hurley parked and idling just past the front door. Izzy and I thank Todd for his help and head outside, where I discover I have missed a gorgeously beautiful and warm spring day while trapped in the dusty, dingy basement of the hospital. I stash my box of papers on the floor of the backseat on the passenger side, and then close my eyes and briefly turn my face to the sun, letting its warmth wash over me before I climb into the truck.

Todd waves good-bye and I waggle a few fingers in his direction in return. As soon as Izzy is in the truck, Hurley takes off, gunning the gas a little harder than is necessary.

Once we're on the road again, Hurley says, "Did you guys find any smoking guns that you know of?"

"Nothing obvious on my end," I say. "But there are several things I didn't look at thoroughly. I want to go over it all again."

"There wasn't anything with the autopsies that jumped out at me," Izzy says. "How did things go on your end?"

"Not much of any use other than the fact that the locals aren't taking too well to the idea that they might have convicted the wrong man."

"It *is* an election year for them," Izzy says pointedly.

"They'd see a killer go free and an innocent man go to prison rather than lose an election?" I say, appalled. "Where is their sense of justice?"

"Hiding behind their ambition and egos," Hurley mutters.

"Well, we got what we came for," Izzy says from the backseat. "Although, I'm not sure what good it will do. Based on what I've heard and seen, I fully understand why Ulrich was convicted."

Hurley sighs. "I'm with you there. What little I was able to review in the police files and evidence was damning, no doubt about it."

"So, where does that leave us with our case?" I ask. My question is met with silence and I wonder if the men thought it was rhetorical. To clarify, I try a different approach. "We can't prove Ulrich is innocent unless we can prove someone else is guilty," I say. "How can we do that?"

Hurley says, "We work our case, look at the evidence, and try to figure out who killed our victim. Maybe it is a copycat killing. Yes, the evidence regarding those flower petals wasn't known publicly, but like Hamilton said, it wasn't a state secret, either. Enough people knew about them that it might have gotten out. If so, we need to prove that. If not, we need to disprove it."

"This doesn't feel like a copycat," I say. "Why do it in a completely different jurisdiction and risk having it go unnoticed? Don't most copycats want attention?" I shake my head and sigh. "It feels wrong to me."

This time my questions are rhetorical, because the three of us are well acquainted with this kind of stuff and I know we don't have answers to any of it yet. Our discussion dies off; we are lost in our thoughts on the subject, lulled by the hum of tires on pavement and the warmth of the late-afternoon sun. The whole copycat theory doesn't sit well with me, but I'm not an expert on these types of things. Fortunately, I know someone who is, someone I need to have a chat with on other, more personal matters.

Once we are back in Sorenson, we drop off Izzy at his house and pick up Matthew. Dom is preparing dinner and the smells of garlic, tomato, and yeast make my mouth water. I don't ask what he's making; I don't want to know. It's hard enough to decline based on the scents alone and I really want to get home, kick off my shoes, and relax.

Hurley seems to sense my need for calm, because once we are home, he takes charge of Matthew and starts fixing dinner with him. Emily is in the living room watching the reality game show *Survivor,* and she smiles at me as I drop into one of the chairs—big and overstuffed—letting the soft comfort envelop me. I've watched *Survivor* before, though I haven't kept up with the current season and have no vested interest in any of the players. I see the show is at the point where the losing team has been determined and the players on that team are all frantically conniving, gossiping, and plotting to throw someone under the bus at the tribal council.

The basic structure of the show strikes me as genius, the interplay of physical strength, social skills, and simple wit making for an entertaining and addictive program. It is not unlike the way things go down in the business and corporate worlds, and other work environments where one's ability to make friends, fly under the radar, and occasionally kiss ass can overcome an inability to do the job. I've seen it happen and have heard some of my friends bemoan their career paths—or the lack thereof—because they didn't or couldn't play the game properly.

I think about the people involved in the Ulrich case: a district attorney and a coroner whose jobs depend on the voting community liking them, since they are elected into their positions. Their dislike of our probe into the Ulrich case and our suggestion that a mistake might've been made is because they don't want to get voted out at the next tribal council. How far would they go to correct the mistake, assuming one was made? Would they sacrifice someone else's life, doom a man to a lifetime in prison, simply to protect their own reputations and jobs?

I don't want to think so, but one thing my job in the medical examiner's office has taught me is that humans are capable of amazing cruelty. If Mason Ulrich is innocent, I have a sinking feeling that any chance the man might have at freedom and exoneration lies with Hurley, Izzy, and me. How can we prove he didn't do it? The only answer is to find the person who did.

I push out of the chair and head for the front door, stepping outside. The warm evening air is redolent with the fragrant, earthy scents of early spring, which in Wisconsin is typically a hint of floral sweetness and fresh earth overrun with the stench of cow manure.

My cell phone is in my pants pocket and I take it out and sort through my contacts until I find the one for Maggie Baldwin. Naggy Maggie, as I once called her, is my shrink. Not that I have regular appointments or need psychiatric care, though I'm sure there are days when my husband would beg to differ on that point. I first met Maggie when Izzy made me go to her as a condition of employment back when things between Hurley and me were crazy mixed-up, and my personal life was about as stable as one of Wile E. Coyote's plans to catch the Road Runner. I balked at the idea, insulted by the implication that I needed such a thing, and worried that maybe I really was crazy. Plus, my opinion of shrinks wasn't a good one. To me, they were all a bunch of pill-pushing charlatans who charged exorbitant amounts of money to sit and listen to people ramble. The pill-pushing thing turned out to be all too true in a couple of cases, because there were three psychiatrists in the surrounding area who were busted during a recent brushup involving some shady dealings by a Big Pharma company.

Maggie survived that roundup, and once I got to know her, I realized she wasn't the monster I thought she was. In fact, I like her. A lot. And I find that her advice—though she doesn't advise me, she just sits, listens, and guides me to the answers that I'm struggling to get out of my own head—has made my life better. She also provided individual and family counseling to Emily, Hurley, and me back in the early days of Emily living with us. Emily was struggling to adapt to a whopping dose of life changes that hit her all at once. When I look back on that time now, I realize we were all struggling to adapt to those changes that disrupted all of our lives.

I also call on Maggie for professional consults on occasion, which is what I'm interested in doing now. I want her take on the Ulrich murders and the person behind them. This is something I could do over the phone, but I want to make an appointment with her because I need some personal time with her as well. I'm struggling with this pregnancy news, and things in my life feel a bit catawampus right now, much like they were when I first went to Maggie.

I dial her number, expecting to get her voice mail, because that's what happens 90 percent of the time, but, to my surprise, she answers.

"Maggie, it's Mattie," I say.

"I know," she says.

Danged caller ID. "Right. Um, I was wondering if you might have an opening anytime soon. There's a case I really want to bounce off you."

"We can do that over the phone, if you want. Though I

suspect you know that. I take it you want to discuss more personal things, too?"

"You know me too well," I say with a nervous laugh.

"As luck would have it, I had a patient cancel on me tomorrow. He was my first appointment of the day. It sounds like an hour won't be enough time for both things, though, so I'm willing to come in early, if you want."

"I hate to put you out."

"Well, I'm leaving at the end of the day tomorrow for two weeks of vacation, so if you want me, you better grab me now while you can."

"*Two weeks?* I'm jealous. Where are you going?"

"To Europe . . . Ireland, Great Britain, the Iberian Peninsula, France, and Germany. A whirlwind tour."

"Sounds nice." It does, and I try to imagine what it will be like. Maggie has no kids, no husband, no ties of any sort. She can go and do what she wants. I envy that, to some degree, but I also know Maggie is lonely at times because of her lifestyle, so I'm not sure I'd want to trade places. Much as I'd love to be able to do a two-week tour of some European countries, I love the life I have, even with its limitations. "What time can we meet?"

"Let's shoot for seven, if that works for you. The appointment that was canceled was my eight o'clock, so that will give us nearly two hours. Will that do it?"

"It should. Thanks, Maggie."

I disconnect the call and then head for the garage. After plugging in the number code for the lock, I duck inside and go to Hurley's truck. I get the file box from the backseat area and transfer it to my hearse, so I can take it into the office tomorrow. I consider bringing some of it inside and trying to look at it tonight, but I'm too tired. I know the break will do my brain some good. Besides, I need to have some family time.

I go back into the house, entering through the connecting door to the garage, which puts me in the kitchen. I see that Hurley has dinner nearly ready, a thrown-together meal of spaghetti with hot dogs for Matthew—one of his favorite combos—and Italian sausage for the rest of us. Not exactly haute cuisine, and it's our second night of Italian food, but that's okay, because it's my favorite food group.

Our dinner conversation revolves around Emily's day, which features her boyfriend, Johnny, a subject that always makes Hurley scowl, and the romantic lives of some of her close girlfriends. Emily is a great storyteller, and she recites her facts with all the drama and angst of a soap opera. Even Matthew is entranced by her tales, even though I'm sure he doesn't understand half of what she's talking about. At least I hope he doesn't.

While listening to Emily's stories, I notice that she pushes her food around her plate a lot and doesn't eat much. When I think back, I realize that she hasn't been eating with her usual gusto lately.

"Aren't you hungry?" I ask her at one point, looking pointedly at her plate.

"I'm trying to drop a few pounds," she says. "Summer is just around the corner."

"You don't need to lose any weight," I tell her. She doesn't. Her build is average, not skinny and not fat. She might have a tiny roll around her middle, but she's far from being in my condition. I have an entire tire factory going on. And it's about to get a lot worse.

"Just a couple of pounds," she says. "I've got my eye on a new bathing suit, so I need to get my beach body. Right?"

I smile at her. "I don't think having a *beach body* means the same thing to me that it does to you, given my line of work."

"Oh, right," she says with a snort.

Hurley rolls his eyes at me, but I see the corner of his mouth creep up.

"If you're going to diet, be sensible about it," I tell Emily, knowing from personal experience that adolescence and dieting seem to go hand in hand.

"I will, I promise," she says, and as if to prove her word, she scoops another bite from her plate and puts it in her mouth.

When we're done eating, Emily offers to do the cleanup in the kitchen and Hurley offers to do the cleanup of Matthew, which will require a bath. Between the food particles, spilt juice, and the dose of dirt he somehow manages to attract every day, he's a sticky, stinky mess.

Finding myself in possession of a rare chunk of time with no demands on it, I head for the master bath and start filling the tub. A long, hot soak with some scented bubbles sounds wonderful, and it will give me some time to think. But then I remember that I'm pregnant, and the sort of hot bath I like to take isn't good for the baby. I settle for a shower instead, and when I'm done, I curl up in bed and pick up the thriller I've had on my bedside table for the past three months. Reading for pleasure isn't something I get to do much, and after ten minutes, it becomes clear that I'm not going to do it tonight, either. My mind won't focus on what I'm reading, and my thoughts keep straying to the Ulrich case. After reading the same page four times, and still not knowing what it said, I put the book aside and turn out the light. I half expect to toss and turn, my mind still whirring busily, but I fall asleep almost instantly.

I awaken the next morning with a throbbing, full bladder and the heavy but reassuring weight of Hurley's arm draped over my midsection. My mind is still muzzy with sleep and I try to ignore the pressure of my bladder, but it's insistent.

Then I remember my appointment with Maggie and look at the clock in panic. It's only ten to six, and I breathe a tiny sigh of relief.

I ease Hurley's arm off me. He mumbles and stirs, but doesn't wake. I slip out of bed and into the bathroom, where I dress quickly and try to tame my hair into something halfway presentable. Going to bed with it still damp last night didn't do me any favors; there are strands of hair that not only have a life of their own, but are seemingly able to defy the laws of physics.

I give up and tiptoe out to the bedroom, hoping to sneak away without waking anyone. I realize then that I never told Hurley about my appointment with Maggie. I make my way over to my bedside stand, where I keep a notebook and pen always at the ready for those late-night calls that come in for work.

In my efforts to tiptoe and be quiet, I manage to stub my toe on the leg of the footboard, drop the pen onto the floor, and let out a tiny yelp when one of the cats attacks my hand from under the bed when I go to pick up the pen.

Given my clumsy attempts at stealth, it's no surprise when I see Hurley's eyes flutter open. "What time is it?" he asks, blinking at me standing there fully dressed.

"Six twenty-five. I was just about to write you a note. Last night, I called Maggie Baldwin and asked her if she'd be willing to talk with me about the Ulrich case, and the only time she had was seven this morning. I forgot to tell you about it."

"That's a great idea," Hurley says, flinging back the covers and sitting on the side of the bed. "I'll go with you."

"You don't need to do that," I say, hoping I don't sound as panicked as I feel. "I'll take notes and tell you everything she says."

"I might have some questions you wouldn't think of. And I'd prefer to hear it straight from the horse's mouth, so to speak. I can be ready in ten minutes."

"What about Matthew? Em's got school, so she can't take care of him," I say, a last-ditch effort. I really don't want Hurley to go with me. I don't want him knowing that I've asked Maggie for some personal counseling time in addition to the professional consult, because I want to discuss my life and my pregnancy with her. And I need to do it without Hurley, at least for now.

He gets up and shuffles toward the bathroom, pausing in the doorway. "If you get him up now, we've got time to drop him at Dom's. Don't worry about feeding him. Dom always has something going for breakfast." And with that, he's in the bathroom, shutting the door behind him.

Cursing under my breath, I step over Hoover, who is sprawled in the bedroom doorway, and head for Matthew's room, surprised he hasn't shown his face yet, as he's typically an early riser. But as I enter his bedroom, I see he has stayed true to form. Not only is he awake, he has managed to dress himself, though not without first emptying every dresser drawer in his room. Clothes are strewn everywhere. His back is to me and he's busy fidgeting with something at his waist. I can't see what he's doing, but I can see some of what he's wearing, and it makes me worried about how he's going to fare in life.

He has on a pair of denim pants, with a pair of green-and-yellow shorts pulled on over them. For a shirt, he has opted for his Spider-Man pajama top, but he has bedecked it with crisscrossed bandoliers, which are made from underpants—Emily's underpants, one red pair, one blue. He has thrust his head through the waistbands and one leg hole from each pair, while he has put an arm through the remaining leg hole. One pair of undies for his right arm, one pair for his left, a lot of material bunched up around his neck like a cowl. Around his waist are the cups of one of Emily's bras, and I gather that his attempts to fasten it in front is what has him so transfixed.

"Good morning, Matthew," I say, making him jump. He whirls around, and I see that I am correct. "What on earth are you doing?" I say to him.

"I'm a superhero," he says with a smile.

"Really?" I say with a chuckle. "Who are you supposed to be? Underwear-Man?"

He pouts at me.

"Why are you wearing one of Emily's bras?"

He spins it around so that the cups are in the front and then reaches up on top of his dresser, taking down a tiny toy truck, which he then stuffs inside one of the cups. "It's my futility belt," he says with an indignant thrust of his chin, like he's daring me to say otherwise.

"You mean . . . Never mind. I like your version better. But you need to take that stuff off. We need to go to Dom's, and we need to hurry. Your dad and I have to be somewhere."

"No."

"Matthew, I don't have the time or the patience to argue with you this morning. Please just do as I asked."

"I don't wanna." He folds his arms over his chest, or rather he tries to. The underwear wrapped around his upper arms limits his movements some. His lower lip protrudes, and I recognize the signs of a pending tantrum. I spin around and leave the room, heading back to my bedroom. Hurley has come out of the bathroom dressed and with his hair wetly combed into perfection, which makes my already-fuming frame of mind even hotter.

"Your son is having one of his moments, or is about to," I say. "And I'm not dealing with it today. There's no reason why you need to come with me to Maggie's. I'll take detailed notes and share them with you later." That said, I turn and leave the room, hurrying down the hall, down the stairs, and to the front hallway. There I grab a jacket from the closet and head for the kitchen. My purse is on the counter by the garage door and I grab it on the way. A minute later, I'm sitting in my hearse, watching the garage door rise at what feels like a snail's pace. I half expect Hurley to appear in the garage any second, holding Matthew in his arms, but he doesn't.

When I can finally back out, I look toward the front door, thinking Hurley might be there, but he isn't. I start to breathe a sigh of relief, but then realize he might simply load Matthew into his truck, take him to Dom's, and then drive to Maggie's office to meet me. While this isn't the ideal way for this to play out, at least not for me, it will at least give me a chance to fill Maggie in on his possible pending arrival and ask her not to mention my personal appointment with her.

It takes me just under thirty minutes to drive to Maggie's office. She isn't located in Sorenson; in fact, her office is in a neighboring town. I consider this ideal, as it lends a certain amount of privacy to my visits there, something I wouldn't have in Sorenson. There are people in Sorenson who consider it their life's duty to spy, observe, eavesdrop, and jump to conclusions that they can then share about town. Gossip is a highly valued commodity in Sorenson, something that tends to be true in most small towns. And I was at the center of that gossip mill for a long time following the breakup of my marriage to David. I have no desire to take center stage again.

When I arrive at the office, I see that Maggie's car isn't there yet. With a wary look in my rearview mirror, I say a silent prayer that she will show before Hurley does, assuming Hurley comes at all. The trip to Dom's should make it hard for him to get here by seven. Then a thought occurs to me. Would he bring Matthew with him? And if so, would he make him take off that ridiculous outfit or let him wear it? Given that Matthew was about to have one of his meltdowns over removing the stuff, I wouldn't put it past Hurley to just let him wear it. I wonder what Maggie will think if Hurley shows up with Matthew outfitted in his superhero underwear.

I hear a motor behind me and breathe a sigh of relief that Maggie is here. Except she isn't. When I look in the rearview mirror, I see the bright blue of Hurley's pickup pull into the lot. And based on the timing, I'm certain Matthew will be in that truck, too.

Pulling in right behind him, Maggie's Mercedes glides in, and I mutter several words I'm glad Matthew isn't close enough to hear.

CHAPTER 15

Hurley parks his truck next to my hearse and climbs out; he's wearing a thunderous expression.

"What the hell was that all about?" he asks me. "You couldn't wait five minutes for us to come with you?"

I decide to use a tactic I've seen him use dozens of times when he's interrogating or interviewing people. Rather than answer his question, I hit him up with one of my own. "Did you bring Matthew in that getup he had on? I hope not."

"Yeah, I did. What's the big deal? He's a kid."

"Wearing underpants on his head," I counter. "And they aren't even his."

"They aren't on his head," Hurley grumbles, "and I don't get why you had to make such a big deal out of this."

I see Maggie has parked and she's coming toward us across the parking lot. "Can we not do this, here and now?" I say to Hurley, my voice low.

He glares at me and, without another word, turns and proceeds to remove Matthew from his car seat. I take advantage of his momentary distraction and hurry over to Maggie. "Please don't mention my personal appointment time with you," I whisper. "Hurley doesn't know and I'd rather he didn't, for now."

She smiles, nods, and heads inside. After a glance at Hurley to make sure he's managing Matthew, I follow her.

By the time Maggie has unlocked the outer door to the building and the inner door to her office, Hurley and Matthew have caught up with us. Matthew does, indeed, still have his underwear outfit on, including his "futility belt" bra, the cups of which are now bulging with secreted items.

Maggie, who has no kids, takes a moment to acknowledge Matthew and admire his outfit. "Oh, my," she says with a broad grin. "Are we experimenting a little with our clothing choices?"

"It's his superhero outfit," I tell her. "The bra is his *futility* belt." I enunciate the word carefully to make sure she hears it and it solicits the expected chuckle. "I tried to make him take it off, but he threatened one of his tantrums."

"And then he had one when I tried the same thing," Hurley says tiredly. "Had I not been in a hurry, I might have stood my ground, but as it was . . ." He trails off, shooting me a mildly reproaching look, which Maggie doesn't miss.

"Well, he certainly is creative," Maggie says. "What superhero are you?"

Maggie bends down to Matthew, who is now sitting on the floor, emptying the pockets of his "futility belt." He removes two miniature trucks, a rubber ball, three marbles, and something I can't quite discern. It's dark, flat, and oddly shaped, and when I bend in for a closer look, I realize it's a dead, desiccated frog. I consider picking it up and throwing it away, but I suspect this will trigger one of Matthew's tantrums, and this is not the time or place.

"I'm Frog-Man," Matthew says.

Maggie, realizing what the last item is, makes a face. "I see," she says, straightening up and giving Hurley and me a wan smile.

"Sorry," I say. "Sometimes the cats catch things outside and bring them in the house."

"Not a problem," Maggie says with a dismissive wave. "Will he be okay sitting here while we sit in my office? We can leave the door open, so we can see him, but it might be best if he didn't hear all of what we need to discuss."

"He should be fine," Hurley says. He removes a rolled-up coloring book and a small box of crayons from his jacket pocket and puts them on the floor next to Matthew. "Here you go, buddy. Draw us some pictures of Frog-Man in action."

"Frog-Man!" Matthew hollers, thrusting his arms in the air. Then he grabs the box of crayons and starts perusing the colors. I make a mental note to keep a close eye on him, in case he decides to color something other than the pictures in the book, like the furniture or walls in Maggie's waiting room. Like some mini Michelangelo on steroids, Matthew has already shown a penchant for turning our walls at home into his own personal canvas.

We settle in Maggie's office with a view of Matthew in the waiting room, where the coloring book is keeping him well occupied. In a low voice, Hurley summarizes the case we have—where the victim was found, what we know about her, and how she was killed. When he gets to the autopsy part, he turns it over to me.

I summarize the stabbing pattern Izzy and I discovered, and the flower petals stuffed into the wound over the heart. Maggie's eyebrows rise at this, and when I tell her I had heard about a similar case at a forensic conference, those eyebrows drop into a frown. Hurley takes over again at this point, giving her a summary of the Ulrich case.

"In conclusion," Hurley tells her once he's done, "we need to figure out who killed our victim, because while some people want to believe ours is a copycat murder, there are things about it that don't make sense."

"I'll say," Maggie says. "The timing for one. The distance for another. Copycats do it for the attention, and if the people in the area aren't familiar with the original case, it kind of defeats the purpose. Plus, there's the business of the flower petals. If it is a copycat murder, your pool of suspects would be a small one, I'd imagine. Who knew about those petals?"

"The defense did," I tell her. "The DA who prosecuted the case seems to think the defense might have killed someone else, solely to throw doubt on Ulrich's guilt and help with the appeals."

"Well, that's possible, I suppose," Maggie says with a doubtful smile, "but it's a bit out there. I take it the prosecuting DA didn't take well to the suggestion that he might have convicted an innocent man?"

"That's putting it mildly," Hurley says with a sigh. "The only way we're going to give Ulrich a chance to be proven innocent is if we can find the real killer and prove he or she did this and the other murders."

"It's a *he,*" Maggie says without hesitation. "And there is some symbolism and significance behind the wound pattern and the flowers that can help in developing a psychological profile of the killer. I can do some research to dig into it deeper, but let me tell you what I know off the top of my head."

Hurley takes out his notebook and pen, then says, "Go."

"Well, to start with, let's look at the stabbing pattern. You have your basic triangle. A triangle that points up can represent male energy, whereas a triangle that points down tends to represent female energy. An upside-down triangle can also indicate instability."

Hurley snorts back a scoffing laugh and I shoot him a dirty look.

"That doesn't mean that female energy is unstable," Maggie adds pointedly, giving Hurley a mildly chastising arch of one brow.

"I didn't say it was," Hurley says, holding his hands up in surrender.

Maggie and I exchange a look that makes Hurley squirm a little in his chair. He knows we know what he was thinking, and that he is now busted.

"Please continue," Hurley says after clearing his throat. Now he isn't looking at either of us; his eyes are totally focused on his notebook and pen.

"The triangle is also a universal symbol for a number of trinities," Maggie goes on. "You have the Christian Trinity of the Father, the Son, and the Holy Spirit. That's a theme that carries into other worship systems, such as the Egyptians, with Osiris, Isis, and Horus, or the Greco-Roman gods Zeus, Poseidon, and Hades. There is the time trinity of past, present, and future, and the human trinity of mind, body, and spirit. Depending on how existential you want to get, there are trinities like emotion, feeling, and thoughts, or love, truth, and wisdom, or creation, destruction, and preservation."

She pauses, takes a breath, and smiles. "I could go on for a long time. The triangle is one of the oldest symbols known to man, and a downward-pointing triangle is one of the oldest symbols of the divine power of the female. It's an ancient symbol used in a number of cultures to represent the genitalia on a goddess."

"It doesn't sound like we're narrowing things down very much," Hurley says with a scowl.

Maggie shrugs. "If you're looking for deep meaning, you could spend hours on this topic alone. However, your triangle could be something very simple and basic, an arrow that starts at the victim's breasts and then points toward her genitalia. Then you have these yellow carnation petals stuffed into the wound over the heart. You've already established that the yellow carnation represents rejection and disappointment with a loved one, so that symbolism seems straightforward. Given all that, a simpler interpretation of everything is that the killer has issues with a past lover who hurt him badly, though it could also be a mother or other strong maternal influence in his life." Maggie pauses a moment and looks at Hurley, her brow furrowing. "You said all of the victims resembled one another in their physical characteristics?"

"They do."

"Then the obvious conclusion to draw from that is that whatever woman triggered this man's homicidal tendencies also shares those physical characteristics."

"That's the basic theory of the prosecution in the Ulrich case," I say. "Ulrich dated a woman who ended up being his final victim, but they broke up before the killings started. The prosecution claims that Ulrich was so upset by the breakup that he killed women who looked like the lover who scorned him, and then eventually killed the lover herself."

"A theory that makes sense from the sound of it," Maggie says. "At least until you take into account your victim." She frowns again, rubbing at her chin with her thumb. "All of the original victims were found in the area of Eau Claire, correct?"

"Correct," Hurley says. He is eyeing her curiously.

"And yet you said that only one of them was actually from the Eau Claire area, also correct?"

"That's right," Hurley said. "All of the victims except for the last one, the one that Ulrich dated, were transients . . . homeless women who were drug addicts."

"And your victim, the latest one, she is also a transient homeless person?"

Hurley and I both nod.

"Hmm," Maggie says, rubbing her chin again.

"What are you thinking, Dr. Baldwin?" Hurley says. He's leaning forward in his seat, an eager look on his face.

Maggie doesn't answer right away, and Hurley's right leg starts bouncing in impatient anticipation. The room is so silent for a moment that I can hear the scribbling sound of my son's crayon in the other room.

"Let's assume that your victim is not a copycat killing," Maggie says finally. "I really don't think it is, because it doesn't make sense. As I said before, copycat killers want the attention. Yet, whoever killed this woman has not only done nothing to draw attention to himself, he's made efforts to hide his work. So we go with the premise that it's the same killer. If we do that, certain other things don't make sense, either. The woman Ulrich dated is an outlier. She doesn't fit in with the other victims, and the only way she makes sense is if Ulrich killed all of them, including yours. And we know he didn't kill your victim."

Hurley leans back in his seat and looks up at the ceiling for a moment, letting out a sigh. Then he looks at Maggie and says, "Do you think the same person killed all these women?"

"My gut says yes, but you need to look very closely at the wounds, the exact positioning and shape of the wounds. Determine if they were made with the same weapon, if you can. Examine any trace evidence you might have and compare that with trace found on the other victims. Tie them together with the evidence, and once you do that, it will help you find your killer. Either the defense team is behind this latest killing, in which case I think you'll find subtle differences between your victim and the others, or one person has killed all these women. If the latter is the case, the victim that Ulrich dated doesn't fit the profile. She's the exception, and therein lies your answer. Why was *she* killed?"

There is another long silence as all three of us contemplate what Maggie has just said. I finally say, "Do you have any theories on why she was killed, Maggie?"

"Either she knew something about the killer and needed to be eliminated, or she was a way for the killer to point a finger in Ulrich's direction, making him a patsy. He was already on the police's radar you said, right?"

Both Hurley and I nod.

"Then it makes sense for the real killer to stack the odds even more against Ulrich, so he takes the fall for it." Maggie pauses and her face lights up. She raises a finger, letting us know she's about to make a point. "And if you go with that theory, the geographic anomaly surrounding your latest victim makes more sense. The killer wanted to stop, but couldn't, so he killed someone outside of the previous jurisdiction with the hope that it wouldn't attract attention."

Hurley's face lights up, too, and he nods slowly.

"Consider who would have had the knowledge and access to the case to be able to set up Ulrich as a patsy," Maggie says.

"Someone with ties to the investigation," Hurley says. "Of course." He beams a smile at Maggie. "Thanks, Dr. Baldwin. You've been a big help."

With that, Hurley stands and looks at me. I stand, too, and say, "Hurley, would you mind taking Matthew to Dom's? I want to get back to my office and get Arnie to help me with examining those wound patterns right away."

"Sure," Hurley says. I help him round up Matthew and his playthings, then carry Matthew to Hurley's truck, fastening him into his car seat and kissing him good-bye. I then get in my car and start it up. Hurley starts up his truck and pulls to the edge of the parking lot, where he waits, idling.

I realize he's waiting for me to follow him and I think fast, trying to figure out a way to get him to go on rather than wait for me so we can caravan back to town. An idea comes to me, and I pull the hearse up alongside his truck, rolling my window down.

"Don't wait on me," I say. "I need to get gas."

Hurley nods and rolls his window back up. I hear Matthew fussing about something just before the window closes, and I breathe a sigh of relief as Hurley pulls out onto the street. I pull out, too, but go in the opposite direction and pull into a gas station that is in the same block. Committed to playing out my scenario, I pull up to a pump, get out, swipe a credit card, and start pumping. It doesn't take long. My tank was three-quarters full already. By the time I'm done, Hurley's truck has disappeared down the road and I breathe a sigh of relief. I get back in my car, drive back to Maggie's lot, park, and head inside.

I go upstairs to her office, and when I open the door, she is still sitting where we left her. She smiles at me and says, "Quite the subterfuge."

"I know. Don't judge me. I really need to talk to you alone and I'm not ready for Hurley to know about it yet. I want to sort some things out first."

"I'm not judging," Maggie says, waving me toward a seat.

I settle into the same seat I'd had earlier. I'm trying to figure out where to begin and decide I will start by telling Maggie that I'm pregnant. No sooner do I open my mouth to do this, when the outer door to the office opens. I hadn't bothered to close the inner door, since no one was expected, so the new arrival has a clear view of me sitting inside.

The newcomer is Hurley, holding Matthew by the hand, his face an angry shade of red.

CHAPTER 16

My mind is whirling with questions, excuses, potential explanations, and a sense of fear akin to what I felt as a child when I was caught doing something I wasn't allowed to do. I sputter for a moment, withering beneath Hurley's expression, which is a weird mix of hurt, confusion, and distrust.

The tension in the office is tighter than a tourniquet, but it is suddenly released when Matthew hollers, "There it is!" He dashes into the room and drops to his knees, bending over to reach under a side table against the wall. He pulls out one of the toy trucks he'd had tucked into his "futility belt" earlier.

"Hurley, what are you doing here?" I manage to say, realizing that I already know the answer. I know how persistent and annoying Matthew can be if he wants something he's left behind and, clearly, the toy truck fit that bill.

Hurley doesn't answer. Instead, he fires my own question back at me. "What are *you* doing here?"

There is a definite hint of suspicion in his voice and I decide that some semblance of the truth is called for. "I had some things that were bothering me that I thought I could talk over with Maggie, things related to the . . ." I point to my belly. "After I gassed up the car, I popped back over here, since I knew Maggie's first appointment for the day had canceled and she would have some open time." This is essentially the truth, though I've worded it in such a way as to fudge with the timeline a little and not make it apparent that this had been my plan all along.

"What issues?" Hurley asks, glancing at Matthew, who is still on his knees on the floor, running his truck over the carpet and making *vroom-vroom* noises. "If you're having issues related to the . . . situation, shouldn't we both be involved in any discussions about it?"

I glance back at Maggie, giving her a wide-eyed look that I'm hoping says, *"Feel free to jump in and help me anytime here,"* but she is smiling serenely and watching our interchange as if it's a tennis match between friends. Realizing I'm on my own, I turn back to Hurley.

"It's just some personal stuff," I tell him, trying to smile, but forcing it so much that I fear I look ghoulish. "Girl stuff," I add.

Hurley stares at me, frowning, and I let my forced smile fade. I decide to go on the offensive. "Is there a problem with that?" I ask, hoping I sound innocently confused. He is clearly upset by the discovery, though I'm not sure if it's because I wasn't totally honest with him in coming back here, or if it's something more.

Silence stretches between us, every second pulling the band of tension between us tighter. Finally Hurley says, "We can discuss it later." He breaks the eye contact, strides over to Matthew in two long steps, grabs him around the waist, and hauls him off the floor. Then, without another word or look, he turns and leaves, carrying Matthew on one hip.

I turn and give Maggie a fragile smile.

"Well, that was certainly interesting," she says. "I gather there is some tension between the two of you?"

"You think?" I say sarcastically.

"And I also gather that you are pregnant again?"

I start to answer, but I am suddenly overcome with emotion—frustration, anger, a feeling of helplessness. My throat is too tight to speak and I burst into tears.

Maggie rises from her chair, hands me a box of tissues, and walks over to shut the door between her office and the waiting room. "Looks like we've got some work ahead of us," she says, heading back to her chair. "Where would you like to start?"

It takes me a moment to get my tears under control enough that I can speak. "I'm pregnant," I say, stating the obvious. "And I'm happy about that. At least I think I am. Hurley is very happy about it."

"You can be happy about it and still have reservations," Maggie says. "That's to be expected."

I nod. "Yes, I suppose that's it. I'm happy, but I'm also worried."

"About what, specifically? List some of your concerns and we'll tackle them, one at a time."

This is one of the things I love about Maggie. She has the ability to distill an overwhelming situation down to its basic core issues, each of which can then be dealt with individually, making the problem seem much less daunting.

"To start with, I have doubts about my abilities as a mother. There are times with Matthew when I feel like I'm doing everything wrong, and I'm going to ruin him somehow. There's no manual on how to do this the right way, and let's face it, I didn't have the best example of motherhood to draw from with my own experiences."

This is an understatement of astounding proportions. My mother has had a list of mental health issues all her life. Her medical record reads like the psychiatric section of the diagnostic standards manual. In addition to being both a narcissist and a hypochondriac, my mother also suffers from obsessive-compulsive disorder, and has claustrophobia, agoraphobia, germophobia, and aerophobia. This means she is afraid to go out of her house, which is cleaner than the OR I once worked in, will never fly anywhere, must have everything done her way and in just the right order, and is dying all the time from some imagined terminal illness.

This latter problem, her hypochondria, which I think is mixed in with a touch of Munchausen—a mental disorder where someone uses faked illnesses to garner attention—colored my entire childhood. As far back as I can remember, I believed my mother was imminently dying of some horrific disease. This belief was reinforced by frequent visits to many doctors, who looked amazed, appalled, and intrigued by the menu of symptoms my mother would relate to them. Mom researched her illnesses well and knew exactly what to say to convince her medical providers of what she had. She never told them outright, even though she always had a specific diagnosis in mind.

Treating my mother was like watching an episode of *House*, where all the answers are a test of one's knowledge of fascinomas—a term for rare and obscure diagnoses that, ironically, often intrigue and fascinate the medical providers more so than the patient who has them. There's a saying in medicine that when you hear hoofbeats, you should think of horses, not zebras. The meaning behind this is a caveat to diagnosticians to look for and rule out the common disorders and diseases before going after the sexier, more obscure ones. But the zebras are much more interesting and alluring, and that's what my mother offered. The lure was more than most could resist.

Of course it was only once the batteries of tests all came back normal or negative that the physicians began to suspect Mom's only illness was in her head. And there is nothing sexy about mental illness. Once the doctors figured out what was really going on, many of them expelled my mother from their practices. By the time I was in high school, I often had to drive Mom to neighboring towns for her appointments, because she'd burned through all the local physicians. Her reputation is well known in the medical community, and I fear it will one day cause her the same fate of that boy who cried wolf one too many times. Someday she will have something legitimately wrong with her and no one will believe it.

Fortunately, my mother's physical health seems to be fine. And I gained an unexpected benefit from her many antics, in that I knew a lot about medicine by the time I went into nursing school. That and the extensive medical resource library my mother has at home—all the books encased in special plastic dustcovers—gave me a definite leg up over the other students in my class.

"I think your mother trained you well," Maggie says. "You've been a caregiver most of your life, and that's essentially what being a mother is."

"That seems rather simplistic," I say irritably, unwilling to be so easily placated, and really wanting to shift most, if not all, of the blame for my insecurities onto my mother. "Though I'm sure it seems that way to someone on the outside, someone who doesn't see the day-to-day trials and tribulations involved with raising a child. Or even just keeping them alive for that matter," I add, recalling Matthew's recent climb to the top of the refrigerator to get the cookies I put up there, all in the amount of time it took me to throw a load of unsorted laundry into the washer. "Someone who doesn't see all that doesn't understand what it's really like. And now I'm about to double my trouble."

Maggie stares at me for a long moment, and at first, I'm afraid that I've insulted her, or hurt her feelings in some way by pointing out her childlessness, something I know wasn't a choice for her. But then she smiles knowingly and says, "This whining about the trials and tribulations is just a smoke screen. What's really behind all this angst? You agreed to having another child, and I know for a fact that Matthew means more to you than life itself. So let's figure out what's really going on, shall we?"

I roll my eyes at her. "Where do we begin?"

"Let's start with Matthew and Emily and your skills as a mother. What, specifically, do you feel is lacking in your abilities?"

I ponder the question and can't come up with any specific shortcomings, though there is a nagging issue I keep trying to bury. Like a zombie, it refuses to die, trying to eat away at my brain instead.

"Emily is fine, and I can't take any credit for the way she turned out. Kate gets the kudos there."

"Not true. Kate has been dead for several years now and you've been the primary maternal influence in Emily's life, true?"

I shrug. "If you can call it that. To be honest, our relationship is more like a sibling one than it is a parent-child one. And let's not forget that Emily hated me in the beginning."

"And yet you won her over," Maggie points out. "That says something, doesn't it?"

"I don't know if I won her over. I think it was more of an acceptance of the circumstances that life threw at us and the establishment of a détente."

"I think you're shortchanging yourself in that regard," Maggie says. "And I have reason to know that." She has a point. Maggie provided a lot of counseling to Emily back in the early days. "But let's shift and focus on Matthew," Maggie goes on. "What are your thoughts on your ability to mother him?"

I let my zombie out. "Sometimes I wonder if I'm shortchanging Matthew by working instead of being a stay-at-home mom."

"Okay, let's explore that a little. You've cut back your hours so you can spend more time with Matthew, correct?"

I nod. "But then I do what I'm doing today, what I did yesterday. I spend what should be my days off, my time with Matthew, working the job anyway."

"You are working one particular case, right?"

I nod.

"Do you always give up your days off to work a case, or is this one an exception?"

"This one is an exception," I admit. "There have been one or two others, but for the most part, I'm happy to hand stuff off to Christopher, my job-share partner."

"What is it about the exceptions that make them *exceptions*?"

I think on this a moment. "Well, the last one was because I knew there was a young girl out there that we had the chance to save if we solved the mystery of her sister's death fast enough."

"That seems reasonable," Maggie says. "What about the current case?"

This one took me longer to parse out. "I'm not sure. I think it's the idea that there is a man behind bars who might be innocent."

"And you think that if you put in the extra hours it will make a difference in the outcome?"

Do I think this? I realize quickly that I don't. So, why am I spending my time off working this case? Why am I not spending the time with Matthew instead? "I'm not sure," I say, but an instant later, I know that's a lie.

Maggie leans forward, cocking her head at me. "What?"

"There was another case, one where I testified against someone who I knew was guilty. Except he *wasn't*. And my testimony played a key role in his conviction."

"Why were you so convinced of his guilt?" Maggie probes.

I explain the situation that occurred with Tomas Wyzinski,

of finding the decapitated head of a murder victim in his refrigerator, a murder victim who happened to be his ex-girlfriend. Like everyone else I've talked to about the case, Maggie assures me that my conclusions were logical and sensible.

"But they were also wrong," I say.

"Has the man you testified against been exonerated, or is he still in prison?"

"He's been freed," I say. "He's in the Witness Protection Program now, hopefully starting a new life."

"But you still feel you owe him something, don't you?" Maggie says, zipping an arrow into the heart of my zombie.

Of course this won't kill the zombie. It's already dead. It might slow it down some, however, and help me preserve some of my brain.

"I do," I admit.

"And do you see how that might correlate to this current case?"

"Of course," I say with a sigh. It seems crystal clear to me now. "Putting in the time on this Ulrich case is my way of doing penance for my mistakes in the other one."

Maggie smiles, and I feel a wash of relief and affection for her, not all that different from what a child probably feels when she achieves a new milestone and a parent bathes her with praise and approval. Or what I imagine that must feel like.

My mother wasn't one for praise or approval. The woman is better at finding faults than a seismologist. She still hasn't forgiven me for divorcing David, "a doctor, for cripes' sake." You might think her ire was over concern for my emotions, or my financial future and security. But it's really about the fact that my mother had reached the pinnacle of her hypochondriacal existence by getting a doctor into the family, and then I went and screwed the whole thing up.

"Should I just get over it and quit trying to appease my guilt at my son's expense?" I ask Maggie.

"Do you honestly believe Matthew is suffering as a result of the extra hours you're putting in?"

I open my mouth to answer, but she stops me.

"Don't give me your first impulse answer. Think about it seriously. Do you believe that picking up these extra hours will somehow damage Matthew?"

I let out a sigh of exasperation, but do what she says. And I must admit, deep down, I don't believe that. Maybe if my childcare arrangements were different, or maybe if Matthew was demonstrating issues with socialization, or doing things other than typical "terrible two" behavior, I might believe that. But I know that Desi and Dom provide my son with the same love and attention I would, maybe even more. And I believe that his exposure to other people and experiences will make him more rounded in the long run. Plus, the lingering dregs of the guilt that I have force me to make the most of the time I do spend with Matthew. I try to make it all quality time—this morning being a notable exception—to compensate for the lack of quantity.

"No, I don't believe that," I tell Maggie.

"Do you think you would enjoy giving up your job and being at home with Matthew all day?"

"No," I say without hesitation. "I love my job. And I think I'd go a little stir-crazy if I was at home with Matthew all day, every day."

"And would Matthew benefit from having you around all the time if you were going, as you put it, 'stir-crazy'?"

"No," I admit.

"Are you comfortable with the childcare arrangements you have for him?"

This makes me smile. I've counted myself lucky so many times because of Desi and Dom. "I am. Very much so. Desi and

Dom are both natural-born caregivers. They're the human equivalent of polar bears and elephants, animals with strong maternal instincts and abilities. Whereas I'm more of a seahorse or an emperor penguin, animals where the father of the species shoulders the bulk of the care."

I shoot a glance at Maggie, checking out her expression, curious as to whether she is judging me on this confession. But her face is its usual placid, unrevealing self. "It's not that I don't love my son. I do," I go on. "As you so aptly pointed out, I love him more than life itself. But that doesn't mean I always enjoy spending time with him. Frankly, the idea of being stuck at home with him *and* an infant all day terrifies me. And that makes me feel guilty."

"It shouldn't," Maggie says. "No one person can be everything to any other person. That's true in adult relationships, as well as parent-child relationships. And everyone is different when it comes to what makes them happy. There is no need to feel guilty because you enjoy your work or time outside the home. It means you'll be happier, more balanced—both emotionally and mentally—when you do spend time with your kids."

"How is that dynamic going to change when we throw another child into the mix?"

"How do you think it's going to change?"

I shoot Maggie an annoyed look to let her know I'm aware that she's using the classic answer-a-question-with-a-question tactic on me. "It will probably double my guilt," I say with a sly smile to let her know I'm joking . . . at least mostly.

"Are you sorry you agreed to have another child?"

"No, not really. I do want another child with Hurley, but I wish there was a way to do it without the pregnancy crap, and the whole sleepless-nights routine when they're little and then these 'terrible twos' Matthew is embracing."

"There are ways to avoid those things," Maggie says in a cautionary tone. "You could hire a nanny."

"God, no," I say. "I don't want some strange woman in my house. I'm sure I'd end up with some cute young thing with a foreign accent, who'd flirt mercilessly with Hurley until he caved and ran off with her, probably after murdering me because Hurley knows how to do that and get away with it, you know, or some elderly iron maiden, with thick legs, no waist, and orthopedic shoes, who oozes withering judgment and condescension on an hourly basis." I pause to take a breath, while Maggie bites back a smile. "I want to be a mother to my kids," I say. I pause and make a face. "Just not full-time."

"And that's okay," Maggie says. "What little I've seen of Matthew during your earlier counseling sessions and later visits, like this morning's, he seems to be a normal, healthy kid."

"Even wearing his sister's underwear?" I challenge.

She smiles. "I must admit it was an entertaining getup. Are you worried that he might be gay?"

"No," I say without hesitation. "I'd be fine with that."

"Then I wouldn't worry. Matthew's use of the underwear is an innocent thing. It demonstrates his ability to visualize things in his world in ways that are outside of the expected norms. That tends to be the case in people with strong artistic leanings."

I think about this, wondering how Matthew could have inherited any artistic talent. Neither Hurley nor I have any. I can barely color inside the lines.

My silence triggers a new question from Maggie. "You didn't have any issues with Matthew's pregnancy, so there isn't any reason to think you will this time, is there?"

"Depends on your definition of 'issues,'" I say. "Pregnancy and I didn't get along all that well. There's the vomiting, the peeing, the weight gain, the painful boobs, the swollen ankles, and the nights where no position is comfortable. And, of course, labor." I sigh wearily. "And I'm pushing forty. The risk of birth defects is higher, and the odds of my body bouncing back from all that stretching is a lot lower." I look at Maggie, then at my hands in my lap. "I'm afraid Hurley won't find me attractive anymore." My voice is lower, timid when I say this.

"Aha," Maggie says. "Now we're getting to the crux of the matter. This isn't really about having another child, or your worries about your parenting skills, is it? You're worried about your relationship with Hurley."

I open my mouth to say "maybe," but she doesn't give me a chance.

"So, what's going on between you two that's caused all this doubt? You've always struck me as a solid couple. What's changed?"

"Everything. We both adore Matthew, but, Lord, that child has changed the dynamic between us."

"How so?"

"The division of work regarding Matthew's care. The division of work that needs doing around the house. The amount of time we spend together alone. Our sex life, or the lack thereof. It seems like I'm tired all the time, and I find myself resenting Hurley sometimes because his work keeps him from being home to help with the housework and the kids. It's gotten a little easier, now that Emily can drive, but there's still so much to do with maintaining the household and keeping the kids fed and clothed. Sometimes I wish we hadn't built the new house. There's so much of it. It takes forever just to vacuum. By the end of any given day, when Hurley and I go to bed, assuming we manage to be there at the same time, which with our jobs is never a given, I'm always exhausted. I feel like we're growing apart. And adding another child to the mix isn't going to help the situation."

"Have you talked to Hurley about this?"

"Not directly," I admit. "I've gone off and snapped a few times with grumbles about how the housework is wearing me down. I mean, look at yesterday and today. I'm supposed to be off work and at home, tending to the household. Instead, though, I spent the time doing work-related stuff and letting the household stuff slide. But that only makes it worse. The laundry piles get bigger, the dust bunnies proliferate the way only bunnies can, and the groceries need buying."

"You and Hurley need to sit down and discuss this together," Maggie says. "It would have been helpful if he'd been able to stay here with you this morning, so we could talk it out in a neutral setting. Now you'll have to do it on your own or wait until I get back from my vacation. And I'm booked up solid for the first two weeks."

I run my hands through my hair, fighting back an urge to cry. "I've made a mess of things," I say.

"I can give you the name of another counselor, if you like, someone who might be able to see the two of you while I'm gone."

I shake my head. "No, but thanks. Hurley and I need to face this together, and you're right that I need to talk to him about it." I sigh and sit up straighter in my seat. "I'll tackle it. I needed you to help me drill down to exactly what it was that was bothering me, but now that I know what it is, I can handle it."

"Are you sure?"

I give her a wounded look. "Are you saying you think I'll screw it up? That it will all blow up in my face?"

"I didn't say that."

"You implied it with your tone."

She considers this for a few seconds and then gives me a conciliatory shrug. "Perhaps I did. I want to caution you to approach this at a time when the two of you are relaxed and alone, without risk of interruption. And it sounds like that might be hard to arrange."

"No, I can do it. Between Desi and Dom, I can arrange for

Hurley and me to have an evening to ourselves. Assuming I can get him to forget work for one night. Only—"

Maggie narrows her eyes at me. "Only what?" she says.

"This case, the Ulrich thing. It's really eating at both of us. I can't see either one of us relaxing enough to have this talk while the case is still pending."

Maggie winces. It's fleeting—there and gone so fast, I wonder if I imagined it. But her next words tell me I didn't. "Be careful, Mattie. The longer you let this go, the worse it's going to get. I understand the appeal of your work, and the possibility of seeing justice brought to bear, and all that sexy stuff, but you need to choose your priorities carefully. Don't put your marriage and your relationship with Hurley on a back burner for too long. If you do, the wound that's there now might fester into something fatal."

"Medical metaphors," I say with a smile. "I love it."

Maggie doesn't smile in return, and eventually mine feels forced enough that I let it go.

"I hear what you're saying, Maggie. I do. Thank you." I glance at my watch and stand. "I appreciate you carving out some time for me this morning. Just send me the bill, as usual. And have a great trip through Europe. I'm a little jealous."

Maggie smiles. "It's been a long time since I've done anything nice for myself like this or taken time off from work, for that matter. I'm practicing what I'm preaching," she adds pointedly.

"I hear you." *No need to beat me over the head with it.* As soon as the thought crosses my mind, I regret it. Maggie is only worried for me. "I promise I'll deal with it sooner rather than later."

Maggie reaches over and places a hand on my arm, giving it a gentle squeeze.

"Call me in a couple of weeks to at least let me know how it's going," she says. "Leave me a voice mail. And if you need me, maybe we can arrange a session over dinner some night, once I'm back. I'll book an appointment for the two of you at my earliest opening, just to be safe. If you don't need it, you can always cancel, okay?"

I nod. I have several weeks. Plenty of time to sort things out and get my marriage and my life back on track. It's also plenty of time to blow both to smithereens.

As I climb in my hearse and drive back toward town, I find myself wondering just what the hell smithereens are.

CHAPTER 17

Since Dom has Matthew for the day (I can't help but wonder whether Hurley delivered him there with his superhero costume in place, and what Dom's thoughts on it will be, if he did), I decide to head for the office and do some work on the Ulrich case. I know myself well enough to realize that I'm too distracted by the case to be able to spend any real quality time with my son if I did pick him up and take him home. My mind would be on the case the whole time.

I drive to my office and pull into the underground garage, using my key card to enter. I park my hearse close to the elevator and haul the file box out from the backseat, where I'd put it last night.

My mind is so focused on the morning's earlier events and that look I saw on Hurley's face when he caught me back at Maggie's that it takes me a moment to realize there is someone else in the garage with me. While driving into our garage requires a key card for access, the area is open to anyone who wants to walk into it, which is why getting into the building from our garage via the elevator also requires a key card. I've realized in the past that it's not the most secure setup, given that anyone who wanted to get into our office could easily accost any one of us in the garage, and either steal our key cards or force us to use them and come along. However, it's not like we're a hotbed of interest for criminals looking to gain something, unless what they want to gain is a dead body or two. We don't have any money, we don't have any drugs, and to be perfectly honest, the place would creep out most people.

I suppose if someone wanted to steal a body that might incriminate them, or destroy evidence of some type, that might be a reason for an attempt to break and enter, but it hasn't happened yet. So when I realize someone else is in the garage, it doesn't panic me much, even though the person is hidden in shadow, standing off to one side just inside the entrance. I stop and stare at the figure, trying to make out detail, but it's too dark where they're standing.

That's what finally raises the hackles on my spine, the fact that whoever is standing there won't come forward. "Hello?" I say, and I give my best warm and welcoming smile. I get no response. "Who's there?" Still, no response, and I debate whether I should turn my back and continue to the elevator, which is only a few feet away, but might take precious seconds to arrive, or be proactive and walk toward the shadowy figure.

I do neither. I stay where I am, shift the weight of the box to one arm and a hip, and with my other arm, I take my cell phone out of my purse. This is a ruse, because our underground garage is a dead zone for cell signals, as well as arriving bodies, but I'm hoping that the shadowy figure won't know that. Holding the phone up so the shadow person can see it, I jab at the screen with my thumb and dial Hurley's number, knowing the call will go nowhere.

I put the phone up to my ear and that does the trick. The shadow suddenly shifts and moves toward the entrance gate. For a moment, the figure is silhouetted by the sunlight outside and I see that the person is wearing a hoodie and track pants. I get the sense that it's a male, based on the general body shape, but there is no way to be sure. In a flash, he or she steps past the arm of the electric gate and onto the sidewalk outside, cutting a sharp left and disappearing alongside the building.

I lower my phone, realizing that my heart is pounding. With several glances over my shoulder to make sure the shadow hasn't returned, and others aren't lurking elsewhere, I hurry to the elevator and call it. It seems to take forever to arrive, but once I'm inside and the door closes, I feel my nerves start to unwind. By the time I step out on the main floor, I've convinced myself that I overreacted to what was most likely some kid who got nosy and decided to explore the garage area. It's happened before. In fact, we had someone tag our walls with some interesting graffiti a year or so ago. They painted a tombstone with RIP written on it, and beneath that, they wrote: FIVE OUT OF SIX SCIENTISTS SAY RUSSIAN ROULETTE IS SAFE.

I make my way to the library, a large room with shelves on two walls and a big conference table in the middle. There are also two desks equipped with computers on either side of the room and these serve as office space for my job-share partner, Christopher Malone, and me.

I know Christopher is in the office before I walk through the door. Christopher is a great employee, who knows the business and is good at it. He has a dark, twisted sense of humor—my favorite kind—and the two of us get along quite well. Both Izzy and his job-share partner, Dr. Otto Morton, like him, too. But he does have one major issue that can make it difficult to work with him at times. He has some sort of metabolic disorder that causes him to produce huge amounts of intestinal gas. It's something he has little to no control over, and though he tries to control it with diet and medications, the man is a hothouse of foul-smelling emissions. We've made efforts to accommodate his condition by adding some fans, filters, and air fresheners, but these have only a minimal effect.

Aside from this, Christopher is a charming and attractive man. Unfortunately, his condition cost him a marriage and a job as a police officer in California. He sued the police department and won a decent settlement, a fact that has made all his future employers—us included—wary of firing him because of his farts. Basically, it's a disability, and as such, he is a protected employee.

I consider it a fair trade-off. Christopher is easy to work with, flexible with his schedule, and fun to be around. He's even managed to hit it off with one of the police officers in town, Brenda Joiner, and the two of them have been dating for several months.

In the beginning, the constant farting did take some getting used to, but I don't notice it anymore. I got used to nasty smells in my work as a nurse, and in my current job, I often encounter smells that are much worse. Besides, I live with a dog and a kid, and either one could give Christopher a run for his money.

"Good morning, Christopher," I say as I enter the library. He is seated at the conference table rather than his desk, several reference books open and spread out around him. I set my box and my purse on the end of the table and shrug off my jacket.

"What are you doing here?" he asks. "Not working again, I hope."

I smile guiltily. "This Ulrich case is eating at me. I want to do a bit of work on it."

Christopher shakes his head. "If I recall correctly, you've used that same excuse several times recently. You don't seem to grasp the idea of this job-sharing stuff."

"I know it must seem that way lately," I say with a sigh. "But this one really is bothering me, and I know that if I don't work on it, I'll just be at home, sitting and thinking about it all day."

"Can I help?"

"I'd love another pair of eyes to go over some evidence," I tell him. "Though it looks like you already have your own hands full." I nod toward the books he has open on the table.

"This can wait," he says with a dismissive wave of his hand toward the books. "I was doing a bit of research on a cold case from twelve years ago."

"Which one?"

Now it's his turn to flash a guilty smile. "To be honest, it's not one of ours. It's a case I worked as a cop before I was let go. The wife of this guy who was employed at a meatpacking plant disappeared, never to be seen or heard from again, and—"

"Stop right there," I say with a grimace as my stomach lurches threateningly. "I don't want to know. I had sausage for dinner last night."

Christopher arches his left brow and grins evilly.

"I'm serious, Chris," I say, swallowing hard.

His grin slowly fades, his eyes narrow for a second, and then his right eyebrow rises to the level of the left one. "Are you . . . ?" He lets it hang there, probably afraid to commit to the question.

I debate my options for two seconds and figure I might as well come clean. "*Pregnant?* Yes, I am."

"That's great!" he says, beaming at me. "Congratulations!"

"Thanks," I say with far less enthusiasm. He doesn't miss it.

"Uh-oh, is it not a good thing?"

"It's okay," I say with a tired smile. "We've been trying. It's just that I have some mixed feelings about it. Pregnancy isn't my favorite state of existence, and I'm just a little worried about adding another kid to the mix of crazy already going on at our house."

"Understandable. Though I have to say, I'm a little envious. I'd love to have some kid craziness in my life."

There is a wistful tone to his voice that makes me feel like a heel for being less than enthusiastic about my condition. "Give it time," I say. "At least with you men, you don't have a biological clock ticking away, forcing or limiting your choices."

"I don't, but . . ." He bites his lower lip, shakes his head, and says, "Never mind."

"You were going to say something about Brenda," I nudge. "How are things going between the two of you?"

"Quite well," he says. "I'm thinking of asking her to move in with me."

"Really?"

He nods, looking at me expectantly, and I realize he's hoping I'll weigh in on the idea. This is dangerous territory. I haven't talked to Brenda about her relationship with Christopher, so I have no idea how she feels about him. But I do know one thing that raises some concerns. Brenda lives in a condo downtown that is modern, relatively new, and requires little to no effort on her part for things like shoveling snow, raking leaves, and mowing grass. Given that Brenda works a lot of overtime, I know this arrangement is one she likes.

Christopher, on the other hand, has purchased a very old, very run-down farmhouse outside of town, which he's in the process of fixing up. Currently it doesn't have any electricity, thanks to old knob-and-tube wiring that has been torn out, without any new wiring being put in yet.

"Maybe you should make a little more progress on the house before you ask her to move in with you," I say. "You know, secure the basics, like electricity and running water. I'm not sure Brenda's the adventurous type."

Christopher frowns. "Yeah, you're probably right."

I feel bad putting a damper on his enthusiasm, and I make

a mental note to have a chat with Brenda as soon as possible and try to feel out her thoughts on Christopher and their relationship.

"Anyway," Christopher says, perking up. "Tell me about this case. Is it related to the Jane Doe you brought in earlier this week?"

"It is."

I then spend the next hour filling Christopher in on the nuances of the case and its ties to the Ulrich murders. I can tell from the expression on his face that he's hooked when I'm only five minutes into it. I've covered most of the particulars, including our findings at Troll Nook, our talk with Dutch, our chat with Ulrich yesterday (including a very detailed description of Barney Ledbetter and his antics), and our experiences with the Eau Claire people involved.

At this point, our receptionist, Cass, comes into the room. It's one of the rare occasions when Cass looks like herself and not whatever character she's currently playing with the local theater group.

"Mattie, there's a gentleman out here asking to see you," she says.

"About what? Did he give a name?"

"Mr. Oliver."

It takes me a second or two to make the connection. "Ah, Todd," I say. "I wonder what he's doing here?"

I follow Cass out to the front lobby and see Todd standing by the front door, staring out.

"Todd?" I say, and he turns around with a big smile. "This is a surprise."

He walks over to me, looking abashed. "I know, I know, I should have called first, but I didn't want you to talk me out of it, and I feared you would."

"Talk you out of what?"

"Helping you with your case . . . the one that's connected to Ulrich. I figured it couldn't hurt to have another pair of eyes on it, particularly a pair of eyes that are intimately familiar with the details and evidence relating to the Ulrich victims."

"Well, your timing is impeccable," I say. "I was just bringing my work partner up to speed on the case, so he can help me sort through the evidence. Come on back and join us."

Cass buzzes us through and I lead Todd down the hall toward the library.

"I don't suppose I could ask you to return a favor and give me a tour of your facility," Todd says.

"Sure," I say. "Let me introduce you to Christopher first." I lead us into the library and make the necessary introductions, watching Todd's face closely to see what reaction, if any, he will have to Christopher's ever-present miasma. The two men shake hands, share a few pleasantries, and then I tell Christopher I'm going to give Todd a quick tour.

Once we're back in the hallway and the library door has closed behind us, Todd says, "Have you guys had some kind of failure in your exhaust system?"

I smile and shake my head. "Nope." I then explain Christopher's condition to him. I expect him to bemoan the situation and express some sympathy for me and the others who work with Chris, but he surprises me.

"Geez, the poor guy," he says. "How awful it must be for him."

"I suppose so," I say, "though he seems to get on well enough, despite it. He even has a girlfriend, one of the local cops. And I think most of us here at the office are so used to it that we don't really notice it anymore." This is a tiny white lie because some of Christopher's emissions are about as easy to ignore or miss as a nuclear blast. I think I got used to it quicker than Arnie, Cass, and Izzy.

I give Todd the nickel tour of the first floor, starting with the autopsy suite and ending with the doc's office. It doesn't take long; the space isn't all that big. I tell Todd that Arnie has a lab upstairs, but don't offer to show that area, explaining to him that both Arnie and Izzy like to limit the people who visit or have access to the lab to ensure the security of any evidence we have there. Todd seems to understand, and less than ten minutes later, we are back in the library.

We dig into the evidence related to the Ulrich case and start sorting and comparing it to the evidence we have from our own Jane Doe case. Even though we're quite certain our victim is Lacy O'Connor, based on her birthmark and other physical characteristics, until we get her DNA back, she will remain a Jane Doe officially.

After looking at the information Todd and Dr. Larson gathered about the knife wounds on the Ulrich victims, we compare it to the knife wounds on our victim. I call Arnie down to the library to join us, and after introductions, the four of us do an in-depth analysis of the wound photos and specs, including depth, width, hilt marks, and other characteristics.

"I'd say it's conclusive," Arnie announces once we're done. "Our victim's wounds match those of the other victims, except the first one, right down to the hilt mark and the amount of force behind the stabbing."

"But that's not enough by itself," Christopher says. "The knife that was identified as the likely weapon is a common hunting knife that any number of people could buy or might already own. It means a copycat is still a viable option. And while it appears that the amount of force used to stab the victims is the same in all the cases, that could be mere coincidence."

Todd and I both nod.

"What else have we got?" I say.

"Let's look at the trace," Arnie says. "That's the kind of thing copycats don't always know about."

"The biggest trace evidence is the flower petals," I say. "In theory, a copycat shouldn't know about those, but there were enough people who did know that we can't rule it out."

"Did anyone ever figure out where the flowers came from?" Arnie asks.

Todd and I both shake our heads.

"That's key," Arnie says. "The time of year for both the Ulrich murders and ours don't coincide with a natural-growing season for carnations. They had to have been grown indoors or ordered from a florist. We need to find a way to connect those flowers."

"But the cops in Eau Claire tried to do that and they couldn't find any connection between Ulrich and the flowers," I say. "They checked with local florists and greenhouses, some outlying florists and greenhouses, and Ulrich's Internet activities. Nothing came up."

Christopher snaps his fingers. "Arnie is right. The flowers are key. And the cops in Eau Claire went about it the wrong way, or rather they went about it in a way that seemed logical at the time, because they had a specific suspect. We need to look at it from a different angle. Instead of trying to tie Ulrich to the flowers, we need to tie the flowers to Eau Claire. At least that's where we start. It means assuming the killer is from the Eau Claire area, but I think that's a reasonable assumption, given the first murders."

"I see where you're going with this," Arnie says, looking excited. "But it's a needle in a haystack. We'd have to research all the online florist sites and find any orders coming to Eau Claire or the surrounding area over a period of several months. We'd have to look at orders to businesses, as well as to individuals. That could take a lot of time."

"Still, it's a place to start," Todd says.

"That sounds like something Laura would be good at," I say to Arnie.

Laura Kingston is an evidence technician and lab rat that

our office shares with the police department. For a while, Arnie and his counterpart in the police department, Jonas Kriedeman, were also sharing Laura. Then they learned that she was secretly dating one of the local cops, Patrick Devonshire, aka Devo, and the two men have since moved on. Amazingly, they've all managed to do this without harboring any bad feelings among them.

"I'll have her start on it tonight when she comes into work," Arnie says.

Laura works mostly night shifts, which is how I suspect she and Devo got hooked up, since he has also been working night shifts for a while.

Todd is looking through a folder that contains notes on our most recent victim. "You know," he says, "the freshest way to look at this thing is this girl's case. I see that her identification hasn't been absolutely finalized, but her parents know we have a body fitting their daughter's description, including a birthmark. And there's a boyfriend, too. We should be talking to them, finding out what we can about the girl, particularly her movements just prior to her death."

"We talked to the boyfriend already," I tell him. "It was a dead end." I grimace, realizing what I just said. "Excuse the pun."

Both Christopher and Todd shrug off my apology, though I notice that both are wearing a hint of a smile.

"What about the parents?" Todd asks. "Has anyone talked to them?"

Christopher says, "I imagine the cops have done that already."

"Maybe not in any detail," I say. "They were waiting for the DNA results. Let me give Hurley a call and see what I can find out." I take out my cell phone and leave the library, preferring my conversation with Hurley to be as private as possible, given the way we parted company earlier today.

I pace in the hallway, listening to Hurley's phone ring until it flips over to voice mail. I'm not expecting this, and for a moment, I'm not sure what message to leave, if any. After stammering for a few seconds, I simply say, "Call me," and then disconnect.

Frustrated and unsure of what to do next, I fall back on my usual fail-safe. I walk back into the library and say, "I'm hungry. Anyone interested in lunch?"

CHAPTER 18

As it turns out, the only person who takes me up on the lunch idea is Todd. Arnie says he brought a lunch and Christopher is a snacker. He rarely eats an entire meal in one sitting, preferring to graze all day long. He's convinced this minimizes the level of his gastric emissions, in quantity if not in quality. I've wondered if by eating all day, he merely spreads his gas production out over the day, creating frequent small but noxious emissions as opposed to a few hearty and robust emissions such as might follow a regular meal. Far be it for me to suggest this, however. The man has been living with this disorder his entire life and I trust that he knows what's best at this point, though what's best for him isn't necessarily what's best for the rest of us.

I ask Todd if he has a food preference and he assures me he does not.

"If it's okay with you then, I suggest we eat at a place called Dairy Airs. It's owned by a farm family that raises dairy cows and most of their menu is related to that. There are lots of cheesy stuff and creamy desserts. Their ice creams and cheesecakes are to die for."

"Sounds perfect for a couple of people who work with the dead," Todd says with a wink.

I offer to drive and escort Todd down to the underground garage. When I walk up to the hearse and open the driver's door, he hesitates, looking from the car to me and back at the car again.

"Oh, sorry," I say. "I forgot that you haven't seen my personal vehicle before."

The corners of his mouth twitch up. "You drive a hearse as your personal vehicle?"

"I do. It's a long story as to why. Climb in and I'll fill you in."

"As long as I don't have to ride in the very back section."

"Not today," I counter with a wink, and without further ado, we both climb in.

The drive to Dairy Airs only takes about seven minutes, but that's long enough for me to give Todd the *Reader's Digest Condensed Books* version of my split from David (though I spare him the gory details of just how I discovered that David was cheating on me), my dire financial circumstances in those first few months, how I came to own the hearse, and the homicidal stalker I had for a while. This is why the hearse has reinforced steel panels, bulletproof glass, and run-flat tires.

"You certainly have led an exciting life," Todd says with amusement as I park in the lot at Dairy Airs.

"Things were kind of crazy for a while," I admit. "It's better now." Even as I say this, a niggling doubt nags at my brain.

Once inside, we peruse the menus and Todd orders the grilled cheese sandwich, with homemade tomato soup, while I opt for a cheese omelet, with spinach and mushrooms, and a side of sourdough toast.

"I've told you some of my dark and dirty secrets," I say, once the waitress takes our orders and disappears into the kitchen. "Tell me about your life."

"Not much to tell," Todd says. "I'm one of four kids, and the only boy, also the youngest, so I'm a bit spoiled. I grew up in Minneapolis, came to Milwaukee for college, and decided to stay awhile. I have a bachelor's degree in agronomy, with a focus on botany." He sees my surprised expression and chuckles. "I know what you're thinking. How the heck did I end up doing what I'm doing now, with that as my background, right?"

"Well, yeah," I admit. "Though that does explain your knowledge of the symbolism behind the carnations," I add with a feeling of unease.

"My father died in a car accident at the end of my junior year in college. Very unexpected."

"I'm sorry," I say.

"Yes, well, dealing with his death was tough. Dealing with the fact that he had a terrible addiction to gambling was a lot tougher, particularly when we learned that he'd gambled away all of his savings, his retirement money, and cashed in his life insurance policies so he could gamble that money, too."

I wince, not only in sympathy for what I imagine Todd went through, but because I have a little problem with gambling myself.

"My mother was left destitute. She had no clue things were as bad as they were. She had to sell the house, and by the time she finished paying off all of Dad's debts, there was nothing left. She had to get a job for the first time in her life, and since she has no formal training or education, and no experience, you can imagine the types of job options she had."

"How awful," I say, feeling genuine empathy for the woman, even though I don't know her.

Her circumstances were similar enough to what mine had been after discovering David's deception that I thought I understood some of what she'd experienced and felt. Granted, I hadn't had to deal with David's death . . . though there were times I fantasized about it. I realized early on that widows are looked upon with sympathy, empathy, and caring, whereas divorcées are looked at with suspicion, scorn, and a certain degree of fear. Both are pitied to some degree, but for different reasons, and the amount of support offered varies widely.

I'd had one advantage over Todd's mother, however; I had an occupation to fall back on, thanks to my nursing degree. This wasn't as simple as it sounds, given that there is only one hospital here in Sorenson, and both David and I worked there at the time. Everyone and their uncle knew all the nitty-gritty particulars about the breakup of our marriage, including the salacious details of David's mostly naked rendezvous with my coworker.

I was humiliated, embarrassed, and too emotionally unstable to continue my employment there, particularly since it would mean seeing David on a regular basis. I'm still amazed that David can continue working there, given that most of the staff knows he has a heart-shaped birthmark on a certain part of his anatomy that I once heard a very drunk ER patient refer to as "some serious Jurassic pork, baby," just before I pushed a catheter into his bladder.

Fortunately for me, Izzy came to my rescue during the destruction of my marriage. I suspect Todd's mother wasn't so lucky.

"What sort of job did she end up with?" I ask Todd.

"Waitressing. She works at a Cracker Barrel restaurant. The money isn't great, but she likes the work. And now that all of us kids are grown and off doing our own thing, it keeps her busy. We all help her out when we can."

"Good for her," I say. "How did you end up in Eau Claire?"

"Well, my education funds dried up literally overnight. I was looking at my senior year with no way to pay for things. I tried applying for financial aid, but the money situation was such a cluster that it took nearly a year and a half to get it all sorted out, so I couldn't prove much in the way of financial need. I thought I was going to have to drop out. Then, just before school started, I saw an ad for a job as a diener. You know what that is, right?"

I nod. The term is an old-fashioned one for a "morgue attendant."

"I didn't know what it was at the time," Todd admits with a cross between a smile and a grimace. "I had to look it up. And when I did, I didn't think it was something I could do. But the money was good, the hours were at night, which worked well with my school schedule, and they were willing to train. So I applied for it and got it. The rest, as they say, is history. I took some classes and training to become a medicolegal death investigator and haven't looked back. When they decided to start the training program for forensic pathologists in Eau Claire, I volunteered to come work it. I was tired of Milwaukee by then and there was a girl I was eager to get away from."

"Oh?" I say, curious to hear more and feeling that hint of unease again.

"Just a relationship that didn't work out. But it was a long-term one and a hard breakup for me. Getting away from all the places and people that reminded me of her was a good thing. I'm sure you can relate, given your divorce."

I certainly can. Reminders of my ex and the life we once shared pop up all the time. It's not much of an issue for me anymore, because I have Hurley, Matthew, Emily, and a great life, but even with that, there are times when I catch a whiff of nostalgic loss.

"Have you ever been married?" I ask.

He shakes his head and smiles, but offers no elaboration as our waitress arrives with our food. The conversation dies for a while as we both dig in, and then our conversation takes a turn.

"I really enjoyed our chat that night in the bar at the Milwaukee conference," Todd says. "I could tell right away that you and I were two peas in a pod with similar career tracks, similar interests, and similar outlooks on life. We even had similar sad-sack love stories."

I have only a minimal, hazy recollection of discussing this topic with him, so I just smile.

"Though yours was a marriage and mine never made it to that point," he adds. "So I guess they were a little different. But a breakup is a breakup, right?"

I smile and nod, my mouth full of omelet.

"And both of us were cheated on," he says. "Though at least I didn't catch my girlfriend in the act." He pauses and chuckles. "I know that had to have been an awful experience for you, and that the pain must have been terrible, but hearing you talk about it that night, well, you had me in stitches. I don't know how you managed to find the humor in a situation like that, but I'm impressed that you did."

Great. In my drunken stupor, I was apparently witty and hilarious on a subject that nearly destroyed my life. I can't remember most of that evening, but there are a few glimmers I can recall. I seem to remember referring to David's genitals as his twig and berries, and thinking that this, and me for thinking of it, was hysterically funny. I recall Todd laughing uproariously, too, so he must have also thought it was funny. Although, now I'm wondering if he was laughing at what I said, or if he was laughing at me laughing at myself.

It doesn't much matter, I finally decide. I like Todd and he seems to like me. We worked well together in Eau Claire, and again this morning at my office, so I think our professional friendship will be good for the long run. We finish up our meal discussing some of our shared irritations with our jobs, and it turns out that we both hate collecting vitreous fluid and the tedious paperwork we're required to do.

I pay for the meal, insisting because Todd is my guest and it's the least I can do to return the favor of him providing us with snacks yesterday. We return to the office intending to spend the next few hours reviewing the evidence in our case. But Chris and Todd start chatting about work-related stuff, and this eventually evolves into stories of unusual, interesting, or weird cases they've seen. The three of us take turns sharing our most memorable cases, reciting the stories in vivid detail and, I suspect, with a small bit of occasional embellishment. It's a lot of fun and restorative to our working souls, though it isn't particularly productive. When I look at the clock on the wall and see that it's almost five already, I'm shocked.

I haven't heard word one either in person, by phone, or by text from my husband, so I step out of the library and call Dom to see if my son is still there, and if so, if Hurley has communicated any plans to pick him up.

"Matthew is here, and your hubby said he'd be by to get him around six," Dom informs me.

"Was he wearing his superhero outfit this morning when they got to your place?"

"Who? Your hubby or your son?"

I laugh. "My son. Wait, does Hurley have a superhero outfit?"

"When he strolls around in his jeans and his white shirt with the sleeves rolled up, and that gun holster of his tucked up under his arm, he looks pretty super to me," Dom says a tad breathlessly.

"Dom, I had no idea!" I say, laughing. "Should I be worried?"

"Heck no, girl. That man has eyes for you, and you alone." He lets out a wistful sigh.

"Does Izzy know you have a secret crush on Hurley?"

"He does. He lets me have my little fantasy, and I let him have his."

"Do tell," I say, wondering who Izzy's crush might be.

"You have to promise not to tell anyone," Dom says in a conspiratorial half-whisper.

"My lips are sealed."

"Izzy's got a thing for our mayor."

"The mayor?" I say with disbelief. "Mayor Kirkland?"

"That's the one."

"Hunh," I say, genuinely surprised. "I never would have guessed."

Our newly elected mayor, Phin Kirkland, short for Phineas—which should tell you all you need to know about his genetic background, because what decent parent would name their kid Phineas in this day and age—is a thirtysomething mass of flesh. He is built just like a Mack truck. His shoulders are broad and muscled, his thighs look like giant bratwursts ready to burst out of his pants, and his hands are the size of one of those canned hams my mother used to always fix for Easter dinner.

Mind you, my mother never ate any of said ham—it was there for my sister, me, and whatever husband was in residence at the time. That didn't stop her from later believing that she had come down with trichinosis, a parasitic worm infection people can get from eating uncooked pork. Apparently, just being in the same household as a piece of pork—never mind that it was precooked and canned—was exposure enough.

Dom forces my mind off canned hams and beefy hands. "If you're referring to your son's fixation with his older sister's underwear, then, yes, he was wearing his superhero outfit. Though I must say," he adds with a chuckle, "the idea of calling a brassiere a 'futility belt' seems highly fitting."

It does for some of us, I think, straightening up and pulling my shoulders back. "You don't think the fact that he used Emily's underwear is a sign of some kind of . . . issue, do you?"

"Gosh, no," Dom says. "I think all boys play with their mom's or sister's underwear at some point. I know I did." Seeming to sense that this might be slightly less reassurance than what I'm seeking, he adds, "And so did my straight brothers. They made slingshots out of my mother's bras." He pauses and then speaks in a more thoughtful tone. "Of course they didn't wear the underwear, like I did."

There is a momentary silence that stretches between our two phones. "Anyway," Dom says finally, "Hurley should be here soon to pick up your son, so you are on your own."

"Great. If he doesn't show for some reason, call me, okay?"

"I will, but you know the little guy can stay here all night, right? Anytime. He and Juliana have so much fun together."

"Thanks, Dom. I'll talk to you later."

I disconnect the call and think about the stretch of free time in front of me, time unencumbered with kids, hubby, or duties. Soon, with another kid added to the craziness that is often my life, such a thing will be more rare than a sighting of Nessie. I should make the most of it. What kind of trouble can I get myself into over the next few hours?

CHAPTER 19

I return to the library and find Todd engrossed in something on my desktop computer. "Christopher just left," he tells me. "He said to tell you good night."

"Thanks. I think I'm going to call it a day, since it's technically my day off. I'm not supposed to be here."

He leans back in the chair and stretches. "Is there a motel here in town where I could stay?" he asks. "I'd like to come back in the morning and work on this case some more. We got a little sidetracked today."

"Yes, we did," I say with a smile. "But it was fun. I think it's important to indulge in some professional bonding like that, from time to time." I consider the idea of inviting him to our house for the night. The couch in the extra bedroom, which we use as a home office, is a sleeper sofa. But given the way things were left between Hurley and me, I decide it's a bad idea to throw a stranger into what will likely be a tense mix at home. Particularly, one whom I had drinks with in a bar last fall.

"There's the Sorenson Motel," I say, worried that I'm being rude by not inviting him to stay with us. "It's owned and operated by a cantankerous old coot who is stuck in the

1980s, something that will be quite apparent when you see the décor of the rooms. But the place is clean and the prices are reasonable."

"Sold."

"I'll drive out there and you can follow me, if you like," I offer as a way of mitigating my lack of hospitality. "It's not far. Just outside of town. I know the owner, so maybe I can wrangle a deal for you."

"That would be great. Are you planning on coming to work in the morning?"

"I am," I say. Tomorrow is supposed to be another day off for me, but the pull of this case is strong, and I know I won't be able to resist.

"I don't suppose you'd let me hang with you again?" Todd says hopefully.

I consider it and shrug. "Sure," I say, unable to come up with any reason to say no. Plus, his insight into the case has already proven useful.

Todd gathers up his coat while I shut down the computer, turn out the lights, and don my own coat. "Could we stop at a local grocery store along the way?" Todd asks. "I'd like to get some snacks and something for breakfast in the morning."

"Sure. Just follow me."

"Easy enough to do. That car of yours is hard to miss. I'm parked out on the street a block over from your garage, so wait for me, okay?"

Four minutes later, I pull out of the garage and idle on the street, waiting for Todd to pull up behind me in the black Honda SUV he drove us in yesterday. I see headlights about thirty feet back on a black SUV and assume it's Todd, but then realize the car isn't moving. Then another set of headlights appears from around the corner and this car comes up behind me—also a black SUV. I'm not great at telling cars apart by their make and so many of these SUVs look alike, so I'm still unsure which one might be Todd. Fortunately, once the car closing in on me gets close enough I can see that it is Todd.

I pull out, noticing as I do that the other car with the headlights on also pulls out into the street, falling in behind Todd's car. The hairs on the back of my neck rise, and I place a palm there, gently kneading the skin, telling myself I'm being silly. But I've been followed before—that homicidal stalker from my past—and the fact that we are investigating a murder case that has made a lot of people very unhappy is uppermost in my mind. I recall Maggie's words earlier, questioning us as to who had access to the knowledge necessary to frame Ulrich. Clearly, we hadn't made many friends in Eau Claire yesterday, but why would anyone be following me?

Certain that I'm overreacting, thanks to my past and the way my day started, I take a circuitous route through town, instead of sticking to the main drag. Todd follows dutifully behind me and the other SUV stays right behind him. The hairs on the back of my neck rise again.

When I get to the grocery store, I head for a parking spot that has another empty one beside it. Todd pulls into it, and to my relief, I watch the other car drive past the lot, continuing down the main road until it's out of sight. Todd raps on my window and I roll it down.

"Want to come inside? You can help me find stuff."

I consider declining, thinking I should watch to see if the other black SUV returns. Then I realize how stupid that idea is, given that there are at least six black SUVs of similar shape and size parked within sight of me right now. If one pulled into the lot, I wouldn't be able to tell if it was the same one that was following me before anyway. If only everyone drove something as distinctive as the hearse.

"Sure," I say to Todd. I get out and lock my car.

Inside the store, Todd grabs one of the hand baskets and makes a beeline for the bakery. "I have a bad sweet tooth in the mornings," he says. "I love sweet rolls for breakfast with my coffee." He looks over at me with a guilty expression and winks. "If I'm going to be honest, I love sweet rolls any time of day."

"You're a man after my own heart," I say with a smile.

Twenty minutes later, we return to our respective cars, Todd laden with a bag of snacks, some sandwich-making materials, a couple of bottles of cheap wine, and a bag of sweet rolls. He opens the box of sweet rolls as we walk through the parking lot, takes one out, and hands it to me. I consider a polite decline, a demure "No, I couldn't," but quickly dismiss it and take the roll.

"Thanks." I bite into it and moan a little as I taste the sweet cinnamon goodness. I get in the hearse, start it up, and back out, using only one hand, since the other is holding the sweet roll. And I drive that way to the motel, finishing off the roll just as we arrive. I pull up in front of the office and Todd pulls in alongside me.

I scan the parking lot, which only has four other cars in it. That's a good sign. "It doesn't look like he's superbusy."

We head inside, where we find Joseph Wagner sitting behind the desk, his head encased in a cloud of smoke from a cigar he's puffing on. He's wearing denim overalls, the only thing I've ever seen him in. I wonder if he has a closet full of them, or if he only changes the shirt and, hopefully, the underwear beneath the same pair each day. His hair, which only grows on the sides of his head, is thick, curly, and gray. He bears a strong resemblance to Larry Fine from the Three Stooges, albeit without the Stooge sense of humor. I'm pretty sure Joseph had his sense of humor surgically removed when he was a kid.

"Hello, Joseph," I say.

He squints at me through the haze of smoke and sets the cigar down in an ashtray. As soon as he recognizes me, he rolls his eyes heavenward. "Oh, great, you again. Are you looking for dead bodies or killers this time?"

"Neither. I'm bringing you some business," I say, nodding toward Todd.

Joseph shifts his puffy-eyed gaze to Todd, giving him a once-over. "I hope *you* don't spend time around dead bodies."

Todd looks at me and says, "I thought you said this guy was a friend of yours."

"No," I say with a smile. "I said I know him. Joseph doesn't have any friends." I turn my smile back toward Joseph. "Do you, Joseph?" Before he can answer, not that he would anyway, I add, "Doesn't look like you have much in the way of business, either."

Joseph scowls at me before turning to Todd and asking, "How many nights?"

"Just one for now," Todd says.

Joseph tilts his head to the side and sighs. "Does that mean you might be staying a second night?"

"I don't know," Todd says. "Does it matter?"

Joseph raises his eyebrows and looks at Todd like he's the dumbest human being on earth. "Son, it matters to me. I can't promise you I'll have a room for a second night if you don't book it now."

"He's bluffing," I say to Todd.

"Am I?" Joseph says, yanking his glare back to me. "I'll have you know that there's a group of gnome painters coming to the Dells this weekend for a mini convention and I typically get overflow guests here."

"*Gnome* painters?" I echo skeptically.

"That's right," Joseph says with a pugnacious thrust of his jaw.

"You know what," I say. "You should remember that I have access to dead bodies. Lots of them. And if one was to mysteriously show up here one of these days, that wouldn't be very good for business, would it? Heck, you might even end up in prison."

Joseph narrows his eyes at me. "Don't threaten me, missy," he grumbles. "I'm over seventy and don't have a pension. Do you think life in prison is a big deterrent for me?"

"Tell you what," Todd says, eyeing us both warily. "I've got off until Monday, so let's go ahead and book for two nights."

Joseph gives me a smug look and then turns to Todd. "That'll be fifty a night."

"That's for one of the end suites with a kitchenette, right?" I say.

"Hell no," Joseph grumbles. "Those go for sixty-five a night."

"You only charged me fifty a night."

"That was three years ago, missy. Ever heard of a little thing called inflation?"

"Can't you give him a break, since I brought you the business?"

Todd starts to say something, but Joseph beats him to it. "No, but I'll return the favor. You'll be the first person I call if a dead body does show up in one of my rooms," he counters. "Tit for tat, right?"

I let my head loll back and look at the ceiling. It's covered with cobwebs. "I give up," I say. "It's up to you, Todd."

He chuckles and says, "I'll take two nights in a suite." He digs his wallet out and slides a credit card across the counter to Joseph.

Five minutes later, we are back outside and Todd is laughing. "He's quite the character," he says.

"Quite the curmudgeon, you mean," I say, shaking my head. "I don't know how the old coot stays in business."

"Speaking of motel rooms," Todd says, "you mentioned earlier today that you have pictures of the room your victim was staying in, the place where you think she was killed."

"I do. They're on our server."

"I meant to look at them before we left and print some copies, so I could study them tonight. I've taken several specialized classes in blood spatter evidence and maybe I can come up with something. Can you log into your file system at work from a remote computer?"

"I can."

"Would you mind doing so on my laptop, so I can print some photos?"

I wince. "I don't think the Wi-Fi here is secure."

"My cell phone has the ability to provide a secure Wi-Fi hotspot and my laptop is one my job provides for me. It comes with some serious virus protection and blocking software. I promise you it will be safe."

"Okay," I say after a moment's thought.

We drive both cars down to the end of the building where Todd's suite is located, and I help him haul his stuff inside. He carries in a small overnight bag, a laptop bag, and a portable printer he has stashed in the cargo area, while I grab the bags from his grocery store haul. While he sets up the laptop and printer on a table in the corner and attempts to log onto the Internet, I scan the suite. It hasn't changed a whit since I stayed in it for a week some three years ago.

"Okay, I have it up and running," Todd says, getting out of his seat. "Can you access the photos?"

I sit down in front of his computer and start typing. Once I've accessed our office server, Todd politely looks away as I type in the password. I locate the appropriate folder, open it, and start clicking through the pictures as Todd watches over my shoulder.

Over the next ten minutes or so, I print the photos Todd requests. The portable printer cranks the pictures out slowly, but in full color and with surprisingly good detail.

"I'm impressed," I tell Todd, looking at the first picture to come off the printer. It's a side shot of the bed in the Troll Nook room showing the headboard, the wall behind it, and a portion of the floor beside the bed. The room is dark, and there are spots of greenish-white glowing light where the luminol has highlighted the blood spatter.

Todd takes the picture from me and adds it to another that has just printed, a view of the ceiling over the bed. "This is the perfect starting point," he says. "With the angles and height of the spatter on the wall, ceiling, and headboard, we can tell what position the killer and the victim were in. I might even be able to tell you how tall your killer is."

"Really?" I'm intrigued.

"Well, the position thing for sure," Todd says. "Think about it a minute. Your first assumption when you look at the bed as the scene of the crime is that the victim was on it with her head and feet where they would be if someone was sleeping. But that wasn't the case here. She was lying sideways with her feet toward your camera, here on the side of the bed."

"How can you tell that?"

"Look at the patterns on the wall and ceiling. Then think about where the killer would have to be to create those patterns."

I try to envision what he's saying, but my brain is having trouble picturing it.

Apparently, Todd can tell this, because he says, "Okay, I've got an idea."

He takes a bottle of red wine from one of his grocery bags and opens it. It has a screw top—good thing, as I'm betting there isn't a corkscrew in the room. Todd pours some of the wine into a motel glass and looks toward the kitchenette area.

I get what he's thinking and walk over to one of the drawers there. "Will this do?" I ask, pulling out a butter knife.

"It will," Todd says with a grin. He takes the knife from me and drops the handle end of it into the glass of wine.

I'm puzzled as to why he put the knife in this way and it must show on my face.

"Safety," he says with a smile. "We're going to act this out, and while this is only a butter knife, the business end of it could still injure, so we'll play it safe and use the other end. It won't be exact anyway, because the wine is a lot thinner than blood would be, but it will do to demonstrate the point." He eyes my clothes. "I want you to play the victim, but it means I'm going to get wine on your clothes. I can't promise it will wash out."

"It's okay," I say. "This is an old blouse and my slacks are black, so it won't show even if it doesn't all wash out."

"Okay, then. Go and lie sideways on the bed."

I walk over to the bed and lie across it on my back, midway between the head and foot, my left side toward the headboard, my feet dangling over the side far enough to touch the floor. "I'm taller than our victim was," I point out.

"That's okay. You're fine like that."

Todd walks over and stands with his legs between my knees, the glass with the knife in his left hand. Then he takes the knife in his right hand, wine dripping off it, and places it against my slacks, just above my symphysis pubis.

"This was likely the first wound made, so it will have less castoff than the others," Todd says.

He raises his arm up quickly and wine flies off the knife and onto the ceiling. Then he makes a stabbing motion toward my belly, stopping just shy of where the edge of my liver would be. He dips the knife in the wine, and then raises his hand up and brings it down again on the other side of my belly, closer to where the spleen and pancreas are located.

He dips again, positions his hand, and raises it once more, coming down this time just above my right breast. One more dip in the wine, and he repeats the arm motions one last time, this time delivering the deathblow just above my left breast. This last stabbing motion leaves a few small spatters of wine on the headboard and the wall above it. It also leaves wine stains all over my blouse.

Todd puts the knife back in the glass and moves away from me, looking up at the ceiling. A fine mist of wine has spattered there, a pattern I've already seen from my position on the bed. The wine pattern on our ceiling is eerily close to the blood spatter pattern we found in the ceiling of the cabin at Troll Nook.

"Joseph will never let me stay here again," I say, staring at the ceiling. Todd laughs and that starts me laughing.

"It's for a good cause," Todd says, still chuckling. "And given the state of the décor and the cobwebs in this place, I don't think Joseph will even notice. But let's be kind and clean up." I sit up as he walks into the bathroom and returns carrying an armful of hand towels and washcloths. He wets the washcloths and tosses one to me. I start swiping at the wine stains on my clothes, while Todd climbs onto the bed beside me, standing, his legs wobbling with his unsteady footing. He tries to wipe at the wine drops on the ceiling, but he can't quite reach them, so he starts jumping and swiping, jumping and swiping. I climb up on the mattress and start doing the same thing beside him, the two of us laughing like kids.

When we are done with the ceiling, we carefully move to the head of the bed, stifling our giggles and trying not to jiggle the mattress too much, our footing wobbly. We each take one half of the headboard and the wall behind it, and ten minutes later, we've done such a good job with the cleanup that there is no evidence of red wine anywhere. Unfortunately, there *is* evidence of our cleaning. The places on the walls and the ceiling where we scrubbed are noticeably whiter than the surrounding wall or ceiling. It seems the Sorenson Motel isn't quite as clean as I thought it was.

We climb down off the bed and I walk over to the kitchenette sink and wet a towel to dab at my wine stains some more. When I'm done and turn around, I find Todd standing there with two glasses in his hands, each one filled with red wine.

"We should celebrate," he says. "It's not the best stuff, but I've had worse. Cheers!" He hands me one of the glasses.

I take it and we clink the glasses together. The wine doesn't taste as bad as I thought it might, considering, but ever mindful of my new pregnant status, I take a few sips and then set it down. "I really need to get home," I say. "But we can start back up in the morning."

"What time will you get to the office, do you think?"

"Let's shoot for eight," I say. "Can you find your way back there okay?"

"Piece of cake," Todd says with a dismissive wave and a smile.

I grab my jacket, put it on, and head out the door. Todd walks with me to the hearse, and as I'm about to open the door, he says, "Thanks for your help with the groceries and the motel room."

"I'm afraid I wasn't much help with the latter," I say. "Joseph is getting quite stubborn in his old age."

I turn to insert my key in the car door and feel Todd's hand on my shoulder. When I look back at him, he takes hold of my other shoulder and turns me around to face him. Then he kisses me.

It happens so fast that my brain can barely comprehend what's going on and I do nothing at first. Then my lips move on instinct, pursing to return what I stupidly think at first is an overexuberant expression of friendship. But then I feel the tip of Todd's tongue probe my lips and panicked realization washes over me. I turn my head and push him away from me.

"What the hell, Todd?" I say, trying to step back away from him. But I'm pinned between him and the hearse.

Todd gives me a look of patient tolerance. "I'm sorry, the

impulse just got the better of me." He smiles, but he doesn't back off.

"That was totally inappropriate," I say, stepping sideways to slide from between him and the car. "What the hell were you thinking?"

He cocks his head, looking confused. "I thought we were hitting it off, having a good time," he says. "Like we were that night at the conference."

"I'm a married woman," I say. "A married woman who loves her husband and isn't interested in any other relationships."

Todd's face pales and he looks shocked. "You're married?" Now he steps back.

"Of course I am," I say irritably, though as soon as the words leave my mouth, I flash back on the time I spent with Todd, both in Eau Claire and in my office today. Did the subject ever come up? I realize with horror that it didn't.

"I thought you said you were divorced," Todd says, his voice sounding wounded and betrayed.

"I am, but I remarried."

His eyes glance at my hands. "You don't wear a wedding ring?"

Oh, God. No wonder the poor guy thought I might be single. "I normally do wear a ring," I explain to him, "but it doesn't fit right now and I need to get it resized. I assumed you knew that Hurley and I were married."

"Hur-Hurley?" he stammers, looking horrified. "You're married to the cop?" His face flushes red and he takes several steps back, raking a hand through his hair. Then he drops his arms to his sides, his expression goes blank, and in a tone of somber resignation, he says, "I'm a dead man."

For some reason, this strikes me as hysterically funny. A giggle bubbles up, and then the giggle builds into a chuckle, and then the chuckle blossoms into a full-blown laugh that continues to grow until I sound like the Joker's crazier big sister.

Todd is staring at me with wide-eyed fascination. Or maybe horror, I can't be sure. "Jesus, I'm sorry," he says. "I . . . You . . . Apparently, I completely misread the situation." He shoves a hand through his hair again and looks heavenward. "Man, you must think I'm a total ass," he says, punctuating it with a humorless laugh.

I get my maniacal laugh under control and give Todd an apologetic look. "I'm sorry, too. I see how easy it was to misinterpret things. I didn't mean to mislead you in any way."

He shoves his hands in his pants pockets, stares at the ground, and does an aw-shucks shuffle of his feet in the parking-lot gravel. "Can we start over?" he says to the ground. "I really do want to work this case with you and I don't want my, well, what just happened to get in the way."

I consider this. His knowledge of the Ulrich case could prove invaluable, and despite recent events, I really do like the guy, just not in the way he thought. Would it be stupid of me to try to continue in any kind of relationship with him, even just a professional one? It should be fine, now that we know where things stand. And I can be careful to avoid being alone with him in the future, to avoid any other misunderstandings or gossip.

He finally looks up from the ground, a sheepish expression on his still-reddened face. My gut tells me I can trust him. "Okay, let's start over."

He breathes a huge sigh of relief and squeezes his eyes closed. "Thank you." He opens his eyes and smiles gratefully. "I promise you I'll be a good boy. See you in the morning." He spins on his heel, hightails back into his motel room, and shuts the door.

On the drive home, I keep replaying the past few days over and over again in my mind, trying to find some point, some event, where my marital status came up in conversation. But

I come up empty. Combine my story of divorce, which Todd knew from the conference night months ago, with the lack of any wedding ring, the different last names, and the fact that Hurley and I try to keep our personal relationship out of all our professional dealings, and it's easy to see how Todd got the idea he did.

I'm minutes away from home when I notice a dark SUV-shaped vehicle behind me. It follows me along the country road to the base of my driveway, staying far enough back that I can't make out any detail. I half expect it to turn into the driveway behind me, but it drives on by instead.

I shake my head and laugh at myself. "You're getting paranoid, girl," I say aloud. And then I remember that I thought that the last time I was being followed.

CHAPTER 20

I find my family gathered in the kitchen. Emily and Matthew are seated at the table in the breakfast nook area, with coloring books and crayons, while Hurley is busy at the stove cooking something that smells delicious. I'm glad to see my son is wearing "normal" clothing and wonder what he's done with his "futility belt."

"Where have you been?" Hurley asks me when I enter the room. His tone is one of mild curiosity and yet I sense an undercurrent to the question.

"Working on our case," I say. I slip off my jacket and hang it on the back of one of the stools lining the kitchen island. Then I walk over and kiss both Matthew and Emily on top of their heads. Next I walk over to the stove and snake my arms around Hurley's waist, pressing the side of my face against the back of his shoulder.

"Smells yummy," I say. "What are you making?"

"Goulash."

"That's a new one."

"Isn't this your block of days off?" Hurley says.

"It is, but this case won't let go of me. In fact, I was wondering if you could arrange for me to talk to the parents of our . . . victim tomorrow." I lower my voice so little ears don't hear. "I'd like to find out more about Lacy's movements before she showed up in this area. If you're too busy to come with me, maybe Junior or Bob Richmond could come along? I'd like to take Todd with me, too."

Hurley shrugs loose of my hold and I straighten and take a step back as he turns to face me. "Todd?" he says, raising his eyebrows. "Are we talking Eau Claire–and–forensic conference Todd?"

I watch as Hurley's eyes narrow ever so slightly. Something in the air feels off, a little dangerous. "Yes, that Todd," I say. "He came down to help us with the case."

"Who invited him?"

"No one," I say, giving him a puzzled look. "Do you have a problem with him helping out?"

Hurley looks at me and I try to read his expression. But he has his detective face on and it's as placid and unreadable as the surface of still water. His gaze drifts down, and I see his nose wrinkle.

"Have you been drinking?" he asks.

"No," I say automatically. Then I remember the two sips of wine I had. "Well, not really. Just two sips of wine."

Hurley reaches for my blouse and points to a dark stain above my left breast, a near twin to the one above my right breast, his eyebrows arched in question. But before he can say anything more, his cell phone rings. His eyes break away as he takes the phone from his shirt pocket, answers the call, and picks up his spoon again, turning his back to me.

I move away from him and settle in on one of the island stools. There is a fruit bowl in front of me and I grab a handful of red grapes and munch on them as I study Hurley's face and try to eavesdrop on his words. This last part is difficult, mainly because he isn't saying much. I get a grunt, one "I see," and an "interesting," before he thanks the caller and asks to be kept posted. He disconnects the call and puts the phone back in his pocket.

"Who was that?" I ask, trying to sound casual, even though my nerves are at full alert. I tell myself it's nothing more than residual nervousness left over from the terse ambiguity created when he found me back with Maggie this morning. Yet it feels like much more.

"One of the guys at work," Hurley says, adding some salt to the pot.

I wait for him to elaborate on the call, to tell me who specifically it was, or what it was about, but he doesn't. I feel certain he's still angry with me and decide to let this sleeping dog lie for now and tackle it later, after dinner, after the kids are either in bed or otherwise occupied. I slip off my stool and join Emily and Matthew in the breakfast nook, where I help Matthew color his picture.

We eat at the dining-room table and the meal goes off without a hitch. The goulash is a big hit with everyone, even Matthew, who eats it exactly as it's served—something that rarely happens with his food. Our conversations are typical, and while they don't feel strained, the interplay between Hurley and me feels forced, like we're actors playing the role of a happy family when, in fact, we aren't one. Emily offers to clean up and do the dishes, and Matthew jumps in to help. The boy has been on his best behavior this evening, eating his food without playing with it and doing what he's told without objection or tantrums. Maybe the Pod People got ahold of him and switched him out.

Hurley gets up from the table as Emily and Matthew are clearing it and says, "I'm going up to the office. I have some reports I need to finish."

I consider following him and trying to talk to him in the office, but I decide to wait until after Matthew has gone to bed. Instead, I spend some time watching TV with my son before taking him upstairs and getting him ready for bed. I manage to find an old Bugs Bunny cartoon with Yosemite Sam in it, and it reminds me of Cory Llewellyn and his vociferous protests about our investigation. I make a mental note to pick Todd's brain tomorrow for more information on the man.

Once I have Matthew tucked into bed and have kissed him good night, I go to the home office and tell Hurley that Matthew is waiting for his good-night kiss from Daddy. Hurley's only acknowledgment of what I've said, of my presence even, is that he gets up and heads for Matthew's room. I'm hoping he'll come to our room when he's done with Matthew, so I plop down on the bed and flip on the TV. An hour goes by, and I know Hurley must have gone back into the office. I get up and go into the bathroom to get myself ready for bed; then I return to my TV watching, waiting patiently for Hurley's arrival. I sit through several reruns of one of the *CSI* shows, fighting the growing heaviness in my eyelids, and groaning at times over the farfetched plots and unrealistic scientific abilities. It proves to be a losing battle, and sometime after eleven, I fall asleep, not knowing or caring who killed the annoying news anchor on the TV show.

When I awaken the next morning, Hurley's side of the bed is empty. The covers are disturbed enough that I can tell he was here at some point, but I have no recollection of him coming to bed or being there at any time during the night. A glance at the clock tells me it's six thirty-five, and I realize that if Hurley is up already, he couldn't have gotten much sleep. I roll over to see if the light is on in the bathroom, but it's dark. Tossing back the covers, I get up and head for the bathroom myself. After using the toilet, brushing my teeth, and running a comb through my hair, I grab my robe off the hook on the back of the door and head down the upstairs hallway. The door to Matthew's room is open and I glance inside as I pass, seeing that he, too, is already up. More surprisingly, Emily's room is also empty. Apparently, I'm the slugabed this morning.

I hear voices in the kitchen and find Emily and Matthew in the breakfast nook, eating bowls of Cheerios: Emily's are done up the traditional way with milk, whereas Matthew has his with apple juice.

A quick glance around the kitchen tells me Hurley isn't here. "Where's your father?" I ask Emily.

"Gone to work. He left about half an hour ago."

"Did he say anything before he left? About me and work, I mean. Or did he leave a note?" I look around the kitchen area and see nothing.

"No, sorry," Emily says with a shrug.

"No, sorry," Matthew echoes with his own shrug. He loves to mimic his older sister.

My spirits take a dive. Hurley's early departure and his lack of a response to my requests for follow-up on the case are telling. Clearly, the two of us need to sit down and talk things out soon, before this standoff gets any worse.

I pour a cup of coffee—a short one, the critter in my belly on my mind—and join the kids at the table. Matthew finishes his cereal and grabs the coloring book and crayons that are still on the table from yesterday. Emily talks about a project she is doing in her art class with clay and how she wants to try and sculpt a face, but her teacher keeps making her do other objects. I encourage her to be patient, and she sighs and rolls her eyes. At seven-fifteen, she gets up, puts on her jacket, and heads for the garage to drive herself to school.

Left alone with my son, I look over at him, sitting between me and the window. "Looks like it's just the two of us, partner," I say.

He doesn't respond. He is completely and utterly focused on the picture he is coloring, his tongue sticking out, the green crayon he has fisted in his hand moving back and forth across the page. It's a scenic picture of a barn with a cow and a horse standing outside. There is a lot of ground in front of the barn, which would be the perfect place for Matthew to exercise his green scribbles. He, however, is coloring the sky green instead.

I give him a couple more minutes to finish with the green while I sip my coffee and ponder the state of my marriage. When Matthew finally sets the green crayon aside, having created an eerie, alien-looking skyscape, I say, "It's time to get dressed, kiddo. You're going to Dom's today."

It's a testament to Dom and his natural ability with kids that my son says, "Goody!" and abandons his art project without a second thought. He loves his Unca Dom. I try to convince myself that Matthew's eagerness to be with someone other than me is a good thing.

For once, the dressing and other prep go off without a hitch and the two of us are climbing into the hearse by seven-fifty. I'm singing the alphabet song with Matthew as I drive, smiling at him in the rearview mirror, when I notice a black SUV behind me. It's far enough back that I can't see the driver or the license plate. As a test, I slow down, expecting the black SUV to come up on my back bumper and then pass me. But it slows down, too, and a seed of fear begins to bloom in my chest.

"Just because you're paranoid doesn't mean they aren't out to get you," I mutter to myself in a low voice. Apparently, I'm not low enough, however.

" 'Out to getcha,' " Matthew says from the backseat. And then he starts a repetitive ditty: *"Gonna getcha, gonna getcha, gonna getcha."*

I give myself a mental slap for not being more careful about what I say around Matthew, and I think, not for the first time, that someone should take away my parent card. I go back to singing the alphabet song in hopes of redirecting him. It works, but my eyes stay on the black SUV behind us until I turn into the driveway at Izzy's house. At that point, it suddenly picks up speed and passes me by. The side windows on the car are tinted, so I can't see who's driving it, and my angle is wrong for getting a plate number.

The drop-off at Dom's is quick and easy. I would love to linger and talk about the black SUV or the state of my marriage with either Dom or Izzy, who is off today and, according to Dom, sleeping in. But I refrain for now, wanting to get to the office in time to meet Todd at eight.

Despite my efforts, I'm five minutes late. I park in my usual spot in the underground garage, get out, and summon the elevator, which arrives a moment later. I step in, and just before the door closes, I see a black SUV out on the street, stopped right in front of the gate to the garage, its engine idling. I grab the elevator door to open it again and get a better look, but as soon as I do, the engine guns and the car disappears.

Had that been Todd? I'd told him to park on the street, since you need a badge to access the garage, but maybe he'd seen my car and followed me, thinking he could sneak in under my badge access. Or maybe it wasn't Todd at all.

The bloom of fear in my chest, which I've been trying to contain, grows bigger. My gut tells me I'm being followed and watched by someone, but who? And why? I've been followed before, and when it happened that time, it was someone who wanted to kill me. Was that incident making me overly paranoid? Or should I trust my gut? Either way, I know I need to mention it to Hurley. Even if he's angrier than he's ever been at me, he'll do something about it.

When I walk into the library, Christopher is there at his desk, but there is no sign of Todd. "Good morning," I say.

"Back at ya," Christopher says with a smile. "Todd called and said he would be a little bit late."

"Okay, thanks." Maybe that *had* been Todd in the black SUV at the garage gate. On the heels of this thought, the door to the library opens and I look, expecting Todd. But it's Doc

Morton, and, as usual, he has arrived for the day bearing a box of goodies that he sets down on the end of the big conference table.

"Welcome back," I say to him, since I didn't get a chance yesterday. "It's good to have you back, and not just because you keep trying to bribe us into liking you with the sweets."

"Thanks," he says. "And admit it, the bribery works. You like me, don't you?"

"I do," I say with a smile and a sniff of the box he's holding.

" 'You like me, you really like me,' " he says in one of the worst Sally Field imitations I've ever seen. The fact that Otto looks like Santa Claus makes it even more of a stretch.

"You know," Christopher says, "that isn't what Sally Field actually said, though the distorted version has been repeated so many times, it's even more iconic than Sally's original words."

Otto looks at Christopher and says, "Apple fritters this morning, killjoy." Then he leaves the room.

My salivary glands go into overdrive and my stomach rumbles loudly as I open the box.

"Did I commit a faux pas?" Christopher says.

"Maybe a little one," I say. "Don't worry about it."

His response is a long, loud release of gas that tells me he's not only worrying about it, but will likely fret on it most of the day. And I know from experience that fretting and worrying make Christopher gassier than normal. That makes me more determined than ever to get out of this building and do some investigating far away.

The library door opens yet again and this time it's Todd. "Good morning," he greets. "Sorry I'm late. There was an incident at the motel involving a chicken," he says. Both his expression and the tone of his voice suggest that he's having trouble believing his own story.

"Oh, yeah," I say, nodding. "I know that chicken. Let me guess. She knocked on your door, and when you opened it, she ran in the room, flapping her wings and squawking like crazy, while dropping feathers and bird poop everywhere she went."

Todd looks at me with surprise. "How did you know?"

"She lives on a nearby farm and she's been terrorizing the motel for years now. Her name is Lolita and she did the same thing to me when I was staying there three years ago. I think she's got some mental health issues."

Todd chuckles.

I gesture toward the fritter box and show him what I have in my hand. "Help yourself," I tell him. "Doc Morton is trying to fatten us up. I think he's related to that witch that got Hansel and Gretel. Other than the chicken attack, how did you sleep?"

"Quite well. Cheap wine is a wonderful sleep aid."

His mention of the wine reminds me of the awkwardness last night. I push it aside and busy myself logging onto my computer. Christopher chats with Todd for a bit about old Joseph and his many idiosyncrasies, taking some of the pressure off me, but I catch Todd watching me several times and my uneasiness grows. I'm not sure I'm going to be able to spend the entire day working with him if I can't find a way to let go of this discomfort.

Hoping to pay a visit to Lacy's parents, I place a call to Hurley and get his voice mail. I leave a message stating what I want and asking him to call me back. My phone rings a few minutes later and I sigh with relief, until I see that it isn't Hurley calling. It's Junior Feller.

"Hi, Junior," I say when I answer. "What's up?"

"Hurley asked me to call you and tell you that you need to wait on visiting Lacy's parents," he says. His voice is strained, and I can guess why. "He says we need to wait on the DNA results before going there and that the local cops have already spoken with them and gotten as much info as they could."

"Okay," I say hesitantly, wondering why Hurley had Junior

call me with this info rather than calling, or even texting me himself. Based on the level of discomfort I hear in Junior's voice, I gather that he's wondering the same thing. "Thanks, Junior."

I disconnect the call, angry at Hurley for his behavior. If he's still mad at me about the incident at Maggie's office, he's holding this grudge much too long.

I don't like being told I can't do things, and I'm tempted to go visit Lacy's parents anyway. But I've been listening to Christopher and Todd talking about the case, and several times they've mentioned how Caroline Helgeson is the key if we work off the assumption that Ulrich is innocent because she doesn't fit the mold of the other killings. The only way Caroline Helgeson's death makes sense is if Ulrich is guilty.

Or if someone was trying to frame Ulrich.

Suddenly Lacy's parents don't seem as important. Dissecting Caroline Helgeson's life is.

Todd casts another look my way and gives me a tentative smile, but there are worry wrinkles in that tanned forehead of his. That squirmy worm of discomfort makes itself known again and that helps me decide what to do. I excuse myself from the room, mumbling something about having to go to the bathroom, and I head for the locker room. Once there, I take my cell out of my pocket and dial the home number for Brenda Joiner, one of the local police officers and Christopher's current paramour. She is also a good friend of mine ever since she did some private protection duty for me back when I had my stalker and ended up saving my life.

She answers on the third ring, her voice laced with sleepiness. "Um, hello?"

"Brenda, it's Mattie. Did I wake you?"

"Nah," she lies. "I was awake, just lounging. What's up?"

"Sorry I woke you. I'm wondering if you might be interested in taking a little road trip with me today. I heard Christopher mention that you're off for the next couple of days."

"What do you have in mind?" She sounds much more awake now, an indication of how much I've piqued her interest. I explain what I want to do, and before I've finished, she says, "I'm in. When do you want to leave?"

"The sooner, the better," I say.

"Give me half an hour to get dressed and caffeined up. Your car or mine?"

"Let's do yours," I say, thinking about the black SUVs. "I'll stop by your place in half an hour."

I disconnect the call and head back to my office. The boys are still working on the case and they've been joined by Arnie.

"Morning, Mattie," Arnie says. He has a smug smile on his face, which I recognize all too well.

"You've got something, don't you?" I say.

"I do, though I'm not sure how much use it will be. You know that gold fiber you found on Lacy?"

I nod.

"It's a type of gold thread that's typically used in things like uniform insignias or decorative emblems on hats, shirts, jackets, and other clothing, that type of thing."

"Interesting," I say. "It might prove useful if we can narrow down on a suspect and show he has such a thing."

"Unfortunately, it's widely used, so I'm not sure how much evidentiary value it will have," Arnie says. "But maybe when it's combined with other evidence, it will help. Laura is working on the flower angle, too. She's got inquiries out to nearly a hundred wholesalers and online shops to get a list of deliveries to the Eau Claire area."

Todd says, "Do you think that will pay off? It seems like searching for a needle in the proverbial haystack."

Arnie shrugs. "All we can do is try."

"Listen, guys," I say. "I'd love to stay here and continue this with you, but my sister called while I was in the bathroom and I need to go and see her right away. She's having a bit of a crisis." Their faces all turn worried and I quickly add, "Girl stuff, you know." A dismissive shrug from me and their faces all relax. I look at Todd. "You're welcome to stay here and continue your efforts. I'm sure Arnie and Christopher won't mind any insight you can provide on the case. You can bring them up to speed on the blood spatter evidence we went over yesterday. I'll try to get back as soon as I can."

Todd frowns, but nods.

"Absolutely, dude," Arnie says. "I love me some blood spatter."

Before anyone can ask any more questions, I grab my coat and hurry out of the room, making my way down to the garage and my hearse. Ten minutes later, I'm standing in the living room of Brenda Joiner's condo, waiting for her to finish applying her makeup.

"Almost there!" she hollers to me. "You're going to have to bring me up to speed on this case during the ride. I heard Junior talking about it yesterday and it sounds like a real can of worms."

"That it is," I agree, looking around the neat and tidy interior of Brenda's place. I recently saw the inside of Christopher's half-wrecked house, when I picked him up to give him a ride to work because his Bug was being serviced. The comparisons are like night and day, and I decide to get that aspect of my plan out of the way first. "Brenda, how are things going with you and Christopher?"

"Oh, okay," she says with less enthusiasm than I expected. "We're chugging along."

"He seems to think you're doing more than 'chugging.'"

She finally comes out of the bathroom, makeup and hair fixed, her small but athletic body outfitted in yoga pants and a tunic-length, lightweight sweater. "You talked to him about us?" she says warily. For a moment, I'm afraid that she's upset about this, but then she adds, "What did he say, exactly?" with a level of eagerness that suggests something else.

"He seems to think the two of you are progressing along quite nicely." I pause, wanting to gauge her reaction so far. She smiles, looking satisfied, and I drop the bombshell part. "And he's going to ask you to move in with him."

Her smile freezes into a rictus worthy of the Joker. "Wh-wh-what?" she stammers. Her hands start to shake.

I sigh, thinking that I should have saved this part of our conversation for later in the day, because getting her to focus on the case will be a challenge now.

"Let me have your keys," I say, doing a "gimme" motion with my hand. "I'm going to drive."

CHAPTER 21

Half an hour into our drive, Brenda is looking a little less shell-shocked and her hands are no longer shaking. I had thought she'd be reluctant to move in with Christopher, but it turns out I was wrong. Brenda is all in, so much so that she's already redesigning some of the rooms in his house and planning a vegetable garden in the mud pit he calls a backyard. To say I'm surprised is an understatement.

"I really had no idea," she squeals for the sixth time. "I thought things were going slow, plodding along. Christopher can be so hard to read sometimes."

"Well, there you go," I say. "One step closer to your 'happily ever after.' "

She gives me a wry, skeptical look, but her smile is beaming behind it.

"Any chance we can focus on the case now?" I try.

"Sure. Of course." She repositions herself in her seat, as if that will somehow make her more serious and focused. "Hit me."

I fill her in on the case, beginning with our local victim, the findings, the Ulrich case, and our trip to Eau Claire. I'm skeptical of Brenda's ability to stay focused, given the level of delirium she's been displaying over the news that Christopher is ready to drive their relationship up a notch; but to her credit, she stays focused on what I'm saying and asks appropriate, intelligent questions. She even eyes me suspiciously when I tell her about meeting Todd at the conference and how he shared the flower petal information with me, and how he has now come down to help us with the investigation. I suspect she has sensed I'm hiding part of the story, but she doesn't ask about it. At least not yet, though I wouldn't be surprised if the topic comes up later in the day.

During the drive, I keep checking the rearview mirror, looking for a black SUV. Oddly enough, given the prevalence of such vehicles on the road, I don't see one. There is a small blue sedan that stays a ways behind us for most of the drive, but it turns off as soon as we reach the city limits.

It's going on eleven o'clock when we arrive in Eau Claire and our first stop is Caroline Helgeson's place of employment, a financial firm that handles investment accounts. Given that our arrival is unplanned, I'm surprised when the receptionist takes us to meet with the woman who had been Caroline's boss.

"Hi, I'm Theda Magnus," the woman says, extending a hand to each of us.

Her grip is firm, though not overly so, and brief. She is a tall, lanky woman, as tall as me, though much thinner. Her gray hair is pulled back in a tight twist and her features are sharp and hawklike, though there is a warmth in her brown eyes that softens the otherwise harsh, angular lines of her face.

"Please have a seat," she says, gesturing toward a grouping of four chairs off to one side of the room. "Did I hear right, that you are looking into Caroline's death?" she says, settling into one of the chairs, once Brenda and I are seated. "May I ask why, given that her killer is already behind bars?"

"Some questions have arisen," I say. "We are looking into the possibility that Caroline may not have been killed by the person who was convicted of her murder."

"Mr. Ulrich," she says, nodding slowly, a troubled expression on her face. "I must confess, I always thought he seemed like an unlikely culprit."

"Why is that?" I ask.

She raises her eyebrows briefly and smiles. "Well, for one thing, the way that Caroline talked about him. I mean, don't get me wrong. He wasn't the love of her life or anything like that. In fact, that was the thing that troubled her about him."

"What do you mean?" I say.

"She said that the two of them were so compatible—they shared the same tastes, they liked doing the same things, their basic philosophies were the same. Caroline kept bemoaning the fact that she felt so comfortable around him and enjoyed his company so much, yet there was no . . . What did she call it?" Theda taps a finger on her temple, looking off to one side. "*Spark*. That was it. She said there was 'no spark' between them."

"Did you ever meet Mason Ulrich?" Brenda asks.

"Once, very briefly. I happened to run into the two of them coming out of a restaurant one evening and Caroline introduced him. He seemed . . ." Once again, she struggles for the right word. *"Polite?"* she says finally, clearly not happy with that choice. "He was solicitous, but not overly so. He opened the door for Caroline, and during the brief time I chatted with them, he only spoke of her and how much she enjoyed her work." She looks heavenward for a moment and sighs heavily. "I know there are people in the world who are good at masquerading. Sociopaths, or psychopaths, or some such. And maybe Mr. Ulrich is one of those people. If he is, he fooled me. I didn't get the sense that he was the sort of person who could do a thing like that."

On that note, I thank Theda for her time and we take our leave.

"Interesting," Brenda says on the way back to her car. "What was your take on the guy when you talked to him in prison?"

In bringing Brenda up to date on the case earlier, I tried hard to share only the facts, not any impressions with her. Given her current question, I must have done an okay job of it.

"To be honest, he seemed sincere and believable. But Theda is right. There are people out there who can fool the best of us, and for all we know, Mason Ulrich might be one of them."

"So where to next?" Brenda asks as we traverse the parking lot.

"I'd like to talk to Ulrich's first attorney, but I don't know who that was. I need to call someone." I take out my phone, google the nonemergency number for the Eau Claire police department, and dial the number. When a woman answers, I ask her if Detective Stetson is in. In true cop-shop fashion, she doesn't answer my question; she fires back with one of her own.

"Who is calling, please?"

"Mattie Winston. I'm with the medical examiner's office in Sorenson."

The woman tells me to hold and then leaves me listening to a painfully tinny but blissfully short segment of Led Zeppelin's "Stairway to Heaven."

"This is Detective Stetson, Ms. Winston. How can I help you?"

"Oh, hi," I say. "I was wondering if you could get some information for me. I'd like to chat with Mr. Ulrich's first attorney, the one who represented him at his trial. Could you give me a name and address for him?"

"I believe that information is in some of the stuff Detective Hurley copied from our files," Stetson says.

"Yes, well, I'm not with Detective Hurley at the moment. I'm here in Eau Claire and—"

"You're back in Eau Claire? Why didn't you call me?"

"I believe I just did," I say, surprised by his harsh tone.

"Why do you want to talk to the lawyer? Are you still thinking Ulrich might be innocent? Because that's crazy thinking."

"Is it?" I say. There is no immediate answer and I can almost hear Stetson's wheels turning.

Stetson finally says, "I think you should leave the investigating to the police, Ms. Winston. Let your local detective do the work and you stick to the autopsies. If you have questions, I suggest you direct them to your detective."

I gather from this that he doesn't know that Hurley and I are a couple. It didn't come up when we were here the other day, a point that was driven painfully home after the whole Todd debacle at the motel. Apparently, it didn't come up while Stetson was with Hurley, either.

"I have a police officer with me," I say. "And part of my job is investigating the deaths that come our way, so if you don't mind, would you please give me the information I asked for?"

"I'll need to look it up and get back to you," he says.

I know he's lying. There is no way he doesn't know the name of Ulrich's lawyer. He's just stalling, hoping to put me off my game. "Okay, please do that," I say, knowing I likely won't hear from the man again. I give him my cell number, thank him as sincerely as I can, and then disconnect the call.

I look at Brenda, my face screwed up in thought. "Here, you drive," I say, tossing her the keys.

"Where to?"

"I'm not sure yet. Hold on." We get in her car and I use my phone to search for Barney Ledbetter's contact information. I find a number and, much to my surprise, Barney himself answers the call.

"Mr. Ledbetter, it's Mattie Winston. We met the other day at Columbia." I offer this explanation as a memory jog, though I feel strongly that Barney doesn't need it. The man did his homework prior to meeting with us and I got a sense that he's a smart cookie.

"Yes?"

"I was wondering if you could give me the name and number for Mr. Ulrich's first attorney. I'd like to speak to him."

"Why?"

"I have some questions I'd like to ask him."

"You can ask me anything you need to know."

I let out an exasperated breath. "For cripes' sake, I'm trying to help your client here. And unless you were present during the early part of the trial and investigation and can tell me how other people reacted and what they might have said, you can't tell me what I need to know."

There is a pause and I can hear Barney's nasal breathing on the other end. "His name is Norman Fowler." He then recites the man's address and phone number, which I quickly scribble down on a pad that Brenda has provided for me. I thank Barney when he's done and then quickly disconnect the call before he can say or ask me anything more.

"Sheesh, it's like pulling teeth trying to get any information out of these people," I say to Brenda.

"It's almost as if they have something to hide," she says pointedly. We exchange a look, but say nothing more. We both know we're on the same wavelength. Brenda plugs the address I've written down into her GPS, and after a moment, the route is calculated for us. It turns out to be a serendipitous moment in our day as Norman Fowler's office is only a few blocks away from where we are now. I debate calling ahead, but instead opt for a surprise drop-in visit, which has worked okay for us so far today.

Norman Fowler is part of a small practice with a group of five lawyers, each with their own specialty. Norman is the only criminal lawyer in the group, and it seems our luck has run out, because he's not in the office.

"I'm sorry, Mr. Fowler is in court today," the skinny, twentysomething receptionist, with skull earrings, tells us. "If you'd like to leave some contact information, I'll be happy to pass it on to him," she says, looking anything but happy at the idea.

With no other options available, I give her one of my cards and tell her that it's about the Mason Ulrich case. I'm hoping this will get me some attention and it does, just not in the way I'd hoped.

"*Mason Ulrich?* That's an old case, closed a long time ago," she says dismissively.

"I'm aware of that," I say. "But it's important."

"Okay," she says, clearly amused by my efforts. She tosses my card off to one side and smiles at us again. "Anything else?"

"No," I say. "Wait, yes. Your name please?"

Her smile falters ever so slightly. "My name?" she says, looking surprised.

"Yes, please," I say, all icy politeness.

"It's Courtney," she says, shuffling some papers on her desk and acting as if I'm taking up her very valuable time.

"Courtney what?" I push.

Her eyes slide from me to Brenda, and then back to me. "Courtney Edwards," she says, the forced smile still in place. Her lips tremble ever so slightly and then she adds, "Why?"

The word comes out in a tone of innocent curiosity that I'm sure is meant to suggest nonchalance. I can tell she didn't want to ask, but her need to know was simply too overwhelming.

Which is why I beam a smile at her, looking much more confident than I feel. I say, "Thank you." Then I turn and leave.

CHAPTER 22

"Sheesh, Winston, you're good," Brenda says when we're back outside. "I'm pretty sure she called you a bitch as we walked out."

"No doubt, but I'm pretty sure she'll tell Mr. Fowler about me now, and that's all I want."

"So, where to next?"

"I'm hungry and there's a restaurant called Cully's, which Caroline and Mason Ulrich went to several times. Let's grab some lunch and see if we can get any information as a side dish."

Brenda searches for the place in her GPS and we are there fifteen minutes later.

Cully's is a restaurant that reminds me of the Red Robin chain, but with a more limited menu. Their focus is solely on burgers and shakes, and the interior décor looks like it was stolen off the stage during a performance of *Grease*.

Our waitress is a woman named Wendy; I guess her to be fortysomething, and she has the weathered assurance and sensible shoes of a lifelong wait staffer. The menu is intriguing, a mix of traditional beef burgers with various add-ons and toppings, plus a few nontraditional burger offerings made from bison, lamb, pork, and, of course, since we are in Wisconsin, venison.

I opt for a basic mushroom beef burger with Swiss cheese and a side of regular fries, while Brenda goes for the more daring area of the menu and gets a bison burger, with a side of sweet potato fries. We both opt for the chocolate shakes based on Wendy's recommendation, and once our order is placed, I ask Wendy if she ever works the dinner shift.

"All the time," she says. "You can't live off what you make here on lunches alone."

"Did you ever wait on the couple from the infamous Ulrich murders?"

"You mean Caroline?" she says with a wistful tone. "She used to eat here a lot, long before she met that Ulrich guy. She was a regular." She narrows her eyes at me. "Are you a reporter?"

"No. I work at the medical examiner's office in Sorenson, Wisconsin. We're looking into a death we have down there that has some similarities to the ones in the Ulrich case. You knew Caroline Helgeson?"

Wendy shrugs. "I guess you could say that. I waited on her a bunch of times and we chatted. She was trying to advise me on a retirement plan, because Lord knows this place doesn't have one." She rolls her eyes at the very idea of it. "Anyway, yeah, I suppose I kind of knew her. Awful thing that happened to her." She wags her head woefully.

"Did you wait on her when she came in here with Mason Ulrich?" I ask.

"Yeah, twice." She frowns, pursing her lips and tapping her pen against them. "I wouldn't have pegged him as a nutjob," she says. "He always seemed so nice and polite. But then they said that about Ted Bundy, too, didn't they?"

We nod, and her expression perks up.

"Well, best get this order in. Back in a flash with your shakes."

I give Brenda a satisfied look and I'm about to tell her what I'm hoping to learn from Wendy, when a male voice behind me says, "Hello again, Ms. Winston."

I recognize the voice and it sends a little chill down my spine. With a curious smile, I turn and look at Pete Hamilton. "How did you know to find me here? Or are you going to try and tell me that you lunch here a lot and this meeting is a coincidence?"

Hamilton grins. It's a crocodile smile, broad, phony, and full of potential menace. "No, not a coincidence," he says. "I was with Detective Stetson when you called him, and he told me what you were asking. It wasn't too difficult to guess you'd eventually get the info you wanted for Fowler's office, so I went there. Then I followed you here."

"I had no idea I was so intriguing."

Hamilton walks over and pulls out an empty chair from a nearby table, swinging it around and placing it at ours. Then he sits down and looks at Brenda with that reptilian smile. How did this guy ever get elected? He gives me the creeps, but then I suppose his public persona comes across friendlier. He probably turns it on as easy as flipping a light switch.

"I'm Pete Hamilton," he says, extending a hand toward Brenda. "I'm the DA in these parts."

"Officer Brenda Joiner," Brenda says, "with the Sorenson Police Department."

Hamilton unbuttons his coat, but doesn't take it off. Beneath it, I see he's wearing another of his whimsical ties, this one with a cartoon character Minion embroidered at the bottom. Ironic, given that he's the head of all the other minions in his department.

"I don't suppose you've heard the latest in the investigation," Hamilton says, turning his attention back to me and still wearing that smile. "We found Ulrich's knife, the one he used to kill the last three women."

His smile is really starting to annoy me.

"What? How? Where?"

"A student found it down a sewer grate in the sidewalk by the high school. The student knew about Ulrich and saw the knife down there glinting in the sun, so he called the cops. We had a lot of rain a few days ago and those sewers were running hard and fast. The knife was probably buried beneath a bunch of old dead leaves, but the rain runoff was enough to wash the debris away. Might have washed the knife away, too, except part of the blade was stuck in a crack in the concrete. Lucky thing for us."

"If the knife was exposed to that kind of water, there isn't likely to be any evidence left on it," I say. "How do you know it belonged to Ulrich?"

Wendy chooses that moment to show up with our shakes. She smiles at Hamilton. "Hello, Pete, are you joining the ladies?"

Apparently, Hamilton does frequent this place.

"Not today, Wendy," he says. "Maybe a glass of water, though?"

"Sure, coming right up." She sets our milk shakes down on the table and hurries off.

Hamilton turns his attention back to me, his cold eyes matching his smile. "The knife is exactly like the one that we know Ulrich purchased, and it matches the wounds and hilt marks on the victims," Hamilton says to me. "It was found down a sewer grate near where Ulrich was working at the time of the murders. You're right, there probably won't be any DNA evidence left on it after all this time, but we are testing it anyway. Who knows?"

Wendy returns, setting a glass of ice water in front of Hamilton. He thanks her warmly, and then turns cold again, once she's gone, confirming my theory about his ability to turn the friendliness on and off with ease. "But you see, it doesn't really matter if we can prove it or not, because we've already convicted Ulrich. The knife is just gravy, in case anyone gets any idiotic ideas about Ulrich's guilt."

"Ulrich is a smart guy," I say. "Too smart to dump a knife so close to where he works. He had to know that area would be searched. Which raises the question of why it wasn't found back when he was first arrested? I find it hard to believe that no one found that knife until recently. Sloppy police work? Or a plant?"

"I'd watch that mouth of yours," Hamilton says, all pretense of a smile gone now. He runs a hand down his tie, and then takes a drink of his water, glaring at me the whole time. He sets his glass down firmly and narrows his eyes. "Take my advice, Ms. Winston, and go back home and tend to your own household. Don't come here and try to clean ours. Maybe you should find yourself a nice, patient man and settle down, spit out a couple of kids. That should keep you busy for a while." With that, he shoves his chair back, gets up, and leaves, the tails of his coat flapping behind him.

"You want to kill that man right now, don't you?" Brenda says.

"Where the hell does he get off saying that stuff?" I seethe.

"I take it he doesn't realize you're already married, and to a homicide detective, to boot. You're not wearing your ring."

"I have to have it resized. My fingers have been swollen." I feel the sudden burn of tears behind my eyes and my confession comes rolling out of me. "I'm pregnant again, Brenda," I say at a half-sob.

"Oh," she says, her eyes growing wide. Then her face morphs into a confused frown. "Is that a good thing?"

"Yes. No. I don't know. Hell, my life right now is a big mess. Hurley and I are fighting, and I've got mixed feelings about this whole baby thing, and this guy kissed me last night, and I—"

"Whoa!" Brenda says, holding her hand up in traffic-cop fashion. "Who kissed you?"

"Oh, this guy from up here in Eau Claire. He's the one I met at the forensic conference last year who told me about the flower petal thing. He's like a version of me in Eau Claire, except he's not completely official yet, because the doc up here is still training. And then there's some legislative crap that has to happen."

"And he kissed you because . . ." Her eyebrows arch expectantly.

"We were at the Sorenson Motel and we were doing this experiment with wine and we kind of bonded, you know? But just in a friend way . . . or coworker way, I thought. Apparently, he thought different."

"You went to a motel with him?" Brenda says, looking like lightning had struck. She leans back in her chair and stares at me. "Who are you really and what have you done with my Mattie Winston?"

Wendy chooses this moment to arrive with our burgers. "Here we go," she says cheerily, setting the plates down. Her eyes go from me to Brenda and back to me again, her expression growing warily puzzled. Clearly, she can sense that something monumental is going on here. "Did Pete leave?" she asks.

That shakes me out of my misery. "He did," I say. "Do you know him well?"

"Pete? Sure," she says. "He comes in here a lot. He's another regular. His office isn't far from here. Plus, he's kind of a big shot in these parts."

"What's his story?" I ask. "Is he married? Single? Seeing anyone?"

Wendy arches one brow. "Are you interested?" she asks.

"Maybe," I say, figuring if I play along with that line of thinking I might get the answers I want. Brenda is staring at me slack-jawed, no doubt wondering where I've hidden my pod.

"Word is, he's on the market again," Wendy says. "He's been married and divorced a few times. I think his job is hard on relationships."

More likely, his smarmy, smart-assed attitude is hard on relationships. "Are any of his exes tall, blond, and blue-eyed?" I ask.

Wendy eyes me critically for a moment and smiles. "Yeah, I'd say you're his type, all right. Maybe a little heavier than some of the others, but I don't think that's a deal breaker. You should go for it, honey. Life is too short."

With that pearl of wisdom, Wendy departs, leaving me with a shell-shocked Brenda.

"Mattie, what the hell has gotten into you?"

I cock my head to one side and give her a get-real look. "I need to clarify a few things, and my questions about Hamilton are for the investigation. Our victims are all of a type. They're tall, blond, blue-eyed."

"Like you," Brenda says.

I nod.

"You're trying to determine if Hamilton might have any grudges against women who fit that mold."

"Yes. And as for the kissing thing, it was just a misunderstanding." I explain the situation with Todd and me, how we ended up at the motel, the experiment we did with the wine, and the kiss afterward. "I set him straight. He didn't know I was married, and when he found out I was not only hitched, but to Hurley, I thought he was going to run away screaming." I chuckle remembering the horrified look on Todd's face.

"Is that what you and Hurley are fighting about?"

"No. God, no. He doesn't know about that, and I don't want him to. That's all I need right now. No, our fight, if we're actually having one, is about the fact that I lied to him about seeing that shrink I go to at times, Maggie Baldwin."

"I remember," Brenda says with a roll of her eyes. And well she should. She was my escort and chauffeur back when I was pregnant with Matthew, unsure about my relationship with Hurley, being stalked by a madman, and making regular visits to Maggie.

"Anyway, I've been having second thoughts about the whole baby thing, not sure I want to do it again, and feeling insecure about my abilities as a mother. It's not that I don't want to have another kid. I adore Matthew and the idea of having another child with Hurley makes me happy. It's the pregnancy part. And the worrying-if-I'm-a-good-mother part. And, frankly, the exhaustion part." I pause and take a bite of my hamburger, which is delicious and juicy and greasy and probably on the list of things I'm not supposed to eat. *Screw it.*

"You need to be careful about this moving-in-together thing, Brenda," I say, covering my mouth partially with my hand, since I'm still chewing. "Men don't always hold up their end of the bargain." I swallow and take another bite, chewing and swallowing this one before I continue. Brenda, despite being the tiny thing she is, has already put away most of her burger and all her fries.

"Take Hurley, for instance," I say. "He's great at taking care of Matthew and sharing those duties, and he cooks dinner sometimes, and even does the dishes on occasion. But he never dusts, or vacuums, or cleans the bathrooms, or does the laundry. And if it's a choice between work and childcare, something that fortunately happens very rarely, there's this assumption on his part that his job is the more important one, and the childcare issues are mine to figure out."

Another bite.

"I mean, Emily helps out some, but in another year, she's going to be moving out to go to college, and by then, we're going to have another kid in the mix. Twice the kid laundry, twice the kid messes, twice everything. And just the idea of it exhausts me. What's the reality going to do?"

"Have you talked to Hurley about any of this stuff?" she asks.

I shake my head, chewing.

"You need to do that."

"Yeah, yeah, so I've been told." I know she's right, but it doesn't make it any easier to swallow. My burger, however, is going down very nicely. I give her a couple of exaggerated nods and take another bite.

By some mutual, unspoken agreement, we drop the topic for the rest of the meal and eat in silence while I do some more research on my phone. When we're done, I have one more chat with Wendy about Mason Ulrich and Caroline, asking her to describe what she observed between the two of them whenever they ate here.

"To be honest, they seemed to get along really well. They laughed a lot, talked a lot, and seemed to genuinely enjoy one another's company. I was surprised when she told me they'd broken up. She said they got along well and liked each other but didn't have the spark." Wendy shrugs and gives us a look that indicates, "*Go figure.*"

I pay for lunch over Brenda's objections and leave Wendy a very nice tip.

When we're back in the car, Brenda says, "Where to now, boss?"

"There's a bar I want to visit. Are you up for a drink?"

"Always, but you can't, can you?"

"No, but I'll be your designated driver."

"Okay, but the drinks are on me." I acquiesce with a shrug and she smiles. "You and I should take road trips more often," she says.

CHAPTER 23

Since Brenda is already behind the wheel, she drives to our destination, handing me the keys once we arrive. The parking lot of the Town's End Bar—an apt name, given that it is literally just past a city limit sign—is surprisingly full for this time of day. Not surprisingly, there are a lot of pickup trucks in the mix.

The building is a large, sprawling affair with a Western theme. The long, wooden front porch is decked out with hitching posts that have likely never seen anything hitched up, other than someone's low-riding, crack-revealing pants. A split front door is made to look like swinging saloon panels, and a couple of old, wooden wagon wheels are propped up against the railing. Several wanted posters are tacked to the wall next to some hooks bearing lassos, an old-fashioned gas lantern, and a couple of bridles.

"We forgot our cowboy hats and spurs," Brenda says to me sotto voce as we climb the front steps. "This could be interesting."

Despite the appearance of the front door, it's a clever disguise for two regular old doors that open with the turn of a knob. Inside, the place is dimly lit like most bars, and we stop to give our eyes time to adjust from the bright sunlight outside. I see tables scattered about a large open area, and on the far side of the room from us, there is a long bar with a mirrored back and stools that have saddles for seats, complete with horns and stirrups.

Someone is approaching us, but the lighting is behind whoever it is. My eyes are still adjusting, so it takes me a moment to realize it's a saloon girl. Yep, a tray-carrying, boot-wearing, feather-in-her-hair, old-timey, buxom saloon girl. Though I think "bar wench" would be the more appropriate term.

"Can I help you ladies?" she coos at us.

"Can we sit at the bar?" Brenda asks.

"Now that *is* a question," the woman says with a light chuckle that sounds about as genuine as those boobs of hers look. "I don't know if you *can.* Those saddles can be tricky, but you certainly *may* sit at the bar, if you wish."

Great. We have a frigging grammar cop disguised as Miss Kitty for a waitress. Then I take a better look at the woman and realize she's quite young, probably in her mid-twenties, which means she likely doesn't even know who Miss Kitty is.

Brenda heads for the bar and I detour to the bathroom. When I'm done, I make my way to the bar and try to straddle one of those saddle seats next to Brenda. They are close enough together and wide enough that I need to turn sideways to get between two of them. The seat is not only awkwardly shaped and positioned, it's slippery and not designed for women who don't have an appreciable thigh gap. I wonder how many drunks fall off these seats each night. And how many of them slap the seat first and holler out a rousing "Giddy-up!" while hanging onto the brass rail.

Brenda orders a gin and tonic, while I try to get into the spirit of the moment by asking for a sarsaparilla after the bespectacled bartender, who is wearing a red vest over a white shirt with arm garters, assures me it's just root beer. The bartender looks to be about thirty years of age and fifty pounds overweight. His name tag reads: CECIL.

Cecil hovers near us after serving our drinks, drying bar glasses and occasionally taking an order from the bar wench. Brenda and I don't talk much at first; I'm busy scoping out the other people in the bar, hoping to see a particular face. When I don't see the person I'm looking for, I ask Cecil if the owner is anywhere around.

"You mean Cory?"

"Yes, Cory Llewellyn. Is he here?"

"He is. He's in the back. Can I tell him who you are? And can I ask what this is in reference to? He'll want to know."

For a second, I'm tempted to tell him that I don't know if he *can* ask, but he certainly *may.* Instead, I simply say, "My name is Mattie. And this is Brenda. And first, we'd rather talk to you. We're working with someone who is thinking of running against Llewellyn for the job of coroner and I'm trying to get some inside intel on the guy. I don't suppose you'd be willing to spill any beans? I promise you absolute confidentiality."

I promise him something else when I reach into my purse and take out a fifty-dollar bill, which I then slide across the bar. That fifty is my emergency money, a folded-up bill I keep in a small, zippered section of my wallet. It was Hurley's idea: "In case you need an emergency tow, or something." I did it to appease him, even though I have credit cards to cover any such emergencies.

Cecil's been polishing the same glass for a while. It's so dry by now that I'm surprised there aren't cacti growing out of it. He continues toweling it, but his actions have slowed some as he eyes the fifty. He tears his gaze away and looks at me, then at Brenda. I can tell he wants to talk, but he's weighing the consequences.

"If you don't want to tell us anything, that's fine," I say.

"To be honest, we've told our candidate that it will likely be impossible to win because it's basically a popularity contest, and who could be more popular than the owner of a bar?"

"Especially one who buys votes with free booze," Cecil says, leaning in close, his eyes temporarily growing big as his voice dwindles down to just above a whisper. No sooner do the words leave his lips than he straightens and looks around guiltily to see who is nearby. His drying efforts speed up again. At this rate, he might rub that glass into nonexistence.

"Oh, dear," I say, looking worried. "That will make things tough. It's going to be hard enough as it is, given how long he's held the position."

Cecil frowns for a moment and scans the room again. "You know," he says in the conspiratorial tone again, "I've heard that they're starting a program with some doctors in the area that will eliminate the need for a coroner, so your friend might want to rethink the whole thing."

"Is that right?" Brenda says. She slides her empty drink glass over toward Cecil, who then thankfully abandons the driest glass in the world in order to serve her another gin and tonic.

"Yeah, Cory says he isn't worried about it, that he has some backup plan in place, but I can tell he's lying."

"You mean he doesn't have a backup plan in place?" I say.

"No, I mean about him being worried. I've heard there have been some territory disputes already."

"Do tell," Brenda says, feigning high interest.

She not only bats her eyelashes, she manages to look alluring doing it. I'm impressed, because whenever I try to do it, I look like I've got a bad nervous twitch.

"I love a good man squabble," she coos. Brenda gives Cecil a flirty look and he smiles, moving closer to her and away from me.

I know I should be glad that we're getting the job done, no matter how it happens, but I feel an inexplicable twinge of rivalry that starts to grow like the Grinch's heart. Maybe it's my pregnancy hormones, and if anyone asks, it absolutely will be that, but I suddenly want to win Cecil's attentions away from Brenda. This has nothing to do with my being attracted to Cecil in any way—I'm decidedly not—but rather with the affirmation of my allure and attractiveness when it comes to the opposite sex. There is something about being married and pregnant that brings both of these qualities into doubt for me.

I run a hand through my hair and sit up a little straighter, thrusting my bosom out there. Brenda may have me when it comes to overall physique, but if Cecil is a boob man at all, I think I stand a chance here. Of course neither Brenda nor I have any serious interest in Cecil as a man, other than the fact that some flattery or flirting is often a way to stroke the male ego and avoid having to stroke anything else.

"Yes, Cecil," I say in what I hope is a breathless voice, "tell us all about these *territorial disputes.*"

Cecil tears his eyes from Brenda, who is running a finger over her lips in an action that is quite sexy, if I do say so myself, and his eyes briefly settle on my cleavage before looking at my face. He frowns, and then looks back at Brenda, who is now twirling her hair. Clearly, the girl knows what she's doing, because Cecil's expression turns beatific.

"Well, I haven't actually witnessed anything myself," he says, "but I've overheard some of the guys in here talking about how Cory pays the dispatcher to give the death calls to him and not to the new doctor who's supposed to be learning. The doc gets to do the slicing and dicing, of course. Cory doesn't do that, but he doesn't want anyone else doing the investigating and decision-making. I heard that this one guy who works with the doc got into a yelling match with Cory not too long ago about Cory trying to keep him from the death calls. Apparently, Cory let him have a death call after that, because it was one of those nasty ones, you know?

Someone who had been dead for a long time. In fact, it was one of them girls that serial killer guy did."

I recall Todd telling me a similar story. I'm about to ask Cecil what kind of car Cory drives, but a male voice behind us says, "What the hell are you doing here?"

I try to turn on my saddle and end up sliding off instead. One of the stirrups tangles around my legs and I manage to catch myself just before I fall. In doing so, I end up with my hips wedged between two of the saddle seats.

Cory Llewellyn stands in front of me, looking like he just ate a mouthful of rusty nails. He is dressed in jeans and cowboy boots, but his top half is pure Packerland. He has a green sweater, with the Packer *G* on the front of it, embroidered in green and gold, and a matching baseball cap, with the same embroidered emblem.

"Hello again, Mr. Llewellyn," I say, mostly for Brenda's benefit. I wiggle my hips to try and get unstuck, but I'm wedged in good. "We just stopped in for a drink. Fancy meeting you here."

Llewellyn isn't falling for it. "You can quit with the charades," he sneers. "I spoke to Pete about you just a bit ago. You're going to keep pushing this damned Ulrich matter, aren't you? You think you're going to waltz in like some great savior and show everyone how us dumb country bumpkins got it wrong, but you're the one who's messed up." He takes a step closer to me and wags a finger in my face. "You need to keep your nose out of things you got no business looking into."

Brenda slides off her stool and manages to insert herself between Llewellyn and me, all five feet six inches of her. Her physique is deceptive. The girl works out like a demon and she's all hard muscle underneath that slender-looking exterior. She juts her chin up at Llewellyn and says, "That sounded like a threat, sir. I'm sure you don't mean to be threatening my friend here. So back off before you force me to do something I don't want to do."

Llewellyn looks down at Brenda and laughs. "You and what army?" he scoffs.

Brenda slips her badge out and shoves it at his face. "This army," she says.

Llewellyn's smile falters ever so slightly, but he doesn't back down. "I'm not afraid of cops," he says. "Nor am I afraid of you."

"You should be," Brenda says with an icy, brittle smile. There is a glint in her eye that I've never seen before. I suspect it's fueled with some gin and tonic. I find it quite off-putting, and, apparently, Llewellyn thinks so, too, because he finally backs up a couple of steps.

"Drinks are on the house," he says. "Now leave." With that, he turns and storms off, disappearing through a door off to one side of the far end of the bar.

Brenda whirls around and looks at me. "You okay?"

"Not exactly. I'm sort of wedged in between these saddles and can't seem to get myself loose." I try again to maneuver my hips, but nothing is giving.

"Hold on a sec," Brenda says, and she manages to slide a hand in between the outside of my thigh and one of the saddles. She does some manipulating of the upper part of the stirrup and I feel a little give. I give a mighty heave of my hips and manage to break free. I stand there, rubbing my hips, which hurt like they've been branded. The last time my hips ached this bad, it was because I'd just been introduced to an evil machine at the gym that tried to rip my legs apart like two halves of a wishbone.

"Ready to go home?" Brenda asks.

I nod. "Just one sec." I fish in my pocket, come up with a twenty-dollar bill, and slap it on the bar. I notice the fifty has disappeared.

"You heard Cory," Cecil says. "Drinks are on the house."

"Then that's for you," I tell him. "But I have one last question for you before we go."

"What?" He eyes the twenty eagerly.

"What kind of car does Cory drive?"

"A Jeep Grand Cherokee."

Great, an SUV. "What color?"

"Black. Why?"

"Thanks for everything, Cecil," I say, avoiding his question. "You've been great."

I follow Brenda out through the fake saloon doors and to her car. "Why were you asking about Llewellyn's car?" Brenda asks.

"I thought I might have been followed the other day, but couldn't be sure."

"What kind of car?"

"A black SUV."

"But what make and model?"

"I don't know. They never got close enough for me to tell. I'm not very good at identifying vehicles by make and model. I don't know how you cops do it."

We get into the car and I start the engine. "I had no idea you were so good at flirting, Brenda. You had Cecil wrapped around your little finger. Or rather your index finger, since that's the one you kept rubbing over your lips."

"I was getting him then, but you stole him in the end."

"What? No, I didn't. He isn't a boob guy. He's probably a leg man."

"Nope, he's an ass man," Brenda says. "When you were wiggling that butt of yours, trying to get out from between those saddles, his eyes were fixed on your tush. He couldn't stop staring and he had this stupid grin on his face. Heck, he was practically drooling."

"Really?" I say.

"Really."

This information has me feeling pretty good for a minute or two. But it vanishes when I slip behind the wheel of Brenda's car and Brenda informs me that I have toilet paper hanging out the back of my pants.

CHAPTER 24

I keep my eyes on the cars behind us for the duration of our ride home. There are quite a few black SUVs that appear behind us at different times, but they all turn off or pass us by eventually. There is a blue sedan that stays a good distance back for the entire trip, until I turn off to head for Sorenson. I wonder if it's the same car that was behind us on the way to Eau Claire, but then remember that the first blue car left us at the city limits and I decide I'm being overly paranoid again.

We're just outside of Sorenson when I get a call from Arnie; Brenda answers for me.

"Mattie Winston's phone. This is Brenda Joiner. How can I help you?"

There is a moment of silence before Arnie says, "What have you done with Mattie?" in a mockingly menacing tone.

Brenda laughs. "Nothing. She's here with me, but she's driving. I'll put you on speaker, okay?"

She does so, and after checking to make sure all involved can hear, Arnie says, "Your friend wasn't very happy when you skipped out. He didn't stick around very long."

"You mean Todd?"

"Yes, Todd," Arnie says, "though I have to admit that it might have been the air quality that drove him away. Sorry, Brenda."

"No need to apologize," she says. "I know how bad it can get."

"Anyway, that's not why I called," Arnie goes on. "Do you remember that small gold fiber you found on Lacy O'Connor?"

"I do."

"Well, I found something on it. A tiny bit of pollen. It looks like it could have come from a carnation, though I'm going to have to send it to a specialized lab to be sure. That's what sent me looking for Todd. Didn't he say he had a special degree in botany?"

"I think he did, yes."

"Well, he was gone, but then I remembered that Laura also specialized in forensic botany for a while, so I got her out of bed and made her look at it. She wasn't too happy with me, but karma's a bitch, you know?"

I chuckle and Brenda gives me a questioning look. She isn't aware of the romantic triangle that recently existed between Laura, Arnie, and Jonas Kriedeman.

"Laura looked at it," Arnie goes on, "and said it looks like pollen from a carnation. That's key, because the presence of the pollen shows that bit of gold thread is connected to the killer, ruling out the possibility that it was from some random source."

"Good work, Arnie," I say, my mind scrambling back to the earlier events of the day. "Thanks for letting me know."

Brenda disconnects the call and says, "Gold thread. That would certainly apply to the getup that Llewellyn guy was wearing with all that Packer green and gold in those emblems on his sweater and hat."

"But why would he kill the women?" I say. "I get why he'd want to stop the investigation we're conducting and have our victim declared a copycat because it sheds a bad light on him, and he's up for reelection this year. Plus, his job is being threatened."

"Maybe his job being threatened is why he killed the girls," Brenda poses. "A big serial killer case with a newsworthy trial and his involvement front and center. That's some good political advertising for free."

"I suppose, but it would take a hell of a lot of planning in advance. I mean, these killings took place two years ago."

"And when did the forensic pathology program start?" she asks, looking a bit smug.

"Two years ago," I admit. "But if we're going to go with that motive, then we should consider Pete Hamilton, too. He's also up for reelection and his face was certainly out there during the Ulrich trial." A memory flashes and I snap my fingers. "He had an embroidered character on his tie, one of those cartoon Minions," I point out. "It was made with gold thread. And when I saw him the other day, he had on another colorful tie. He might have several with gold fibers of some sort in them. And I've noticed he has a habit of stroking his ties, which would make it easy for a fiber to come loose."

Brenda frowns. "This investigation could get very dangerous, Mattie," she says. "Neither one of those guys was very happy to see you today, and they clearly don't like the fact that you're pushing for Ulrich's innocence. You need to be careful."

I return the frown. "You don't think either of these men would develop some elaborate serial killer scheme and then carry it out . . . actually murder people, just to make sure they're reelected, do you?"

"I don't know. People have killed for lesser reasons." She's right. "But even if we don't think they're the killers, those two men obviously don't want you investigating and reopening the Ulrich case. That *could* cost them the election, particularly if it comes out that Ulrich is innocent. And situations like that make men desperate."

"I think they're all huff and bluff," I tell her. She gives me an exasperated look and I quickly add, "But I'll be careful. I promise."

"Thank you. And now give me the background on Arnie and Laura and tell me why he's seeking revenge on the girl."

We've arrived at Brenda's condo building, so I pull into her lot, park, and then tell her about the Arnie-Jonas-and-Laura debacle. When I'm done, she shakes her head in dismay.

"That was mean of Laura," she says. "I don't understand why men and women have to play so many games when it comes to matters of the heart."

"Do you and Christopher play any?" I ask, thinking about the current riff between Hurley and me.

"A few," she admits with a roll of her eyes. "But for the most part, Christopher is refreshingly forthright and honest about things. And he's not very moody, which is a good thing, because I'm moody enough for both of us. He speaks what's on his mind, and I find that's a rare trait in men."

"Tell me about it. I wish Hurley would do that more. Sometimes that guy is tighter-lipped than a ninety-year-old nun."

Brenda shoots me a bemused look.

"Sorry, nursing humor," I say. "It has to do with catheters and older women and . . . Never mind. Anyway, Hurley likes to keep things close to the vest. He doesn't open up to me all the time, and I hate having to try to guess what he's thinking."

There is a shared silence while we both contemplate the enigma that is men and women, Mars and Venus.

"Do you think you and Christopher will go the distance?" I ask Brenda.

She gives me a tentative smile. "It could. I'm almost afraid to think about it. We're a strange couple, with surprisingly little in common. He likes news and documentaries, and I'm a chick-flick, dramedy, and thriller kind of gal. He has a lot of dietary restrictions, and I eat anything I want. He doesn't exercise much, and I work out regularly. He likes old-fashioned styles, and I'm into modern." She sighs and gives me a fearful look. "It's a wonder we hooked up at all, given all the differences, but we did, and we get along surprisingly well, to boot. On the important things, like our overall relationship philosophy, our future goals for the relationship, and mutual respect, we agree. I suppose that's the most important part of it, right?"

She looks at me hopefully, wanting me to confirm her theory, but I have no idea if she's right.

"I don't know, Brenda," I say apologetically. "When it comes to relationships, I don't have the best record. But I know that every relationship requires work, compromise, and forgiveness at some point. If you let them, little pet peeves can build into monster peeves. I think if you're honest with one another, speak your minds, and always treat one another with respect, then you'll be okay. Heck, look at my mother and William. If you want to see a strange relationship, there's a doozy. Yet they've made it work. Not without conflict, mind you. One of the things that binds them together is their mutual OCD issues, yet even that has its limits. Last fall, my mother tried to make William rake the leaves in her backyard into piles designated by color. He rather liked the idea, as it appealed to his need for order, but once he got started with the actual task, he realized how ridiculous it was. And how tired he was. He and my mother argued over it, and they didn't speak for several days—all over how to rake the leaves!"

Brenda chuckles and shakes her head woefully. "I assume they worked it out eventually?"

"They did. They hired someone to rake the leaves for them and had him come when they weren't home. That was a challenge in and of itself, since my mother rarely leaves the house. But William managed to arrange things so that the raking fellow came when my mother had one of her doctor appointments. Those take some time, because my mother has burned through all the local docs with her histrionics and hypochondria, so now she travels nearly an hour to see one. That allowed plenty of time for getting the leaves raked up and gone."

"If Christopher and I get to arguing about something as trivial as that, then I think we're done for," Brenda says with a laugh.

"I hear you, but keep in mind that this issue wasn't a trivial one for William and my mother. To them, it was as big a deal as, say, the decision to have kids."

Brenda stares at me for a moment and then says, "So, are you going to practice what you preach and go home and have a chat with Hurley?"

"I suppose we do need to talk," I say.

Brenda's eyes grow big. "Oh, God, don't start it off by saying, 'We need to talk.' Go with 'Can we talk?' World of difference. 'We need to talk' is code for 'This is so over, and I'm about to dump your ass.' "

I chuckle, though there is some truth in what she just said. "Thanks for coming with me today, Brenda." I turn the car off and hand her the keys.

"Hey, it was fun. Though I owe you for the drinks at the bar. It was supposed to be my treat."

"No worries. You can make it up to me later. We can do lunch or something."

"Sold. Good luck with Hurley."

With that, we get out of her car and lock it. I head off to my hearse and try to call Hurley, but the call goes to voice mail, ramping up my irritation level. Ignoring me won't work for very long.

I drive over to Izzy's house to pick up Matthew. Izzy, Dom, and Sylvie are all seated in the living room, and Juliana and

Matthew are on a blanket on the floor. The TV is on and the kids are mesmerized by the colorful characters of *SpongeBob SquarePants* and the denizens of Bikini Bottom.

I put a finger to my lips when Izzy sees me. I don't want to disturb this tableau, but I do want to speak to Izzy, and to Dom, though not on the same matter. I wave a hand toward myself and nod toward the kitchen. Izzy gets up and comes toward me, and then Dom sees me and does the same. By some tacit agreement, we all three move into the kitchen.

"Is it okay to leave those three in there alone?" I ask them.

"It will be fine," Dom says. "Sylvie is having a very lucid day today, and they love SpongeBob. Besides, they can't go anywhere. The front-door dead bolt is locked, and I have the key."

"I spoke to Arnie today," Izzy says. "He said you left the office on the pretext of your sister having a crisis? I'm guessing that wasn't the real reason."

Izzy knows me too well. "No, it wasn't. I went back up to Eau Claire to do some digging around. I wanted to get a better feel for Caroline Helgeson, what she was like, how she lived her life, how she behaved when she was with Ulrich, that sort of thing."

"And?"

I slide onto a bar stool at the island as Dom sets out a platter with raw veggies and some dressing or dip, low-cal, no doubt. Izzy sits next to me and we both start out with a carrot stick dipped in what turns out to be ranch dressing. If it is low-calorie, it's good.

"None of it makes any sense. Everyone I talked to, everything we know about her, indicates that she and Ulrich were good friends, even though the romantic angle didn't play out for them. I didn't get the sense that there was any animosity between them at all. And some of the locals clearly didn't like me poking around."

I fill him and Dom in on my encounters with Pete Hamilton and Cory Llewellyn, leaving out the part where I got stuck between two saddles and imitated a horse's ass with a toilet paper tail. Then I add in the information about the gold threads. Dom listens raptly, though he periodically walks over to the door of the living room to check on its occupants.

"Why did you go up there with Brenda?" Izzy asks when I'm done. "Why didn't Hurley go with you?"

I hesitate to answer, mainly because I don't know the answer. "He hasn't been answering my calls today."

Izzy's brow furrows at this; Dom gets an all-knowing look on his face.

"What are you two kids fighting about?" Dom asks.

Izzy looks at him with surprise.

"Well, it's obvious that they're fighting about something," Dom says with a Captain Obvious tone. He walks over and pats my hand. "How about some ice cream while you tell me all about it," he says in a calm, soothing voice. He walks over to the fridge and takes out a pint of Ben & Jerry's Cherry Garcia, one of my favorites. The guy knows my weaknesses.

I pop the lid off the ice cream and look around for a spoon about the same time Dom is getting a bowl out of the cupboard. The container says it contains four servings, which is a laugh. Within minutes, I have half the container emptied into the bowl and Dom serves himself a few scoops.

"Has Izzy told you I'm pregnant?" I ask Dom.

"Not exactly," he answers, shooting Izzy an odd look.

"He guessed it," Izzy says. "When we came home from that trip to Eau Claire, one of the first things he said to me was 'Do you think Mattie might be pregnant again?' "

I spoon some cherry goodness into my mouth and give Dom a curious smile. "How can you tell?"

"It's something in your face. You look . . . richer, creamier . . . I don't know how to describe it. I just know it when I see it."

"Really?" I say, intrigued by whatever it is that Dom sees.

I run the back of my free hand over my cheek and wonder if my ice-cream fetish might be paying off in the complexion department.

"And, of course, there's the bigger boobs, too," Dom adds. "I take it you aren't happy about the pregnancy?"

"I'm not unhappy about it, not really," I say. But no sooner do the words leave my lips than I start doubting them. Both Dom and Izzy give me looks that suggest they're doubtful, too. "Okay, let me clarify. I'm happy about having another child with Hurley . . . in theory, but I'm also afraid. Afraid of what it's going to do to my life, to our relationship, to my sanity, to my body. I feel taxed to the max a lot of the time as it is, and that's with me working only part-time."

"And how many hours have you put in this week?" Izzy asks.

I give him a look of annoyance. "I know, I know, but this case is unusual. It's an exception. That's going to happen sometimes. I need to have flexibility for things like that, and I don't know that I will, once we add another child to the mix."

I pause and draw a deep, shuddering breath, then spoon more ice cream into my mouth. Dom peeks into the living room and then returns to his spot across from me at the kitchen island. "I think I'm just overwhelmed," I say finally. "Hurley is great at sharing the child-rearing duties, but not much at the household stuff, like vacuuming, dusting, and laundry. And if this child is a girl, I'm not sure if he'll be as attentive as he is with Matthew."

Dom looks skeptical. "I don't think that will make much difference."

"It might," Izzy says. He is sitting at the table, eyeing us enviously as we chow down on our respective bowls of ice cream. He gets up, walks over to a drawer, takes out a spoon, and comes over to sit next to me. I slide my bowl toward him and he digs in. We both look at Dom, waiting for him to object or chastise, but he does neither.

"There are studies that show gender preference exists in parenting," Izzy says. "In general, mothers tend to spend more time with their daughters than with their sons, and with fathers, it's the other way around. If you do have a little girl, you might give her more attention than you do Matthew."

"No way," I say as our spoons momentarily collide in the bowl. "I couldn't possibly love another child more than I do Matthew. If anything, I'm afraid I won't love another child as much as I do Matthew."

"I think nature has a way of working it all out," Izzy says.

"Does nature have a fix for my marriage?"

"I think you're on your own for that one," Izzy says.

"Have you talked to Hurley about this stuff?" Dom asks. "He's always struck me as a reasonable guy. If you tell him you need more help around the house, I'm sure he'll find a way to do it."

"But he already works full-time, more than that. It's not fair to ask him to do more if I'm only working half the time that he is, is it?"

"It's absolutely fair to ask," Dom says. "The help doesn't have to come from him. Not directly anyway. You can hire someone to clean your house and do your laundry. That way, you have more time for the kids."

For the kids . . . plural. The sound of that phrase both excites and frightens me. Technically, we've been a kid-plural house for some time already, but I've had little to do with Emily's upbringing. She's more of an asset than a liability.

"I don't know if I'm ready to have another kid."

In a surprise move, Dom tosses his spoon in the sink and hands the remainder of his dish to Izzy. "You already have two," Dom says. "Adding a third to the mix doesn't make a big impact after that. You've done the hard adjustment already."

"Except Emily counts more on the help-us-out side of the equation as opposed to the be-a-burden side." I hear what I just said and feel instant remorse. "Not that Matthew is a burden," I add quickly. "But he is a handful at times. I mean, there are good things, too. Oh, hell, this isn't coming out right at all." I drop my spoon into my empty bowl and run my hands through my hair. "I'm a terrible mother. How can I possibly think I can parent another child?"

"You are not a terrible mother," Dom says. "Matthew even says so."

"He does?"

Dom nods.

"What did he say?" I ask.

"He said his mammy was the best one in the whole world."

I give Dom a doubtful, suspicious look. "He just popped that one out for no reason?" I ask skeptically.

"Not exactly. We were watching something on TV—I don't remember what exactly—but the character was talking about how great a mother he had. And Matthew suddenly turned and looked at me and said his mammy was the best one in the whole world."

"There you go," Izzy says. "Little kids are known for telling the truth."

"Yeah, so are yoga pants," I say. "That doesn't mean the truth is pretty."

Dom cocks his head to one side and gives me the stink eye. "Girl, you're making this thing a lot more complicated than it needs to be. Quit your whining, get your pregnant ass home to that gorgeous husband of yours, and have a talk with him." He makes a shooing motion with his hand. "Go. Now. Get a move on." He snatches my ice-cream bowl from in front of me and drops it in the sink.

I gather up my son and his accoutrements, leaving Izzy in the living room with Juliana and Sylvie. Dom walks me to the back door, and just as I'm about to leave, he leans over and whispers in my ear. "My advice? Have sex first. Then do the hard talk. Pillow talk seems to soften the blows."

"Got it," I say with a smile.

He doesn't smile back. In fact, he looks very serious. He wags a finger in my face and then says, "And don't ever tell Izzy I said that, okay? It's our little secret. We girls need to stick together."

I mime locking my lips and tossing the key. Matthew hears this last statement from Dom and he repeats it to me. "Yeah, Mammy, we girls have to stick together."

Dom slaps a hand to his chest and gives Matthew a look of amused adoration. "He's such a funny kid."

I'm not sure if he means funny ha-ha or funny weird. I'm about to ask and then decide I don't want to know.

On the drive home, I notice there is a black SUV on my tail, though it stays some distance back. I'm not too worried about it, until I hit the country roads and it's still there. My gut is screaming at me that I'm not being paranoid, that this is a matter of some concern. For a moment, I'm tempted to stop my car sideways in the middle of the road and wait for the SUV to come upon me. But I have Matthew in the car.

As I pull into my driveway, the car drives on past. I get a brief glimpse of the driver as it goes by: male, receding hairline. That's all I can discern, and he seems utterly uninterested in me. I think about turning the tables and pulling back out onto the road and following him, but again, I remember that I have my son in the car. If it was just me, I might risk it, but I won't take any chances with Matthew.

CHAPTER 25

It's nearly five by the time I get home. Hurley isn't there, but Emily is, and Johnny is with her. The two of them are seated at the kitchen table doing math homework. Matthew is excited to see Johnny and he runs over and hurls himself at the boy.

"Hey there, little man," Johnny says.

"I'm a big man," Matthew protests. He bends his arm in a classic Popeye pose and squeezes his upper arm through the sleeve of his jacket. "Feel my muscles."

Johnny obliges and looks suitably impressed. "Wow, good work there, little man. You'll be beating me at arm wrestling any day now."

"I beat you now!" Matthew says.

"I don't think so, buddy," Johnny teases.

Matthew climbs down, doffs his jacket, and then climbs up in a chair across from Johnny. "Let's go," he says, kneeling on the chair and leaning over the table. He plants his right elbow on the tabletop and wiggles his fingers.

"If you insist," Johnny says with a shrug. He puts his right arm on the table, his elbow some distance back in order to be able to grab Matthew's hand. "You do the count. I'm ready when you are."

Matthew repositions himself a little, his butt wagging the way Hoover's does when he's about to get a treat. "One, two, three!"

Matthew strains with his entire body. Johnny puts on a good show of struggling, though it's obviously an unfair match. He lets Matthew think he's pushing him down a little ways, but then he gains some strength and pushes back, making Matthew's arm go down. Desperate, Matthew grabs Johnny's wrist with his other hand and puts his full body weight into it.

The door to the garage opens and Hurley walks in just as Johnny says, "Hey, isn't that cheating?" with a smile and a wink at Matthew.

Matthew barely spares his father a glance, fully focused on taking down Johnny's arm, and rather than greeting anyone, Hurley walks over to the table and watches the ongoing spectacle for a few seconds, a scowl on his face. Johnny smiles at him, but when he sees the look on Hurley's face, his smile falters.

Suddenly Matthew lets go of Johnny and cries out, "Owie, owie, owie!" He pulls his arm back, cradling it in a bent position against his chest, kneeling back in his chair. Tears well up and course down his face as he starts to sob. "*Owwwwii-ieeee.*"

I hurry over to Matthew and run my fingers along the length of the arm he's favoring, feeling for any irregularity from his hand up to his elbow, and then from there to his shoulder. All feels normal. There is no obvious swelling or deformity, but he clearly doesn't want to move the arm and cries out if I try.

"What the hell did you do?" Hurley snaps, giving Johnny a thunderous look before turning to me. "Did he break Matthew's arm?"

"No, it's fine," I say, but Hurley's anger is already built up to the point that he's past reason.

"Get out of here," Hurley says to Johnny. He doesn't yell it or raise his voice at all, but the low timbre of the words is even scarier.

"Dad," Emily whines. "Don't."

Johnny gets up and sidles past Hurley with a wary look, like he's expecting to get punched any moment. "I . . . I'm sorry," he says, his expression horror-stricken.

"Hold on," I say, my voice louder than intended, though it's probably necessary at this point to get through to Hurley. "Matthew's arm isn't broken. He subluxed his radial head." Everyone looks at me like I just spoke in tongues. "He has a nursemaid's elbow. It's a common injury in little kids and one I can fix if you'll just calm down and give me a minute."

Everyone freezes in place and stares at me. Realizing I have the moment, I turn to Matthew, take the hand of the injured arm in one of mine, and then grab his upper arm with my other hand. I do a quick manipulation: straighten, rotate, flex.

"Ow!" Matthew hollers as I feel a pop in his arm near the elbow. His eyes widen and then he slowly straightens his arm. Looking surprised but wary, he bends it again, and when that doesn't hurt, he tries several other moves.

"Better?" I ask him.

He nods and looks at me with awe. "Thank you, Mammy." He flings himself at me and wraps his arms around my neck, though he's still a bit tentative with the one that was hurt. He hugs me tight with his good arm and I do the same.

I glance up at Hurley, who still looks angry. It seems he's in a mood, so I figure it's best if Johnny leaves for now.

"You guys will have to take a break from the arm wrestling for a while," I tell Johnny. "Give his arm some time to heal." Johnny nods his understanding, a spastic motion that makes him look like a jack-in-the-box that's just flipped its lid. I look over at Emily and make a side motion with my eyes toward the door. She catches my meaning immediately.

"Come on, Johnny," she says, gathering up the books on the table. "I can't do this anymore today. My brain is mush and we have all weekend still. You should head home. Your mom said dinner was at seven."

"She also said you're invited," Johnny says. He looks from Emily to Hurley, swallowing hard. "Can she come to our house for dinner?"

Hurley's face is still a thundercloud of emotion. This isn't typical for him and I wonder what it is that has him so riled up. Surely, he still can't be that upset over the thing at Maggie's. And while I know he's not crazy about Johnny, he's never been quite this vociferous with his disapproval before.

"I think that will be okay," I say to Emily with an almost imperceptible nudge of my head that says, *"Go, get out now."*

Once again, Emily gets my meaning and she and Johnny make quick work of disappearing. Hurley says nothing, but he walks over to the fridge and takes out a beer. He twists the cap off, tosses it at the garbage bin, and misses. The cap skittles across the floor and Tux suddenly appears from the living room, barreling into the kitchen and swatting at the cap. Rubbish's attention is caught by the motion and he joins the fray, the two of them playing a game of cat hockey.

Hurley shakes his head in disgust and walks out of the room, heading upstairs.

I'm still holding Matthew, and I feel his little body vibrate as he starts to giggle over the cats' antics.

"Those cats are pretty silly, aren't they?" I say to him.

And then my son does something so unexpected, it takes my breath away. He leans back ever so slightly, looks me straight in the face, sandwiches my face between his tiny hands, one on each cheek, and says, "I love you, Mammy." Then he kisses me on the lips, releases his hold, and hugs me again for all he is worth.

It's the best feeling in the world, one that fills my soul with love and joy, my eyes with happy tears. "I love you, too,

Matthew. More than anything in the world." I bury my face in his neck and inhale his little-boy scent, feeling his hair tickle my face.

How could I not want more of this? My heart is bursting with love. Surely, there is enough in it for another child, maybe even more than one. I need to make amends with Hurley, to bring peace to the household and our relationship. I'm about to go upstairs, and attempt to do just that, when my cell phone rings. It's from my sister, and I set Matthew down to answer it.

"Mattie? It's Desi. I'm at the hospital."

"*Hospital?*" I echo, feeling an instant twinge of worry. "Are you okay?"

"I'm fine. It's Da . . . Cedric."

Desi's hesitation on the appropriate term to use says everything about the state of our relationship with the man, our father. "Is he okay?" I ask, realizing I'm hoping to hear he is. I've been trying hard to convince myself that I have no feelings for him ever since he popped back into my life. But it's complicated. I grew up thinking he'd abandoned my mother and me when I was a toddler. He did, but for reasons I never understood until recently. I also grew up thinking that Desi was my half sister, when it turns out my father is also her biological father, though until recently he was as clueless in that regard as we were. The deceptions came from both of my parents for reasons, I'm sure, they felt made sense at the time, but now Desi and I are left to try and sort it out and deal with it. And I'm struggling.

Desi has adapted quicker and better than I have. She is a kind and forgiving soul—though you couldn't have proven it by me when we were kids and she was my primary torturer—whereas I have an amazing ability to distance myself from things that make me uncomfortable. In the past, Maggie has helped me to see that this trait isn't always a healthy one, so

I've been trying to do better. Though it seems the current state of my marriage might suggest otherwise.

"What happened?" I ask Desi.

"He was at our house helping me carry out some boxes of stuff to my car, which I had packed up for Goodwill, when he developed chest pain suddenly. We called an ambulance and he's here in the ER now. They said both his EKG and some enzyme test they did on his blood were negative, but they want to keep him overnight to repeat those tests and then do something to stress him in the morning. I don't know what all that means, but it doesn't sound good. That's why I'm calling you."

"They're talking about a stress test," I explain. "It's a normal part of the process in determining if his heart is okay, assuming the lab and EKG tests continue to be negative. Let me hand Matthew off to Hurley and I'll be there quick as I can, okay?"

"Okay. Thanks."

I disconnect the call and take Matthew by the hand, leading him upstairs. Hurley is in the home office, seated at the desk, working on the laptop computer. He closes the computer as soon as I walk in, an action that rouses my suspicions, but I don't have time to fret over it now.

"I need to go out," I say.

"Why? You're not on call," he says with a hint of irritation.

"I know, but Desi just phoned me from the hospital and my father is up there after developing chest pain. So far, things look okay, but Desi really wants me there."

He arches his brows at me. "What's with this sudden concern for your father? Just a few days ago, you were saying you didn't know if you wanted him in your life, that he complicated things too much." His tone is provocative, taunting, and unexpected. It's not like Hurley to challenge me this way.

I stare at him, wondering what happened to the man I married. This behavior is so unlike him that it scares me. I don't know what to do or say about it and there is nothing I can do now anyway. Not only do I need to leave, Matthew is at my side, listening to our conversation, and studying the two of us intently. I can tell he has sensed the undercurrents. Not wanting to escalate things in front of him, I simply say, "Matthew hasn't had dinner yet. I'll be back as soon as I can, but if you need to go out for some reason, call me."

With that, I turn and leave, not giving him a chance to object. I'm angry, but I push it aside and try to shift my focus to Desi and my father. I drive to the hospital in my hearse, checking my rearview mirror regularly. There are headlights that fall in behind me a short way from my house, but it hangs back, and I can't see the car well enough to tell what kind of vehicle it is. When I pull into the hospital parking lot and it doesn't, I dismiss it from my mind.

I cruise through the hospital lobby on my way to the ER, passing by the gift shop. Knowing that the upcoming visit will be somewhat awkward, I stop and backtrack, peering through the glass walls at the merchandise inside, thinking I might dash in and get a little something to use as a distraction. And then I see something that takes my breath away.

CHAPTER 26

I stand outside the gift shop, gaping, my mind whirling as I take the realization that just slammed into my brain and expand on it. An older woman, one of the hospital volunteers who works the shop, sees me and smiles. I enter and head straight for the refrigerated floral display.

"Can I help you?" the volunteer asks in a pleasant voice. "Are you looking for an arrangement for someone?"

"Do you work here often?" I glance at her and see her name tag reads: DOTTIE.

"Three days every week," Dottie says proudly.

I survey the floral arrangements currently on display. Three of them have carnations in them, one with white ones, the other two with yellow. "Do you put a lot of carnations in your arrangements?"

"Oh, we don't do the arrangements. They come prearranged. But now that you mention it, they do tend to use a lot of carnations, probably because they last a long time."

"What color do you see most often?"

"White," she says without hesitation. "But pink, blue, and yellow run a close second. Of course there are some seasonal variations. And the blue ones are dyed. The pink and blue ones are popular for baby gifts."

I stare at the arrangements, my brain whirring madly.

"Does one of these arrangements meet your needs?" Dottie asks.

"No. Sorry to keep you. Thanks for the information." I leave a perplexed and disappointed Dottie behind, and start to head for the ER, but then a thought hits me and I take a detour toward the elevators.

I ride up to the third floor, a general medical surgical floor that cares for a variety of patients, and make my way to the nurses' station, peering into patient rooms I pass along the way. Several of the rooms have flower displays sitting on the windowsills, one of them with carnations in it. At the nurses' desk, I see Terry Bishop, a nurse I've known for years.

"Hey, Terry, how are you?" I say, a big smile on my face.

"Well, I'll be. Mattie Winston. I'm just fine. How the heck are you?"

"Good as can be expected."

"What are you doing up here? Do you have a family member in the hospital?"

"Not up here, though I might before the night is through. My father is in the ER right now with chest pain. I think they're going to admit him for serial troponins and a stress test in the morning."

"Your father?" Terry says, brow furrowing. "I thought your father was a mystery man."

"He was for most of my life, but we met recently. Lots of interesting family secrets."

"I'll bet," Terry says, leaning closer. No doubt she's hoping I'll spill the beans and give her some good gossip she can then use to elevate her social status. I'm going to disappoint her, but if my father does end up on this floor, I expect Terry will do her best to get what she can out of him and share what she can without violating the HIPAA laws. It may be harder than she thinks. My father spent a good amount of time in the Witness Protection Program, and while he left it voluntarily, he's still pretty good at hiding secrets and keeping things to himself.

"I have a question," I say to her, and she doesn't even try to hide her disappointment. "Do a lot of patients who are admitted to the hospital get flowers?"

"Oh, sure. It's a common gift."

"And do most of them take the arrangements home with them?"

"Most do, I suppose," Terry says with a shrug. "It depends on how much they like the arrangement and how old the flowers are. If they've started to wilt, they'll often leave them behind."

"And then what happens to them?" I ask. "Do they get thrown away?"

"It depends. Occasionally we'll pick out the flowers that are wilted and keep the ones that are still good and put them out here at the nurses' station for a little morale booster. But a lot of the time, they get tossed."

"Good to know. Thanks, Terry."

She gives me a bemused look and says, "You're welcome?" Her tone makes it sound like a question.

I leave and once again head for the ER, but my thoughts are racing. I stop in the hallway outside the entrance to the waiting room to call Hurley. Once again, he doesn't answer, which irritates me, so I don't leave a message. I think a moment and then look up the nonemergency phone number for the Eau Claire Police Department.

A chipper female voice answers.

"Hello, my name is Mattie Winston and I really need to get in touch with Detective Stetson. It's urgent."

I don't expect anything more than a transfer to his voice mail; but to my surprise, the woman says, "Hold on and I'll put you through to him."

The hold time feels like forever, but finally I hear a ring and after the second one, Stetson answers. "Ms. Winston? Our dispatcher said you have an urgent matter?"

"I do. I had a brainstorm I wanted to share with you."

"Is this about the Ulrich case?" he asks in a tired voice.

"Yes, but please hear me out." I know he's going to be closed to any suggestions that someone other than Ulrich committed the murders, at least initially, so I decide to approach things from that angle for starters. "You said the flower petal evidence didn't come out during the trial because you couldn't connect the flowers to Ulrich. But did he have a connection of any sort to the hospital?" There is a long pause, long enough that I think the call might have dropped. "Detective?"

"I'm thinking," he says. "I'm not aware of any connections, but I'd have to look into it. Why?"

"Carnations are frequently used in flower arrangements used for hospital deliveries. I'm at the hospital here in Sorenson right now, and I just talked to someone in the gift shop who said that carnations are frequently used in the arrangements they sell there, and the yellow ones are common. That means anyone working in or even visiting a hospital regularly would have access to them without ever having to order them. They wouldn't even have to buy them. They could remove them from arrangements in patient rooms, or in the trash even. Heck, there might be flowers in the Dumpsters that are still good, since carnations tend to last longer than some other flowers."

"Interesting idea," Stetson says. "I'll have to look into it."

"While you're looking into it, would you consider looking into Todd Oliver as well?"

"*Todd Oliver?* The morgue assistant?"

"Yes."

"Why would I look into him?"

"If Ulrich isn't guilty"—I hear Stetson let out a sigh and I talk faster—"I know you don't want to go there, but please indulge me for a moment. Let's assume he isn't guilty. Who else makes a likely suspect? Todd Oliver."

There is a long silence and I start to think Stetson has hung up on me. But then he says, "Fine. Why would Todd Oliver be a suspect?"

"Well, he has easy and ready access to the hospital, and he came to Eau Claire around the time the killings started. He told me that he had a girlfriend in Milwaukee and things with her didn't end well. I don't know what she looks like, but it would be worth checking to see if she was tall, blond, and blue-eyed. He also knew about the flower petals, not just that they were present, but the symbolism behind them. He was able to monitor the investigation you did up there, and he could have easily set up Ulrich. Plus, he has inserted himself into our investigation down here."

"What do you mean he's 'inserted himself' in your investigation?"

"He's here," I tell him. "Or at least he was. He showed up here yesterday and came to my office, asking to help. We let him review the evidence as a professional courtesy."

"Do you know where he is now?"

"No, but I can find out." Then I remember something. "Wait, I might know where he is, because he booked a room at the Sorenson Motel for two nights, last night and tonight. I don't know how much time he spent in our office today. I'd have to check with my coworker, because I spent the day in your town, as you well know."

"Hunh," Stetson says.

"It might bc a long shot, but don't you think it's worth checking?" I say.

"I'll look into it, Ms. Winston. Thanks."

I start to ask him if he'll let me know what he finds out, when I realize I'm talking to dead air. Stetson has hung up on me.

My next call is to Christopher, who answers after three rings and in a breathless manner. "Christopher . . . *puff* . . . Malone . . . *puff*."

"Chris, it's Mattie. Did I catch you at a bad time?" Before he can answer, I hear a familiar female voice in the background: Brenda Joiner. And I have a good idea what I just interrupted.

"No problem, Mattie," he puffs, recovering quickly. "What's up?" There are some grunting noises from Christopher, and some rustling sounds. I feel my face grow red with the images filling my brain. Then I hear a loud, long fart and Brenda's muffled giggle in the background.

"How long was Todd Oliver in the office today? Did he say anything about the case? And do you know what he did while he was there?" I fire the questions at him, eager to end this call.

"He didn't stay long at all. I think he took off, right after you did. He didn't say where he was going, just that he wanted to investigate some things outside the office. Why?"

"Nothing major," I lie. "There was something I wanted to ask him and he's not answering his phone. Sorry to bother you. Have a good night." With that, I hang up and let him and Brenda get back to whatever fun shenanigans they'd been up to when I called.

For a moment, I can't decide what to do, or where to go next, but when my phone buzzes and I see a text message from my sister, the decision is made for me. I enter the ER waiting area and check in with one of the registrars, who then buzzes me through to the back. Before going to my father's bedside, I scan the staff members on duty, searching for a familiar face. It's been almost ten years since I left my job here in the ER and many of the folks I used to work with have since moved on. There is a high level of burnout among ER staff. Fortunately, I recognize one face, Mitchell Hough, sitting behind a computer at the nurses' desk.

"Hey, Mitch," I say, walking up to him.

He smiles when he sees me, but then looks confused. "Did we have a death I don't know about?"

"No, I'm not here on official duty. My father is a patient here. Cedric Novak?"

"Your father?" he says, his confusion growing. Mitch knew enough about me back in the day to know my family history.

"Yep, it's a long story," I say with a tired smile, hoping he'll let it go at that. "Can you tell me how he's doing?"

Mitch shifts awkwardly and looks uncomfortable. "Given your, um, relationship, or lack thereof, I need to ask him if it's okay first."

"Of course," I say with a sigh.

Today's HIPAA laws make it doubly difficult to get information that at one time was easily obtained. My feelings on this are mixed. In some ways, I think it's a good thing. There are complicated relationships where a patient might not want a close family member to know anything at all about their physical condition. They might not even want anyone to know they're in the hospital. And many people don't want their friends, coworkers, or employer knowing they are ill or in the hospital, particularly if it's for a condition or treatment they consider embarrassing. It does protect people's privacy to a degree. Unfortunately, in situations like mine, it can also put the staff and occasionally the patient in awkward positions.

"I didn't mean to put you on the spot, Mitch. Do you have time to come with me to his room, so we can ask him if it's okay for you to update me?"

"Sure," he says, looking relieved.

He leads me to my father's room, and when we enter, I find Desi sitting in a chair at the bedside. My father, a tall, large man with dark hair he wears in a comb-over, is sitting in the bed, looking as healthy as his naturally pale complexion will allow.

"Mattie!" he says happily, breaking into a smile.

"Mattie," my sister says at the same time, though hers comes out more like a sigh of relief. She hops up and hurries over to give me a hug.

"Hi, Cedric," I say, and I see Mitch shoot a curious glance my way. "I asked Mitchell if he could give me an update on what's going on with you, but we need your permission for him to do that. Do you mind if the staff here talk about what's going on with you in front of me, or with me?"

"Hell no," Cedric says. "I not only don't mind, I welcome it." He looks over at Mitch. "My daughter Mattie is one sharp lady and she knows her stuff. Anything you guys want to do with me or to me, you run it by her first."

"Good enough," Mitch says. He looks at me. "Should I do it here in the room?"

I shrug and nod.

"Okay, then, here's the scoop." Mitch switches into his professional mode. "He came in with substernal chest pain, rated six out of ten, onset with activity, no shortness of breath, no diaphoresis, but some radiation into the left arm. His initial EKG and troponin level were okay, and the pain subsided with the administration of four baby aspirin and one nitro. Since his symptoms were apparently brought on during an episode of physical exertion and alleviated with nitro, the cardiologist recommended admitting him for serial enzymes and a stress test to make sure his pain isn't heart related. We're waiting on the results of his second troponin now and his repeat EKG was unchanged. He has a small bundle branch block, but otherwise his EKG is normal. He's being admitted upstairs to the fourth floor, and as soon as I can get a bed assignment, we'll get him up there."

"Sounds good. Thanks, Mitch."

Mitch nods and leaves the room.

"What does all that mean?" Desi asks, looking worried.

"What's that 'tree branch' thing in his EKG? Is that something to worry about?"

"It's called a 'bundle branch block,' and, no, it's not anything to worry about. The blood tests they are doing are for an enzyme that the heart releases when it's under duress, so if he is having a heart attack and it's not showing up in the normal way on his EKG, that enzyme value will rise, letting us know that something is going on."

"And the stress thing?" Desi asks.

"Since his chest pain came on during a period of physical exertion, they will put him on a treadmill in the morning and stress his heart with some exercise to see if it happens again, or if there are any changes in his heart rhythm."

Desi nods, her brow still furrowed with worry. I look at Cedric and he doesn't seem worried at all. In fact, he looks relaxed and happy.

"Do you have any questions about what they're doing?" I ask him.

He shakes his head, smiling at me. "No, I don't. Thanks for explaining it, and thanks for coming. I wasn't sure you would."

"Desi asked me to," I say, and when I see his smile falter, I immediately regret the words and want to take them back. I walk over to the side of his stretcher across from Desi and take hold of his hand. "I'm glad things are looking good so far."

His smile returns. "Can you stay with me awhile?" he asks, and for a moment, I see and hear the fear he's trying to hide. It's subtle, but my years of nursing experience have honed my ability to detect and interpret those slight voice inflections and tiny muscle twitches. The realization gives me a strange feeling in my chest, like my own heart is being squeezed ever so lightly.

"Of course, I will," I tell him. "I'll stay with you until they get you settled in upstairs, and I can come back in the morning before your stress test, if you like."

"I would," he says. He looks relieved, but then his brow furrows. "What happens if I flunk this stress test?"

"Then you get a trip to Madison and a cardiac catheterization," I tell him.

"Catheter . . . You mean a tube in my . . ." He doesn't verbalize what he's thinking, but his eyes briefly shift to look down at his crotch before looking back at me.

"No, not there, though they do insert something in that general region. The catheter goes into an artery in your groin."

He looks horrified.

"It's not as bad as it sounds, and I'm not sure it will even happen at this point. I'll explain it in more detail if, and when, it comes to that, okay? For now, let's focus on getting you settled in for a decent night's sleep, so they can get you on that treadmill in the morning." Even as I say this, I know he won't get much sleep—not only because he'll be anxious and worried, but because they'll have him attached to a heart monitor and they'll be waking him every few hours for checks, vital signs, and blood draws.

"Will they let me have anything to eat?" Cedric asks.

"They will, but nothing that tastes good," I say with a smile. "You'll be on a cardiac diet that limits fat, salt, calories, and—"

"Taste?" he finishes for me.

"Pretty much."

We all share a chuckle over that; then Mitch returns to the room to inform us that the second troponin test result was also negative and Cedric's room is ready upstairs.

Half an hour later, we are in a private room, listening to a floor nurse named Brittany review Cedric's health history. She then performs her assessment by examining him, listening to his lungs and heart, checking his vital signs, and connecting him to a telemetry heart monitor, a unit that will monitor his heart, but not require him to be hooked up to a wall-mounted monitor. At least this way, he will have the freedom to get up to the bathroom during the night if he needs. By the time all this is done, we've been in the room for nearly an hour already.

"Any chance of getting something to eat?" Cedric asks the nurse, and I feel my own stomach grumble at the mention of food. I never got dinner, either—assuming ice cream doesn't count—not that I'm in any danger of starving to death. Of course I am eating for two now.

"Sure," Brittany says. "But it's after hours for our kitchen, so it won't be anything hot."

Cedric assures her he doesn't care, and she scurries off, only to return about fifteen minutes later with a turkey and cheese sandwich on wheat bread, a fruit cup, a carton of fat-free milk, and the ubiquitous cup of hospital gelatin in the flavor of the day: orange. The sandwich comes with low-fat mayo and the cheese on it is also low-fat. Unfortunately, most of the flavor in a lot of foods comes with the fat content, so it's not surprising when Cedric leaves half of his sandwich uneaten, commenting that he's eaten cardboard that tasted better. He does finish off the fruit and the gelatin, however, while regaling Desi and me with tales of his days with "the family," the traveling Gypsy relatives who raised him when he was a boy.

It's a fascinating bit of insight into an unfamiliar culture and way of life that gives me a different perspective on my father and his personality. It was a culture of con jobs and well-coordinated stings that took my father away from my mother and me. It also included an untimely run-in with a pharmaceutical company that landed him in the Witness Protection Program, though my mother's decision not to enter the program with him also played a large part.

His actions all those years ago came to bear on us recently. It ultimately resulted in a huge sting on some Big Pharma companies and several doctors in our area. My ex, David, got caught in the trap, but he was lucky enough to turn state's evidence and serve as a confidential whistle-blower. It saved his reputation, but the whole mess destroyed the reputations of a lot of other people—deservedly so—and worse, it cost my previous coworker, Hal, and his fiancée, Tina, their lives, very much undeserved.

My lingering resentment and anger over all of it is a large part of why I've had so much trouble getting close to my father now, though it helps to know that I was wrong in my belief for all those years that my father simply abandoned my mother and me.

"Leaving you was the hardest thing I ever had to do in my entire life," he says, looking at me, tears brimming in his eyes. "But I knew I had to do it in order to keep you and your mother safe." He shifts his gaze to Desi. "And you . . . I didn't even know that you existed." He swallows hard, looking down at his lap as a fat tear rolls down one cheek. With his next words, his voice is fraught with barely controlled emotion. "When I think about all the years I missed, all the birthdays, and milestones, and . . . and . . . life that I missed with you two . . ." His head drops to his chest and he starts to sob.

Desi looks at me, her eyes wet and wide with her own emotions. Ever since Cedric's return, she has been gently nudging me to be more open to the man, inquiring as to why I'm determined to remain so distant and unforgiving. I'm not sure why I'm still resisting. Maybe it's fear. Maybe it's stubbornness. Maybe I'm an idiot. But over time, I have softened toward him, and tonight might have been a turning point for me. Desi senses it, too. She doesn't need to say anything; I can read her thoughts in her expression: *"How can you not be moved by this?"*

I *am* moved, profoundly. I'm moved enough that I feel that icy wall that's been hanging around my heart since Cedric's return finally begin to melt. I'm moved enough that I share the news about my pregnancy, which delights both Cedric and Desi. I'm moved enough that when I finally leave my father for the night, just after nine o'clock, I kiss him on his cheek, give him a hug, and say, "Good night, Dad." I'm moved enough that I feel a lump in my throat when I think about the possibility of losing him again.

Desi and I agree to meet back here in the morning at seven, so we can see Cedric . . . Dad . . . before he goes for his stress test. I hug my sister tightly, and smile at her parting words to me: "Don't be afraid to let him all the way in, Mattie. He's a kind, loving man, when you get to know him."

When I get in my hearse, I check my phone, annoyed and disappointed that there's no message from Hurley, not even an inquiry as to how my father's doing. I sit for a moment, thinking about what to do next, and the Ulrich case seeps back into the forefront of my thoughts. Solving this case would go a long way toward freeing up my mind, and probably Hurley's, too, allowing us to focus on more pedestrian issues, like our marriage.

Now that I've got Stetson interested, I need to tell Hurley about the hospital flower idea and my suspicions about Todd. Had Stetson found out anything yet? Maybe Hurley and I should question Todd on his whereabouts on the night that Lacy was killed. Was he still here in town at the Sorenson Motel? We should try to catch him before he has a chance to check out and return to Eau Claire in the morning. Hurley and I always do well together in situations like that: questioning suspects, working cases, interpreting evidence, and setting traps. Todd might be just the thing we need to start smoothing over the rough patches Hurley and I have run into of late.

I shift the hearse into drive and I'm at the Sorenson Motel in less than ten minutes. A quick drive through the parking lot should tell me if Todd is there, and if he is, maybe I can convince Hurley that we should talk to him tonight.

The place is much busier tonight—Joseph's gnome

painters, perhaps?—and there are a lot more cars in the lot. I drive the hearse down to the end where Todd's room is and see that there is a black SUV parked in the lot, though it's several cars up from his door.

The curtain on the window to his suite is pulled closed, but there is a slight gap where the two halves meet, a dim light coming from inside. I pull over to the far side of the parking lot and shift the hearse into park. Leaving it running, I climb out and tiptoe toward the suite window. After checking to make sure no one is out and about to see me peeping in through the window, I approach and bend down to look through the gap.

A hand wraps around my mouth and I let out a muffled cry.

"Hush, please, Ms. Winston," a voice whispers in my ear.

I recognize the voice right away. It's Detective Stetson. I relax and he takes his hand away. Then he crooks a finger at me, indicating I should follow him. He walks around the end of the building toward a field that lies alongside the motel.

"What's going on?" I whisper.

"You were right," Stetson says in a low voice. "Todd Oliver's mark is all over this case. I can't believe we didn't see it before. He set up that poor man to take the fall, and the rest of us got suckered into it. I came down here to arrest him, but it dawned on me that I don't know if the guy is armed. You've been working with him, you said."

"That's right."

"Did you notice if he carries a gun of any type? Or any other weapon, for that matter?"

"I never saw one," I say, thinking back. "But he had a suitcase, an overnight bag kind of thing, and I never saw what was inside that."

Stetson rubs at his chin, looking off in the distance. "I'm wondering if you could help me out here," he says. "I don't want to spook Oliver, and if I just go up and knock on his door, he'll likely ask who it is. If he knows it's me, he might barricade himself inside there and make things a whole lot more complicated. But if he thought it was you, he'd open the door to you, wouldn't he?"

"Yeah," I say with a shrug. "I imagine he would."

"Would you mind doing that? I'll go with you and we can go into the room together. Once we're inside, I think it will be straightforward enough to arrest the guy. He won't know I'm coming, so even if he has a weapon, he probably won't have it at the ready."

"Sure," I say. "Anything we can do to make this simple and safe. There are a lot of other people here."

Together we walk back over to the suite, and after a nod from Stetson, who is standing just off to the side of the entrance, I knock on the door.

"Who is it?" Todd hollers from inside.

"It's Mattie Winston," I say.

Seconds later, I hear the locks being undone and the door opens. Todd greets me with a smile and a look of relief. "I wasn't sure you were still speaking to me," he says.

I step inside, and Stetson steps over and through the door, shutting it behind him. He draws a gun and aims it at Todd.

"What the hell is going on?" Todd says, staring at Stetson. "Have you lost your mind, man? Put that thing away."

Todd shifts his eyes toward me and I give him an apologetic but unforgiving look. "We know, Todd," I say.

"You know what?" he fires back angrily, his eyes darting between Stetson and me.

"Ms. Winston here figured out that you're the one who killed all those women that Ulrich took the blame for," Stetson says.

I glance over at the detective, surprised to see a smirk on his face. And then I notice something else that makes my internal alarm start to clamor. The vest he's wearing has an Eau Claire Police Department emblem sewn onto it over the heart. It's navy blue with a white eagle head on it, and a gold ribbon across the middle. It's worn and frayed. That, in and of itself, isn't what alarms me. Beneath the vest, he's wearing a blue denim shirt, the sleeves rolled up to the elbows. And on his forearms are several areas of red, raised bites in little groupings of three.

Bedbug bites.

I look at Todd, trying to hide the sudden sense of horror I feel, but he sees it. He gives me a quizzical look that makes Stetson look at me. At first, he still looks amused, that smirk firmly planted on his face. But in the next second or two, his expression changes.

I have one thought circling through my brain, a loop like the lyrics of a stuck record.

I need to get out of here. I need to get out of here. I need to get out of here.

I turn and make a mad dash for the door, but I've hesitated too long. Stetson is on me in a flash, and then my head explodes in a bright burst of light followed by an all-encompassing darkness.

CHAPTER 27

I sense that I'm in my bed, but when I open my eyes and look up at the ceiling, it doesn't look right. I look to my left, searching for my alarm clock to see what time it is, but that's all wrong, too. This isn't my bedroom. This isn't my bed. I roll my head to the right and immediately regret it as a white-hot pain shoots through my brain. I squeeze my eyes closed until the pain ebbs to a tolerable level and then I open them and try to focus. Hurley is lying there next to me.

Except it isn't Hurley. The hair is blond, not black. My eyes refuse to come into focus and I blink hard and try again. Gradually I recognize the face: Todd Oliver.

Memory comes rushing in and a wash of panic raises gooseflesh along my arms, which I realize are extended above my head. A shiver shakes me, and I try to sit up and get off this bed away from Todd, but my hands and feet won't move. *Am I paralyzed?* I focus and realize I can feel my clothes against my skin, and the pressure of the mattress beneath me, and something chafing and confining around my wrists and ankles. I realize then that I can move my hands and feet, just not very much. I arch my neck and look up at my hands. They are tied together with a length of yellow nylon rope, the other end of which is tied to the headboard of the bed. I look down at my feet and see the same situation there. A few attempts to move and pull loose of the ties tell me they are too tight to escape.

"You can't escape," says Todd. Except his voice sounds wrong. I turn to my right and look at him. He is lying on his side, facing me. He doesn't move, his blue eyes staring at me. There is something wrong with his eyes. There are three of them and they aren't blinking or moving. I blink hard to make up for it and try to get my eyes to focus better.

"You made a good case for Todd, Ms. Winston," says the voice, and now I realize it's coming from beyond Todd, whose mouth didn't move any more than his eyes did. His three eyes. A head rises behind Todd's like a moon coming up on the horizon and I see Detective Stetson standing there. I look again at Todd, at his face, at those three eyes, the third one nearly centered above his other two. Not an eye then, just a hole. I look at his throat, and then at his chest. Nothing is moving.

"Is he dead?" I ask.

"Sadly, yes," Stetson says. "After killing you in his usual ritual manner, he decided to kill himself, knowing that the truth would get out." He sighs. "I suppose this means that Ulrich will eventually go free and there will be hell to pay for those who wrongly convicted him."

"*You* wrongly convicted him."

"No, I merely collected evidence and then arrested the man it pointed to. The decision to prosecute the man came from the DA. Of course the evidence was rather overwhelming, wouldn't you agree?"

Things are beginning to gel in my mind, my whirling, chaotic thoughts coming together. "You set up Ulrich, didn't you?"

He shrugs and smiles. "The man basically set up himself. He had the misfortune to be in the wrong place, at the wrong time, when he went fishing and was careless enough to lose his license. That was all I needed to begin directing the investigation toward him. After that, it was easy to plant evidence. I checked the carpet in his car and got a sample of the threads, I looked up his credit card purchases and saw what kind of fishing knife he'd bought, and then I stole it." He reaches into the back of his pants and comes out with a sheathed knife. He slowly removes the sheath and then holds the knife up to the light, turning it first one way and then another, watching the reflection off the shiny blade. "I have to admit, it made a much better murder weapon than the first knife I used," he says.

I recall that the autopsies showed a difference in the wounds of the first victim as opposed to those of the others. Now I understand why. Now I understand far too many things that I wish I didn't.

"Pete Hamilton said they found the knife Ulrich used," I say, recalling our conversation earlier.

"Yes, they did. Except now it will be the knife that Mr. Oliver here used. It just happens to be the same type as the one Ulrich owned." He gazes at the light bouncing off the blade again, a smile on his face. "I had to get a new one but it will do the job all the same."

He flips the knife into his other hand, holding it by the handle in a way that suggests he's ready to stab something.

"You killed the girls?" I say. "All of them?"

Stetson grins at me.

"Why?"

"They were whores and drug addicts who served no useful purpose."

"Caroline Helgeson wasn't a whore or a drug addict."

He makes an equivocal face, bobbing his head from one side to another. "True, but I needed to kill her in order to seal up the case against Ulrich. Fortunately, she had the right look. Rather serendipitous, wouldn't you agree? It was just her bad luck that she agreed to go out with Ulrich, and my good luck that they then broke up."

"You killed Lacy O'Connor, too?"

"Who?" He looks genuinely puzzled for a few seconds; then enlightenment hits. "Oh, you mean that heroin addict you pulled for a case?" He clucks his tongue. "I suppose I should have gone farther out to find someone, but I really thought this would be far enough. If it hadn't been for Todd here and his loose lips, no one would be the wiser. So I suppose it's fitting in a way that he'll be the next patsy to go down for the crime. The next and the last."

I search through my brain for something to say, to stall him, to keep him talking, and I remember something Maggie had said.

"I'm not a whore or a drug addict," I say, searching desperately for some line of conversation to keep him talking, to try to reason with him, though I'm certain reason plays no role in his life right now, and probably hasn't for a long time.

"I'll take your word for it," Stetson says with a shrug of indifference. "You wrote your own death certificate, lady, by sticking your nose in where it didn't belong. Now you know too much." He pauses and a grin splits his face, a grin that freezes my blood. "And there's that serendipity again, because you fit the physical parameters, just like Caroline did. It makes it so much easier for me, because I can set things up so that it looks like Todd killed you before killing himself."

"Who are you really killing?" I ask. "Who screwed you up, Stetson? Was it your mother? An old girlfriend? Your wife?"

His eyes widen when I mention his wife and I know I've hit on something. "Her hair is red now, but it's obviously a dye job, and given those two towheads you have for kids, I'm guessing she's a natural blonde. What did she do? Have an affair?"

Stetson scoffs at the suggestion. "How pedestrian," he mutters. "No, she did much worse than that. She killed my mother."

I'm shocked by his comment and it must show.

"I know, surprising, isn't it?" Stetson says. "She's a nurse, and nurses are supposed to be compassionate, caring people, not murderers."

I'm not sure I can believe what he's saying. Has the man gone off the deep end? "If she killed your mother, why didn't you arrest her?"

"Arrest the pregnant mother of my twin children?" he scoffs. "I couldn't do that. Kids need their mother. Besides, she said she did it in a way that would be unprovable, undetectable. She knew what to do and how to do it so there'd be no trace and it would look like a natural death." His face flushes red. "But it wasn't natural, not at all. And she killed the only woman who has ever truly loved me." His anger is building, his words coming out with a spray of spittle. "She betrayed me. They all betrayed me. All of them!"

His voice rises in anger and he walks around the bottom of the bed and comes to stand alongside me, the knife still in his hand. My heart is racing, beating so hard I can see my chest moving with each beat. Stetson runs the side of the knife along his leg, front to back; then he runs it the other way, back to front. He is staring at Todd and suddenly his face breaks into a smile. The quicksilver change of emotions fills me with dread.

"That idea you had about Todd's girlfriend in Milwaukee?" he says. "That was a stroke of brilliance on your part. Kudos to you." He lunges toward my pelvic area and I flinch reflectively, yelling out in anticipation. But rather than stabbing me, Stetson merely positions himself atop my tied-together legs, straddling them. "It turns out that Todd's old girlfriend was a tall, blue-eyed blonde, just like Todd himself." He glances over at Todd and clucks his tongue, shaking his head. "He was rather vain, that boy. I think that's why he went for that type. She looked like him, and he was in love with himself."

"And why did you go for that type?" I ask, eager to keep him talking.

He looks back at me, studying my face, his head cocked to one side. I can't read him, and I'm afraid he's going to plunge that knife into my lower belly any second. An image of Matthew, the way he held my face between his hands and told me he loved me, flashes through my mind. An image of Hurley from the other night when I interrupted his reading in bed comes next. And then Emily, sitting at the kitchen table and smiling. A rapid montage of faces follows: my sister, her kids, Erika and Ethan, my father, Izzy, Dom, little Juliana. Was this what it was like when people said their lives flashed before their eyes?

Tears run from the corners of my eyes and down the sides of my face into my hair. Stetson isn't answering my question and desperation overtakes me. I get an idea based on something he said, and I figure what I'm about to say next will either buy me more time or be the last words I ever utter. I almost wait too long, as Stetson suddenly raises his arm up, the knife pointing at my lower belly, ready to bring it down.

"I'm pregnant!" I blurt out, my last gambit.

It works, at least for the moment. Stetson's hand freezes in midair and he stares at me, his brow furrowing. I'm breathing so hard and fast that my entire body is heaving, even my legs. Stetson rises and falls with each breath, making it appear as if we're engaging in a sex act. We remain frozen in this tableau, rising and falling like the waves in the ocean, for what seems like an eternity.

Then Stetson shrugs and I squeeze my eyes closed and tense my body in anticipation of the pain that is about to come. I pray it will be a quick death. I spare a second to mourn the child within me, the child I'll never know. And I use what I assume will be my last good breath to let out a bloodcurdling scream.

There is a loud crashing sound and the bed shakes beneath me. I open my eyes just as another deafening sound echoes inside the room. Stetson is still straddling me, but he's tipping over to his left, toward Todd. His arm, the one that was holding the knife, is hanging oddly at his side. And then a dark mass comes flying from my left, colliding with Stetson in a cacophony of grunts and smacking flesh. I feel the weight of Stetson briefly lift off me, only to have another heavier weight take its place.

The next sound I hear is one of the sweetest ever. "Squatch, are you okay?"

I turn my head to my left and see Hurley's face inches away from mine. His hands reach up and start scrabbling at the ropes around my wrists. The weight on my legs finally lifts, though the grunting and groaning continues somewhere off to my right. I tune out everything in the room, every sensation I feel, everything except the sight of Hurley's blue eyes, full of love and concern, staring into mine. And then I burst into uncontrollable, body-wracking sobs.

CHAPTER 28

I'm sitting across from Maggie Baldwin, who looks refreshed and content after her whirlwind tour of Europe. I feel tired and haggard by comparison, and Hurley, who is sitting next to me, doesn't look much better.

"You need to realize that what happened likely would have happened regardless of how you behaved or reacted to things," Maggie says to Hurley. She then looks at me. "You need to realize it, too. Sometimes stuff just happens. There doesn't need to be a causal event and it isn't necessarily because of anything you've done."

I nod slowly, and from the periphery of my vision, I see Hurley do the same. On some level, I know that what Maggie is saying is true, but on another more visceral level, I'm not buying it. I suspect Hurley feels the same way.

"Let's talk about where you go from here," Maggie says. "I think the two of you need to draw up a future plan, separate ones to start with, and then we'll look at them together and come up with one that both of you can agree on."

"It's hard to think about the future, until we resolve the current stuff," I grumble. I look at Hurley. "You had me followed. You didn't trust me. And that hurts me."

"It also saved your life," Hurley grouses, but he looks remorseful. "If that PI hadn't been on your tail, Stetson would have killed you. We were almost too late, even with that."

"I realize that, and I'm not ungrateful. But that doesn't take away from the fact that you had me followed, night and day, apparently. That's a huge violation of trust, not to mention an invasion of my privacy. You even had me followed when Brenda and I went to Eau Claire."

"How was I supposed to know you were going to Eau Claire?" Hurley counters, throwing his hands up. "The guy almost didn't follow you there because it was so unexpected! Fortunately, he had associates who could help out with the tailing duty."

"Whatever," I say impatiently. "If you'd answered my phone calls, you would have known what was going on."

"I was busy with work, meeting with the chief, helping the county guys with a case they had, and trying to follow up on the Lacy O'Connor case. You could have left messages."

"None of which takes away from the underlying fact that you hired a PI in the first place." I pause, sighing. "Look, I'm forever grateful that your guy was there at the motel. I really am. He saved my life, and I don't want to belittle that point or seem ungrateful. But if you had just talked to me, asked me questions, and answered my damned phone calls, none of it would have been necessary."

"I said I was sorry," Hurley snaps. Then he sighs with regret, his shoulders sagging. "What was I to think? You were lying to me and—"

"I didn't lie to you," I interrupt.

"Well, you sure as hell didn't give me all the facts. That became clear when I discovered you'd come back to see Maggie alone last month, after putting on this big pretense of leaving."

"I wanted to talk to her," I say. "Without you, and about you. About us."

"And you couldn't tell me that be*cause* . . . ?" He drags the last syllable out as if he's drawing a blank for me to fill in.

"I didn't tell you about it because I knew that most of the doubt I was harboring was self-doubt, not doubt about you or us. I didn't want to worry you unnecessarily."

"Yet you ended up doing just that."

"And your first reaction to that is to hire a private detective to follow me around?" I say, my anger building again. "Why didn't you talk to me?"

"Clearly, you didn't want to talk to me, as evidenced by that little subterfuge you pulled here. Granted, I may have overreacted in hiring the PI, but the combination of that episode here with Maggie, and discovering that you had drinks in a bar late at night with some stranger you met at a conference, triggered a jealous streak in me. I'm not proud of it, but there it is. And it didn't help matters any that the PI not only saw you drive to the Sorenson Motel with that Todd guy, he saw you kissing him after being in his room for a length of time. You came home that night smelling of alcohol, your shirt halfway untucked, and then I get a call from the PI telling me about the motel and the kiss. What was I supposed to think?"

"You were supposed to trust me, Hurley. I already explained all of that. I misread Todd, and as a result, I may have made some bad decisions. I own that, but it wasn't intentional. Todd misread things, too. It was all a big misunderstanding and we sorted it out. Nothing happened." I pause then as a pained realization washes over me. "Well, that's not totally true. Something awful did happen. Todd paid the ultimate price."

"And I feel bad about that," Hurley says, looking grim. "But none of it would have happened if you'd been more open and honest with me."

I give Maggie a desperate look: *"Aren't you going to help me here?"*

"He has a valid point, Mattie," Maggie says, and I shoot eye daggers at her. I adore this woman and I value her skills, but right now, I'm silently calling her every bad name I can think of. "Why didn't you share your concerns and doubts with Hurley?"

"Because my doubts were about the pregnancy. Hurley was clearly so excited about it. Plus, it was my birthday gift to him. How could I tell him that—"

Maggie holds her hand out toward Hurley, like he's a showcase on *The Price Is Right*. "Tell him now."

I let out an exasperated breath and turn to face Hurley. "How could I tell you that the one thing that made you so happy, the thing that I had gifted you, was something I wasn't sure I wanted? How could I tell you that some small part of me wanted to take it all back? How could I disappoint you like that?"

Hurley's brows draw together in an expression of pain. "Squatch, I admit I was excited when you agreed to have another child, and over the moon about the pregnancy. But as much as that meant to me, it doesn't compare to what *you* mean to me. You will always come first. You have to know that."

I feel tears pressing behind my eyes and I struggle to keep them in check. It's a losing battle. "And now it's a moot point," I say. "I can't help but wonder if I willed this pregnancy to fail."

Now it's Maggie's turn to be exasperated. "It's not your fault," she reiterates. "It's no one's fault. Miscarriages happen all the time, especially as we women get older. You know that, Mattie."

That was the same thing my obstetrician had said when I called and told her I was bleeding two days after Hurley and his hired PI had rescued me.

"There isn't anything I can do to stop this pregnancy from miscarrying if that's what's happening," she told me over the phone. "Most of the time, it happens because there is something wrong with the pregnancy or the fetus. It's nature's way of taking care of things. And as you get older, the likelihood of things going wrong increases. We discussed this."

We had. On an intellectual level, I knew that everything she'd said was true. But on an emotional level, logic and scientific knowledge held little sway. The miscarriage had done one thing for me, though. It cemented the desire for another child in my heart and mind, eliminating my doubts once and for all. The loss of this pregnancy hit me harder than I expected, and I found myself mourning an imaginary child that never existed. My heart still aches for the lost child that will never be, but it also has plenty of room for another child to move in and secure a spot. It took a tragedy of epic proportions to make me realize this.

I explain this to Hurley and Maggie, tears running down my cheeks. Hurley reaches over and takes my hand, squeezing it in his. I see tears building in his eyes, and it makes mine come faster and harder. When he leans over and kisses my hand, I want to go to him, curl up in his lap, and rest my head against his chest. Instead, I mouth the words *"I love you."* Hurley smiles and mouths back, *"And I you."*

Maggie clears her throat and says, "I have some homework for the two of you. I want each of you to work out a plan for your relationship, and by plan, I mean how you see your interactions and relationship evolving. You can include the roles you see each of you carrying out, and since Mattie has already expressed some concern about feeling overwhelmed by the amount of household tasks there are to do, I want you to each include a list of those tasks and who you see owning them. Include work goals in the plan. Include sex and intimacy in the plan. Include family time—how, where, and when it will occur—in your plan. It's imperative that you be honest." She looks at Hurley. "If you know you're not going to do the laundry on a regular basis, don't list it as one of your tasks." She shifts her gaze to me. "If you know you have no interest in cooking meals regularly, don't list it in your tasks."

The woman obviously knows us well.

"I want you to do these plans separately," she goes on, "without any discussion between the two of you. No sharing or sneaking peeks before you meet with me next time." She shoots a pointed look at me when she mentions the peeking thing; for a moment, I'm convinced she really can read my mind.

"Does it have to be realistic, or can it be our fantasy life?" I say. I'm asking as a joke, but Maggie considers it seriously.

"For it to be useful, it needs to have some level of practicality," she says. "It does no good if you put down that you want to be seated on a throne and have Hurley worship at your feet while you eat bonbons all day."

"I would never want that," I say. "It would have to be ice cream, not bonbons."

Maggie smiles. Hurley snorts back a laugh and says, "Mainly Cherry Garcia, right?"

I look at him lovingly. "You know my soft spots well," I say.

Hurley arches one brow as his eyes start to smolder. "Yes, I do," he says in a sultry tone. We share an intense and wonderfully heated moment of nonverbal communication, which is broken when Maggie again clears her throat.

"Any other questions?" she asks.

The last few seconds between us have been enough to take my breath away, and I grip the arms of my chair in an effort to recenter myself.

"Make your plan realistic," Maggie says, "but feel free to slant it your way. I will be the only one who sees them, and I will use them to come up with future topics for discussion and negotiation, and to determine the areas where we need to work on more compromise. Okay?"

Hurley and I exchange another look, this one more pedestrian. I kind of like the idea of writing out my ideal plan. It will be the romance novel version of my life. "I'm game," I say.

"Me too," Hurley says, and he sounds genuinely intrigued by the idea.

"Okay, that's settled," Maggie says, glancing at her watch. "Have them for me when we meet again in two weeks." She smiles and sets aside the notebook she's been writing in since the start of our meeting. "We have some time left, so let's switch gears," she says. "Fill me in on the Ulrich case. I'm dying to hear the details."

"We have them," I say. "It turns out our killer loves to talk." I look over at Hurley and give him a nod. "You start."

"Well," he begins, "it turns out Ulrich was innocent, after all. I'm sure you've heard by now that it was Detective Stetson who committed all the murders. He had an ideal situation going for him until he killed Lacy O'Connor. He tried to stifle his urge to kill, but couldn't, so he traveled outside his jurisdiction, thinking that would keep people from making any connections to the Ulrich case. Had he not done the bit with the flower petals, he might have gotten away with it. But as it turns out, those flowers had a very strong significance for him."

"And it had nothing to do with all the ritual stuff associated with the flowers," I add. "As you guessed, as we all guessed, there was a woman behind the motivation to kill—two women, in a way—but it wasn't poor Carolyn Helgeson. She was targeted by Stetson as the ultimate frame for Ulrich."

Maggie nods, her eyes bright with interest.

"You nailed it when you told us that we needed to look at Caroline and how she didn't fit," Hurley says. "And you also pointed out that we needed to look at who had the wherewithal to frame Ulrich. Who better than the detective in charge of the case?"

"Indeed," Maggie says with a smile, leaning forward eagerly.

"Stetson manipulated the evidence with ease after he committed his first killing and dumped the body down by the river," Hurley goes on. "When the local cops found Ulrich's fishing license, it gave Stetson the idea of setting the man up for any subsequent deaths. And that's exactly what he did. He started stalking Ulrich. He stole Ulrich's fishing knife and used it to commit the other killings. He took carpet fibers from Ulrich's car and planted them on one of the bodies. He watched Ulrich night and day, learning his habits, discerning when he would be home alone and therefore without an alibi. He timed the killings for those periods. Then he almost got caught dumping the body of his third victim, and that scared him into trying to stop. But before he did, he targeted Caroline Helgeson as the final nail in Ulrich's coffin. Fortunately, she fit the physical parameters of the type of women Stetson was looking for."

"And what was it about the physical parameters that was so important to him?" Maggie asks. She is leaning forward, elbows on her knees, chin resting on her interlaced fingers.

"It's pretty twisted," I warn Maggie, but this only makes her look more interested. "Stetson's father died right around the time he was entering puberty. His mother latched onto him to fill the void that was created, expecting him to fix things around the house, act as her protector, handle the so-called manly chores, even start earning some money, even though he was only thirteen. Eventually, as his body started changing, she had him fill other voids," I say with a grimace.

Maggie's eyes grow huge. "Sex?" she says.

I nod grimly. "And it went on for years, well into Stetson's adulthood. They both knew the outside world wouldn't approve. Apparently, the woman did a number on her son, because he was completely and utterly brainwashed. They continued their relationship through his college years, the police academy, and his job."

Hurley takes over. "They lived together all that time, but everyone just thought that Stetson was a dutiful son who looked after his mom. No one suspected just how twisted their relationship was."

"Until his mother got sick a few years ago," I say. "She was diagnosed with ovarian cancer, and with the surgery, chemo, and radiation that followed, her relationship with her son changed. It took on more of a normal mother-son characteristic. Stetson met Susan at the hospital while visiting his mother there, and for the first time, he began to think that he could have a more normal relationship with another woman. They dated, Susan got pregnant, and then they got married, all of it while Mrs. Stetson was undergoing her treatments."

Hurley picks up the story again while I take a sip of water. "Mrs. Stetson was too ill during the early stages of her son's courtship of Susan to realize what was going on, but once she did, it didn't go over well. But by then, Susan was pregnant and she and Stetson had had the modern-day version of a shotgun wedding. Apparently, Mrs. Stetson was furious and the hold she had on her son was stronger than he realized. As she recovered from her treatments, she lured him back to her bed. Susan found out and threatened to expose them both."

"Oh, my," Maggie says. I can tell from her expression that she's eating this up.

Hurley continues: "Faced with the shame and embarrassment of the situation, Susan came up with an alternate plan, one that would solve the problem, save face, and keep the awful family secret under wraps. When Mrs. Stetson had a setback and ended up back in the hospital, Susan confronted her and told her she was going to expose them. According to Susan, the two women had quite a row, and Mrs. Stetson accused Susan of sleeping around and even went so far as to say the twins weren't her son's. Susan expected Stetson to side with her, of course, but he didn't. When she saw how strong a hold his mother had over him, she realized he would never come around—as long as Mrs. Stetson was alive.

"According to Stetson, Susan was working at the hospital when his mother was readmitted and had to have emergency surgery. He claims Susan found a way to kill the woman and make it look like a natural death. She supposedly admitted to Stetson that she did this, though the woman is adamantly denying it now." Hurley pauses and shrugs. "Whether or not she did kill the woman, Stetson believed she did, and he went nuts."

"I take it that Mrs. Stetson, the mother, that is, was blond-haired and blue-eyed?" Maggie says.

"Nope," I say. "She was short, dark-haired, and had brown eyes."

Maggie looks confused.

"Hold on, it will make sense in a minute," I say with a smile. "The loss of his mother hit Stetson hard and he blamed Susan. He wanted to kill her for it, but he couldn't bring himself to kill the mother of his daughters. Still, the whole thing destroyed their marriage, and it also destroyed any sanity Stetson had left after what his mother had done to him all those years. He couldn't kill Susan, so he killed women who represented her—women who looked like her, women with no morals, and, out of self-preservation, women he thought no one would miss. Caroline Helgeson was the only exception, a necessary one if Stetson was going to get away with it and lay the blame on Ulrich."

"But I saw a news clip that showed Stetson's wife recently," Maggie says. "She had red hair."

"She does now," I say, "but she's a blonde naturally. She didn't start dying it red until very recently. I should have realized that when I saw the twins. They're both towheads."

"Where did Stetson kill the women?" Maggie asks. "And how?"

"He killed all of them out at his family home," Hurley says. "He inherited an old farm from his mother. It was easy to lure the women to his vehicle and drive them out there with the promise of more drugs, which he apparently provided. The cops found blood evidence all over the floor of a barn that sits on Stetson's property, and they also found an old truck that had blood evidence in the bed. It's what he used to transport the bodies, that and an old rowboat he towed out to the one site where he left Darla Marks's body. He grabbed a sample of the river grass in that area, working off a mistaken belief that that area was the only spot along the river where it grew. He then planted the grass on Ulrich's boat, thinking it would be one more piece of evidence against the poor man."

Hurley pauses and chuckles before continuing. "The irony of the river grass story is that the DA on the Ulrich case, a man named Pete Hamilton, used that river grass in another earlier case to prove someone else's guilt. Some expert had testified that it could only be found in one spot along the river, but it turned out he was wrong. The defense team in that case never challenged it, as there was so much other evidence against their client that it didn't matter. Stetson had heard the original testimony about the grass, but never knew it had been disproven, so he believed it to be true."

"As for how Stetson killed," I say, "he had a definite pattern. Based on the heroin levels in the blood of all the victims, they were unconscious when he finally got around to the stabbing part. I suppose that's some small consolation. His victims likely felt little to no pain because of all the heroin in their systems.

"The one exception to it all, as you so wisely pointed out, was Caroline Helgeson," I continue. "She had a huge amount of heroin in her system, too, and only one needle mark on her arm. She wasn't a regular user, and at first, the cops couldn't figure out why she would have let anyone do that to her.

There was no evidence of any restraints being used, and no defensive wounds of any sort. And unlike the other women, she wasn't already under the influence of illicit drugs, at least not any she self-administered. It turns out they found GHB in her vitreous fluid."

"He slipped her a dose of the date rape drug?" Maggie says, looking surprised.

"Yep, Stetson admitted to it," I say. "Of course, originally the cops thought it was Ulrich who gave it to her, even though they couldn't prove how he got the stuff, or that he ever had it."

"We're not sure how Stetson got the drugs, either," Hurley says. "But there have been enough drug raids and confiscated materials by the Eau Claire PD that it wouldn't have been all that hard for him to have stashed some aside for his own use."

"Our Sorenson victim had a high level of heroin in her blood, like the other victims, but in her case, we think it came from her own stash," I add. "Stetson admitted he had some heroin on him that he brought along with the intention of using it on Lacy, but he took advantage of the score she and Dutch had made earlier and saved what he had for another day."

"So the Sorenson victim was stalked?" Maggie asks. "She wasn't a victim of circumstance?"

"A little of both, but he definitely stalked her," Hurley says. "He traveled around looking for potential victims, feeling the need to kill again, but smart enough not to do it in his own area. Lacy O'Connor and Dutch Simmons happened to walk into a convenience store where Stetson had stopped to gas up his car and he saw Dutch score some drugs outside the store a few minutes later. Since Lacy fit the physical parameters Stetson wanted, he followed her and that idiot boyfriend of hers. He saw that they had a cabin at Troll Nook and he went home to Eau Claire and came back the next day. It took three nights of stalking the two of them before he got his chance. Their car broke down and Lacy took the drugs she and Dutch had scored that day and started walking to Troll Nook. Dutch was passed out in the car and later ended up in the ER. Lacy wasn't so lucky. Stetson offered her a ride and she accepted. He took her back to her cabin, shot her up with more heroin, laid out the plastic sheet he brought with him on the bed, and killed her."

"And then he dumped her on the side of a road?" Maggie says, wincing.

"Right," Hurley says. "I guess he figured taking her to his home in Eau Claire and killing her in the barn like all the others was too risky and impractical. That would have been a long drive with a comatose drug addict in the car. The likely reason he took Lacy's body and dumped it alongside the road was to try to keep the actual murder scene from being discovered, fearful that he might have inadvertently left evidence behind, like DNA, that would point to him. We theorized that it was while dumping her body that the gold fiber got caught in Lacy's teeth. They were quite jagged, and her face was against his chest when he carried her. Her tooth probably snagged on the police department emblem on his jacket and pulled loose a gold thread."

Maggie leans back in her seat with a satisfied smile. "Quite the intriguing and sordid story," she says. "How is poor Mr. Ulrich doing?"

"As good as can be expected," I say. "He's talking about moving away, heading back east to Vermont, I think he said. It's where one of his sisters lives."

"That's probably a good idea," Maggie says. "He'll never have a normal life in this area if he stays." She looks troubled for a moment. "Is he going to be here for Stetson's trial?"

Hurley shakes his head. "For now, there isn't going to be one. The shrinks—" Realizing what he's said, he grimaces and mutters, "Sorry."

Maggie smiles and waves him off. "I'm not that sensitive."

"The doctors," Hurley says instead, "all agree that Stetson

is insane. He hid it well, but once they started digging into that man's brain, they discovered how truly messed up he is."

"And his wife?" Maggie asks.

"Ah, there's the rub," I say. "No one knows for sure if Stetson can be believed when he says Susan claimed to have killed his mother. Susan denies it, of course, and Mrs. Stetson was cremated a long time ago, so there's no way to check. And the medical records for Mrs. Stetson right before she died showed multiple medical conditions that could have caused her death and would have in short order, regardless."

"So she just gets away with it, if she did do it?" Maggie says, looking appalled.

Hurley and I both nod.

"To be honest," I say, "I'd rather see someone like her get away with murder than see someone like Mason Ulrich falsely accused. And from the sound of things, Mrs. Stetson's death was no big loss to anyone other than her son. I know it doesn't justify murder, but that woman was seriously twisted and disturbed."

"We disagree on that point," Hurley says, giving me a wan smile. "It was the death of Mrs. Stetson that led to all the murders. If Susan Stetson killed the woman, she's as guilty of those deaths as her husband is."

"Not if you can't prove it," I say.

Hurley sighs, but with a smile. We've discussed this case six ways from Sunday over the past month and realized that we're never going to agree on all the issues. Given the current tension in our relationship, one might expect such disagreements would be a potential hazard. But the truth is, Hurley and I love debating the issues, arguing our respective points, and philosophizing on things in general. We're both passionate and animated during these discussions, but also respectful of one another. Often as not, the debates lead to sex. At least that part of our relationship is still functioning well.

"What about the carnations? And the stabbing pattern?

Were you able to get any explanations out of Stetson for those?" Maggie asks.

"We did," I say. "The stabbing pattern was basically Stetson venting his rage at all things female. He said he wanted to destroy the essence of their femininity, or some crazy crap like that, and that meant one stab in the uterus, one in each ovary—though his knowledge of anatomy was off by several inches in that case—and one in each breast."

"Makes sense," Maggie says. "If that kind of thing can ever be considered sensible. And the carnations?"

"Yellow carnations were his mother's favorite flowers," I say. "Simple as that. It had nothing to do with all that symbolism, though it ended up being quite apt. Stetson had access to the hospital, so it was easy enough for him to get the flowers for his own use without ordering them. Sometimes he took them from arrangements that patients had, sometimes he got them from the garbage. He visited the hospital often under the guise of going to the morgue or visiting Dr. Larson, and the hospital trash was located outside a basement door not far from the morgue."

A buzzer sounds, and Maggie smiles and says, "That's my next patient, so we'll have to call it a day. Thanks for filling me in. See you in two weeks and don't forget your homework."

Hurley and I thank Maggie and leave, walking out of the building hand in hand, silent until we reach his pickup.

"We're okay, Squatch, aren't we?" he says, not releasing my hand. "Because you . . . us . . . our family . . . they're the most important things in my life. I hope you know that."

I look deep into his eyes, into his heart. *God, I love this man.* "I do know that," I say honestly. "There will always be challenges, but I'm confident that we can meet them together. I'll do better at being more open and honest with you."

"Me too." He tears his gaze away and looks out over the

parking area. "I do trust you, Squatch. I don't know what came over me. I'm sorry I got so jealous. It was a stupid thing to do."

I smile and run a hand over his chest. "It's probably very un-PC of me to say that I kind of like that you did."

He looks at me again, his expression serious, his eyes locked on mine. "Are you sure, absolutely sure, about the baby thing?"

I nod. "I am. Losing this pregnancy made me realize how much I want another kid with you, Hurley."

He arches one eyebrow and cocks a half-smile at me. "Want to go home and practice?"

I feel a funny little quiver in my nether regions. "Absolutely."

With that, we go speeding homeward into a hopeful but unknown future.

CHAPTER 1

I awaken and peer out of one eye at the clock on my bedside stand, hoping for another hour or two of sleep. Sadly, it is not to be. The clock reads 7:28—two minutes before the alarm is going to sound. I want desperately to close my eyes and go back to sleep, to snuggle down in the warmth of the covers and hide from the morning cold, to cuddle up next to my sleeping husband, bathing in the feelings of love and sanctuary he instills in me. Instead, I reach over and turn off the alarm before it starts clamoring. Bleary-eyed, I ease out from under the covers and sit on the edge of the bed, giving my senses a minute or so to more fully wake up. I listen to the sounds of the house and the gentle snores of Hurley behind me, feeling the coolness in the air, and letting my eyes adjust better to the dark.

Eventually I grab my cell phone and unplug it from the charge cord; then I slip off the last of the covers and tiptoe my way to the bathroom, hoping not to disturb my husband. He's a homicide detective here in the Wisconsin town of Sorenson, where we live, and he works long hours a lot of the time. Plus, we are working parents of a teenager and a toddler, so sleep is a precious commodity for us both.

In the bathroom, I brush my teeth, don a robe against the morning chill, and tame my blond locks as best I can, though a cowlick on one side refuses to stay down, sticking out near my right temple like a broken, wayward horn. I eventually give up on the hair and tiptoe back the way I came, through the walk-in closet, and across the bedroom to the hallway. Our dog, Hoover, is asleep on the floor in front of the fireplace—a fireplace whose warmth I could use right now, though at the moment it's dark and empty—and the dog gets up and falls into step behind me. I shut the door as quietly as I can, and then Hoover and I pad down the hall toward the bedroom of my two-and-a-half-year-old son, Matthew. I'm surprised he isn't awake because he's proven himself to be an annoyingly early riser who is typically anything but quiet. But when I reach his room, I realize he has stayed true to form and is, indeed, awake; he just hasn't bothered anyone yet. His silence doesn't bode well, and sure enough I find him standing stark naked, busily becoming the next Vincent van Gogh by drawing on his bedroom wall with an assortment of crayons.

"Matthew!" I say in an irritable tone that loses much of its effect because I don't raise my voice. "Why are you drawing on the wall?"

Matthew looks guilty, but not enough so that he stops the scribble he's currently making, something that looks like a giant purple cookie. He doesn't answer me. I shake my head, walk over to him, and take the crayon from his hand, dropping it in a box at his feet that contains an assortment of crayons in all colors and sizes. When I pick up the box and place it on top of his dresser, Matthew lets out a bloodcurdling scream loud enough that a passerby might think he was being physically tortured. Some dark corner of my mind briefly entertains the possibility, before I take a deep breath and slowly release it, coming to my senses.

"I want crayons!" Matthew screams, pounding his fists on the wall.

"Hush before you wake up your father!" I rummage through his dresser drawers and grab some clothing for the day, and then take Matthew by the hand and head for the bathroom down the hall. As soon as we reach the hallway, he pulls free of my grip, runs back into his room, and resumes his crayon mantra, growing louder and more infuriated with each rant. I'm about to pick him up and haul him bodily to the bathroom when my cell phone rings.

"Damn it," I mutter, taking the phone out of my robe pocket. I swipe the answer icon and back out into the hallway so I can hear above my son's screeches. "Mattie Winston."

"Hey, Mattie, it's Heidi." Heidi is a day dispatcher at the local police station.

"What's up?" I plug a finger in my free ear to try to block out the sound of my son's meltdown. I hear the bedroom door open down the hall and see our two cats, Tux and Rubbish, come flying out of the room as if the hounds of hell are on their heels. Behind them, Hurley, or "the hound of hell in our house," shuffles and rubs his eyes. Hurley hates cats.

"The ER has a death to report," Heidi tells me.

"Okay," I say, stifling a yawn. "I'll call them." I disconnect and give Hurley an apologetic look. "Sorry about the noise." I walk over and kiss him on his cheek. His morning stubble feels scratchy on my lips, and I note that he, too, has a cowlick on one side of his head. His, however, looks adorable. But then with that dark hair of his and those morning-glory blue eyes, how could he look anything but?

Hurley looks in at Matthew, who has decided to halt his screams now that his father is here. For some reason, Matthew saves most of his meltdowns for me. "I have to call the hospital," I tell Hurley. "And your son over there has decided he's Michelangelo and his bedroom wall is the Sistine Chapel."

"I got it covered," Hurley says, mid-yawn. He ventures into the room barefoot, clad only in his pajama pants, and I take a moment to admire his physique.

"I pulled some clothes out for him," I say, setting them on top of the dresser.

Hurley scoops Matthew up in one arm, props him on his hip, and grabs the clothing with his free hand. The socks that are in the pile drop to the floor.

"Damn it," Matthew says, looking down at the socks.

Hurley shoots Matthew a chastising look. "Hey, buddy, we don't talk like that."

"Mammy does," Matthew says, using his unique combination of "Mattie" and "Mommy," fingering me with no hint of guile or guilt.

Hurley looks over at me, eyebrows raised.

I flash him a guilty but remorseful smile, and make a quick escape back to the bedroom, where I shut the door and dial the number for the hospital. A minute later, I'm on the phone with a nurse named Krista.

"Sorry for the call," she says, "but I have a young girl here in the ER who came in badly banged up. Shortly after arriving, she coded, and we weren't able to bring her back. She was dropped off by this guy who was acting really weird. He disappeared sometime during the code and hasn't come back."

I close my eyes and sigh. I had hoped the death would be something straightforward, like an older person with a history of heart disease who came in with a myocardial infarction and died. Something like that I could have cleared over the phone after a quick consult with my boss, Izzy, the medical examiner here in Sorenson. But this death sounds like it won't be a simple one.

"Okay," I say. "I'll be there in fifteen minutes. In the meantime, don't let anyone into the room. If the guy comes back, see if security can get him to stay."

"Got it." She disconnects the call without any further niceties. All business, this dead stuff.

I strip off my robe and pajamas, and don some slacks and a heavy sweater. The February weather has been harsh of late, and I can hear wind howling through the trees beyond the bedroom window. I head into the bathroom, wishing I had enough time to take a shower and wash my hair. Instead, I wet a comb and attempt once again to make my cowlick lie flat. It refuses until I saturate that section of hair thoroughly, plastering it down to my head with my palm. But a few seconds later, it begins a slow rise again, the Lazarus of cowlicks.

I shrug it off, knowing I've gone out looking far worse. My job as a medico-legal death investigator often requires me to go out on calls in the middle of the night, and there have been times when my sleep-addled brain lacked the ability to accomplish basic tasks during those first few minutes of wakefulness. I've gone out on calls with my shirt inside out, wearing mismatched shoes, boasting Medusa hair, and displaying the remnants of makeup smeared beneath my eyes that I was too tired to remove the night before. I'm always fully awake and alert by the time I get into my car and head out, but by then the damage is done.

I find my boys in the kitchen, Matthew standing next to his father, who is tending to something in the toaster. I have a good guess about what's in there, since there is a box of toaster waffles on the counter next to him. The smell of freshly brewed coffee hits me, and I take a moment to relish the smell. Then I indulge in what has become a morning ritual for me of late—I look around me.

Hurley and I have only been in this house for two months, and the newness of it is still a treat for me. We had it built after spending almost two years crammed into his small house in town. As a family of four—Emily, Hurley's teenage daughter from a previous relationship, also lives with us—his house was crowded and uncomfortable. And for whatever reason, it never felt like my home. The entire time we lived there, I felt like a guest who had overstayed her welcome. Almost nothing in the house was mine, or even anything I'd had a say in picking out. I'm not sure why I felt this way, because when I left my first husband, a local surgeon, I abandoned, with nary a regret, all of the furnishings I had purchased and the décor I had chosen. I moved into the small mother-in-law cottage behind the house of our neighbor and my best friend, Izzy, and paid Izzy rent. The place was already furnished, so nothing there was mine, either. But I didn't share it with anyone and it felt like mine, making it different somehow.

After bumping around together with Hurley in his house for a year or so, we bought a five-acre parcel of land just outside the city limits and built a house on a bluff that overlooks the countryside. We were able to move in right before Christmas, and while we didn't have much time to decorate—not to mention an inability to find all the right boxes—I still reveled in our first Christmas here and knew I'd remember it forever. I love our new home; it is a place uniquely ours, a perfect blend of our ideas, tastes, and needs. Despite the fact that it is a large house with an open floor plan, it feels warm, cozy, and comfortable. Part of that comes from the design and décor, but another part of it is the sense of safety and family that it provides for me. Our house is my sanctuary, the place I go to when I need to escape the sadness and the sometimes-hectic pace of my job.

I step around Hurley so I can pour myself a cup of coffee to go. The hospital has coffee, but it's rotgut stuff. I know this because I used to work there. I spent six years working in the emergency room and another seven in the OR. I loved working in the emergency room and had it not been for meeting David Winston, the surgeon who would eventually become my first husband, I probably would've stayed in the ER. But I made the change to the OR so that David and I could spend more time together. Unfortunately, David eventually decided to spend some very intimate time with one of my coworkers instead, and I caught the two of them one night in a darkened, empty OR. As shocking as this was—and it shocked my life into a state of major chaos for quite a while—the fallout from it led to both my current job and, via a rocky, roundabout trail, to my marriage to Hurley.

There are times when I regret making the change from the ER to the OR, though I have to admit that the slicing and dicing I learned how to do in the OR was good preparation for the job Izzy offered me when I fled both my marriage and my hospital job. David's dalliance was well timed in one respect, because Izzy's prior assistant had just quit. And since Izzy was offering me his cottage to stay in, it benefited both of us for him to offer me a job as well. It's hard to pay rent when you're unemployed.

I will be forever grateful to Izzy for taking a chance on me. I wasn't trained in the intricacies of the investigative and forensic aspects of my new job, but I'm a quick study. It didn't hurt that I'm also nosy, and fell into the investigative portion of things quite easily. Now, three years and a number of educational conferences and classes later, I have graduated from my original job as a diener—a term used to describe folks who assist with autopsies—to a full-fledged, medico-legal death investigator, trained in scene processing, evidence collection, and a host of investigative techniques.

As I reach for the coffeepot to fill my cup, I notice something on the door of the cupboard below. It is yet another of Matthew's artistic creations, this time in Magic Marker.

"Matthew!" I say, pointing to the scribbled lines. "Did you do this?"

Matthew looks at the cupboard door, then at me. Without so much as a blink, or a hint of hesitation, he says, "No."

"I think you did, Matthew," I say. "Who else could have done it?"

"Hoovah," he says.

"Really? Well, I guess I better punish Hoover then. What should I do to him?"

Matthew's eyes roll heavenward for a moment, and he sticks his tongue out, a sign that he is thinking. Then he looks over at Hoover, who is lying beneath the table in hopes of a dropped morsel. "Bad dog!" Matthew says, apparently willing to throw Hoover under the bus if it will get him out of trouble. He wags a finger in the dog's direction and repeats his admonition. "Hoovah bad dog!"

Hoover looks over at me and sighs, as if he knows the kid has just fingered him for a crime he didn't commit. I look at my son, trying hard not to laugh. His antics and quick-on-his-feet lies amuse me, but I don't want him to know it, lest it encourage more such behavior.

The toaster pops, revealing four waffles, and Matthew's attention is instantly diverted, his crime forgotten. The kid inherited his father's dark hair and good looks, but his food fixation is all from me.

"Awful," he says, reaching up with one hand and doing a *gimme* gesture with his fingers.

Hurley takes one of the waffles out, puts it on a plate, and says, "It's hot. Go sit at the table and I'll bring it to you when it's cool enough to eat."

Matthew pouts, mutters, "Damn it," and walks to the table with a scowl on his face.

Hurley shoots me a look. I smile and shrug, and then I give him a kiss on the cheek. "Can I beg one of those from you?" Taking a cue from my son's clever diversionary tactics, I don't wait for an answer. I snatch a waffle from the toaster, plug it into my mouth, and then head for the coat closet.

"Tell Richmond I'll be in around nine if he picks up this, or any other case," Hurley says to me.

"I'm sure he'll be involved with this one," I say, donning my coat. "Sounds like it may be a case of domestic abuse."

I put on boots, gloves, and a hat, tearing off bites of the waffle as I go. It's not much of a breakfast, but it will do for now. As soon as I'm fully armored against the elements, I walk over and grab my coffee cup from the counter, kiss my husband on his lips, kiss my son on top of his head, and head for the garage.

I start up my car—an older-model, midnight-blue hearse with low mileage—and hit the garage door opener. Outside, the sky has a heavy, leaden look to it, a harbinger of what is to come. I flip on the radio and listen as the morning-show host tells everyone that a huge winter storm is headed our way, due to hit our area tomorrow afternoon. "This one is going to be a doozy," he says with a classic Wisconsin accent. "Expect heavy winds, freezing rain followed by snow, with up to a foot or more of accumulation." Then, after issuing this forecast of gloom and doom, he says in a chipper voice, "Get those snowmobiles tuned up, people. And make sure you stock up on brats and beer."

Despite his cheery tone, he's promising this will be an impressive storm, even by Wisconsin standards. And that's saying something.

I hope it's not an omen for the day ahead of me.